Eve Devon writes sexy heroes, sassy heroines and happy ever afters…

Growing up in locations like Botswana and Venezuela gave her a taste for adventure and her love for romances began when her mother shoved one into her hands in a desperate attempt to keep her quiet during TV coverage of the Wimbledon tennis finals.

When she wasn't consuming books by the bucket-load, she could be found pretending to be a damsel in distress or running around solving mysteries and writing down her adventures. As a teenager, she wrote countless episodes of TV detective dramas so the hero and heroine would end up together every week. As an adult, she worked in a library to conveniently continue consuming books by the bucket-load, until realising she was destined to write contemporary romance and romantic suspense. She lives in leafy Surrey in the UK, a book-devouring, slightly melodramatic, romance-writing sassy heroine with her very own sexy hero husband. Eve loves hearing from readers, so if you'd like to get in touch you can find her at one of these places:

🐦 @EveDevon
f https://www.facebook.com/EveDevonAuthor
www.EveDevon.com

Also by Eve Devon

Her Best Laid Plans
The Love List
It's In His Kiss

The Little Clock House on the Green

EVE DEVON

A division of HarperCollins*Publishers*
www.harpercollins.co.uk

Harper*Impulse* an imprint of
HarperCollins*Publishers*
The News Building
1 London Bridge Street
London SE1 9GF

www.harpercollins.co.uk

A Paperback Original 2017
2

A catalogue record for this book
is available from the British Library

ISBN: 9780008212179

This novel is entirely a work of fiction.
The names, characters and incidents portrayed in it are
the work of the author's imagination. Any resemblance to
actual persons, living or dead, events or localities is
entirely coincidental.

Set in Birka by Palimpsest Book Production Limited,
Falkirk, Stirlingshire

Printed and bound in Great Britain by
Clays Ltd, St Ives plc

MIX
Paper from
responsible sources
FSC www.fsc.org **FSC® C007454**

*For anyone who ever brought a dream back up to the surface,
dusted it off and made it come true*

'Hope is the thing with feathers that perches in the soul,
And sings the tune without the words,
And never stops at all.'

Emily Dickinson

Chapter 1

Accidental Selfie Hell

Kate

Jiminy Cricket! It was hotter than Hades in the shade. Kate didn't think Tobago was ever supposed to get this hot. Arching her neck, she held the water bottle she'd been eking out for the last quarter of a mile to her skin and rolled it back and forth in the hope of teasing out the last condensation-filled cooling properties.

Honestly, how couples even – you know – coupled in this heat she had no idea. Not that she was here for coupling, which was probably why she was attracting attention and almost certainly what was making her job reviewing the luxury resort's facilities so difficult.

Was there anywhere on earth more guaranteed to make you stick out like a sore thumb than at a couples-only resort when you weren't part of a couple?

If she'd still been seeing Marco, she could have invited him along. But she wasn't. And besides, Marco would have hated it. He was more Rough Guide than Forbes list. Weirdly, all the time she was with him she would have sworn she was the same, enjoying reporting on some of the more out-of-the-way and definitely cheaper destinations for the holidaying masses. But now, despite the fact that she was a singleton in couple-land, she couldn't help remembering how she'd used to subscribe to the notion that a little luxury in everyday life was no bad thing.

'Are we nearly there, yet?' her body whined at her brain as she walked back from the local markets. She'd had it in mind to write an article for a travel blog she freelanced for, but as the sun had beat down all she'd been able to think about was that thing about frogs being slowly boiled alive.

When the road became familiar landscaped gardens and she realised main reception and more bottles of water, together with blissful air-conditioning wasn't far away, she celebrated by opening the bottle she was carrying, peeling the neckline of her t-shirt away from her hot skin and chucking a generous amount of the liquid down inside her top.

The water splashed down her front and had a cooling effect for about a nano-second. With her free hand she slipped her phone from her shorts pocket. At 2pm there was a cocktail-making lesson with her name on it. Squinting against the glare from the sun dancing merrily across the screen, Kate held the phone aloft, twisting and turning, trying to find the right angle to read the display, pouting with impatience when she couldn't and splashing more water in the direction of her now transparent t-shirt.

'Oh my goodness, Richard, look – I think that's that Kardashian selfie-woman.'

At the not-so-sotto-voce comment, Kate looked up, eager to catch a glimpse of her. Instead she found a couple in their sixties walking towards her, the man with a friendly grin on his face, the woman with the kind of disapproving frown that suggested *she* was the Kardashian in this little scenario.

Kate followed the woman's pointed stare at her chest. Oops! She lowered her phone back to her side at the realisation that she was doing a good impression of a selfie-obsessed wet t-shirt entry in a club 18–30 holiday instead of a guest at a seven-star complex. Timing never had been – probably never would be – her strong suit.

Still. Kate felt herself bristle.

Did the woman really have to look at her like she'd been put on this path to corrupt all men?

She offered up a smile, yet more heat blooming across her décolletage, creeping blotchily up her neck and landing prominently on her cheeks when the woman didn't appear interested in accepting it. Fabulous, Kate thought, feeling foolish under the disapproving regard.

#SneeringWoman's inability to give her the benefit of the doubt had Kate wanting to lean towards the man, drench the both of them with the rest of the water, and go all *Pretty Woman* on them with a, 'Fifty bucks, Grandpa – for seventy-five, the wife can watch.'

But by the power of Greyskull, she managed to rein herself in.

Just.

Because while she might have an impulsive streak running a mile wide through her, adding grist to the mill was almost certainly going to land her in even more hot water, and right now she was hot enough, thank you very much.

Lifting the heavy swathe of mahogany hair off her shoulders, Kate twisted it up into a knot on top of her head, slightly worried someone from staff was going to pop out from behind a palm tree and accuse her of trying to make a mini-porn phone video. In public. On their premises.

She stepped off the path in order to let the couple pass and when the woman protectively manoeuvred herself between them, Kate glanced down to double-check that her clothes hadn't somehow magically melted away. Nope. Her cleavage might be rocking the *Flashdance* drenched look, but she was still wearing ninety per cent more than anyone on the beach… and had she mentioned how hot it was?

As if those last words had formed on her lips instead of inside her head, the couple glanced back and Kate couldn't help herself – she lowered her oversize shades, gave an exaggerated wink, and, yes, finished off with a bit of a shoulder-chest shimmie. The look she received from both of them as they left her – presumably on the highway to hell – was priceless and went a little way to restoring her sense of humour.

She headed along the curving trail through the tropical gardens. Even the geckos were trying to avoid the direct heat of the sun, their little splayed feet barely seeming to touch the concrete as they scurried off the path, through the bougainvilleas, and straight for the shade of the palm trees.

Kate squinted down at her phone. The time said that she was due at the largest of the resort's five poolside bars in thirty minutes, which left her plenty of time to check for messages at reception, and then nip back to her room for a quick shower and a change into her bikini.

The thought of alcohol in this heat had her fingers tightening around the now empty water bottle. She'd ask to make mocktails instead.

It occurred to her she couldn't remember the last time she'd held a mug of tea in her hands or felt the comforting sting of a strong, sweet brew against her tongue and palate.

A strange little pang hit beneath her breastbone, surprising her. Who in their right mind would swap sherbet coloured drinks, in happy bulbous shaped glasses, complete with cute little umbrellas rammed in at jaunty angles, for mugs of builder's tea?

At the main building she walked into reception, the piercing bright sunshine of the day immediately giving way to the darker, cooler tones of the interior.

The blast of air-conditioning had her shivering in delight; the man-made chill wrapping itself around her and freezing that unsettling pang for home in its tracks.

Shoving her sunglasses high into her hair, Kate made her way across the huge expanse of marble flooring to reception and smiled. 'Hi, any messages for 103?'

The receptionist glanced briefly at the transparency of Kate's top before adopting a neutral expression and turned to check a wall of numbered pigeon-holes. Kate wished she had the same kind of game-face that the staff at the resort had, but unfortunately emotion tended to use her face like it was under spotlights and centre stage in a one-woman show. With a mortified look down at her top, she pulled the material so that it wasn't plastered to her curves and rested her forearms against the polished surface of the desk. Her fingers tapped out a silent tune. Her left foot came out of her flip-flop to rub against her calf. She chewed the inside of her cheek.

She was fidgety.

Restless.

Which was disconcerting because since when did the prospect of checking out a hotel's facilities make her fidgety? Granted, she didn't usually get offered the honeymoon destinations, but after four years' reviewing all kinds of venues, she was up to the challenge. Plenty of people would love to have her job. If she hadn't found it quite so fulfilling lately, well, she was almost certain she could avoid dwelling on that this evening, with the aid of a Planter's Punch and a good book.

Popping her foot back into its flip-flop she forced her hands to still on the countertop. Beside her was a stack of glossy white leaflets advertising the hotel spa services. She had a handful of them already tucked in a folder back in her room. She even knew which treatments she was scheduled to have the next day. But concentrating on reading the leaflet would stop her fidgeting. Maybe halt the whisper of anxiety accompanying the restlessness – *the loneliness*. Definitely stop that pang for home from darting unexpectedly through her again.

'Here you go, Ms Somersby,' the receptionist said with a broad grin as he held out the hotel's blush-pink letterhead paper containing a reminder that the fire-alarms would be tested at 11am the following day, together with a postcard.

A postcard? Wasn't the sending of postcards supposed to be the other way around?

Kate smiled her thanks and looked down at the picture of

quintessential rolling English countryside. With shaking hands she turned the card over.

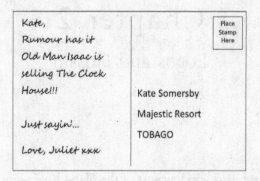

Kate,
Rumour has it
Old Man Isaac is
selling The Clock
House!!!

Just sayin'...

Love, Juliet xxx

Place Stamp Here

Kate Somersby

Majestic Resort

TOBAGO

Kate's sunglasses slipped back down her head as she stared at her cousin's handwriting.

Old Man Isaac was *selling*...?

A horrible tilting sensation had her reaching out to grab a hold of the edge of the reception desk.

Wow.

Okay.

And Juliet thought she needed to know because...?

Before memories could swirl into focus and the charming old brick building could fully form in her mind, Kate shoved the postcard into the darkest, deepest recess of her bag and headed off in the direction of her room, one clear thought making its way to the top of the jumble in her head: she was absolutely, positively, going to ask the bartender how to make the most alcoholic cocktail on the bar's menu. And then she was going to drink it. Stat.

Chapter 2

Logos and Gossip

Kate

In the cramped window seat of the plane, Kate was oblivious to the fact that if she looked out of the window, past the thin layer of cloud, she'd be able to make out the Atlantic Ocean below. Instead, she was completely focused on her laptop screen. Using the tracker-pad, she dropped the image of the little friendly looking bee over the letter 'e' in the word 'Beauty'.

Hmmm.

It didn't look quite right.

Maybe she should change the word 'at' for the 'at' sign?

Making the change, she tipped her head to the side and re-read: Beauty @ The Clock House.

That looked much better. Simple and contemporary. Although... maybe she should work on a tagline to explain the bees?

'Clever,' declared the passenger in the seat beside her. 'Do you design logos for a living, then?'

Dragged from her state of intense concentration, Kate turned towards the woman sitting next to her. 'I'm sorry?'

The woman nodded her head towards Kate's laptop screen and turning a little red, said, 'It's me who should be sorry. I shouldn't have been looking.'

Kate swung her gaze back to her laptop screen.

Caught red-handed.

Darn it!

She *was* supposed to be working. On coming up with the last three points of her 'Travel Hacks' article for The World's Your Oyster travel blog. She certainly wasn't supposed to be designing logos for a pipe dream she'd thought she'd successfully buried four years before.

It was all Juliet's fault.

Six weeks after receiving the first postcard, she'd received another.

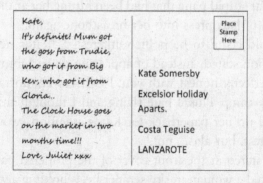

Kate,

It's definite! Mum got the goss from Trudie, who got it from Big Kev, who got it from Gloria...

The Clock House goes on the market in two months time!!!

Love, Juliet xxx

Place Stamp Here

Kate Somersby

Excelsior Holiday Aparts.

Costa Teguise

LANZAROTE

Two postcards in and Kate had an inkling these things were going to find her wherever she was. Honest to goodness, it was like being on the Dursley end of receiving owl post.

After the first one, she'd emailed Juliet and explained she wasn't interested in hearing about the clock house, but clearly her words had been lost in translation. Admittedly they'd been shoved into the middle paragraphs about how beautiful Tobago was and all about the stunning humming-birds and the tranquillity of the rainforest areas and this gorgeous callaloo soup she'd tried because obviously she didn't want to appear too weirded-out about The Clock House being up for sale.

But maybe she was going to have to stop sending Juliet postcards, e-cards or any other kind of card that kept her in touch with where she was and how she was, if this was the sort of payback she was going to receive.

Her cousin was the only person from Whispers Wood who Kate kept in loose contact with and the thought of not checking in with her every now and then... the thought of severing that connection with the place she used to call home, made that stupid pang that had been hitting her at the oddest of times of late, press into her breastbone again.

'I could claim to be politely interested,' Kate's new travel companion stated, 'instead of appearing downright nosy, but to be perfectly honest with you, I fall very comfortably into the nosy camp. Plus, I hate flying and I thought this book,' she held up her paperback for Kate's attention, 'would hold my interest, but alas... not.'

Kate stared at the front cover of the proffered paperback. It depicted a woman in sky-scraper heels holding a whip and standing over a man lying on a bed. Kate grinned. Who didn't love gawping at what other people were reading? 'Too much whipping action?' she sympathised.

'Not enough,' the woman said, making Kate's smile grow wider. 'So much for the "What to read after *50 Shades*" list, but don't mind me. If you're not in the mood to talk... or if what you're working on is confidential...'

'No, it's all right,' Kate reassured, glad of the interruption, because what if, after she'd finished designing logos for a business she didn't have, in premises she has absolutely no intention of owning, she'd actually moved on to designing the packaging too? 'What you saw,' she gently closed her laptop, 'well, that wasn't work. I was just–' *Getting carried away? Testing myself?* 'Doodling,' she finished lamely.

'I see,' said the woman, with a look that clearly said she didn't and as Kate hardly understood it either, she couldn't really blame her.

For the thousandth time Kate told herself that just because Old Man Isaac was finally selling The Clock House, didn't mean she should be the one to buy it...

Yes, she might, technically, have the funds sitting in a bank, largely untouched for four years, and, yes, she might have the idea.

But, and as buts go, this one was a doozy... the person she was supposed to implement the idea with, wasn't here any more.

Her hand moved unconsciously to rub at her sternum and encountered the filigree-silver locket watch she never took off.

There were some wounds that time couldn't heal, so to be even contemplating going home to Whispers Wood and buying The Clock House was madness.

Determined to shake off the melancholy, Kate turned more fully to her new-found friend and asked, 'Have you been to La Rochelle, before, then?'

Her companion shook her head. 'My son-in-law is French, and he and my daughter moved back two years ago now. We Skype and all that business, but I haven't been to see them because I hate flying so much. But–' The woman pulled out her phone. 'I decided the arrival of one's first granddaughter merits a change in attitude and so here I am. Prepare yourself, this is where I now bore you with photos.'

Kate stared dutifully down at the slide show on the woman's phone, right into the eyes of a cherubic newborn swaddled in baby-pink waffle-textured blanket. 'She's so sweet. And tiny! Looks as if Granny's in for a lovely visit.'

'Doesn't it? When my daughter first told me they were moving I was determined to be happy for them. It was a bit of a shock. We'd only lost my husband two years before.'

'Oh, I'm sorry to hear that.' Kate watched the grief flash in the woman's eyes before acceptance remembered to make its appearance and, without even thinking about it, Kate reached out to squeeze her hand.

The woman stared into Kate's eyes and after a moment squeezed back and heaved in a breath. 'Anyway, it was hard, but I had work and my friends and I knew I'd be okay. And then, oh, I don't know, you go about your daily routine, being okay and you think that okay is fine. Okay is good. And then, out of the blue, you get some news and suddenly you're realising things can be better than okay. And such joy floods in,' the woman shot Kate a look. 'Do you know what I mean?'

'Oh, completely,' replied Kate, lying through her teeth, because compared with before, her life being 'okay' was already more. Except... *maybe* when she'd received that first postcard from Juliet... Mixed in with that gravity-shifting experience – before she'd tamped it down so forcefully – had been a feeling of joy. Joy at the possibility of a second chance. Joy at the possibility of more.

'So what about you?' the woman asked, stroking a finger over the photo on the screen before sliding the phone back into her bag. 'Meeting someone the other end?' The woman glanced down at her book and grinned. 'Ooh, tell me you're jetting over oceans to meet your lover?'

Kate grinned back. 'Where I will naturally whip him into shape?'

'Naturally,' the woman laughed.

'Sadly,' Kate answered, 'I'm just going to be working.'

She wasn't sure why she'd accepted the job, really. Possibly to prove something to herself? She would really rather not have realised that every flight she took of late seemed to bring her closer to England. And this was the first trip back to La Rochelle where she wouldn't grab a taxi and whiz through the port's busy harbour streets to meet Marco. There would be no falling into bed with him. No late-night stroll down the Rue Saint Pierre afterwards, holding hands and chatting about their latest work assignments before stopping in at his favourite bar and, after a drink or four, going back to his tiny apartment to fall back into bed again.

She tested a breath and found that it wasn't lodged too deeply in her throat after all. The last few months had eased the ego-crushing aftershock of her last visit, when Marco had sat her down and gently told her that he'd met someone. Someone who wanted to be with him. Wanted to live with him.

Wanted to commit to him.

She'd been stunned. He'd never once intimated he'd wanted more and hot on the heels of the shock had been an automatic need to tell him she was sure she could commit to him too – especially now that she knew that was what he was looking for.

Big mistake.

Huge.

The realisation that the gravel-laced reverence in his voice when he talked about Clara was definitely not, and indeed, had never been, present in his voice when he'd talked to her, coupled with the excruciatingly gentle manner he'd used to explain why it was never going to be her, had had her salvaging her pride and high-tailing it out of there.

She'd gone down the tried-and-tested route when she'd left on that jet plane, completely certain she wouldn't be back again. Throwing herself into work she'd crossed so many time zones she hadn't even bothered unpacking. Not that she usually unpacked. That was her ultimate life-hack, but Kate knew that didn't look great, so she kept it to herself.

'Work?' said the woman disappointedly. 'So the doodling...?'

'Was for someone else.' Another her. A different her. A lifetime ago. 'My job involves travelling and reviewing for airlines, tourist boards, resort owners, etc. It's a tough job...'

'But somebody has to do it,' her new friend replied, with a generous smile. 'You get to travel. Experience new things. Share them with others. I like it.'

'Exactly.'

'You're probably too young to settle down anyway.'

Exactly.

'So where is home for you?' the woman asked.

Kate's heart missed a beat. 'Oh, you won't have heard of it. It's a small village in West Sussex.' Determinedly she reached out in front of her, opened up her laptop and, with only a moment's hesitation, hit the delete key on the logos she'd been tinkering with.

Home was where the other her had lived. The different her. A lifetime ago.

Opening up the blog article, she took a deep breath and glad to have this lovely person sitting next to her, a person more than capable of distracting her from pipedreams, Kate put her fingers on the keyboard and asked, 'Hey, what's your top tip for travelling?'

Chapter 3

Within the Sound of Silence

Kate

Kate sat cross-legged staring out to sea, Juliet's latest post-card tucked away in her over-the-shoulder bag. Out of sight. And weighing on her mind and tempting her as if it was gold and ring-shaped and called 'The Precious'.

No matter how she turned it all in her head, she couldn't come up with a way of getting her mindset to return to life before the postcards.

The third postcard, a.k.a, The Precious, was succinct, to say the least:

Kate,	Place Stamp Here
Seriously! Three	
weeks to go...	Kate Somersby
Read between	Hotel Pierre
the lines!!!!	14 Rue Saint Pierre
	La Rochelle
Love, Juliet xxx	FRANCE

She *had* read between the lines. She'd read above the lines and below the lines and the actual lines themselves.

Over and over and over.

And now her head was so full of possibility she could barely breathe.

She tried to remember exactly when had been the last time she'd felt this wealth of ideas rushing forward, this sense of future slotting quietly into place?

Her fingers flexed involuntarily as her heart clutched against the memory.

It had been the 9th October 2013.

Kate squeezed her eyes shut and shook her head helplessly. She wasn't going there.

And yet if she did this, if she went home and looked into buying The Clock House, she was definitely going to have to 'go there'.

Be there.

Back in Whispers Wood.

Without Bea.

The sister who'd dreamed up that future right alongside her.

Kate stared hard at the wide ocean in front of her.

Bea was gone and was never coming back and Kate missed her every blessed day.

And every day she tried to get okay with missing her.

If she returned to Whispers Wood, Kate would be saying that she could deal with being back without Bea.

Or, at the very least, she would be saying she was going to try.

Again.

Because it wasn't like she hadn't gone home before. Over the years since Bea's death, she'd made plenty of duty visits to see her mum. Visits where the only view was that of watching her mum exist silently on the fringes of life – not ready to re-engage – not *able* to re-engage. Well, not with Kate, anyway.

'Okay. Not plenty of visits,' Kate admitted, imagining Bea's snort of laughter floating to her on the sea breeze. 'But I've been back a few times. Enough times,' she ended with.

But each visit she'd avoided the village green and The Clock House.

She was too fanciful. Too sentimental. Too scared that in looking up at it she'd imagine it winking back at her – stirring everything up.

Dazzling her.

Kate blew out a breath.

It was silly to be even considering returning to Whispers Wood on a more permanent basis and yet all she'd done since she'd received the latest postcard from Juliet was consider just that.

How could what she had always thought of as her last option, suddenly seem like her only true option?

'What do you think, Bea?' Kate whispered into the sea breeze. 'Should I go back?'

Silence.

Kate's ears strained past the sound of the ocean waves lapping against the shore and past the odd cry from a seagull. Not one sound that could magically be made into her sister's voice giving her approval.

A tear rolled down her cheek.

As much as she still felt the gaping chasm Bea's passing had left behind, she knew something had to change. She'd spent four years expecting, hoping, *needing* to hear Bea's voice telling her what to do. Never once had she received an answer.

Kate swiped a hand under her nose and sniffed.

She had to make a decision on her own. End this stupid purgatory with the postcards.

She tried to think of how she'd feel if Old Man Isaac sold to someone else? Or even of how she'd feel if Juliet mentioned in casual conversation, during one of her visits home, that The Clock House had been sold. But it was as if those reactions and emotions were protectively inaccessible. All she had to base her decision on was the spark that Juliet's postcards had struck inside of her.

And all the hours of regret that had walked doggedly beside her for four years.

'So make a decision, already,' Kate muttered, looking around at the pebbles scattered across the sand. She leant over slightly and picked one up. It was mauve in colour with a white vein running across one side.

Perfect.

'White vein I go back. Plain I go on.'

She tossed the pebble up into the air and tracked its plummet back to the ground.

As it lay motionless on the sand before her, there, in between the beats of her heart, she stared at her answer, and then, with a wry, 'Sod it, then,' she picked up the pebble and slipped it into her pocket.

Chapter 4

Boys and Their Toys

Daniel

As Daniel sped around the leafy lanes with the top down on his absolute pride and joy, Monroe – a Triumph Spitfire in phantom grey, it finally occurred to him why his face was aching.

He was smiling.

Had been for maybe the last fifteen miles or so.

Happy days, he thought. As improvements to his state of mind went, smiling had to be right up there with that first gulp of an IPA beer at the start of a hot summer's evening.

He shifted gears, pressing down on the accelerator, the dappled sunlight creating fast-moving reflections of the tree-lined country roads in his Wayfarers.

Two hours before, when he'd been grabbing clothes from a cheap freestanding clothes-rail in his studio apartment and shoving them into a leather holdall, he definitely hadn't been smiling.

He'd been swearing.

Profusely.

He'd actually managed to shock himself at being able to string so many different swear words together. Granted, the sentences had been neither grammatically correct, nor, he was pretty sure, anatomically possible, but the flow of them had brought a certain sense of surprising satisfaction.

Don't get me wrong – Daniel Westlake wasn't some advocate for anti-profanity. But when he swore it was usually short and succinct and relating to a mild frustration that he determined to quickly get past – and did.

It had been a really crap year, though.

The crappiest, in fact.

At first, he'd dismissed that sly prickle of awareness… that amorphous inkling, that something at his accountancy firm, West and Westlake, was wrong.

The clients had to be satisfied, the way they kept introducing more business to the firm. The money was coming in and the projections for the following year were great. And he was working sixty/seventy-hour weeks, week in, week out.

Any real time to pause over a feeling, a premonition, a sense of impending doom, whatever you wanted to call it, was nil. Tinkering-with-Monroe time had dwindled to maybe one afternoon a quarter and the only time available to focus on anything other than his accounts was when he was out running.

Daniel loved running. Loved the discipline. Loved the rhythm.

But it had been on one of those early-morning runs – you know, the ones where the sun is just breaking through and the roads are that kind of pre-zombie-apocalypse eerie-quiet, and your mind flits and floats as your feet pound the pavement, that the worry that everything was *a little too good* at West and Westlake had stretched and yawned, and this time, refused to lie back down, dormant.

Another mile in and the awakening had become a nasty, sweat-inducing growing suspicion that had had him circling back in the direction of his offices at 5am on a Sunday, letting himself in, downloading every single set of accounts, and back at his three-bed penthouse at 2:17am the following morning, had led him to the very conclusive and very shitty discovery that, yes, his scumbag partner, was, to put it bluntly, cooking the books.

The betrayal had felt like a herd of elephants doing Buddha-spins on his chest.

Not least because Daniel and his business partner, Hugo West, had been friends since school.

Good friends. Even though, to be fair, Hugo had always been a bit of a dick.

He was that friend, who, growing up, always had to do everything first. First to climb the tree, first to crack the crass joke in class. First to ace a test. First to get fall-down drunk. First to lose his virginity. First to come up with an idea.

But he had also been the only friend to stand up for, and to stand beside, Daniel, when Daniel's life had imploded at nineteen.

It was hard to discount that kind of loyalty and then there was the fact that Hugo teamed playing hard with working hard. The hardest. Maybe he'd had to. That need of his to be ahead in everything, probably. But Daniel had always admired his friend's drive and determination and, in the beginning, where Daniel might have given up on their fledgling accountancy firm, it had been Hugo's grit that had seen them through that crucial first two years. Hugo who had the guts to go for the big clients straight off. Hugo who helped the company fly so high.

So high and, seemingly, so successfully that Daniel had completely forgotten Hugo's dick-like tendencies. That was on him – and lesson learned. He'd *never* make the same mistake.

After the bloody awful court case and the dissolution of their business partnership, Daniel had one priority and one priority only: starting afresh.

The swear-fest, record-breaking packing-gig had been a result of reconfirming that decision after the letter had plopped onto his doormat that morning.

Postmarked from Ford open prison, Hugo obviously hadn't lasted two weeks into his sentence before 'reaching out'.

Daniel couldn't imagine what there was left to say and although opening it would have relieved his curiosity, the letter had sat sealed on the sparse kitchen breakfast bar while he'd consumed bland instant coffee and stared at the offending article, conflicted.

Swallowing down the last gulp of coffee it had met the choking anger rising up, making Daniel realise there was no room for misplaced loyalty. After what Hugo had done, he was now in the category of forever-dead-to-him dick.

End of.

So after the swearing and the packing, Daniel had written 'Not at this address' across the front of the letter and tossed it into the first postbox he'd come across after leaving London.

Driving with no particular destination in mind had eased that grinding knot in his stomach, but now, as he down-shifted to hit an approaching bend in the road, Daniel realised he could hear a grinding noise above the roar of the engine. The smile on his face disappeared. That noise wasn't a grinding stomach-ulcer noise. That noise was Monroe-speak for 'Um, Houston, we have a problem'.

He nursed the car around the corner and felt the engine slow even as he tried to accelerate out of it. 'Come on Monroe – you can't fail me now, not in the middle of–' he twisted his head to try and catch what the signpost he had driven past had read, but was too late. 'Nowhere,' he said, not too upset to discover he had no idea where he was.

It had been the whole point.

Get in the car and drive.

Get away from London.

Away from the last year.

And end up somewhere where he could think.

But thinking of any sort was put on hold the instant he saw the woman with the long, *incredible* legs, hauling a suitcase out of the back of a taxi.

You didn't see a soul for miles and then, POW, some Diana Prince goddess was standing at the side of the road in front of a row of stone cottages.

The thought of stopping and offering help – of getting a chance to meet this gorgeous woman was enough to put the smile back on his face. He was just starting to slow when Monroe chose to emit a put-put-puttering noise.

'Christ, Monroe – not cool,' he muttered and got an over-way-too-quickly impression of huge eyes as Wonder Woman's head popped out from the boot of the taxi to check on the strange noise.

Time slowed. But not in a hero-walking-down-the-road-slow-mo-movie way – more in a let's-get-a-full-look-at-the-idiot-who-doesn't-know-how-to-drive-a-classic-car kind of a way.

Daniel actually found himself hunkering down in his seat as he brought his arm up to rest on the window frame so that his hand could shield his face from her inquisitive gaze.

Bunny-hopping past a beautiful woman in his beloved Triumph Spitfire was definitely not how he'd imagined his fresh start beginning.

Neither was sounding like he couldn't find a gear if his life depended on it.

All ability to appear cool having disappeared out of Monroe's exhaust pipe, Daniel opted not to stop after all. Wonder Woman looked like she had everything under control and he... didn't.

His gaze shifted to his rear-view mirror, where he allowed himself one last look at her, before concentrating on not driving into the hedge.

Thankfully a few yards further and the narrow country lane opened out so that on his right was a large village green with some sort of stately-home affair at the end of it and on his left were yet more stone cottages, this time with roses rambling up them.

As he sputtered through the picture-postcard-perfect village a few choice words came to mind. Should've checked the oil before leaving London, shouldn't he? He usually did, but today he'd done what he assumed all people did when attempting an impromptu getaway from life in their classic car. He'd glanced dutifully up at the sky, noted the lack of rain clouds, chucked his holdall onto the passenger seat of the car, hopped in and revved the engine. Tearing out of London as fast as the speed limit permitted.

Giving up before he did irreparable damage, Daniel steered safely towards the thick hedgerow on the other side of the green. He cut the engine and hopped out of the car. At the edge of the green a proud wrought-iron sign twisted into the form of a row of trees read: Welcome to Whispers Wood.

He'd never heard of it. With a sigh he wandered back up the road in the opposite direction from which he'd come until he found another signpost which read: Whispers Wood 1/4 mile, Whispers Ford 2 miles.

He hadn't heard of Whispers Ford either and now wished he'd been paying attention when he'd driven through the last town.

Which village would have a garage?

A cow mooed, making him jump. Daniel turned around and looked at the field of cows beyond the hedgerow. One of the cows had its head poking over what he considered to be – although he wasn't exactly an expert – an insubstantial fence-line, considering how big cows were close-up. The cow was looking at him like it had initiated conversation. Daniel found himself holding his hands up to placate as he backed carefully away a couple of steps. The cow watched him with a sort of doleful look on its face before it mooed again.

Since the cow was so talkative Daniel held his hands back

out. 'Garage?' he asked. 'That way,' he pointed left. 'Or,' he pointed right, 'That way?'

Damned if the cow didn't bow its head as if to say, yes there was a garage, before it then swung its head to the left before turning around and ignoring him.

Countryfile hadn't exactly been part of Daniel's 'on demand' viewing schedule so he had no idea whether it was possible to get pied by a cow, but just in case he was going to take cow-conversing with a giant pinch of salt.

Of course, he could always wander back through the village, to where he'd seen Wonder Woman, and ask her if there was a garage and mechanic he could trust Monroe to, but let's face it, being that asking for directions wasn't part of a man's make-up, he was never going to ask a human who could actually judge him.

He took out his phone and Googled.

Bingo.

It looked as if a garage was one of the few facilities Whispers Wood did have.

With a last glance to check the cow was on the right side of the fence, or at least the one the other side of him, Daniel strode off down the lane to try and locate Ted's Garage.

'So, when you say it could be the gearbox or the transmission...?' Daniel asked.

'I mean it could be the gearbox or the transmission,' Ted, the portly overall-wearing, mechanic, repeated. 'Won't know until I look at it proper. Need me to tow it in for you?'

Daniel wasn't sure. The tow truck parked up on the verge

looked as if it had seen better days. Monroe would probably take one look at it and refuse.

'No, don't worry,' Daniel replied. 'I think I can get it here without doing too much more damage.' It could only be three hundred yards or so up the gentle incline to the garage. If he put it to Monroe nicely, he was pretty sure she'd oblige instead of suffering the indignity of a tow.

Twenty minutes later, Ted was staring at the car appreciatively. 'Well, now, it's not every day I get to see one of these.'

'Do you think you'll be able to find out what the problem is?'

'I reckon it'll be a pleasure. If it is the gearbox, though, I'm going to need to order the part special. Not going to be cheap. Might take a few days.'

This past year anger seemed to have top dog status in Daniel's emotional repertoire and now he waited for it to pipe up. He was a lot relieved and a little surprised when it failed to rise up to bite.

Must be the country air.

'I don't suppose there's anywhere to stay in Whispers Wood?' he asked.

'There is,' Ted answered, giving Daniel an assessing look. 'Have to say, you look like you'd be more comfortable in the posh hotel in Whispers Ford.'

'I'm happy to stay here in the village.'

'Yeah?'

Ted didn't look convinced, but Daniel was hardly going to tell a stranger about to get intimate with Monroe that despite the shirt on his back being a slim fit, double-cuff from

Burberry he was pretty much broke, bar his seed money for starting again. 'Well, then,' Ted continued, 'you should try Sheila Somersby's B&B. It's about a ten minute walk, on the outskirts of the village, but I know she has a couple of vacancies at the moment.'

'Thanks. What's her number? I'll phone her now while you're looking Monroe over.'

'Monroe?' Ted turned in the direction of Daniel's stare, his expression suddenly clearing and becoming warm. 'As in Marilyn?'

'Hadn't actually meant to say that out loud,' Daniel admitted. Not that there was anything wrong with naming your car. Just, maybe, not out loud! And maybe not Marilyn if you ever wanted to get girls into it.

'Don't you worry, Mr...?'

Daniel hesitated and hated himself for doing so. He'd worked hard for years to be able to give his surname without worrying. Telling himself he wasn't going to let Hugo take that from him as well, he cleared his throat and held out his hand, 'Westlake. Daniel Westlake.'

'Well, don't you worry, Mr Westlake,' Ted said shaking his hand. 'I'll take care of your Marilyn Monroe. I'll even warm my hands up first,' he added with a wink.

Daniel smiled. He got out his phone to ring the woman who owned the B&B and ten minutes later he had a room booked and a promise from Ted he'd phone as soon as he knew what was wrong with the car.

Following the lane back down to the village, Daniel stopped, his gaze taking in the lush green grass surrounded by a foot-high chain link fence, with a building at one end and the stone cottages at the other. To the left was what looked like woods and to the right a small parade of shops.

So this was Whispers Wood.

It looked nice.

Pleasant.

Soothing.

A good enough place to hole up and think about where the hell he went from here.

Chapter 5

Back – From Outer Space

Kate

Kate winced as her Aunt Cheryl skewered her scalp with what was surely bobby-pin number one hundred and one. After the first couple of eye-widening stares into the mirror, Kate had decided it was probably best to avoid the reflective surface and simply allow Aunt Cheryl's 'Prom Look No. 3' to develop into all it was meant to be.

How she'd ended up as the practice hair model for Wood View High's prom, she wasn't quite sure. Although having said that, she had just sat down with a cuppa, and her mum's sister was famous for turning dead time into 'doings' time.

'So how long are you back for?' Aunt Cheryl asked, sectioning off the front of Kate's hair and proceeding to back-comb it to within an inch of its life.

Back.

Home.

Ignoring the fact that they were both four-letter words, Kate concentrated on answering truthfully. Confidently. Brook-no-argument-ly. 'I was thinking... permanently?' She winced as she heard herself. Okay, so she still had a little work to do on sounding convinced.

You could hear a pin drop.

Literally, because the one in Aunt Cheryl's mouth fell out as her jaw dropped open and it made a tiny ping as it hit the floorboards Juliet had painted white in an effort to make the room appear bigger.

As her aunt bent down to retrieve the pin, Kate's panicked eyes sought out Juliet's in the mirror and she was grateful for the double thumbs-up of encouragement, before her cousin tactfully went back to the crafting magazine she'd been leafing through.

'Back permanently?' Aunt Cheryl asked, reclaiming the pin and shoving it back into her mouth along with a few others. 'As in you've come home, home?'

'Mmmn,' Kate fixed her smile into place. The one she'd practised all the way over on the plane. Back two days and already she was discovering that, apparently, Kate Somersby coming back to Whispers Wood permanently had been one of those beyond-the-realms-of-possibility things.

'And have you let your mum know?' Aunt Cheryl wanted to know.

Kate shifted uncomfortably on the chair she was perched upon and avoiding the question, put a hand up to her hair. 'I thought this year prom hair was sort of romantic half-up, half-down affairs?'

'And, see,' Aunt Cheryl nudged Kate's shoulder until she was looking in the mirror again, 'isn't that what I'm doing?'

Kate stared at the half-up, half-down beehive that had some

sort of fishtail plait going on at the back. Apparently, Look No.3 was a party-in-the-front *and* party-in-the-back affair.

It wouldn't be fair to describe Aunt Cheryl as a novice when it came to hair. She was a perfectly acceptable and qualified mobile hairdresser, who for the last twenty-five years had been dispensing opinions she'd gained from her first-class honours degree in sear-you-to-your-bones honesty along with a good set and blow-dry. If you were a certain age, you really had no complaints. If you were from *this* millennia, though, you knew to ask Juliet to do your hair.

Juliet was amazing with hair and, privately, Kate always wondered if it was loyalty to her mum or shyness that stopped Juliet from striking out on her own.

'So have you, then? Seen your mother, that is,' Aunt Cheryl repeated.

Kate began singing Abba's 'S.O.S.' under her breath as once again her gaze sought her cousin's in the mirror.

Fortunately Juliet spoke 'awkward' and with a gentle smile, stood up and crossed the room to pass her mother the hairspray. 'Give it a rest, Mum. She's only been back a couple of days.'

'Well, she can't hide out with you forever, can she? Where's she sleeping? You can't even swing a cat in here, although God knows, you've got enough of them.'

'It won't be for forever. Although,' Juliet turned and put a reassuring hand on Kate's shoulder, 'You know the sofa's yours for as long as you want it. I love having you here.'

'Thanks, lovely,' Kate said.

'Because, honestly,' Aunt Cheryl demanded as if neither

had spoken, 'What's Sheila going to say if she bumps into you?'

That was actually a tough one.

Kate had been worrying more about *if* her mum was going to react, rather than how.

'Is she going to bump into me, though? I mean, does she actually leave the house now, then? Other than to pop out for something one of her beloved guest's might need, I mean?'

'Kate,' her aunt reproved.

'Sorry. Sorry. Habit.'

'A bad habit.'

'Yes,' Kate whispered. 'Bad habit.'

Kate wanted to add that it was a habit she hadn't wanted to learn, but now that she had it was one she seemed incapable of unlearning. But if she was back to stay she was going to have to. Being back meant seeing Sheila Somersby. Talking to Sheila Somersby. Trying to have a relationship with Sheila Somersby.

At least she was pretty sure it did. In the quagmire of grief after Bea dying, Kate had begun to refer to her mum as The Shell because when Bea died she'd, rather unhelpfully, in Kate's humble opinion, taken their mum with her, leaving behind only a hulled-out shell of skin and bone. Any energy her mum was able to drum up was spent on keeping her B&B guests comfortable.

In the moments Kate could apply perspective, she got that – she really did. Her mum had a business she needed to keep going. A business she'd started after Kate and Bea's dad had upped and left. A business that had enabled Sheila Somersby to block out the humiliation of his leaving and operate under a super-polished veneer of stoicism.

Back then, Kate and Bea had had each other to soften the fallout and share their concerns their mum would never rekindle the sharp wit and curiosity for life that she'd used to share with her sister, Cheryl.

But after Bea had died...

Well, there was just Sheila.

And there was just Kate.

Separated by a wall of grief Kate wasn't sure could ever be knocked down. Wasn't even sure her mother thought either of them was entitled to.

'I do understand, you know,' Cheryl said gently. 'But think about it from her point of view. How would you like it, the whole village knowing your daughter was back and you the only one not to have been told.'

'Has she... Is she–?' She shook her head to silence the questions threatening escape and marvelled slightly at the fact that not one hair on her head moved as she did.

'You'll never know if you don't go and see her, will you? I think you'll be surprised by what you find. Good surprised.'

Hope took a breath.

Fear that she'd be responsible for setting her mother back extinguished it.

She couldn't do it.

Not yet.

She had another visit she had to make first.

'Maybe I'll go now,' she said, shooting to her feet the moment Aunt Cheryl reached for the next can of hairspray.

'Oh, but I haven't–' but as if she could sense Kate's wings threatening to take flight, Aunt Cheryl nodded her head. Reaching out she pulled some of Kate's long brown hair over her shoulder and tipped her head to the side in consideration. 'Yes. I think this look will be received well at Wood View High.'

'I'd say definitely if your motivation is to help curb teenage pregnancy,' Kate said, thinking no one in their right mind would find this look attractive.

Cheryl winked. 'With great talent comes great responsibility. Give your mum my love and tell her I'll pop over on Friday, usual time, to take her to bridge.'

Juliet waylaid her as she was sticking her feet into Juliet's bright, happy, purple-skulls-and-orange-daisy covered festival wellies. Kate hadn't exactly unpacked, yet. Not that there was much room to in Wren Cottage. At least, that was her excuse.

'Sorry,' Juliet muttered, pulling the front door shut behind her. 'She just wants the two of you to–'

'It's okay,' Kate answered, cutting her off with a, 'And I know. Your mum's been completely Switzerland about all of this, which I know must be hard. It'll get better. I'll get better at dealing with it.'

'You're going to have to if you're staying.'

'I know. I just–'

Juliet gave a brief nod of understanding. 'Didn't need this all in your face from the moment you walked through the door? I'm sorry I haven't been around since you've got back. It's wedding season and I've been flat out. But I promise we'll talk tonight. Hey,' she looked down, her red hair falling over her shoulder as she noticed Kate's foot attire for the first time. 'It's a little hot for boots – you want to borrow something else and take the car?'

'No. The walk will do me good. And where I'm going I don't need to dress up.' Kate's denim cut-offs, buttercup-yellow gypsy top and festival wellies would be perfectly acceptable for where she was going.

'You're not going to visit your mum?'

'Nope.'

'Then, where – oh,' Juliet flushed scarlet. 'You're going to see Oscar?'

'Nope. God, Juliet, if I can't pluck up the courage to see mum, you can be damn certain I haven't got the balls to see my brother-in-law, yet.'

'Right. But, well, you'll have to see him eventually. Tell him you're back and what you're planning to do.'

'Why?' Kate asked, her bottom lip poking out sulkily.

'What do you mean, why? Don't you think he's going to notice if you buy The Clock House and open it up as a spa?'

'No... yes...' Kate looked around for something handy to hang her subject-change on and looked right into Juliet's flushed face. 'What's with the red face?'

'What?' Juliet swallowed.

'You,' Kate answered, waving her hand in her cousin's face, 'and the blushing thing you've got going on.'

'Hello?' Juliet pointed to her ginger hair. 'Daily occurrence, with this mop, isn't it?'

'I suppose,' Kate said, not sure whether to delve deeper or leave Juliet to her poor excuse.

'So, if you're not going to meet Oscar, where are you going then? Oh–'

'Yep.'

'Do you want me to come with you?'

'Nope. And don't look so worried. This madness was your idea, remember?'

'I don't know what I was thinking,' Juliet ran her hands down the front of her pretty white embroidery anglaise dress and gave Kate a rueful look. 'Well, yes, I do know what I was thinking. It had a kind of two-birds-with-one-stone sort of symmetry.'

Should've delved deeper, Kate realised. 'When I get back we'll have a cuppa and you can tell me all about the birds and the stones, okay?'

'Okay,' Juliet said, sounding not okay, at all.

Leaning over, Kate gave her cousin a quick reassuring kiss on the cheek. 'Hey, it's going to be fine. Promise.' And before Juliet could say something else heartfelt that would stop her from getting her first look at the whole reason she'd come back, she waved cheerio.

Turning left, she walked down the path that would take her to the cut-through into Whispers Wood and allow her to emerge onto the village green. In a bid to settle the butterflies she took a deep breath and inhaled a lungful of freshly mown grass and early summer flowers.

The scent helped her feel happier. Less weighted-down. Until she started thinking about how she'd have to walk past the little parade of shops on the other side of the village green. Well, she said parade – there were five units and two of them were permanently empty these days. The other three consisted of the Post Office, a dentist and Big Kev's corner shop.

Should she pop in and say 'Hi' while she was out and about? Casually mention that she had re-entered the Whispers Wood atmosphere and had touched down permanently?

Her pace automatically slowed at the thought.

She was such a coward.

It was only going to get more difficult if she kept letting herself off the hook, wasn't it? Maybe if the first person she'd bumped into as she was heaving her rucksack and wheelie-case out of the taxi after it had pulled up outside Wren Cottage hadn't been Sandeep, the postman. And maybe if he hadn't looked agog at her when she'd told him she was back to stay...

And maybe if she wasn't secretly smarting from every one of the staggered-disbelief expressions she encountered when she went all 'full-disclosure' she could keep it up.

As she entered the woods she exchanged the scent of freshly cut grass, with its hint of creeping roses and honeysuckle for the smell of dry, dusty, musty earth and trees. Here, she automatically followed the well-beaten dirt track right through the centre and noticed that street lamps had been installed either end since she'd last used the cut-through.

She wondered how long the village meeting about street lamps versus the existing wildlife's quality of life had gone on for, because she was betting Whispers Woods' unofficial 'mayor', Crispin Harlow, had called a meeting to discuss the issue.

Crispin Harlow had become the unofficial village head-honcho ten years ago, when he'd moved in, promptly formed the Whispers Wood Residents' Association, and Aunt Cheryl and Aunt Cheryl's best friend, Trudie McTravers, had used the AOB section at one of his meetings to present him with 'robes' they'd run up from leftover material from the nativity play Trudie had helped put on at the local primary school. Crispin didn't really do irony and, you know that Shakespeare saying: 'clothes maketh the man'? As far as Kate was aware he'd been unstoppable ever since.

If Old Man Isaac still allowed Crispin to use The Clock House for 'all things village-related' meetings, Kate wondered how she'd deal with Crispin when it was time to tell him she owned the building and meetings would need to be booked through her.

Kate stopped mid-stride.

She mustn't start thinking of it as hers.

Not yet.

Chapter 6

Voice of the Beehive

Kate

Kate emerged from the cut-through into brilliant sunlight and couldn't understand why there was a lot of shouting going on. As her eyes adjusted, there, under the shade of the oak trees lining the right hand side of the green was her answer... Someone had gone and let the army in to train on the green.

Her first thought was, did Crispin know about this?

Her second thought, as she looked closer, was that the army would probably be full of fitter, younger individuals, who wouldn't give away their position by training in varying eye-watering shades of neon Lycra.

So the noughties had truly arrived in Whispers Wood. Prior to this, outdoor exercise in the village was usually of the T'ai Chi pace, rather than full-on, cardiac-arrest-inducing (by the looks of some of the participants), sergeant-major-style-y circuit-training.

'Kate? Kate Somersby? Sweetie, is that you?'

Kate looked over in the direction of the voice, a smile breaking out over her face. 'Hi, Trudie – looking good.'

'Oh, thanks, sweetie. Trying to lose these last fifteen pounds is killer,' she puffed out as she lunged not so much gracefully as disgracefully across the green towards her.

'I see that,' Kate replied.

Kate always thought of Trudie McTravers as the Eddie to Aunt Cheryl's Pats because whenever they got together and alcohol was involved, mayhem wasn't usually far behind.

Wonderfully larger-than-life and the self-appointed creative director of the local Whispers Wood am-dram society, rumour had it that during the eighties Trudie had starred in several Alan Ayckbourn plays in the West End.

Rumour also had it that before quiet and reserved bank manager, Nigel, had snapped her up she'd also starred in several films of an adult nature. Trudie never confirmed nor denied the rumours and as her Twitter ID was: @ AFlairForTheDramatic, Kate suspected she wasn't only the star of such rumours but the source as well.

'You just get back?' Trudie puffed out.

Kate nodded. 'A couple of days ago.'

Trudie's gaze strayed to Kate's 'do' and grinned. 'Cheryl?'

'Cheryl,' Kate confirmed.

'How long are you back for?'

'Oh, this time I was thinking,' she leaned forward conspiratorially and whispered, 'of forever'.

Trudie's laugh took on a braying quality before she brought herself under control. 'Okay, but actually, that's got me thinking... How long are you back for really, because we're doing *Midsummer Night's Dream* again, and you always made a fabulous Titania.'

Kate winced at the disbelieving laugh and determined not to gently remind Trudie that it had been Bea, not her, who had played Titania, to everyone's delight.

Some years Trudie 'encouraged' (begged and bribed) so many of the Whispers Wood inhabitants into her production that she had to rope in the residents of Whispers Ford to make up an audience. But the year Bea had played Titania and Oscar Matthews had played Bottom, everyone had agreed it had been Trudie's most inspired production yet. Of course, that was the year that Bea had finally got Oscar Matthews to notice her, so...

'McTravers, are you chatting or exercising?'

Kate glanced over in the direction of the booming voice. 'Oops,' she whispered out of the side of her mouth to Trudie, 'I don't think Private Benjamin is allowed to talk.'

'I'm a woman,' Trudie shouted back at the fitness instructor, 'I can talk and exercise.'

'Prove it,' ordered Mr Sergeant Major, 'and give me fifteen star jumps while you're standing around chatting the day away.'

'Is he for real?' Kate asked in equal parts scared and impressed as Trudie duly obliged.

'Trust me, he is definitely for real,' Trudie puffed out. 'Last week, he caught Crispin chatting to Sandeep and made him drop and give him twenty.'

'No! And Crispin did it?'

'Managed twelve before he passed out.'

'Oh my God, that's barbaric.' Although, darn, because she would have loved to have seen that.

She looked over at the rest of the class, hanging out in the shade of the trees, doing burpees. Burpees! On Whispers Wood green. It defied all village logic. Or maybe she'd been away too long. 'Trudie, are you sure this guy isn't violating your civil rights or something?'

'Sweetie, I can't afford to care if I want to lose the fifteen pounds. Besides,' she gasped mid star-jump. 'Have you seen the way his butt looks in those shorts?'

Kate couldn't help it – she looked over at the fitness instructor and, yes, checked out his butt encased in the kind of white shorts last seen in an eighties Wimbledon final. 'Wow. Um. Very Magnum P.I.'

'Such a shame that the face was made for radio.'

'Trudie,' Kate admonished.

'At least I get to spend one hour three mornings a week doing a little butt-staring,' Trudie wriggled her eyebrows appreciatively.

'And what does Nigel have to say about this new hobby of yours?'

'Oh he's far too busy reaping the rewards to complain.'

Kate screwed up her face. 'Euw! T.M.I.'

'What can you possibly mean,' Trudie said, adopting an innocent expression. 'I'm talking about having the stamina to help Nigel out in the garden – what are you talking about?'

Kate laughed.

'Now all I have to do,' Trudie added, her attention on the fitness instructor, 'is to convince Mr Butt that after helping out backstage at the summer play, he really wants to be in the Christmas one.'

'Playing what? The back end of the pantomime horse?'

'Trudie McTravers, do not make me come over there,' came the voice from the other end of the green.

'Help,' Trudie said, not very convincingly.

'Run!' Kate advised. 'Run like the wind.'

Trudie finished her star-jumps and turned to give Kate a mock salute. 'Back for forever, you say?'

'Uh-huh,' Kate murmured, saluting back, convinced she heard Trudie mutter a, 'well, just when you think you've heard it all,' under her breath as she sort of yomped back to the rest of the class.

Kate's smile faltered when she realised she had nothing left to distract her from what she'd come to see.

She blew out a breath to prepare for her first proper glance... and turned to face The Clock House.

There it stood.

Rising up from the far end of the village green. Strong and straight and true.

Her gaze roamed greedily over it.

The three-storeys-high, Georgian red-brick building with the ornate clock perched proudly on top was finished off with a lead dome and brass weathervane.

The sash windows still had their white trim, and the matching double doors, gleaming in the sunshine, looked as if they'd only recently been re-painted. In the brick space between the second and third floors, simple, no-fuss, wrought-iron lettering spelled out 'The Clock House'.

Her gaze sought out the face of the clock.

Without even being conscious of it, her hand moved to stroke over the locket watch she wore.

All this time, and, incredibly, a part of her had still expected the time on The Clock House clock to state 1:23pm.

She squeezed against the cool metal in her palm, the chain cutting into her neck slightly.

So selfish to think that here time would have stood still for four years.

Bold roman numerals in the same material as the signage, reigned stately over the white face of the clock and the fact that after more than a hundred years it kept good time at all was a testament to Old Man Isaac's family of clock-makers.

Kate stared and breathed.

Deeply and evenly.

Right up until she clapped eyes on the For Sale sign staked to the low brick wall in front of the building. For the second time in twenty-eight years her little world came to a grinding stop.

So this was how it felt to be blown apart that the building she'd grown up loving was up for sale.

Thank goodness that pebble had landed vein-side up.

Because maybe she really wanted this building... maybe she really *needed* this building... She took a shaky step forward, and then another, and then another, so that by the time she'd hopped over the low brick wall and stepped onto the gravel drive, her heart was pounding clear out of her chest.

She hesitated and then rallied. She'd come this far, hadn't she? Silly to turn away now.

With trembling hands she reached out to the key-safe Old Man Isaac had fitted years ago. Everyone in Whispers Wood knew the combination because everyone used the building for village events. Flipping open the cover to expose the keypad, she entered the code her mother used before she had started the B&B, when she'd been responsible for cleaning the building, and prayed it hadn't been altered.

Seconds later and the key-safe opened to reveal a set of brass keys.

In for a penny in for a pound.

Kate put the largest of the keys in the lock, turned it, pushed open the door and stepped across the threshold.

The shouting from the exercise group was drowned out by the whooshing in her ears as mine after mine dropped into her field of memory and exploded. Too quick for her to check for injury – too sharp to doubt she would escape unscathed.

The Somersby Sisters.

Bea and Kate.

Five years old and wearing summer school dresses of green and white check. White ankle socks with frills and scuffed black shoes. Chasing each other round the building. Screeching with glee as they cartwheeled across the parquet flooring. Collapsing in a fit of giggles when they were told off for being too loud, too happy, too exuberant.

The Somersby Sisters.

Bea and Kate.

Fifteen years old. Their school uniform skirts rolled up short, their long socks rolled down. School ties shoved into their bags. Lying in the gardens behind The Clock House, bitching about Gloria Pavey and whispering about boys.

The Somersby Sisters.

Bea and Kate.

Twenty. In the main foyer, clearing up after Bea and Oscar's engagement party. A little drunk and talking nineteen to the dozen about how, one day, they were going to open their own business – a little day spa that would use only the best organic treatments and would be set in the most perfect premises. Premises as perfect as The Clock House.

A Somersby Sister, 15th October 2013.

Kate.

Twenty-four and staring up at The Clock House.

Dressed in black.

Blind with tears.

Filled with rage.

And completely and utterly finished with dreams.

The sound of a door closing brought Kate back to life. She whirled around, the echoes of memory so strong she half expected to see a replay of a five-year-old Bea disappearing around a corner. But there was no movement. No sound. Nothing.

Heaving in a breath she realised she'd been so caught up she'd been moving through the building by rote and now she was standing in the largest of the main rooms on the ground floor – the one that Trudie used for productions because you could erect a stage at one end and still have space for at least twenty rows of seating for the audience.

Kate's gaze wandered from the soothing eau de nil paint on the walls, up to the high white painted ceiling with its ornate coving and now-naked ceiling-rose. At one time there'd been a *Phantom-of-the-Opera*-worthy chandelier hanging from the rose. Kate had seen photographs of it from when the building had belonged to Old Man Isaac's great-grandfather – a famous clockmaker who'd settled in the village and built this place. If she did get to open this place as a spa she was determined to bring back a little of that opulence for customers to appreciate.

It was sad Old Man Isaac didn't have anyone left in his family to pass the building on to, but given the chance, she'd make him proud with what she wanted to turn it into.

With the memories she'd been so worried about facing starting to fade, Kate walked back through the large open foyer and into the next main room. This room was slightly smaller because of the kitchenette. Kate knew that contained within the Formica cabinets were topsy-turvy towers of teacups with matching saucers and plates in what she was fairly certain Farrow and Ball would name 'Catering Crockery in Hospital Blue'.

In the far corner of the room there was a lonely spinner of leaflets, their print faded with time and the sunlight that poured in through the floor-to-ceiling double doors. Soft-play mats in primary colours were stacked in the corner. Evidence that the local nursery still used the room.

Kate was going to need to work out how to zone the areas so that there was still plenty of space for village functions. Her mind drifted to thoughts of building regulations. What if there was some sort of covenant on the land that meant you couldn't use the building for a commercial enterprise?

She thought of Bea's box files. Ever since Kate had come up with the hare-brained scheme to open a day spa one day, Bea had got fixated on opening it in The Clock House. Not that they ever envisaged having the funds to buy the building. But still. The dreams had had to be corralled somehow and so Bea had collated files of research and made business plan after business plan.

If Kate was going to do this, she'd need to ask Oscar if he'd kept all of Bea's files.

If she did this?

It hit her then how big a thing this was to do. And who was she, with her zero experience, to have a go?

The doubt she'd managed to bat away the moment she'd put that pebble in her pocket gathered and swooped, to peck at her.

What on earth had she been thinking? Had she even *been* thinking? If she really wanted to resurrect past dreams, she should do it in a place that didn't know her. Somewhere where if she failed, that failure wouldn't strike at the heart of those she loved.

Needing air, she unlocked one of the patio doors and stepped out into the walled garden. She walked towards the intricately carved wrought-iron moon-gate in the wall, overwhelmed with feeling.

She hadn't realised how much she yearned for the opportunity to settle and build something. Something that would end all the regret and the running.

She'd toyed with this future like a cat toys with a mouse too many times to count and now she wasn't sure she'd ever believe she deserved it.

How had she managed to convince herself that Old Man Isaac selling and Juliet sending her the postcards were signs from Bea? Now that she was actually here, standing in front of the moon-gate, and faced with the reality of what running a business would entail...

She should let it go.

It would find lovely owners. Old Man Isaac would make certain of that, she was sure.

And maybe whoever owned it next would turn it back into a house.

A home.

And on her visits back to Whispers Wood, she'd be able to walk past it without feeling so divided.

Without feeling.

With her heart heavy in her chest she opened the moon-gate and walked through, thinking she'd take one last look and then explain to Juliet that she was very sorry, but she wasn't the right person to take over the place.

She stopped to take in the scene before her.

Oh my.

So ironic that here time had absolutely stood still, she thought, as she looked around.

It always looked best in spring and summer. The wild meadow on the other side of the moon-gate. Where tall grass vied for space with poppies, cornflowers and buttercups.

And there, tucked away amongst the large shrubs of buddleia, was what Kate had been unconsciously looking for since opening the main door of the building.

As she stared at the roofs of the white painted hives, the tears finally spilled from Kate's brown eyes.

She'd found Bea's bees.

Chapter 7

Then I Saw Her Face, Now I'm A Belieber!

Daniel

Daniel was finishing his cool-down when the lady with the crazy energy from the exercise class approached.

Impish blue eyes, fire-engine-red lips and dressed from head to toe in a pink so bright it hurt his eyes, she bounced up and greeted him with a 'Cooee,' and a hand-wave.

'Morning,' he replied cautiously.

'I don't think we've seen you around here before, have we, sweetie? I'm guessing it's you that owns that beautiful car that Ted is working on?'

Daniel tried to remember that outside London it was perfectly acceptable to talk to complete strangers. 'That's right.'

'So, I suppose you'll be with us until Ted fixes you up?'

'I guess so,' Daniel agreed, although, truth to tell, he'd enjoyed the last couple of days enough to have thought about staying on. He hadn't had a holiday in years and the change of pace had reminded him that not everyone in the world was caught up in that 'concrete jungle where dreams are made of', mentality.

When Ted had intimated that Daniel would rather be in a five-star hotel than the local village B&B, he hadn't been that far off the mark. He'd hot-footed it out of London with his only thought being to get away, but if Monroe hadn't broken down, it wouldn't have occurred to Daniel to stop in a village, or even small town. He'd have carried on driving until he'd hit the next major city and paid a lot of money to stay in an impersonal hotel.

He'd really lucked out at the B&B, though, because in addition to the fabulous breakfasts and scrumptious cream teas, he would swear his host had instantly picked up on his need for anonymity. Other than some quiet and polite greetings, he'd been left to his own devices. Kicking back and mulling things over had been something he'd needed to do for weeks.

'What a shame you're not staying the summer, at least,' the woman in front of him said and Daniel felt her gaze slide interestingly over him from head to toe. He took an awkward step backwards. Was she... hitting on him? Surely not. She was at least twice his age.

'I guess you probably don't get a lot of newcomers to the village?' he asked, attempting to stretch the conversation and prove he wasn't feeling the pressure of small talk.

'Too true, sweetie. But you mustn't mind me – I'm always on the lookout, that's all.'

The lookout? He was just wondering if there was any tactful way of telling her he wasn't interested but that he could show her how to set up a Tinder account when he saw *her*.

It was the third time he'd spotted her in two days.

The first time, she'd been hauling case out of the back of

that taxi and Monroe hadn't exactly shown herself in her best light. The second time, she'd been pacing back and forth across the small front garden of the cottage the taxi had pulled up outside of. The last time he'd seen her had been a few moments before – talking to the woman now standing in front of him. He'd spotted the boots first before lifting his gaze to notice the legs were out again. By the time he'd reached the daisy-dukes he'd been so distracted he'd nearly run into a tree. Righting himself and concerned he might end up doing something else embarrassing, like tripping over a leaf and face-planting right in front of her, he'd elected to pretend he hadn't seen her and concentrate on getting the rest of his run in.

'I have to be on the lookout,' the woman in pink told him, 'I'm casting for *A Midsummer Night's Dream* and really want us in rehearsals by the end of this month.'

Daniel wasn't listening. He was too interested in watching the gorgeous brunette with the dynamite legs hop over the low brick wall in front of the building at the end of the village green and... wait, had she just kicked that For Sale sign?

He grinned as he watched her give it a second kick before she disappeared into the building.

'...and I'm always on the lookout for fresh talent. I don't suppose you can act, sing or dance as well as you look?'

Daniel whipped his attention back to the woman in front of him. 'I'm sorry, cast members?'

'Oh, sweetie, don't worry, I can see your mind is elsewhere,' she said, with a chuckle, as she turned in the direction of his gaze.

She wasn't wrong. With a nod of his head towards the building in front of them, he found himself asking, 'Is The Clock House a private residence?' Maybe she kicked the sign because she lived there and didn't want to move.

'I guess technically it is. Old Man Isaac – that's the owner, moved out a few years ago when he turned eighty. Got a bit much for him,' the woman confided. 'Moved into one of the cottages opposite,' she explained, pointing in the direction of the charming stone cottages at the other end of the green. 'He never did get married nor have any children, so he sort of keeps the building open for the village to use it. You know, for toddler groups and the local flower-arranging class, that sort of thing. It's a fabulous space. My am-dram group meets there every week.'

'I see. So if the door was open I would be free to go in and take a look around?'

'Of course. On a Thursday morning it should be empty. I'm going to need your name, though.'

'My name?'

'And a few other details,' she said, grinning from ear to ear.

Oh, she was good. He smiled and held out his hand. 'Daniel Westlake. And you already know I'm in the village because my car broke down and I'm waiting for Ted to get the part he needs and then fit it.'

'And where are you staying while you're here?'

'At the little B&B on the other side of the village. Sheila Somersby's place?'

'I know it. Sheila has a lovely place.' And apparently deciding he was harmless, she finished with, 'Well, Daniel

Westlake, it's been lovely to meet you. Enjoy your visit at The Clock House. I'm Trudie McTravers. It's a small place, so no doubt we'll run into each other again.'

'Don't forget to stretch and cool-down properly before you leave the green.'

She smiled and in a flurry of pink and red, jogged back across the green.

Daniel walked towards The Clock House and bypassing hopping over the wall, opted for the perfectly accessible gated entrance. Three strides across the gravel and he was poking his head inside the front doors.

'Well, I'll be damned,' he muttered as he stepped across the threshold into the large foyer that was so much more grand than he had been expecting.

He turned in a circle, blowing out a long whistle when he saw the beautiful sweeping staircase which curved up to the next floor. The stick balusters were painted in thick creamy gloss, and the handrail and stair-treads had been left in their original dark wood, though stained with a clear protective varnish. All the walls were painted in a watery green, right up to the cornicing, which was painted in simple white.

Daniel couldn't believe the owner, this Old Man Isaac fellow, had let the village use such a stately place for meetings and what-not. Or that the villagers had kept it so lovingly maintained. Said something about the people of Whispers Wood, didn't it?

As he crossed the parquet floor he wondered what it would have been like to grow up in a house like this one. He'd spent most of his childhood in a crowded semi in Stevenage with his mum, his aunt and uncle, and their two kids, because his father was away such a lot. It hadn't been a bad upbringing, but he'd rather have been on the road with his dad. At least in those early years, Daniel reflected, before automatically shutting his thoughts down.

Taken with the welcoming ambience, he stole up the staircase to explore, forgetting he was supposed to be looking out for a glimpse of his 'wonder woman'.

He guessed once upon a time the rooms on the second floor would have been one-room deep, in keeping with the traditional Georgian layout. Reaching out, he knocked against one of the walls in the same way he'd seen the woman with all the scarves do in that property programme – and concluded that most of the walls were partition. If it was up to him he'd keep some of them divided and open some out.

To use as what, though?

And that's when it hit him.

If it was him he'd open this place up as office space... conference facilities... something that would bring people who worked in isolation together.

Within minutes, the creative side of his brain, held in check for far too long, was firing like a Nerf gun at a seven-year-olds birthday party. Inspiration flexed back to life like an old and wasted muscle and as he continued his tour he focused on the fact that the place was for sale and how he needed something to do.

What would it be like to get to come to work in a space like this every day?

Hadn't he been looking for a fresh start?

Maybe Monroe breaking down was fate. Daniel came to a sudden halt halfway back down the stairs to the ground floor. He wasn't sure he believed in fate. Believing in fate would surely render the last year as being unavoidable and Daniel couldn't accept that. He was too certain that if he'd been paying proper attention – been looking at the whole picture – he would have spotted what Hugo had been up to earlier.

By the time he'd made it back down to the foyer Daniel had all but totally convinced himself that one weird flight of fancy was allowed after everything that had happened lately. To truly consider buying this place when he already had one failed business under his belt was career suicide.

Except… he couldn't imagine working for someone else. Couldn't think how to transition from accountancy to anything else without having to explain this whole sorry year and as soon as anyone discovered what had happened at West and Westlake, it wouldn't matter that he was the innocent party. He'd be considered a risk.

Trudie McTravers had said the village used this place for functions. All he'd be doing, if he bought it, would be guaranteeing that even more people could use it. He remembered all those fruitless hours searching for affordable business premises when he and Hugo had located to London. For the first eight months, they'd had to run West and Westlake from a combination of Hugo's front room and the Starbucks down the road.

There must be people in the surrounding villages who worked from home. Sole business owners having to ask their kids to keep the noise down because they were working. Or people trying to find a place to hold a meeting. Setting up this place as a pop-up and pop-in work premises would make the perfect small business.

A business where the only faith he'd have to have would be in himself.

He wandered into a room with a small kitchenette, thinking that he was crazy.

A business like he was thinking of wasn't about numbers. It wasn't accountancy.

It was... sexier.

More appealing.

But who swapped numbers, facts and assurances for a creative small business that would depend on getting people in to turn a profit?

Straight-down-the-line Daniel Westlake certainly wouldn't. Would he?

Shoving a hand through his nut brown hair in frustration, he sighed. He probably couldn't afford it anyway.

There was something about this place, though. He'd only been in it for a few moments.

Only been in the village for a handful more.

Crazy.

Yet he had his phone in his hand with half a mind to check house prices in the area before he realised that it was actually ringing.

'Hello?' he said, answering the call, grateful for the interruption because there was working out what to do next business-wise and there was getting completely carried away without doing a shred of research into a field he knew nothing about.

'Mr Westlake? It's Ted... said I'd ring you when–'

Daniel couldn't hear a thing over the music playing in the background. 'Sorry? What? I can't hear you.'

'...I just wanted to let you know that it's going to take a few more days to fit it.'

'So, what exactly was the problem with her, then?' Daniel shouted. 'Sorry – can you turn the music down your end? I can't make out – oomph–'

Daniel felt a sudden impact against his back.

'What the–' he stopped mid-sentence because then there was softness pressed up against him.

Instinctively he turned, his arms coming protectively out and around the warmth that had ploughed into him.

The fall was so unexpected he didn't have time to twist and soften the other person's landing.

His breath whooshed out of him as he landed and then didn't quite make it all the way back into his lungs because that was when he registered that the person on the hard parquet floor with him, was *her*.

Outstanding!

Because falling *on* her was so much better than falling down in front of her.

'I'm so sorry,' he finally managed, growing concerned when she didn't move or make any kind of sound as she lay under him. 'Hey?' he whispered, leaning forward to check for signs of life, his heart speeding up when she didn't respond. 'Hey, hey, hey,' he repeated, each word getting a little louder and more panicky when she continued to lie silent under him.

His hand came out to gently sweep across her cheekbone

and without giving him any time to prepare, her huge, sparkling brown eyes suddenly flashed open to stare up at him.

Daniel swallowed. He wasn't sure he'd ever seen such big, such beautiful, such emotive brown eyes. 'Are you all right?' he asked.

'I'm not sure.' She lifted a hand to the back of her head and groaned. 'I think I might be dead.' She blinked a couple of times and then frowned. 'Although I have to say it's a huge surprise if I am – I mean, I always thought there'd be harp music or bells in heaven... I definitely didn't figure on The Big Man being a Justin Bieber fan.'

Chapter 8

The Whirling Dervish in the Wild Wellies

Daniel

'A "what" fan?' Daniel asked, unsure she was making sense. Maybe he'd really hurt her when he'd landed on top of her.

'You can't hear music?' she asked, wincing slightly as she moved her head to the side, as if to check she could hear properly.

Over the sound of his thumping heart, Daniel suddenly registered a voice singing the words, 'Is It Too Late For Me To Say Sorry Now', and in a smooth, and let's face it, basic accountancy move, put two and two together. 'Oh, hell. The music you can hear is coming from my phone. Hold tight,' he said and with one hand anchoring her to him, he reached out to grab the phone that had fallen from his hand when they'd hit the ground. 'Ted? I'm sorry, I'm going to have to call you back, okay?' and without waiting for a reply, he ended the call.

'So, I'm not in heaven, then?' she asked.

'I hope that's not too disappointing for you.'

An almost sorrowful expression that he couldn't hope to decipher the meaning behind flitted briefly into her eyes before she chased it away with a determined, 'Nah, I'm a glass half-full kind of gal.'

He smiled and wondered how long he could leave it before mentioning her long legs clamped around his hips.

Giving in to the urge to touch her again, he reached out and repeated the stroke of his thumb gently across her cheekbone. Her skin was like velvet and was it his imagination or did she tremble under him? 'So.' He blew out a soft breath. 'You're really real.'

'As opposed to...?'

'I've been wondering if you were a ghost,' he admitted.

She looked intrigued. 'Are we talking about the "Don't Cross the Streams" kind, or the standing behind a pottery wheel, kind?'

'The second one, I think,' he answered.

She nodded. 'Right, because who doesn't love clay?' And then that same haunting expression of earlier came back before she closed her eyes briefly, as if to smother it. When her eyelids fluttered open again, she said quietly, 'It's this place. It'll do that to you. Bring back ghosts.'

He wondered what ghosts she'd been running from when she'd hurled herself through the open door and into him and he wanted to lift the heaviness from her words. 'Ah, but when I first saw you, you weren't in here.'

'I wasn't? Where did you first see me, then?' Her expression took on an exaggerated thoughtful pose before she suddenly snapped her fingers, 'Oh wait... was it... in your dreams?'

A laugh rumbled out of him. 'You never say what's expected, do you?'

'And you do, I suppose?'

'Plus, you have really weird hair,' he replied, without missing a beat.

She sniffed. 'I'll have you know that my current deconstructed/reconstructed Amy Winehouse do is all the rage. At least, it will be for prom,' she added, as if that explained everything.

It really didn't, but being as he was lying on the floor in a building he'd just decided to buy, with a girl averse to talking in normal sentences, he was so far past surreal it would be silly to care.

Hell, maybe the knock had rendered him unconscious and *he* was the one hallucinating. As if to double-check the woman lying under him was indeed really real, he stared back down at her. That was when he noticed the tear tracks.

'You've been crying,' he accused.

The fun that had come back into her eyes left again.

'Hey, your hair isn't that bad,' he added, trying to soften his claim about her crying.

Her full lips twitched. 'It really is, but it was made with love, so I had to go with it. Are you going to let me up, then?'

'Thinking about it,' he replied, trying to come up with an excuse that meant he didn't have to. 'Why?' he asked. 'Are you uncomfortable?'

She gave him a look that said, not entirely, which he took as encouragement.

Fine by him to stay on the floor with her.

'So are you going to tell me why you've been crying?' he prodded, wanting to know what it was that had sent her whirling into his arms.

Immediately the shields came up. He shouldn't have pressed it. He felt bad for landing on top of her, though – wanted to make sure he hadn't put some of the sting in her eyes.

'It's fine. I'm fine,' she said, her voice flat. 'Let me up, will you?'

'Or, we could do the Snow Patrol thing and let me lie with you and just forget the world.'

'So tempting. And yet...' This time there was a note of steel in her voice that had him holding his hands up in surrender.

'Okay, letting you up now... Although I feel obliged to mention, that in order for me to let you up, you're going to have to unwrap those gorgeous long legs of yours from around me first.'

For a second, she looked like she didn't really want to and he really liked how that made him feel, so much so that when, a few moments later, he felt her legs loosen their hold around him, disappointment punched him in the gut.

Rising to his feet, he pulled her with him.

'Are you sure you're feeling all right?' he asked. 'No wooziness? No sprains? No serious damage done?'

She smoothed her hands over her torso and then down her long, long legs, making him completely lose his train of thought. 'I think I'm good. You okay?'

'Me? Oh, I'll live. Had a perfect landing, didn't I?'

'I guess it's not every day you get taken down by a whirling dervish in wild wellies. Sorry about that, by the way.'

'Apology most definitely accepted. Daniel,' he said, by way of introduction, taking her hand to make a formal handshake.

'Daniel,' she said, as if testing out the feel of his name on her tongue. She shook his hand firmly and then, with a tip of her head, queried, 'Not Dan? Danny?'

Daniel went from being super-aware of the sound of his name on her lips to being on the back foot. He never went by Dan and certainly never Danny. Danny Westlake was his father. 'Just Daniel,' he reiterated, waiting to see what she made of that.

She hesitated, as if she could tell there was a story behind his insistence, and then seemed to accept that it wasn't her right to know that story. It only made him like her more.

'Okay, Just Daniel. I'm Kate.'

'As in, *Kiss me, Kate?*' he rallied, determined to settle his heart-rate back to a more normal rhythm. Unless he had the worst luck in the world and Kate was a racing-car fan, he doubted she'd have put the name Danny and the name Westlake together and come to a confirmation that meant their budding acquaintance was over before it had really begun.

'As in, just Kate,' she answered, although he could swear she was holding back a smile.

'So, Just Kate, are you the owner of this beautiful building?'

'I am. Well, what I mean is that I'm going to be.'

'You're interested in buying it?' He tried to hide the disappointment, worried he could feel so let down at the news when he'd only been in the building less than thirty minutes.

'I'm *going* to buy it,' she said, with complete confidence.

She couldn't be more than mid-to-late twenties. He wasn't

much older than that. His gaze slid over her attire. She didn't look like the horse-and-hound set, who came from money, were schooled privately and then lived in Chelsea for a few years before moving back home to add to the country pile, so how could she possibly afford it?

'Sounds like you have some sort of special advantage,' he said, shoving his hands into his pockets.

'I guess you'd call it a home advantage.'

Daniel frowned. 'Is that what the current owner is looking for? Someone who knows the area? I'd have thought they'd be more interested making as much money from the sale as possible.'

She shook her head. 'The owner of this particular building isn't like that. At least, I'm banking on that being the case,' she admitted.

So maybe she didn't have the funds and was getting a little ahead of herself? Daniel let the prospect sink in. If the owner wasn't looking for top market value – just wanted to get shot of the property as quickly as possible, he was probably still in with a chance of buying it himself. His inner-sensible did a double-take. Buying a building because someone else was implying he couldn't was even crazier than wanting to buy it in the first place. 'Maybe the owners are more interested in someone being able to make something of this place,' he said, almost to himself as excitement in his business idea notched up a gear.

'That's what I intend to do. Make something of it, I mean,' Kate declared, sliding her hands into the frayed pockets of her exquisitely short shorts.

She looked so wonderfully brave and naively defiant standing in front of him that he found a grin starting at the corners of his mouth and spreading.

'Well, this is going to make life interesting,' he told her, 'because so do I.'

Her jaw dropped open. 'Excuse me?'

'I intend to make something of this place too. Soon as I walked in, I knew,' he said, making himself ignore the shock streaking naked through her eyes. Telling himself that business was business and if he'd been more assertive with West and Westlake then he might have stopped everything from turning out like it had. 'This place is perfect.'

'Perfect for what?'

'For me.'

'For you? You're seriously interested in buying The Clock House?'

'I'm seriously *intending* to *buy* The Clock House.'

'But you can't,' she spluttered.

'Why not?'

'Because...'

'Because?' For a moment he was worried those lovely chocolate brown orbs were going to fill with water and he'd be lost, but after a few seconds a fire sparked the amber flecks reminding him of a phoenix bursting into life again.

'Because I know the owner. And I know he'll sell to me.'

'Yeah?'

'Yeah,' she answered.

'You're convinced then that you can get together the capital needed to buy a place of this size?'

She smiled.

No, grinned.

Like a Cheshire cat.

And he should not find that sexy!

He began to revisit his theory that she was some sort of multi-millionairess. Maybe this is what she did – went about playing at businesses, trying to find one that took her fancy. Well, not this time, sweetheart, he thought, as resolve settled in his guts.

'You should probably start looking at other properties,' she said, her tone consoling.

'But I like this one.'

'I'm quite sure that there are other fabulous properties all over the country.'

'And I wish you luck in finding one,' he said, grinning.

Her eyes narrowed. 'You know, it occurs to me we haven't bumped into each other before today. Exactly how long have you lived in Whispers Wood?'

His grin slipped a little. 'Technically, I guess it would be fair to say I don't actually live here.'

'Really? Well, good luck. I hope you know how to deal with disappointment.'

'Disappointment's not something I've really had to get used to in life,' Daniel lied as the last year flashed before him in ego-smashing 4-D detail. 'Disappointment' didn't even begin to cover this last year... and yet he'd come out the other side eventually, hadn't he? And now he felt the fight lift him. 'So, I certainly hope you won't be too upset with me when I buy this place.'

'You're really that sure that you will?'

'You're really that sure that *you* will?' he countered.

Again, that super-sexy smile transformed her face, making her button-brown eyes sparkle with delight.

'I guess this is "Game-On"?'

'I guess it is,' she said. She moved towards the front doors, almost as if she knew he wasn't going to pass up the opportunity to watch those hypnotic hips swaying as she walked out on him.

When she turned and found him staring she gave him a cheeky smile. 'Oh, in case I forgot to say it already, welcome to Whispers Wood.'

Daniel tipped his head in a thank you, his eyes glued to her as she turned and walked out of The Clock House. He stared after her for a couple of seconds after the door shut and then, with a shake of his head and a huge smile on his face, he got out his phone and punched in the number on the front of the For Sale sign. He hadn't felt this upbeat and optimistic about things in ages. When he got through to the independent estate agents he was told that if he wanted to discuss terms they would be happy to make an appointment for him with the owner.

It was a little strange, but he actually liked the idea of taking a business meeting for the first time in a year. At least this one would be about new beginnings instead of wrapping things up.

He was about to leave the room when he saw something glinting on the floor, where he and Kate had tumbled to the ground.

Walking over, he picked up the necklace, and intrigued, opened the locket dangling from the chain.

On one side was a watch. The screen had a huge crack running right through the centre of it and he was only just able to work out that the time had stopped at 1:23pm.

Well, damn.

He felt awful that he'd obviously broken her watch as he'd fallen on top of her.

He frowned as his gaze fell on the photo on the opposite side of the watch.

It was a photo of a man and little girl, arms wrapped around each other and staring up at the camera laughing.

Well, double damn.

He could have sworn there'd been some chemistry between him and Kate. But thinking about it, she hadn't said anything overly flirty at all. All the smiling had been about buying this property.

God, his instincts really were shot to hell.

Chapter 9

Letting the Cat Out of the Bag

Juliet

'Exactly how long are you going to leave it before you tell Kate why you put the idea into her head with all those postcards?'

'Mum, please.' Juliet fished out the teabag from her Cath Kidston 'Garden Birds' mug and stuck the teaspoon into the hedgehog mug with slightly too much vigour. As the teabag split, she swore softly under her breath, poured the whole lot down the kitchen sink and stuck the kettle back on to boil. 'I appreciate your concern, but I have to do this in my own way, and in my own time.'

'You wait much longer and you're going to lose that offer from the bank.'

'So then I'll go and get another one,' she said, moving to open the fridge for the milk and staring inside at the contents, kind of hoping her eyes would light upon a jar labelled 'patience'.

She loved her mum, she really did. They had a wonderful relationship, especially considering they worked together every day. But some days... The days where her mum was usually right... They were sometimes the hardest.

Juliet was super-aware that time was running out on the loan offer she had from the bank and she wasn't exactly confident she'd be able to get another if this one expired, but now that Kate was actually home? Well, it felt only fair to give her at least a couple of seconds to adjust to being back.

Setting down a fresh mug of tea in front of her mum, she joined her at the small kitchen table. 'Kate and I are going to talk tonight. I promise.'

'Good stuff. And I'm sorry. I know you're not the sort to intentionally keep secrets, so I know you'll get around to telling her.'

Juliet's mouthful of tea hit her windpipe at completely the wrong angle and splurted back out of her mouth. As she tried to drag in air, Cheryl jumped up to grab a couple of pieces of kitchen roll for her.

Head down, unable to look her mother in the eye, she took the proffered kitchen roll and set about mopping up. When her mum remained silent as she sat back down again, Juliet wondered if maybe she *did know* her daughter's dirtiest secret, but out of motherly love, chose to keep quiet.

'I'm trying to think about everyone,' her mum said as Juliet took another careful sip of tea, grateful when it went down the right way. 'I don't like keeping this from Sheila. It should come from Kate, anyway, even with everything they need to work through and, well – I don't want you getting caught in the middle and getting hurt.'

'I know.' Juliet laid a hand over her mum's and squeezed

it gently before returning it to her mug. 'But I really think Kate wouldn't have come back to stay if she hadn't thought carefully about what that would mean. I know she's impulsive but she's never ridden roughshod over people's feelings.'

'True,' Cheryl agreed and then added almost to herself, 'if anything, everyone has tended to ride roughshod over hers. Or ignore them entirely.' There was a small sigh and then Juliet felt her mum studying her carefully. 'You really think Old Man Isaac is going to go for all of this?'

'Of course,' Juliet answered, determined to keep the faith. 'It's a brilliant idea and who else is going to buy the place?'

At the sound of the front door slamming, Juliet looked automatically at the kitchen door, where Kate appeared. From her breathing and the glow about her, she looked as if she'd run all the way back from The Clock House.

'Okay,' Kate asked them, 'so who on earth is the guy who arrived in the village, like, three seconds ago?'

Juliet looked at her mum, who looked at Kate and said with a mystified expression, 'You're going to have to be more specific.'

'Mr Tall Dark and Handsome,' Kate said, staring at both of them. When neither Juliet nor her mum said anything, she added, 'Mr I'm All Done Working-Out So Now I'm Just Chilling Until Marvel Films Call.'

'Do you know who she's talking about?' Juliet asked, turning to her mum and getting more interested by the second at the look in Kate's eyes.

'Nope. Don't know of any superhero lookalikes around here,' chimed in Cheryl.

'That's it?' Kate pouted, her face getting redder. 'What's happened to this place? A complete stranger waltzes in and none of you thinks to start up the phone-tree? Nobody finds out where he's staying, assembles the SWAT team, goes in and applies the thumb-screws and switches on the spotlight so that they can watch him sweat as he slowly divulges every credential to his name?' She stared in askance at both of them and then, in true Kate fashion, a look of determination came into her eyes. 'Well, somebody has to take responsibility here. Auntie Cheryl, I want you to phone Trudie and find out what she knows. If it's nothing, I want you to get straight on the phone to Crispin Harlow.'

'And should I use your exact description...?' Cheryl asked, with a raised eyebrow.

'Oh,' Kate faltered. 'No. Um, he said his name was Daniel,' she tacked on helpfully, and Juliet was surprised to see the pink still hanging about on her cousin's cheeks deepen a shade further.

'So where did you bump into this Mr TDH? Was it at,' Juliet mouthed her last words, 'The Clock House?' even though her mum's back was turned as she grabbed her bag to look for her phone.

Cheryl opened the kitchen back door and stepped outside, presumably for peace and quiet when she delivered the gossip to Trudie that her niece hadn't even been back a week and had already quite possibly lost the plot.

Kate nodded. 'He was standing in the open doorway, presumably waiting for someone to walk into him. I mean who does that?'

Juliet had to hide her smile when Kate belatedly looked around, realised she was standing right in the doorway and moved to take her mum's place at the kitchen table.

'I didn't stand a chance,' Kate continued. 'There I was, wandering back in through the garden doors at a completely leisurely pace when I, well, I ran right into him. You'd think he'd have had the good sense to remain upright, because it isn't as if he isn't well-built – but no – instead he tries to do the hero thing and reach out to help me and instead we both fall to the ground.'

'Wow. You called him Mr Tall Dark and Handsome,' Juliet said, grinning delightedly. 'You said he was well-built. You're all... breathy and flushed.'

Kate grimaced. 'Yes, well, it's unusually hot for the middle of May.'

'You think he's gorgeous,' Juliet sing-songed. 'You want to date him... you want to hug him... you want to kiss him... you want to marry him.'

'Oh my God, thank you, Gracie Hart, can you bring Juliet back now,' Kate pleaded with a roll of her huge brown eyes.

'Sorry, not sorry,' Juliet shot back, laughing and trying to remember if she had ever seen Kate so flustered about a man. She'd occasionally talked about Marco in her emails, but only lightly. In fact, so lightly that by the time Juliet had realised she'd stopped mentioning him altogether, so much time had passed that Juliet hadn't wanted to open up any wounds by asking what had happened. 'So what was this guy doing at The Clock House, and how did it go when you got there?' Juliet's hand snuck under the table to tightly cross her fingers.

'He–'

'Right,' Cheryl said, coming back into the kitchen, and cutting Kate off, 'Trudie couldn't actually remember this Daniel's last name.'

Kate threw her hands dramatically up into the air. 'Fabulous. How am I supposed to Google him now?'

'Why do we need to Google him?' Juliet asked.

'So, if I could finish…?' Cheryl said, nodding her head when Kate and Juliet turned to look at her. 'She can't remember his last name, but if you had actually gone to visit your mum like you said you were going to, you could have found out everything you needed to know for yourself because this Daniel chap is staying with her as a guest while waiting for his car to be repaired.'

Kate's eyes widened to saucers. 'Oh my God,' she whispered, 'he's infiltrated enemy camp already. Oh, this is not good. Not good at all.'

'Okay,' Juliet interrupted calmly. 'Let's suppose both Mum's and my Kate-interpreting skills are a little rusty. Start at the beginning. You went to The Clock House and…?'

Kate took a couple of calming breaths. 'Sorry. And sorry, Aunt Cheryl – I know I said I was going to see Mum, but I–' she dragged in another calming breath, 'I went to The Clock House instead. I haven't been back there since,' she swallowed and Juliet's heart broke at the bleak light that had crept into her cousin's eyes. 'I haven't been able to go back there since Bea died and so, well, that's where I went. At first the memories where overwhelming but, then it was almost as if it knew what I could handle, you know?' she looked up at both Juliet

77

and Cheryl for confirmation and all Juliet could do was smile gently back. 'Anyway, it was good. Great actually...'

Juliet's heart leaped.

'...I mean there was a middle bit where it wasn't,' Kate continued. 'Where I started thinking I can't do this. I can't be here. And I definitely can't follow old dreams and open the place back up as a business. And I was thinking how on earth am I going to tell you, Juliet?'

Juliet felt Kate looking at her and hoped she couldn't see the blood draining from her face. Kate was the strongest person she knew and she really thought that tempting her into coming back was the right thing to do. But the angst in her voice, the fine tremble in the hands she'd clasped together in front of her...

'But then,' Kate continued, 'I walked out into the courtyard and through the moon-gate – and I saw Bea's bees. They are Bea's, aren't they?'

Juliet nodded.

'Are you looking after them?' Kate asked her.

Juliet shook her head and tried to find her voice. The pretty little beehives that had stood in the meadow backing onto The Clock House remained because of one person. And darn it – why did she always lose the ability to speak when it came to him?

'Is it–' Kate looked from Juliet to Cheryl, 'Is it Oscar that's looking after them?'

Juliet felt the weight of her mother's stare, despite it being so gentle. Oh, good grief, she knew.

'It is, Oscar, yes,' Cheryl said.

Juliet watched Kate's eyes close as if to absorb what that meant and her hand snuck under the table again, this time to pick nervously at the hem of her dress.

'Okay, well, that's good,' Kate eventually whispered, shaking her head a little, presumably to put the unshed tears back in their place. 'It's good to think of them being looked after. Bea loved them so.'

Juliet couldn't bear it. Getting up from the table, she said, 'It's got to be wine o'clock somewhere in the world, right?'

Kate sniffed. 'Don't bother on my account. I'm okay. It was just a shock to see them, that's all. But, oh – I haven't even told you... It was seeing the bees that made me think everything might be okay after all.'

'It was?' Juliet felt those little wings of hope flutter inside her chest.

'Yes. I don't know if Bea ever told anyone, but she came up with all these wonderful recipes for using honey in her organic beauty treatments. That's why she kept the bees.'

'That hair conditioner she used to make,' Cheryl murmured. 'She was always telling me there was a secret ingredient. Must have been the honey.'

'It was,' Kate admitted. 'And when I saw the bees it reminded me about how she went to see Old Man Isaac to ask him if she could site them there and how he was so kind to her. After seeing them, all I could think was that I wanted to use Bea's honey. I want to open the day spa. I have to do it. Somehow. Which brings me to the teeny-tiny thorny problem...'

'Whatever it is, I'm sure we can fix it,' Juliet immediately said. 'I'll help.'

'You have no idea how much I love you for saying that,' Kate replied. 'It's this Daniel... he wants to buy it!'

'Buy what? Bea's bees? The honey?'

'No. He wants to buy The Clock House.'

'But whatever for?' Juliet asked, feeling all her plans slip away.

'Not sure. Can't let him get it, though. I need to phone Old Man Isaac and organise a meeting, or do you think it would be more professional to go through the estate agent? No. Business is all about using your contacts, right?'

Juliet's mum stood up. 'I think I'll love you and leave you both. You have a lot to talk over together.'

Juliet winced. She would have to be blind and in another room not to pick up on her mum's pointed comment.

As Cheryl went to leave she put a reassuring hand over Kate's. 'I'm so happy for you, lovey. You've done all your firsts now. I think you've picked a lovely reason to stay. And I know your mum will want to hear about this. But when you're ready, okay?'

Kate quickly wiped a tear away. 'You really think she'll be okay with me being back? I don't want to hurt her – make it worse for her.'

'Give it time. You have that if you're back now. I know it's easier on you not to expect anything. But she is trying. Truly. Juliet, if you need to go to any business meetings with Kate phone me early enough that I can shuffle my day around and fit your clients in.'

'Um, thanks, Mum.'

'Thanks, Auntie Cheryl,' Kate smiled up at her and then

Juliet felt her turn her attention to her. 'And thank you, Juliet. If you hadn't sent me those postcards...' and then, as if what Juliet's mum had just said had filtered through, she frowned and then laughed, 'I appreciate your support, but you certainly don't have to come to any meeting with me.'

'Actually,' Juliet said, clearing her throat, 'about that...'

Chapter 10

And the Cats Just Keep on Coming...

Juliet

'Juliet?' Kate asked, the moment her mum had left the cottage. 'What was your mum going on about? Why would you want to be in on a meeting about buying The Clock House?'

Juliet let out a breath and wondered how on earth to explain, without having to really, you know, explain.

'Sod it,' she muttered and got up to search for that bottle of Dutch courage. She pulled an opened bottle of white wine out of the fridge, but it was when she went to pull the cork out with her teeth that she realised Kate was staring at her with a mystified expression on her face.

'Is the alcohol for celebrating with or commiserating with?'

'Can it be both and still be okay?'

'I don't know,' Kate said carefully. 'Have I got this all wrong? Did you not send me those postcards because you wanted me to come home and buy The Clock House?'

'No, you haven't got that wrong,' she answered and with a sigh stuck the cork back in the bottle because maybe it would be better to save the alcohol for Kate's reaction, rather than being half-sozzled before she'd even finished explaining.

'Okay,' Kate said warily. 'I know it must have been hard not telling anyone about the money and where it came from,' she waited a heartbeat and then added, 'you haven't, have you?'

'No. I kept your secret.' It hadn't been that difficult. Telling anyone would have just made them hurt for what could now never be changed.

'Thank you. You're mum must be wondering what the hell is going on, though, and worrying. I mean, me suddenly talking about how I could afford to buy that building and open up a business in it.'

'Actually, she probably doesn't,' Juliet admitted. 'And that's probably on account of her thinking that I'm going to be buying it with you.'

'Buying it with—'

Juliet heard her kitchen chair being scraped back from the table as Kate hopped up. 'Did I just hear you right?'

Juliet nodded and pulled the cork out of the bottle of wine again.

'Wait,' Kate stopped her. 'You're serious, serious?'

'Serious, serious. Fancy that wine, now?'

'Forget the wine, have you got any honey lying around? I'll make us both a couple of honey martinis while you tell me why on earth your mum thinks you want to buy The Clock House?'

'Honey martinis? I haven't had one of those since…' Juliet shut her mouth when she remembered it had been after Bea's funeral. 'I don't think I've got any vodka.'

'We'll do it gin-based, then. You still have that bottle sitting on your bookshelf in the lounge, gathering dust?'

'Yep.'

'So go get it and start explaining.'

'Okay,' Juliet wandered out into the lounge, throwing a, 'It's all because of the cats,' over her shoulder.

In the lounge she reached up to the top shelf of the book-shelf and grabbed a hold of Gordon. One of her Musketeer cats, Porthos, stretched lazily on the sofa beside her as if he knew that sooner or later he'd be talked about.

'Well, of course it's because of the cats,' Kate said, as if the statement made total sense to her, when Juliet walked back into the kitchen with the bottle. 'Continue,' she said, taking the gin from her and then moving to the small workspace area to set out the rest of the ingredients. 'Or is the deal with the cats big enough that you need the alcohol first?'

'I can probably survive, but only if you hurry. So the thing with the cats...' Juliet replied hovering over Kate's shoulder. 'I overheard Gloria Pavey–'

'Gloria Pavey is a complete bitch and no one should pay any heed to whatever she says. Ever. Wait – she is still a bitch, right? Please tell me she hasn't morphed into a national treasure and I'm going to have to feel guilty for every horrible thing I ever said about her?'

'Oh rest assured, she hasn't changed one little bit. Well, actually, now that she's become the ultimate cliché, she's worse.'

'The ultimate cliché? Do tell.'

'Her hubby went off with a younger model,' Juliet explained, pushing aside the guilt for gossiping.

'No! After all the work she had done to make sure that wouldn't happen.'

'I know. But it turns out that instead of having her boobs done she should, in fact, have had them reduced and had a completely different part retrofitted instead.'

'Retrofitted?'

'The younger model is an actual model... called Bobby. As in short for Robert.'

'Bobby? Truly? Bob Pavey has left Gloria for another guy... A guy called Bobby?'

'You forgot the male model part.'

'The Bobsters... Bob and Bobby Pavey,' Kate tried the names out and Juliet watched her computing the hugeness of the gossip that had been delivered. 'God, it must be killing Gloria that she made Bob take her name when they got married.'

'I know. And you can hardly blame her for being bitter and twisted now.'

'You're right. That's, wow, a lot. I mean, Gloria's always done the competition thing with just about everyone she comes into contact with, but competing for your husband's affection against another man? How is she still even adulting?'

'She's not, really. And that's why we've all been cutting her a little slack.'

'Oh my God, I just thought – this must mean I'm officially no longer the only screw-up in the village.'

'You've never been thought of as a screw-up and *anyway...*' Juliet added, because if she didn't get the words out soon she would definitely be too drunk to filter what she was saying.

'Sorry – yes – so what did Gloria do?' Kate asked as she took a lemon from the fruit bowl and cut it in half.

'It sounds so silly now,' Juliet murmured.

'It's not silly if it hurt you. Come on, out with it.'

'Okay. So. I overheard her declaring me the 'Girl Most Likely To Become Whispers Wood Official Crazy Cat Lady'.'

There. She'd said it. And with that she opened a drawer to search for the honey drizzler stick thing she was sure she owned.

'*What?*' Kate said, spying it in the drawer and fishing it out for her and then brandishing it like a sword. 'Is she still living in that converted barn? I am going to track her down and pull her hair and kick her shins and steal her conkers and, hang on, she called you a name?'

'I know,' Juliet nodded, squishing half the lemon juice into the cocktail shaker. 'It's pathetic. I shouldn't have let it get to me. Except. Well, Kate, do you know how many cats I have now?'

'One,' Kate answered loyally, calmly chucking a shot of gin into the shaker and looking at her for confirmation.

Juliet shook her head.

'Two?' Kate asked, chucking in another shot of gin.

Juliet shook her head.

'Right, right,' Kate added, measuring out one more shot, 'I saw another one that looked like it doubled for Grumpy Cat.' She reached for the honey. 'So, you have three cats, big deal.'

'Five. I have five cats.'

The honey drizzler that Kate had plunged into the jar of

honey paused mid-air. 'Wow, Juliet... That's a lot of fur-babies to feed.'

'I know,' Juliet agreed, sliding the cocktail shaker under the spoon of honey before the contents could ooze and drip onto the countertop. 'And I swear the last two found me, I didn't find them. I've officially run out of names. There are only three musketeers, Kate. Four if you count D'Artagnan. And you know how I hate it when things don't match. Do you know what I ended up calling the last one, the one that could stunt-double for Grumpy Cat?'

'What?'

'Catty McCatFace. And now it has a complex–'

'Because it thinks it's a boat?'

'No, because, because other cats probably hear me calling it in at night and probably go all Gloria Pavey on it when I'm not around.'

'Oh Jules,' Kate said sympathetically.

If Kate was using her pet name for her, she really was sounding pathetic. Annoyed with herself, she threw open the door of the freezer and tossed a bag of ice onto the countertop. Taking a rolling pin out of the drawer, she smashed the bag and tipped some of the contents into the cocktail shaker, slammed the lid down on top and began to shake it vigorously.

'So why would buying The Clock House stop you from being the Crazy Cat Lady of Whispers Wood?' Kate asked, as she stood back to allow Juliet to reach into an overhead cupboard and grab two jam jars.

Juliet stared at the jars. It had taken hours to build up the lace-effect Washi-Tape evenly.

'Jules?'

'Having a business to work on will help take my mind off it. Cheers,' she said, passing one of the jars to Kate and clinking hers against it before taking a huge gulp.

Lemony-honey-alcoholic goodness slipped down Juliet's throat, making her think she could do this. She could make Kate understand without having to go into soul-despairing detail.

'You're going about this the wrong way,' Kate said after taking another sip. 'What would take your mind off thinking you're going to end up old, alone, mad and with a house full of cats, is to find a man.'

Juliet stared hard at her cousin and then nodded at the genius of it all. 'Yes. Thank you. I can't believe I hadn't thought of that.'

Kate winced. 'I get that pickings are slim around here, but maybe it's time to try online dating.'

'You think all my problems will disappear if I do online dating?'

'I know it's not easy–'

'Oh you do, do you?'

'Okay. I don't. And I've obviously oversimplified. Obviously there's more to this than the cat thing.'

'I've tried online dating.'

'Seriously?'

Juliet put down her drink. She'd only had half of it and couldn't believe the words had popped out like that. 'It was a disaster.' A serious disaster. She didn't think she could ever do it again. She was too shy. Too reserved. Too tentative. Too unattracted to every man bar one…

'You never wrote to me about this.'

'You never wrote to me about what happened with Marco.'

Kate stared into her drink. 'So we've been keeping secrets.'

'Yes. Secrets.' Juliet felt the familiar weight of hers and, not for the first time, thought that if she could just once shout it out at the top of her lungs, everything would be better.

'If I tell you about Marco, will you tell me your secret?' Kate asked.

'Is it so wrong to want to concentrate on something other than a man?' she asked, fully prepared now to sulk. 'The world doesn't revolve around them, you know. Maybe I want a new challenge in my life.'

'Okay. Who is he?'

'What?'

'Someone's done a number on you.'

'No they haven't.'

'Rubbish. Some guy has done a number on you and frightened you off all men.'

'No. He really hasn't. Wouldn't. Couldn't.'

Kate's eyes narrowed. 'You sound like you're talking about someone specific.'

'Nope,' Juliet answered, shoving more alcohol down her neck.

'You want to talk about anything else, don't you?'

'I really do.'

'Okay. You have ten minutes.'

'Ten minutes?'

'Ten minutes to talk about anything else and then we're going back to this because something's going on here.'

'And to think I was thinking of going into business with you!'

'Business?'

'Yes. The Clock House. Business. Together. You and me. You running the day spa. Me...' she took a much-needed sip of her cocktail and then rushed out, 'and me running a hair salon.'

'You want to open a hair salon in The Clock House?'

'Not anymore, I don't.' She sniffed. 'I changed my mind.'

'This is about the "killing two birds" thing you were talking about earlier this morning? You want to stop being thought of as the Cat Lady and you want to open a hair salon?'

'Finally. She gets it. So, what do you think?'

Kate took a sip of her drink.

Juliet wasn't completely surprised to discover she'd already finished hers.

'I think it's the most brilliant idea in the world.'

'You do?' Juliet let out the breath she hadn't even been aware she'd been holding. 'I mean, you really do?'

'I really do. But Juliet, let's be serious for a moment. We have zero experience...'

'That's not true,' Juliet defended, suddenly feeling a lot more confident now she hadn't been laughed out of her own house.

'Right,' Kate said. 'I totally forgot the part where we've both had oodles of manis and pedis and the part where we've both had our hair cut.'

'Exactly. Plus, what with your *business degree* and me *actually being a hairdresser...*'

Kate smiled. 'Oh yeah. This calls for more honey martinis.' She grabbed the shaker out of the sink and pulled the bottle of gin towards her. 'So, we're really about to think about doing this?'

'Seems like. Oh. Wait here. I need to go get my business plan.'

'You have a business plan?'

'Of course.'

'Am I the only one who hasn't actually done a business plan?'

'Yes, but that was probably because you needed to be here first and, you know, see if you could, do it.'

'I guess.'

She left Kate happily hacking the rest of the ice into tiny shards while she raced upstairs to get her laptop and files. Catty McCatface was sitting on the bed and looked up at her when she burst through her bedroom door.

'What?' Juliet whispered as she looked at the cat's permanently dour expression. 'A girl has to grow up. Move on. Make a life for herself. Find a dream that could actually come true, and work towards that. Oh, you know I'm right,' she added when the cat merely sniffed and put its head back down on its paws and closed its eyes. Quietly she left her bedroom and jogged back down the stairs.

'So what's the other reason you want to buy into The Clock House?' Kate asked before Juliet had even set the laptop on the kitchen table.

The file Juliet was holding slid to the floor. 'What happened to me getting ten minutes?'

'They've been and gone and I'm onto my second cocktail of the morning and suddenly I'm thinking something doesn't add up.'

'It d-doesn't?' she stammered as she dropped to the floor to pick up the file.

'No. It doesn't. For starters, what does your mum think?'

'You know she's always encouraged me to go it on my own one day. And the timing couldn't be better,' she rushed out, blowing a strand of hair out of her face as she rose to her feet.

'Really? Why is that? And don't tell me it's because of cats, because it can't be.'

'Well, then let me show you my plan. Let me pitch to you.'

'Okay, but I get a full Q and A, after.'

'Fair enough.' Juliet put down the file, switched on her laptop and then tucked her hair behind her ears. 'So, as I was saying, mum has always encouraged me to think long-term. You know we've always been a team, so in the beginning it felt super-logical to work with her when I qualified. But then I kept working with her because it was easy. Too easy. I find it difficult to...'

'Push yourself forward?' Kate inserted.

'Yes. Push myself forward. Thank you.' She pulled up some graphics and turned the screen towards Kate. 'Obviously I didn't tell the bank manager any of the personal stuff. This is just to help explain to you.'

Kate nodded and then sat forward in her chair, not looking at the screen but looking at Juliet with a serious expression. A completely business-like expression. 'Juliet, have you thought about how much starting a business is about pushing yourself forward?'

'I have and... hey, I thought we were going to do the Q and A after.'

'Okay, Miss Bossy Boots!'

'I'm sorry, it's just that I can't do this if you're going to interrupt – and I've been practising.'

'No more interrupting. I promise.'

'Good. So, you know how much I love doing hair and you know how hard I've worked to get where I am. But it's not enough. Not any more–' she broke off when she saw the questions enter Kate's eyes, but to Kate's credit she kept to her promise and didn't interrupt.

'Mum's not going to want to work forever and I know I could take over her clients. Spend my days doing semi-waves and sets. But I want more than that. I appreciate that this is Whispers Wood and the clientele is somewhat older. But with the right location and the right ambience... which is The Clock House all over if you buy it and open it as a day spa... Well, in a nutshell, I want to be able to rent some space from you. If I open in The Clock House I could attract clients from outside Whispers Wood. I know I could.'

'I know you could too. That's not what I'm worried about.'

'Oh.' From her earliest memories Juliet had somehow understood she'd always be just on the periphery of the bond Kate and Bea had shared. She fiddled with the corner of the file she'd been clutching. 'Is it – is it that this was all yours and Bea's dream? Not the salon part but the spa, and you think to do it with anyone else wouldn't be right. That she wouldn't have liked it?'

'No. No not at all. I'm worried that you're incredibly

polished and professional... and I'm not. I have the idea and that's it. I need to spend hours working out if this is all properly doable. I guess I'm worried that if it isn't... there wouldn't be anything to hold me here.'

'If you don't want to take the risk, I need you to know I'm going to do this anyway. That's how serious I am about this. I have a loan from the bank – it's not huge, but it would be enough to open a tiny salon in one of the empty shops on the green. It won't be the same, but this is what I really want.'

'You see? You've spent proper grown-up time coming to this conclusion. I'm pretty sure pebble-tossing didn't even enter your head as a decision-making process.'

'But Kate, you have thought about this more than that. All those years you and Bea dreamt about opening up the spa. You haven't forgotten all of that. You've just filed it away in a box marked 'difficult'. You access all of that thinking and you'll find you're already halfway there. And I bet you've done some thinking these last few weeks. You just don't want to admit how much.'

'Okay. Say you're right – say I've had some... thoughts about what it would be like running my own business. Say I think that having a hair salon along with a day spa would only benefit us both...What happens now?'

'You phone Old Man Isaac and make an appointment with him.'

'It's as simple as that?'

'I think it has to be. If we keep focusing on how big a thing this is, then we might not follow through. And, Kate? I really want the both of us to follow through on this.' Juliet knew she had to do something to drag herself out of fantasy-land and into fulfilling-a-lifelong-dream-land.

'I guess there's no time like the present,' Kate said, suddenly standing up so that she could push her hand into her pocket. Out came a folded-up piece of paper. 'It's the estate-agent deets. I'll make the call now.'

Juliet smiled. 'I'll get us set up in the lounge, there's at least another four inches of space in there!'

She could hear Kate on the phone as she set about clearing her sewing machine from the coffee table. They were really going to do this. She hadn't felt this fluttery, excited feeling since... a pair of sinfully gorgeous green eyes popped into her head and with practised concentration she shooed them away again so that she could focus on the task at hand.

'I'm all set for visiting Old Man Isaac tomorrow morning at ten,' Kate told her when she re-entered the kitchen. 'We're going to have to work our arses off to prep before then. I need to come up with a solid plan as polished as yours in case he asks what I want to do with the place. Hey, you know what we need?'

'Another batch of martinis?'

'Nope. Cake. Can you make one of your famous Victoria sponges? Is that still his favourite? I'll take it with me when I go tomorrow.'

'Ooh, good idea.'

'It's these kinds of little touches that are going to help win him over.'

'That and the fact that I'm going to lend you one of my dresses.'

'No daisy-dukes at the meeting?'

'You want to impress him with your business prowess, not give him a heart attack.'

Kate tipped some of her remaining honey martini into Juliet's jam jar and slid it back to her before picking hers up and holding it aloft. 'To Gloria, then' she said, making a toast.

'To Gloria,' Juliet agreed, holding her jam jar aloft. 'And all the cats,' she added, as Catty McCatface made an appearance in the kitchen.

Kate grinned as she looked at him and then started singing, 'Memory, all alone in the moonlight...'

Juliet tipped the last of the alcohol down her throat and joined in.

Catty McCatface looked derisively at the humans as if to say that the sooner cats developed opposable thumbs, the sooner the human slaves would remember their place.

Chapter 11

Birdsong, Baskets and Business Plans

Kate

Kate stood in Juliet's kitchen, nervously trying to make sure that every single one of the butterflies swarming inside her stayed inside her and under control. If she could just keep a lid on them a while longer, then she had every chance of getting through this meeting and coming out the other side of it with her offer on The Clock House being accepted.

So, no biggie, then.

When she'd been standing in front of the full-length mirror that hung on the back of Juliet's bedroom door, staring at her reflection with a critical eye, she'd thought that she looked good in the white dress covered in tiny violets. She'd thought she'd looked pretty and professional or at least pretty professional.

But now that she was waiting for Juliet to get back with the cake all she could see as she smoothed her hands down the front of the nineteen-sixties-styled dress, with its gorgeously swishy skirt and nipped-in waist, was her chest.

She frowned. She was a little, and for a little, read a lot, fuller in the bust area than Juliet and as she dragged in a shaky breath and felt her diaphragm push tightly against the material of the dress, she was very grateful there weren't any buttons that could ping off mid-meeting.

'I'm back, panic over,' Juliet said, breezing in through the cottage.

'Who was panicking?' Kate harrumphed, feeling sick. She'd only glanced at the kitchen clock eleven million times in the twenty minutes that Juliet had been gone.

'My bad,' Juliet said dryly, putting the box she'd purchased down on the kitchen counter in front of Kate. 'There you go. One perfectly factory-formed Victoria sponge from Big Kev's.'

Kate stared at the box. Even the photo on the front didn't look as good as the kissed-by-angels, light-as-air, yummy-licious Victoria sponge stuffed with home-made strawberry jam and clotted cream that Juliet had made yesterday. If only they hadn't eaten it at one o'clock this morning when they were tired, hungry and had needed the pick-me-up.

'Right, open it up and pop it on this plate,' Juliet said, putting a pretty floral china plate down on the counter, 'we'll have this ready to go in a jiffy.'

Leaning forward, Kate slid her finger under the corner of the cardboard box and pushed it along until the flap popped open. A quick tussle with the cellophane wrapping and then she was plopping the cake onto the plate.

She stared down at it. 'Um... maybe it would be better to forget the cake,' she told Juliet. 'This doesn't look like it could be placed on the "altar of gingham" or be in with a shot of winning Star Baker.'

'It will in a moment. Here – hold this,' Juliet shoved a lace doily into her hand.

'Again, I'm no Mary Berry but shouldn't this go under the cake?'

'No. Hold your hand up higher. Good – now hold it there while I–'

Kate watched as Juliet, her tongue caught between her teeth, shoved her hand down onto one side of the cake to make a dent.

'Hey,' Kate swiped at Juliet's arm. 'What did you go and do that for? It's all lop-sided now.'

'Authenticity,' Juliet said and then, holding Kate's hand with the doily a good six inches above the cake, she reached over with her other hand and swiped a shaker off the sideboard and proceeded to waft icing sugar over the whole affair.

When she stopped, Kate moved the doily and stared in wonder at the now pimped-up sponge. 'Where did you learn how to do all this stuff?'

'It came with the folder marked "How to be a Crazy Cat Lady",' Juliet answered, with a small smile, before she picked up the plate and popped it into a wicker basket so that it was nestled prettily alongside the small posy of flowers she'd picked.

Kate watched as Juliet continued to fuss with the basket. She could honestly kill Gloria for paying out on Juliet and making her in any way doubt herself or her ability to meet some guy and fall in love with him and set up a forever home with him.

'Seriously, Juliet, it all looks beautiful. You realise one of these days you're going to make one of those mums that the Mummy Mafia hang around at the school gates discussing how to make disappear, right?'

A wistful expression crossed her cousin's face, causing Kate to regret her words. Juliet was definitely the get-married-first-and-then-have-babies type, so talking about her being a mum when she wasn't even dating wasn't very helpful. She bit down hard on the inside of her cheek because sometimes it felt like she wasn't very good at being kind – Bea had always been the kind one. After she'd died Kate had often consciously mirrored Bea's personality so that she could feel kind in letting her mum get away with ignoring her. But now that time had passed she knew she'd simply been taking the easy way out. Four years of focusing solely on getting herself through the days had made her too inward-facing. She was going to have to work on that.

'How about,' Juliet said, 'before attempting the Super Mum thing, both of us concentrate on attempting the "highly successful, running our own businesses" thing, yes?'

'Yes,' Kate answered, unable to stop the thought of how much Bea would have excelled at combining career with being a mum. Sudden grief rose up to take a healthy chunk out of her.

Juliet glanced at the clock. 'If you leave now you'll be perfectly on time.'

'Good. That's good,' she said, struggling past the sorrow. 'Especially as I'm visiting a retired clock-maker.'

'Exactly. You look lovely, by the way.'

Kate twirled a little. 'It feels weird wearing clothes that

come past my knees, but I feel gorgeous in it, so thank you.'
She hadn't realised how much she'd got used to casual beach
attire or the comfy pashmina and cashmere t-shirt coupled
with stretchy leggings that she'd learned worked best on long
plane journeys.

'You can totally do this,' Juliet told her with a warm smile.

'Uh-huh. Totes,' Kate whispered.

'Now say it like you mean it.'

'I can totally do this,' she said, putting everything into it
so as to take some of the nerves out of Juliet's eyes too. 'I'm
not coming back without my offer being accepted.'

'Atta girl.'

Kate picked up the presentation that she and Juliet had
worked on all night. It contained a proper business plan for
opening and running a day spa along with her projections
for how she would grow the business over the first two years.

Her brain still hurt from all the statistics she'd amassed,
but now she had a plan she knew could work. It had amazed
her to discover how little she'd been put off when examining
the pitfalls. If anything, it had reinforced how much she wanted
to do this.

And that was all down to Juliet and her own dream and
her insights with the postcards.

'I'm going now, then.'

'I rang Mum this morning and told her to take all my
clients for the day, so I'll be right here waiting for you when
you finish.'

'Okay,' she said, picking up the basket and walking towards
the front door.

'Break a leg.'

'Distinct possibility in these shoes,' Kate murmured and with a wave she headed down the lane towards the cut-through.

As she entered the woods she shivered and hugged the basket to her as if the delicate scent of the tea roses and the artificial sweetness from the cake could warm her as well as comfort her. She picked up her pace, wishing she'd thought to add a cardy or a cape. A giggle escaped. A cape? Really? Must be the woods and the wicker basket that had her going all Little Red Riding Hood.

Right on cue a bird burst into song.

Had to be an omen, right?

She chose to think of it as a good one.

Birdsong, baskets and business plans.

She had this.

Besides, she'd always got on really well with Old Man Isaac. Wily, wise and interesting, she liked to think of him as a person who everyone always found time for because he always made time for them. She knew he'd pay her the service of listening attentively to her today, so she wanted to repay him by presenting her idea well.

Emerging from the cut-through she crossed the green to walk up to the entrance of Rosehip Cottage. One quick flick of her hair over her shoulder, one last yogic breathing exercise that was supposed to help calm the nerves jangling around in her stomach but unfortunately only served to remind her how tight the dress was on her, and she was giving the letterbox a rat-a-tat-tat.

It felt like an eternity before he answered the door and she tried to reassure herself that was only because when you were waiting to secure your future, every moment felt like an hour.

Finally the door opened and there he was. A short, balding man with thick-rimmed glasses, a cream shirt, fawn-coloured trousers, a walking stick, and, her favourite part, a whimsical dickie-bow.

For some reason she found a lump forming in her throat.

Her thoughts scrambled as the lump grew larger. She couldn't afford to fall apart before she'd even laid out her offer. It had to be that it was so familiar. So comforting. So much had changed about Whispers Wood and so this small thing staying the same was like another good omen. An omen that said it was okay to mix the old with the new.

Old dreams. New future.

She breathed as deeply as the dress would allow and determined to swallow past the lump in her throat.

'Kate Somersby. Well look at you, standing at my door, looking pretty as a picture.'

Kate smiled. 'Thank you so much for agreeing to see me today, Mr—' Holy Face-Palm, her welcoming grin was chased off her face by utter consternation. She'd only known him all her life and yet, what on earth was his last name? Frantically she ran through names in her head. Isaac... Isaac Bell? Isaac Newton? Isaac... Asimov?

'Oh, I think you can get away with calling me, Isaac, dear,' he said, saving her bacon and making her feel like maybe she could do this after all.

'Are you sure? I mean—'

'Between you and me, I'm rather feeling my age these days, so the less of the "Old Man" the better.'

'Okay. Then, thank you... Isaac.' It felt strange. It felt grown up. It felt as if he knew how nervous she was and was helping her all he could. Another lump formed in her throat as it dawned on her that today wasn't so much about 'Going Big or Going Home' as it was about 'Going Big and Coming Home.'

If she bought The Clock House she wouldn't be able to leave. She'd have to stay and see it through. All that roaming, searching... running... that she had hardly been able to admit to herself had become so tiring, would simply stop.

'Come in, come in,' Isaac said, ushering her in through the door.

'Thank you,' she said, forcing the lump further down into her windpipe as she stepped into the narrow cottage hallway.

Rosehip Cottage was like all the two-up, two-down cottages in Whispers Wood, except for the Alice in Wonderland feel Old Man Isaac had accidentally created. All the furniture, having come from The Clock House, looked huge in the tiny home. She paused beside the imposing grandfather clock in the hallway and stared up at it wide-eyed.

'I remember this clock used to stand in the foyer by the stairs in The Clock House,' she commented, noting that she was one minute early, and awarding herself a brownie point. 'Is it one of your family's designs?'

'It is, yes. I kept a few of the family's clocks when I moved in. But this one will always be my favourite. It was made by my grandfather.'

'It's wonderful. I've seen the famous astronomical clock in

Prague... you know the one where the skeleton "Death" strikes the hour?' As the last words left her mouth, Kate stared forlornly down at the carpet runner. *Good one, Kate, why not spend the entire meeting today talking about old stuff and death!*

'Ah, you've seen the Orlej in Prague? It's quite something, isn't it? Please, go on through to the lounge. I have another guest, but we're just finishing up.'

'Another guest? Oh–' she broke off as the clock beside her – along with what felt like a hundred other clocks in the small cottage – started to chime the hour.

'I'm not sure you've met Mr Westlake?' Old Man Isaac asked as he walked ahead of her into the lounge.

'Mr – sorry, who?' she said, unable to hear a thing over the clock chimes. Lawks, how was she going to be able to concentrate if all the clocks kept clanging as they ticked off the minutes?

She followed him through to the lounge and came to an abrupt halt.

Oh. My. Tick-Tock. God.

'Mr Daniel Westlake,' Old Man Isaac said as he introduced her to the other guest and pointed to the only other available seat in the room. A perfect Kate's butt-sized space on the sofa next to... *Daniel.*

This couldn't be happening. Surely she wasn't supposed to have the most important meeting of her life sitting next to the man who could take it all away from her?

As the clock struck the hour, she couldn't help but look heavenwards with suspicion. The first time she'd met him there had been music. This time... the clanging chimes of doom.

As the lump in her throat disintegrated into dust and absorbed every drop of saliva she could have produced, unhelpful thoughts flashed neon in her head.

Why did he have to be so distractingly good-looking?

What was with her heart pitter-pattering?

Why wasn't anything ever simple?

Get it together, get it together. Get. It. Together.

Her tongue cleaved to the roof of her mouth. Her hands remained wrapped tightly around her basket. The wicker basket that had so reminded her of Red Riding Hood.

And then Daniel was standing up to greet her.

And smiling all wolf-like...

'My, Grandma, what big teeth you have,' she muttered under her breath as she reached forward with her hand.

Chapter 12

It's All in the Timing, Mr Wolf

Daniel

So this was Sheila Somersby's daughter?

If he hadn't have heard Isaac say her name he would never have believed it. She was so completely cheese to the B&B owner's chalk. But then there was that certain look in her eyes that matched Sheila's identically. A look of quiet determination that flashed whenever she was challenged.

His breath caught at the impression she made in a flowery dress. If yesterday was sexy boho-chic. Today was vicar's tea-party meets a day at the races. She wore both styles with ease, making him wonder how many sides to her there were.

In her eyes he saw part-devastation that he'd got here before her today, and part Fool Me Once, Shame on You, Fool Me Twice – Nah, Never Gonna Happen...

He was fairly sure he shouldn't find that entertaining or challenging.

'I'm sorry? I didn't catch what you said,' he told her as he reached over and enclosed her delicate hand in his. No way could she just have likened him to the wolf in Red Riding

Hood. He might want The Clock House but he didn't feel the need to act like some city wolf prowling in and scooping up whatever took his fancy. Although, now that she was standing so prettily in front of him...

He remembered the photograph in that locket he was getting fixed and though it was impossible to stop his fingertips from stroking lightly across the pulse point of her wrist, when she trembled and tugged her hand free to wipe it nervously down her killer-dress, he couldn't help noticing she wasn't wearing a wedding ring. Still. Chances were she was attached, so following through on an attraction wasn't appropriate and definitely not what he should be concentrating on anyway.

He watched as she dragged in a breath and pasted on a smile. 'I said: Daniel Westlake, what a wonderful surprise to find you here.'

He grinned and couldn't resist telling her, 'I had the nine o'clock slot.'

'Of course you did,' she said, smiling back in a way that meant he discovered even her fake smiles could cause a bolt of awareness to shoot through him.

'The two of you know each other, then,' Isaac noted, lowering himself into the armchair in the corner of the room.

'Yes,' Daniel said, staring into Kate's magnificent eyes.

'No,' Kate said at the exact same time. His left eyebrow must have done the shooting-up-into-his-hairline thing because in the next second she was admitting, 'That is, we met yesterday.'

He felt as if he'd won a small victory when she was the first to look away.

And then felt as though he'd lost again when she raised her eyes back up to him and dismissed their meeting with a for-his-ears-only, 'So brief, I'd almost forgotten it.'

'We met at The Clock House,' Daniel told Isaac.

'I see,' Isaac said. 'Well this is a tad unusual, but then I always find the unusual is worth a second look. Mr Westlake, here—'

'Daniel, please,' he insisted.

'Daniel here has been telling me that he plans to buy The Clock House and make it into a going concern.'

'Like I said,' Daniel said, upping the wattage to his smile, 'I had the nine o'clock slot.'

The look of desolation in her eyes when she realised he'd already spent a good hour negotiating with Isaac had him almost backing down.

Almost.

'Well, you know what they say about going first?' Kate asked in a determined sing-song voice.

'It sets the bar?' he quipped.

'Never gets remembered,' she countered.

Daniel felt her gaze travel over him from head to foot, in what he suspected was a deliberate attempt to make him feel forgettable again. Would have worked well, he realised, feeling the sting that he might not even be worth a second glance, until he saw her pupils dilate.

'Isaac,' Kate said turning towards him, 'I'm sure the estate agent will have told you that I'm interested in buying The Clock House, too.'

Isaac rested his elbows on the arms of his armchair and

steepled his fingers together. 'I did wonder if that might be the case. You'd better pour yourself a cup of tea and sit down, then.'

Daniel watched her gaze sneak to the dainty china laid out.

'Shall I be mother?' he prompted when she continued to stare at the refreshment.

'Will you be staying that long?' she asked him.

Oh, he had absolutely no intention of going anywhere until Isaac made it clear his meeting with him was over and let her know that by taking his place back on the sofa.

'Um, Isaac?' Kate began, inclining her head frantically in Daniel's direction, when Daniel remained where he was but now with a huge grin on his face.

'Are you well?' Daniel asked out of the side of that grin.

'Completely, thank you.'

'You're sure? Only the head-twitching is beginning to look a little Regan-Pazuzu there.'

A look of horror crossed her face. 'Thank you William P. Blatty, but I do not need an exorcist. I – look Isaac,' she turned and her skirt made a little swishing sound that Daniel's ears seemed especially attuned to, given the base level of all the ticking clocks. 'Daniel has had his hour to talk through his plans with you... so...'

'If you don't mind,' Isaac said, 'I'd like Daniel to stay while you outline your reasons for wanting to buy The Clock House. I think it would be beneficial for both of you to hear each other out and I'm sure he won't mind outlining his proposal again afterwards'

'Afterwards?' she whispered, clearly horrified she was being asked to pitch her offer in front of him.

'It's a little unorthodox, I know,' Isaac confirmed. 'But humour an old man, eh?'

Daniel watched Kate's eyes narrow a fraction at the 'Old Man' term and her thoughts probably matched his. Old Man Isaac was certainly old but he had lost none of his cognitive ability.

'You don't have to disclose offer price in front of each other,' Isaac made clear, 'but I would like to hear what you intend to do with the building. In the interests of a fair competition, so should Daniel.'

'Competition,' Kate mumbled with a sort of dejected finality as she stared down at her basket.

Daniel had to hand it to her; she hardly wasted any time at all pulling herself together and while he found that pouting thing she did when she didn't immediately get her own way, way too attractive, he definitely admired that she didn't prolong the sulking.

'Okay,' she said, gathering up her basket and walking over to the low coffee table in the centre of the room. 'Before I start, it would be silly of me not to take out the cake that I brought for you, Isaac.'

Daniel followed Kate's movement as she bent over and delved into the basket she'd set at her feet.

'It's a little on the small side – obviously I wasn't expecting a third party, but I'm sure it can stretch to three,' she said, sparing Daniel a brief look that told him if she had thought she could get away with it, he'd be wearing the cake. 'I hope I remembered right – is Victoria sponge still your favourite?'

'It is,' Isaac said with an indulgent look on his face. 'What a thoughtful gesture, thank you.'

'Daniel, if you'd like to pour me a cup of tea, now?'

Daniel blinked as he moved his gaze from Isaac back to Kate. In one fell swoop she'd managed to please Isaac with some cake and make him, Daniel, feel like the hired help.

He reached over and poured her a cup of tea, watching as she delved back into the basket and withdrew a small crystal vase of flowers.

It was like watching a sexy Mary Poppins in action. Why had she brought flowers? It honestly hadn't occurred to him to bring anything other than himself to his meeting today. If this was how deals were arranged in the country he needed to learn faster.

'You got anything else in there?' he asked, staring suspiciously into the basket as he passed her the cup of tea.

She smiled as if he'd have to wait and see and damned if anticipation didn't wash over him so that he couldn't take his eyes off her as she accepted the cup of tea, popped it immediately down on the coffee table and somehow managed to do some twisty-twerky thing that meant that when she next bent over the basket it was right in front of him. Thor could have appeared through the Bifröst and he wouldn't have noticed, although, he realised with consolation, neither would she with her head stuck in that basket of tricks she'd brought along.

Finally she came up for air, holding in her hand a sheaf of printed pages.

The only way this could go better for her, Daniel observed,

was if she'd brought along a wad of cash. He stared at the basket hard before bringing his gaze back to Kate.

'So,' she began, before glancing down at her papers and then lowering them to her side, pulling her shoulders back and addressing Isaac as if he was the only person in the room. 'You should know, first of all, that as soon as I heard that The Clock House was up for sale, I came back.'

Daniel frowned. Where had she been? He remembered her mentioning Prague in the hallway, so maybe she'd been on holiday. In which case, how had she even heard about the sale? Village grapevine, he supposed.

'Perhaps I hoped that you would,' Isaac said.

Daniel inhaled sharply. Was he wasting his time here? Were the two of them having some warped kind of laughing-at-him tea party? Had Isaac always intended to sell to one person and one person only?

'I know I haven't been around,' Kate added, her voice softening as she bit down hard on her lip. 'But I haven't been idle while I've been away.'

'Kate, please,' Isaac consoled, 'I never thought you would have wasted your time for a moment, dear. Of course, I've often wondered if you stayed away because of what the building might represent–'

'Oh, please don't think that,' Kate said, cutting him off. 'I think of The Clock House in a positive light and feel very in tune with it.'

'You have no idea how relieved I am to hear that, Kate.'

'I'm so sorry. I should have thought... When you saw me that day... I was...'

What day? How was she? Daniel found himself leaning forward, wanting to wipe the uncertainty from her face and bring back that spark that came with the challenge of battle.

'I completely understand, dear. No explanation necessary at all,' Isaac told her.

Damn, really? Because Daniel would have loved one and to try and facilitate that he settled back comfortably in the corner of the sofa, interested to hear everything Kate had to say.

Five minutes into her presentation and all Daniel could think was: She was good.

Really good.

As she talked about the services she would offer at her day spa: Beauty @ The Clock House, he shifted on the sofa uncomfortably, so completely wrapped up in her sales spiel that when she talked about full-body massages he could actually imagine her hands on him. But more importantly by the time she got into her stride and he'd managed to separate his body from the conversation, she had him totally believing in her business proposal.

He could see it perfectly and he believed her completely when she talked about how it would bring more business to the village from outside Whispers Wood. He hadn't thought about that enough or he'd have highlighted it when he'd been talking his idea through with Isaac. And he hadn't known about the hotel in Whispers Ford stealing most of the business from Whispers Wood or he'd have addressed that as well.

As she concluded her presentation, he was under no illusion that her idea was directly comparable to his.

Finally she turned to look at him. 'So, what's your idea, then?'

He hesitated because she was looking at him like she'd just slam-dunked her way into The Clock House.

Underlying all her bravado was a confidence built upon her personal relationship with Old Man Isaac. It had shone through as soon as she'd been able to effectively dismiss Daniel as being in the room and it left him wanting to ask her why it was so ridiculous that a stranger could wander into the village by accident and fall in love with the place. Or at least fall in love with what could be created here.

Maybe it was because she didn't know where he'd come from, before he'd arrived here. He loved a lot of London, and maybe if what had happened to West and Westlake hadn't happened he could have fooled himself for another few years that he was happy living there. That he was happy running a firm of accountants. That he was ecstatic about casual dating because who had time to meet anyone via a conventional channel or the time to turn that meeting into a relationship.

But five minutes of distance had shown him he hadn't put down roots and it was past time for him to find a place that could become home.

'What's my idea?' he repeated, remaining seated and keeping his posture relaxed. 'It's simple; I want to use The Clock House to provide co-working office space and hot-desking for home workers – a sort of office away from home.'

She frowned and then her eyes brightened with victory and her tone could not have been more patronising as she said, 'You mean... like a Starbucks?'

Ouch.

'I *mean,* I want to provide an inspiration centre in great surroundings where individuals can come and book space to work and break the isolation that comes from working on their own. I *mean* I want to provide premises where those individuals can chat with other business owners and gain better knowledge, help and expertise. I *mean* creating office and meeting room facilities for small business enterprises and start-ups. A professional space that's rentable and affordable and taps into the co-working culture.'

'Oh.'

He could get used to watching her lips form that perfect 'o' of surprise and couldn't resist adding, 'But yes, of course, I will provide coffee. I may even branch out and include tea. And perhaps, even more than one type of biscuit.'

She had the grace to blush like he had wanted her to, but damn it, it only made her prettier.

Isaac cleared his throat and broke the silence. 'I think both of your ideas hold merit. But here's the problem. Neither of you has been in the village recently, so I'll be perfectly frank. Whispers Wood has lost its mojo and I want the two of you to get it back.'

Chapter 13

The Clock House Challenge

Daniel

Daniel took in the expectant look on Isaac's face, but for the life of him couldn't really understand what he meant. 'Someone's stolen the village's mojo and you want us to...?'

'Get it back,' Kate supplied, as if it was the most normal request in the world. 'I suspect it went by way of the next village over?' she checked with Isaac.

'Whispers Ford?' Daniel asked, with a frown.

Kate nodded. 'Apparently they won the Best in Bloom this year?'

Isaac nodded.

'We won it twelve years in a row,' Kate explained. 'Then, last year Whispers Ford opened a hotel and promptly covered it and their entire village in flowers.'

Daniel thought for a moment and then immediately tried to bring things back to his advantage. 'Isaac, once the village gets wind of what I intend to do with The Clock House, the excitement that new business always brings to an area will grow, and I'm sure that will help, um, restore mojo.'

'Nothing restores one's mojo like a little pampering and that's what this village needs,' Kate added, jumping on his bandwagon. 'And they'd have access to that with my day spa. I'm sure you're already aware of this, Daniel,' she said, turning to face him, 'but the key to a successful life is not making it about work, work, work.'

'I do know that, actually. But if you think running your own businesses is going to afford you any time to use your spa facilities – think again. It's literally going to be work, work and work for you.'

'Well, I'm totally up for the sacrifice.'

'Shouldn't even feel like a sacrifice if you're doing something you love.'

'Yeah? You've run your own business before, have you?'

'As a matter of fact, I have,' he shot back, eager to see one of her sexy, enlightened 'Oh's' form on her lips. Not that he wanted to go into details of how spectacularly he had failed that business and how long it had taken him to extricate himself from all of it.

'The Clock House has been in my family for a long time,' Isaac interrupted. 'And for a long time I've enjoyed it representing the heart of our village and so... of course, I would get a kick out of seeing it remain so... but let's not forget that the real heart of the village are people.'

'So what exactly are you saying? Are you stipulating that the purchaser of The Clock House continues to provide community facilities? Because I don't have a problem with that,' Daniel stated.

'Of course, the building should provide community space,'

Kate added with a quick glance at him. 'I've already factored that into my proposal.'

Isaac held up his hand. 'Forgive me, but providing a few facilities as part of your business isn't good enough. This isn't about bricks and mortar. This community deserves to feel equal, not second best. That is why,' Isaac paused for dramatic affect and Daniel wondered if Kate's heart rate had sped up like his.

'I have a little challenge for the pair of you,' Isaac continued. 'I want Whispers Wood to have a summer fete this year. One like we used to have, where the entire village gets involved and enjoys the day. I'd like the pair of you to raise funds for it. Whoever of you raises the most funds, earns the right to buy The Clock House.'

Daniel wanted to laugh out loud.

Kate actually did.

'Let me see if I understand this right,' Daniel said, 'you want the two of us,' he pointed between himself and Kate, 'to compete against each other in order to prove to you which one of us wants to buy The Clock House more?'

Isaac shook his head. 'I want the two of you to prove you have the staying power for building a business you love by showing me how much you love the community you're going to start that business in. Raising funds for a village fete is a perfect way to test that. The more money invested in making the fete great – the more money we'll make from the fete. I want to see this village fired up and actually looking forward to what the fete – *their* fete – can bring to Whispers Wood. I appreciate the challenge is a little on the eccentric side, but if you're really serious, you'll–'

'Humour an old man?' Daniel finished for him, wishing he knew him well enough to decide if the twinkle in his eye was always there or reserved for particularly bizarre notions.

'Say we agree,' Kate was asking, 'you'll take The Clock House off the market so that no one else can register interest in buying it?'

'All right,' Isaac said, nodding his head.

'Only Kate and I will be raising funds – the challenge is kept to two entrants?'

'I'll allow you help. After all it's going to take the whole community to restore our spark.'

'Those are the only rules?' Kate wanted to know. 'Whichever of us – and our team – raises the most money to put on a spectacular village fete gets to buy The Clock House?'

'That's it.'

Daniel's gaze swept around the room for cameras because he had to be being punked, right?

He heard Kate whisper under her breath, 'I'm in some sort of *The Apprentice* hell.'

Daniel smirked. This wasn't about whether one of them was going to be fired for not raising enough funds to put on a fundraiser. It was going to be a lot more like starting a community crowd-funding project but where the currency wasn't money, but mojo.

Was he stupid to be even considering this?

He wanted to make a home.

He wanted to grow a business.

He wanted to build a reputation that stood for something weightier than status.

Whispers Wood felt real. Solid.

And he felt real and solid here.

And he had absolutely nothing to lose by entering into this challenge wholeheartedly.

Daniel thought about the people he'd met so far in Whispers Wood. There was Kate who, actually... probably best not to bring Kate into his decision-making paradigm!

But there was Ted, the mechanic, who went the extra mile to make Daniel feel Monroe was in good hands. Sheila Somersby, the perfect hostess, who quietly let him go about his business. Trudie McTravers, who was, admittedly, a little larger than life, but obviously protective about the place she lived in. Crispin Harlow, who may or may not have been wearing a wig, which had transfixed Daniel so much he couldn't really remember what he was like. And, today, Old Man Isaac, a man who cared so much about the village he'd lived all his life in he'd been worrying about how to restore its heart.

Maybe Daniel felt happy here because the residents had largely left him alone and given him the space he'd needed to think, and maybe that was because they *had* lost their mojo, so that stereotypical everyone-in-each-other's-business vibe was missing, but Daniel couldn't find enough about the place or the people not to recommend taking the risk.

He'd promised himself the next thing he started as going to be risk-free.

But how difficult could it be to raise funds to put on a village fete – he could already feel ideas forming and all the while he got to know the residents of Whispers Wood properly he could be working on getting the business ready to go when he won.

'So, what do you say?' Isaac asked, excitement and anticipation present in his tone. 'Are you up for the challenge?' Isaac asked.

Daniel reached over and helped himself to a slice of Whispers Wood homeliness. 'Piece of cake,' he said, biting into the sponge.

Chapter 14

Winner, Winner, Chicken Dinner

Kate

'*Piece of cake,*' he says.

Kate stomped across the village green, her kitten heels stabbing into the dry earth, her grip rigid against the wicker handle of her basket, her gaze fixed firmly on the prize sitting regally at the end of the green, The Clock House. *Her* clock house, if she was to have anything to do with it.

Boy, was she certainly glad she hadn't wasted some of Juliet's prize-winning cake on the source of her malcontent, Daniel-bloody-Westlake.

Confession: it didn't seem right or respectful to blame her mood on Old Man Isaac on account of him turning the purchase of his building into a challenge, which if she was hearing about it from anyone else, she might have found just a little bit adorable.

It did seem entirely sensible, however, to blame the fact that her sense of humour appeared to have been flattened into one of Gertrude's (Whispers Wood's resident runaway cow) cowpats, on the only pair of broad shoulders around here... Daniel-bloody-Westlake's.

Okay. In the interests of being completely fair, she could concede to the sense of being flattened as partly her fault as well. Somehow, possibly during the hours she'd been using her brain on non-man-fantasising tasks, like working out how to kit out a building the size of The Clock House, she'd managed to convince herself that Daniel couldn't possibly have been as good-looking as she'd first thought. Couldn't possibly be the owner of intelligent navy-blue eyes with impossibly long Spanish lashes. And definitely couldn't be the possessor of full-shaped lips that stretched sexily into the kind of wolfish grins you knew would have you blushing from head to toe if they started whispering into your ear.

Confronted with him being at Rosehip Cottage, instead of nailing her indifference, she'd been desperate enough to look for signs of thinning hair or a paunch. But his thick, brown, slide-your-hands-through-and-cling locks looked like they belonged in a 'You're Worth It' commercial and as he'd stretched lazily across the small sofa, the fit of his shirt had told her that he was about as far away from an I-eat-sushi-for-lunch-but-grab-a-stuffed-crust-every-night-for-dinner city-slacker as you could get.

The whole realisation had thrown her because considering it had only been yesterday she'd convinced herself that the heart-fluttering she'd felt lying under him had probably been from the shock of the fall, it was disgustingly rude of him to make her aware of more heart-fluttering the very next morning.

Honestly, the way he'd delighted in shoving a whole slice

of vanilla-sweetened sponge into his mouth and chomping down on it, I mean, had it really been too much to sincerely hope he'd choke on it?

And then, of all the nerve... for him to produce that sexy little frown and ask politely if it was homemade. As if he could tell cake made with love, as opposed to cake made in a factory.

Kate stopped right in front of The Clock House and slapped her forehead. Of course Daniel could tell. He was living at her mum's B&B. He was probably provided with afternoon tea made by her every day. Her mum was unwittingly feeding her business rival and now Clock House Challenge rival and Kate couldn't even warn her because a) no way could she drop around unannounced now that she knew *he* was living there and even more importantly b) there was the whole awks/emosh/mother-daughter no longer knowing how to deal with each other, thing anyway.

She'd have to get Aunt Cheryl to go over and explain – maybe do a little recon on a certain guest while she was there and then report back to her and Juliet.

Oh, God.

Juliet.

She'd promised she'd return to Wren Cottage with her offer accepted.

How was she going to tell her cousin that as well as the two of them having to work their arses off organising the opening of two businesses, they now needed to raise a shed-load of spondoolies for a village fete as well? Because there was absoposilutely no way she was losing out to Daniel and his stupid Let's All Come Together to Work and Drink Coffee All Day idea.

'*Piece of cake.*' Kate repeated Daniel's throwing down of the gauntlet out loud and as she stared up at the brick building knew she had to do whatever it took to make the place hers.

How difficult could it be to raise a few thousand pounds to put on a village fete in a village where apparently everyone was feeling down and crappy anyway?

Kate felt her fighting spirit waver.

Last night she'd created a spreadsheet overflowing with things to do in order to get the business up and running. But having to come up with ideas for fundraising events for a village fete didn't seem like it would be covered by inserting one more line at the top of that list. It overwhelmingly seemed like it should have a spreadsheet all of its own.

She sniffed and focused on the moss she could see clinging to some of the gravel in the driveway.

Had she really thought that making the decision to come back home in the first place was going to be the hardest part of all of this? Because she hadn't even made that decision properly, had she? She'd used a pebble. Maybe if she'd used her lucky magic eight-ball instead she wouldn't be crumbling at the first hurdle.

Flatness poured on top of flatness.

She couldn't crumble.

Coming home was a line in the sand.

A crossing over into acceptance that she couldn't act like everything she didn't like in life would simply change if she wished hard enough.

Wishes were for horses, not for humans – no matter how much humans started believing in them again when someone died.

She'd wished every day for too many days that Bea wouldn't be dead. And when the wishing, the praying, the begging hadn't changed the fact, she'd simply switched her denial and bargaining to wishing that living without her wasn't so hard.

But Juliet had been right when she'd talked about putting one foot in front of the other and following through. She'd tried so hard to do that when she'd left Whispers Wood and living *had* eventually become less hard.

Surely the longer she stayed in Whispers Wood, the less hard coming home would be too?

So.

She'd raise some money. *The most money*, she vowed.

To do that she probably needed to stop thinking like a defeatist and start thinking like a boss. There was probably an app she could download to help her with that. Or at the very least she could adopt a Katy Perry song as her mantra. Delving into the basket to locate her phone, she pulled it out and brought up Juliet's number.

Juliet answered on the first ring with a, 'Hi, how did it go? Tell me everything? God, do you realise how long you've been? I could have crocheted a pair of knickers!'

'Quick,' Kate said, clutching the phone to her ear. 'Tell me I'm a firework.'

'What – why on earth… oh, so I can see your colours burst?'

'Yes!' Kate tried to go for an air-grab moment but with her

127

hand still attached to her basket, settled for a tiny side-to-side victory dance instead. 'I knew you'd get it. This is why we're going to work so well together. Because we can turn each other into Katy Perry Roaring, Rising, Fireworking winners.'

'Brilliant,' Juliet said loyally. 'Shall I pop down to Big Kev's for some celebratory champs, then?'

'Wouldn't hurt.'

'Because we're getting the keys to The Clock House...?' Juliet asked, obviously awaiting clear and concise confirmation before she went into squee-mode.

Kate patted the gravel down with the toe of her shoe and mumbled, 'Or because there's never a wrong time to drink bubbles.'

There was a pause and then, 'Kate? Why do I get the feeling this isn't a ten-from-Len moment?'

'Maybe because it's more of a seven-from-Craig moment?'

A longer pause this time and then, 'Oh. Well, a seven from Craig is actually—'

'I know,' Kate inserted. 'Still cause for huge celebration.'

'What's going on?'

'It's all good. There's only one teeny-tiny glitch before I can give you the go-ahead to choose glam mirrors for your hairdressing station kits.'

'And that is?'

Kate heard the apprehension in Juliet's voice and felt awful. 'Don't worry, crocheted knickers will not be needed, well, unless we decide to do a craft afternoon... which, now I think about it, isn't a bad idea...'

'Okay, are you, or are you not, buying The Clock House?'

'I am. I totally am. Right after you and I get the people of Whispers Wood all gung-to-the-ho about everything village fete-y.'

Juliet sighed, probably as a result of realising she was going to require a full explanation before she knew what was really going on. 'I'll get the Prosecco in,' she said finally.

'Baby, you're a firework,' Kate insisted. And then, remembering she needed to start thinking more like a boss, it occurred to her that she was going to have to keep her plans for opening Beauty @ The Clock House running alongside raising funds and mojo or she'd never be in a position to open when she won. 'Actually, don't worry about popping out,' she told Juliet. 'I'll buy a bottle from Big Kev's on my way back. I'm going to stop off and see Oscar and grab all of Bea's files from him first, okay?' It was a brave move, but speaking to Juliet and taking action made her feel brave.

'Um… 'kay.'

At least it would have done if Juliet's lacklustre response didn't immediately take the wind out of her sails. 'What? You sound funny…?'

'Nope. Not me,' Juliet defended, clearing her throat. 'Nothing funny to see here.'

Kate's heart squeezed with sympathy. 'I swear no more rookie mistakes. I intend to get us The Clock House, which is why I'm stopping by Oscar's first and picking up those files.' She swallowed as a new thought occurred to her. 'If he still has them, that is.'

'Well, let's hope he's in and that he does.'

'And that he's willing to give them to me.'

'He will – just – don't go in too hard, okay?'

'What's that supposed to mean?'

'Just that, you know, you'll be catching him totally unawares. He doesn't even know you're back, right?'

'Right. Got it. Softly, softly approach.'

Juliet snorted, as if the very idea that Kate could do subtle and softly, softly was an oxymoron. 'I'm not sure I told you, but he and Melody aren't at the old place any more.'

Kate felt the ground shift under her feet. Oscar and Melody weren't living at Sunflower Cottage any more? They'd... moved on? 'What do you mean? Where have they gone?' She swallowed hard. Bea had loved that cottage. She'd spent hours doing it up. Kate had helped her repaint every wall and piece of furniture in it.

'He bought the old barn in the grounds of Knightley Hall and has spent the last year converting it.'

The last year? She'd been in Whispers Wood five months ago. She'd managed one night at the B&B before the silences had got too much for her. No way her mum could have failed to notice her son-in-law and granddaughter moving, so the fact she hadn't even been able to use the information as an ice-breaker with Kate, ripped into her. Was she so very hard to deal with, then? And was it any wonder that instead of fighting fire with fire, she'd resorted to fighting avoidance with more avoidance?

Anger, hurt and embarrassment that she hadn't known went into the way she said, 'Right.'

'Kate, come on,' Juliet whispered gently. 'It's been four years.'

Kate let Juliet's words sink in. Maybe in moving away she'd

effectively stopped herself from moving on, while everyone back here hadn't had a choice working through the impact of Bea's passing. 'Well, it's going to take me longer to walk there and back, but I'll be back with the files and the bubbles before you know it, okay? You going to be all right on your own? I know it's been a long morning waiting.'

'I'm sure I'll find something to do to keep me out of trouble.'

'Good. But, Jules? I want to hear you say "no to knitted knickers" before I hang up.'

'No to knitted knickers, before I hang up!'

Kate giggled and, feeling lighter, popped her phone back in her basket and set off for Oscar's.

Chapter 15

Let the Right One In

Oscar

Oscar Matthews was sitting at his dining table, having taken a sip of boiling hot coffee from his 'Yoda Best Dad, Yo Are' mug, when a shadow popping up in the giant window to his right caught his attention.

Jesus Christ!

It definitely wasn't Jesus Christ appearing in his window, but coffee flew out of his mouth nonetheless, spluttering across all the papers he'd laid out in order to prepare his quote for Crispin Harlow's single-storey extension.

He stood up, his chair scraping across the wooden floor, as he automatically reached for the sheet of kitchen roll he'd popped his stack of chocolate biscuits on. Quickly, methodically, he started mopping up the worst of the spillage. Damn it, he was going to have to print this all out again before he gave it to Crispin.

When he next looked up at the window there was nothing, but still he craned his neck, reluctant to think he'd imagined the whole thing. Other than the odd nosy visitation from

Gertrude the cow poking her head through an open window, Oscar wasn't used to anyone lurking around his property.

Not that he was here often to see if anyone was lurking. This was a rare morning off-site before he picked up Melody from school and took her to her dental appointment.

Walking over to the kitchen area to dispense with the sodden kitchen roll he walked back over to the window to stare out.

Nothing.

No one.

Bovine or human.

Idiot.

Pushing a hand through his hair, he wandered back over to the table and was just about to sit down and force himself to concentrate on Crispin's quote when he saw movement, this time at his front door.

For an instant, with the sun shining from behind, silhouetting the person, well... he thought it was his wife, Bea, and stupidly wondered why she was just standing there instead of walking in through her own front door.

But then ghosts didn't need doors opened for them, did they? Not that Bea being dead automatically meant she was a ghost.

What he had actually reconciled himself to believing was that she was an angel in the sky watching over their daughter, Melody. Those were the terms he'd placed on the situation so he could deal with her being gone and deal with her leaving him alone to look after their four-year- old daughter.

Angels helped.

Ghosts didn't.

Ghosts were prone to have you thinking you could see them. And for a while he had. Everywhere. Tantalising glimpses in crowds full of strangers.

No. Ghosts weren't helpful. They messed with reality and brought you closer to insanity and he'd learned that the yearning they made you feel took you further from the people who needed you.

The person in front of the door pressed the doorbell, dragging him out of his half-frozen state and as he walked towards it to answer it, he thought that at least the time-lag between thinking he'd seen his wife, registering that he couldn't have, and being okay with all of that was now reduced to a wave of emotion that crashed over and then receded pretty much as soon as it arrived.

Not that he was still at the stage where everyone resembled her or everything reminded him. It was that this particular person – the way she stood...

He opened the door and stared.

The way she looked...

'Hello, Oscar.'

His heart bottomed-out. The way she sounded...

'Kate,' he acknowledged, his voice sounding like gravel even to his own ears.

'I hope it's all right to stop by.'

He wondered what she'd do if he said 'No' and could almost hear Bea's gentle tsk in his ear. Reluctantly he opened the door wider and Kate took his silent gesture for the welcome she needed and stepped forward to hug him.

Whoa.

He couldn't do hugging.

Was too worried that if he hugged back he'd hold on and that vice around his heart would tighten unbearably. So instinctively, automatically, he stepped backwards, out of her way, and then pretended not to see the streak of red stain her cheeks as she wobbled and held onto the wall for a moment to regain her balance.

Great! Self-protection was obviously only for wusses because now he felt like a right churlish plum.

It was that he wasn't expecting it – her.

Here.

In his new house.

The house he and Melody had created without Bea.

As if she knew that, she said as she walked past him into the large open-plan living area, 'You didn't let me know you'd moved.'

'I let Sheila know,' he shot back, shoving his hands in his jeans pockets.

He watched her absorb the low blow and while he felt guilty again, he was at a loss as to where to locate his manners. This was how he was with her now. All his anger that she'd found it so easy to walk away still unreconciled, still too acute. Because who did that? Who left when people needed you? Specifically told you they needed you?

Bea would have told him not to get so riled up. She would have told him people were human and that humans made mistakes. He knew she would have told him that because that was how she'd explained the process of forgiving a father who'd turned out to have another family other than Sheila, Bea and Kate waiting in the wings. A family that he'd decided he preferred and had gone to live with all those years ago.

Bea would have urged Oscar to forgive Kate for turning out to be just like her father and upping and running to something she considered better or easier or whatever the hell foolish reason she'd come up with to go when the going got tough.

But Bea wasn't here to tell him to temper his reactions now and maybe he'd never had to deal with a parent not wanting anything to do with him for the rest of his life, so maybe he'd never had to deal with working out that forgiving was easier than holding on to the hate, but regardless of all that, or maybe because of all that, he couldn't get his head around Kate having come from that... and then becoming that.

His gaze rested on the old-fashioned station clock he'd hung from one of the kitchen beams. He had an hour before he had to pick up Melody. If he was lucky, Kate would be long gone by then and he wouldn't have to deal with Melody getting all excited about seeing her aunt again and then deal with the heartache when she left.

Again.

'You've created a lovely space,' Kate ventured as she looked around.

He didn't know what to say to that and tried out a, 'Thank you.'

'I saw Gertrude lolling around in the upper field next to the big house.'

'Yes,' he said and then because she didn't fill the gap he

searched for something akin to the small talk that would save him from telling her what he really thought of her turning up here unannounced. 'She does that. Someone from the farm will come and make sure she gets back to the rest of the herd by the end of the day. Actually,' he added, 'what you really saw was Gertrude Mk 2.' At least that's what Jake Knightley, inheritor of the Tudor mansion, Knightley Hall, had let slip when he'd been selling off the barn and third of an acre plot that came with it. Gertrude Mk 2, like Gertrude, the original, definitely hadn't inherited the herding instinct and Jake had wanted to check Melody wouldn't be scared of bumping into a cow who wandered around the estate every now and then.

'So what happened to Gertrude-Gertrude?' Kate asked.

'What do you think happened?' Oscar replied, unsure he was willing to talk about cows for the duration of her visit.

Kate looked at him, appalled. 'Please tell me she didn't wander out of the village and into the first Golden Arches she came across and end up as dinner for the post-clubbing crowd or breakfast for the pre-scaffolding crew?'

'It's all right. She was old and died of natural causes. I suspect she has full roaming-rights and all the grass she can eat in that big field in the sky.'

'Oh. Well. Phew.'

'Although, out of respect,' he found himself saying, 'maybe swap out the quarter-pounder with cheese tonight and go for a salad instead.'

In a moment of complete unguarded normality between them, Kate laughed and so did he. As if all the awkwardness, grief, anger and hostility between them had fallen into the water under the biggest bridge imaginable.

But then he remembered how it was with her now and all laughter abruptly stopped.

Kate stared at him for a moment, an expression of being at an utter loss on her face, before her eyes sparked and she broke eye contact to start looking around his home with the usual curiosity she had for everything in life. Apparently unable to stand still, she wandered around the huge open-plan living, dining, kitchen area, taking everything in.

She paused as she took in the mixture of cushions in duck-egg blue, gold and ecru that were lined up like soldiers across the large L-shaped grey sofa in front of the wood-burner. He saw a frown cross her features and wanted to explain that it was nigh-on impossible not to learn a thing or two about interior decorating since he'd been running his construction company, and that Melody liked burrowing into them when they sat down on Sunday afternoons for movie time together.

His hands came out of his pockets, but tension immediately filled him again the moment she stopped in front of the chunky timber mantelpiece he'd put in over the wood-burner. His gaze narrowed as she leant forward to look at the collection of photographs.

Melody in a graduation hat and gown, even though she was only five. Melody draping a daisy chain Juliet had helped her make around Gertrude's neck. Him and Sheila sitting with his parents in the beer garden of the new hotel in Whispers Ford. His parents had driven down from Exeter to check on him and Melody under the guise of gawping at the newest hot-spot.

Oscar watched as Kate reached out and stroked a finger over the photo of Melody blowing out candles on a giant pink birthday cake in the shape of an eight, at her birthday party a couple of months ago. As if the shock of seeing her niece for the first time in over a year was too much, she brought her hand to her mouth and pressed it against her lips. A tiny shake of her head and then her gaze was roaming repeatedly back over the photos and Oscar knew the exact moment she registered that there weren't any of Bea.

He refused to feel guilty, or, at least, he tried not to.

Melody had several pictures of her mum in her room. Treasured photographs that she had picked out especially.

'Melody looks so grown up,' Kate announced, turning to look at him.

'Mmmn,' he answered, now feeling as if he deserved to be hauled over the coals for not having pictures of his dead wife up everywhere.

'That's a nice photo of you with Mum and your parents,' she said, jerking her thumb back to one of the photos on the mantelpiece. 'Do you see a lot of her, then? Mum, that is?'

'Melody and I go over to hers for Thursday night dinner every week.'

'Every week?'

'It's a new arrangement we've come to.'

'Wow. That's... great.'

'Yes. It is.'

For the longest time immediately after Bea had died, just the sight of Melody had been enough to send Sheila sinking back down into her abyss. After the numbness of his own grief had worn off, he'd realised Melody needed to know her grandmother, mess or not, and so rather than giving up, he'd presented Melody to her at every opportunity.

It had worked.

A little too much, though, because then, suddenly, Sheila had wanted to spend all her time with Melody and Oscar had begun to worry that instead of Melody dragging his mother-in-law out of her grief, Sheila was going to take Melody down with her.

Oscar had had to have several frank talks with her about how she could not and how he *would not* let her take Melody into that black hole of grief with her. Melody was the most beautiful link to Bea, but first and foremost she needed to be treated as a little person in her own right. His daughter and Sheila's granddaughter, yes. A little Bea or a little Kate, no.

He and Sheila had worked their way up to a visit every week, and, actually, things between him and his mother-in-law were the best they'd been. Sheila had put in a lot of work into coming to terms with his boundaries and he wasn't about to let Kate come back and upset all of that.

'Kate, why are you here?' he asked her now, looking her directly in the eye.

'Can't a sister-in-law pop around for a coffee?' she asked, nervously.

With a sigh, he turned and walked over to the kitchen area to grab mugs. Plunging his hand into a glass bowl filled with different flavoured coffee pods that Melody liked picking out for him, he plucked one from the bowl and held it up for

Kate to either approve or disapprove of. When she nodded her head he popped it into the coffee machine and pressed the button.

As coffee dripped into the mug, he crossed his arms again, leant his hip against the granite counter and resumed staring at her. Waiting.

'I know you've found it difficult to be around me but I–' she broke off and he scowled as she cleared her throat, and tried again. 'I wanted to tell you I'm back and to also tell you–'

'Sugar? Milk?' he interrupted, annoyed with himself that his stone heart had started to crack and beat out a very human, very apprehensive beat.

'Oh, um, the usual, please.'

'So is that sugar? Milk?' he asked tightly. *Say 'just like Bea took it'*. Say it so that I can stay mad, he thought.

'Um... no sugar and a little milk, please.'

Silently he followed the instructions that would make it like Bea had drunk it and, picking up the mug, walked with it over to the coffee table and plonked it down.

'Melody isn't here?' She said, sitting down.

'She's at school.'

'Right. Of course. I knew that.' She paused and then asked, 'Do you know if she got my letters? I mean, I didn't know you'd moved, so I would hate to think that she hadn't–'

'Sandeep knew, though, so he delivered them here instead.'

'Great. That's great. Do you know if she wrote–'

'Wait here a minute,' he said, standing up, walking away and refusing to give in to social nicety and offer her a tour of the place he was so proud of rebuilding. In Melody's room he went over to the only thing in the room that wasn't pink – and thank God there was at least something in the room that wasn't – a white jewellery box that Sheila had given her granddaughter for her birthday. Before the pop-up ballerina inside could produce a full pirouette, he whipped out the three envelopes Melody had told him she had kept in there, slammed the lid shut and wandered back out to find Kate.

He passed them to her silently and she read the careful child's printing on them, smiled and held them to her chest. When she looked up at him it was with watery eyes that undid him a little.

He cleared his throat. 'Obviously we didn't have your address, so Melody and I came to an agreement that she would write when she wanted to and I would give them to you when I next saw you. *If I next saw you.*'

'Juliet always knew where I was,' she whispered.

'I didn't realise I was suppose to interrogate every member of your family to work out if anyone knew where you were.'

Vivid crimson stained her cheeks again. 'Thank you for saving them for me. I can't wait to read them. Can't wait to see Melody, either. I – I don't know if you know – I mean, of course you know... that The Clock House is for sale?'

Oscar stared as her words petered out uncertainly. Anger was swift to find its voice again. Full and justified and burning hot as he worked out where she was going with the information. 'You have to be joking,' he ground out.

'Oh, you know me,' she said, picking up her coffee and taking a healthy sip, 'I never drink and jibe.'

'You're back because The Clock House is for sale? That's what's brought you back? Not people. Not family. But a bloody building?'

'I realise this might be hard to believe, but to me that building does represent people – family.'

'For God's sake, Kate–'

'And maybe deep down you recognise those ties too,' she was quick to jump in with. 'Because I know you've been looking after Bea's bees there.'

He stared at the floor. No way was she going to get him to admit that he enjoyed looking after them. That after the first grief-filled grudging treks to check on the apiary, he had started to care what happened to them. And then, somehow, it had become a therapy of sorts and somewhere he could retreat from constantly being asked if he was all right, or constantly being talked to as the Young Widower of Whispers Wood.

'Somebody had to look after those bees and patently it wasn't going to be you or Sheila, was it?' he said, looking back up at her.

'No, neither Mum nor I were in any fit state to–' she stopped and shook her head as if chastising herself for implying that he had found it in any way easier to recover from what had happened in comparison to her mum and her. 'Anyway, I'm very glad it's you looking after them.'

'Why?'

She shrugged helplessly. 'I guess you're good for them. Quiet. Calm. Patient. Loyal.'

'What do you want, Kate?' he asked again, feeling none of those things.

'I was wondering if you had kept all of Bea's journals and files relating to The Clock House.'

He could see them neatly stacked in the clear plastic container boxes in the cupboard in his office. 'And if I have?' She couldn't really be thinking of going over this same ground again, could she?

'I was wondering if you might lend them to me. When I said I was back – I meant that I was back, back. I intend to buy The Clock House and open it as a day spa.'

'No.'

'No?' She licked her lips. Fiddled with the handle of the coffee mug and then took a deep breath. 'No, you don't have them any more. Or, "no" you have them but I can't have them?'

'No, you're not buying The Clock House and opening it up as Bea's business.'

She blinked, but couldn't hide the flare of anger in her eyes. 'I wasn't aware I needed your permission.'

'I'm not handing over Bea's things to you so you can play at being a grown-up before you decide it's too tough and end up leaving again.'

His arrow obviously hitting its mark, he watched as her hand flew up to her chest to hover over her heart. Watched some more as her fingers then scrabbled around the neckline of her dress and he continued to watch as her fingers then clenched and unclenched as all the colour leached from her face.

She shot up to her feet, grabbed her basket and started rooting around in it, before her hand went to her throat once more.

'I have to leave,' she said, pale and stiff as she walked towards the front door.

Probably for the best, he thought, yet was unable to completely stamp out the concern as she wrenched open the front door. She couldn't even look at him and as she ran down the path away from him, Oscar felt the overwhelmingly shitty sensation that he'd gone too far.

Chapter 16

A Lot Like Losing a Locket and Finding a Pebble

Kate

Panic clambered up Kate's spine, unfurled and then flooded her nervous system as she retraced her steps down the drive.

Where was it?

Where was her locket?

Not even her locket, but Bea's locket.

Her breath scythed in and out in short, sharp, painful puffs and there was a weird dull-pitched sound in her ears, like the sound of hope flatlining.

Okay. It was okay. She whispered the words over and over as her gaze darted left and right.

The important thing here was not to lose it.

Like she'd lost the locket!

Over the horrible, continuous ringing sound in her head, Kate heard Gertrude moo and looked up to watch the cow disappear around the corner. An utterly horrific thought slammed into her, making her whimper as she worried – what

146

if Gertrude had found the locket and eaten it and was going to die from ingesting it and ended up joining Bea and Gertrude Mk 1 in the sky?

She forced down the ball of emotion threatening to turn into sobs. Life couldn't be cruel enough to have allowed Gertrude to find the locket and eat it. It just couldn't. She had to calm down. Chances were it was either at Old Man Isaac's, Wren Cottage or The Clock House.

She'd simply search all of those and she'd find it and as soon as she did she'd start to feel better again.

Because it couldn't be lost, lost.

No way would she cope if she'd lost the one thing of Bea's that she'd kept.

By the time she made it to the end of the drive leading up to Knightley Hall, huge, fat raindrops were falling from the sky.

She looked up and watched one dark rain cloud join up with another. 'Great,' she muttered. 'You go right ahead and pour water on troubled oil. I mean, it's supposed to be the other way around, but obviously I haven't got enough to worry about.'

Like the fact that seeing photos of Melody had only reinforced what she'd been missing out on. All the beautiful places she'd worked in and right now she'd swap every one of them for having memories and photos of sweet and simple family gatherings from the last few years.

In each time-frame exposed by the shutter's release she'd seen not the occasion captured but the healing that was taking place and now her breath was a fiery constriction in her throat at her exclusion from that process.

Her fault, she knew.

But she'd thought she'd been making it better for everyone. Easier.

The rain started falling harder and quickly she removed the precious letters from her niece and her phone from the basket and stuffed them all down the front of her dress, hoping they'd be protected as off she tottered down the road, with her basket upended and perched on her head like a giant wicker pith helmet.

She'd known it was going to be tough seeing Oscar again, she reasoned, as she squinted ineffectually down at the uneven country lane underfoot, in case the locket had fallen off and was lying in wait for her to find it and never let it out of her sight again.

She just hadn't counted on him not mellowing towards her one iota. He was so bloody pig-headed. She couldn't begin to see what Bea had seen in him – aside from the fact that he used to be a friendly, warm, happy-go-lucky, family-minded guy, who, it was obvious to everyone, absolutely adored Bea.

Kate hopped over a puddle and sighed. Lord knew she'd changed since Bea's passing, so was it really any wonder that Oscar had as well?

But from the moment he'd left Kate hanging in Hug Land, to his chopping and changing between pinched-lipped sarcasm and lecturing tone... she'd been left in no doubt she'd lost his respect.

And now she'd gone and lost Bea's locket too.

She remembered Oscar coming up to her in the kitchenette of The Clock House after Bea's funeral. She'd been counting out cups and saucers, trying to remember who had said 'tea' and who had said 'coffee' when he'd quietly asked her to make a list of the things she might like of Bea's. She'd stared down at the parquet flooring, poking at a loose briquette, wondering how to tell him she wanted everything of Bea's, while at the same time knowing that that was a ridiculous answer.

Instead she'd told him, just as quietly, that she would have a think and get back to him. For days she'd thought and thought and thought and when she'd realised that the one thing she truly wanted and had plucked up the courage to tell Oscar, she'd immediately seen from his face that it had been completely the wrong thing to ask for.

Yet he'd honoured his offer and given her the locket.

That's how cool a guy he was. Before, that was, she'd left Whispers Wood and had come back on visits to find him uninterested in what she was up to at best, and really angry with her at worst.

Halfway back to Wren Cottage her arm finally lost circulation from where it had been holding the rim of the basket out of her eyes. No longer caring if she resembled a drowned rat, she took the basket off. All she could focus on was the sick feeling filling up her insides. Why hadn't she immediately realised she hadn't been wearing the locket? And, the way she had left Oscar's house, like that? Not staying, not fighting, not proving to him that she was the right person to buy The Clock House. God, if he thought she was fickle already, her leaving in the way she had would have only reinforced his opinion.

By the time she was standing in the lounge doorway of Wren Cottage she wasn't sure she could feel more wretched.

'Wow,' said Juliet. 'The least Oscar could have done was offer you a lift back in this rain. Or was he not in?'

She opened her mouth to explain that the rate she'd run out of his house, he would have had to turn into The Flash in order to catch her first, when the tears that had been threatening rose up and spilled over. 'I've lost Bea's locket,' she whispered, wiping at the tears and trying desperately to stop fresh ones from forming.

'What? Oh, Hun.'

Kate felt the air around her displace as Juliet jumped up from the sofa and immediately wrapped her up in a hug. The warm compassion had her feeling as if she was on the brink of unravelling and to try and combat the sensation she started talking. 'Daniel Westlake wants to buy The Clock House for definite and Old Man Isaac has pitted us against each other to raise funds for a summer fete as a way of proving we love the village, or something equally adorable yet ridiculously complicated, and Oscar was a complete giant ball of arse to me and, and, it feels like the r-rain has p-purposefully p-pissed all over my f-firework,' she hiccupped, and stared exhaustedly down at the puddles of rainwater appearing at her feet. 'I didn't even realise I was walking straight back here. I should go out again and look for it.'

'You will not,' Juliet ordered, tightening her grip when Kate made to turn around and go back out and search. 'You're absolutely soaked. Forget about The Clock House and this fete-thing and whether Oscar is or is not an arse-ball. Let's have a think about where you could have lost the locket… do you remember wearing it this morning?'

Kate closed her eyes and pictured herself standing in front of Juliet's mirror. She shook her head sadly and when she opened her eyes again more tears slipped out. 'God, Juliet, I've been halfway around the world with that locket and I've never lost sight of it. Never. Five minutes back here and I can't find it. It has to be a sign, doesn't it? Do you think Bea's trying to tell me something?'

Juliet pulled back to look at her carefully. 'Has Bea ever told you anything before?'

'No. No she hasn't,' Kate sniffed. 'And that's the whole problem, isn't it? How can I do this without her blessing? How can I?'

'Kate, stop. You've had a big day. I get why you're so upset, but waiting on a blessing or a sign for everything you do in life isn't going to help. What's going to help is you going upstairs, having a nice hot shower and changing into dry clothes while I ring Old Man Isaac and check whether he found your locket after you left there this morning. Okay?'

'Okay. I'm so sorry to get in such a state...' She hated anyone seeing her not in control or at least giving a good impression of being mostly in control. It was bad enough that people looked at her mum and worried; she didn't like feeling as if they were looking at her and worrying as well.

'Don't be silly,' Juliet ordered. 'Now, how about I make us a plate of sandwiches while you freshen up?'

As if on cue, Kate's stomach rumbled. 'That sounds good.' Walking tiredly over to her bag she took out her wash-kit and fresh clothes and before making her way up the stairs, turned back around to Juliet and determined to reassure her, cheekily asked, 'Can I just hear you say arse-ball one more time?'

Juliet rolled her eyes and shooed her up the stairs. 'Go. I will make phone-calls and sandwiches.'

At the top of the stairs, Kate was rewarded by a softly spoken, 'Arse-ball,' from Juliet.

Smiling and thinking how strange it felt to have someone championing her and how lucky she was to have that, she opened the door to the cosy bathroom with its mosaic white and aqua tiles. Popping the fresh clothes and her wash-kit onto the white painted Lloyd Loom chair next to the sink, she dragged in a breath and stared at her reflection in the tiny mirror above the bijou basin.

More tears leaked out, to run unheeded down her cheeks.

She let them fall for a few more moments, indulging in the cleansing feeling that letting out emotion that had been stored up for way too long gave you before she finally gave a giant sniff and endeavoured to rein in the excess.

Unzipping her wash-kit she automatically started searching to see if she'd tucked the locket safely inside. No locket, but when her hand located something hard and cold she took it out and stared down at it sitting in her palm.

One purple-hued pebble with a white marble vein feathering through it.

She closed her hand around the stone, warming it with the heat of her skin.

The need to get on her laptop and check for any work assignment that would take her away from Whispers Wood to somewhere where no one knew her and she could pretend to be this person with no back-story, or at least someone who had everything in perspective, was so strong she nearly turned around and snuck back down the stairs to pick up the bags she still hadn't unpacked.

She opened up her fist and stared back down at the pebble, thinking about the people who wouldn't want her to run and the people who wouldn't be at all surprised if she did.

She sniffed one more time.

It was going to get better. It was, it was, it was.

No way was she letting down Juliet or proving Oscar right or being bested by Daniel.

Chapter 17

Support Groups

Juliet

'Feel better?' Juliet asked, glancing up from stacking sandwiches onto the cake-stand that had been last month's craft project.

'Heaps,' Kate replied. 'Thank you for stopping me from going full-on hysterical.'

Juliet popped two plates down on the small kitchen table and snagged two napkins out of the matching napkin holder to the cake-stand. 'You do know its okay to do the Kermit flail occasionally, right?' She had a sudden image of Kate in a different country, all on her own, upset and with no one to hug her and didn't like it one bit.

'Course.'

'Now say it like you mean it, please.'

Kate grimaced. 'I guess I'm not used to anyone seeing me like that.'

'Not even the odd boyfriend?'

'I thought the trick was to keep them interested, not send them packing.'

'I thought the trick was to be yourself?'

'I am myself with men,' Kate insisted.

Juliet highly doubted that. Kate had said that way, way too quickly. Maybe what had happened with Marco was to do with Marco figuring out that Kate hadn't completely been herself around him.

'And don't try and convince me,' Kate added, pointing to the cake-plate and matching napkin holder, 'that you unleash your "craft" on every man you meet.'

'Hey, every relationship I enter into gets the full "made with love" me.'

Kate snorted as she helped herself to a sandwich. After a few bites she said, 'I know you know I was still grieving when I left Whispers Wood, but seriously, do you really think every man I met wanted to see that side of me?'

'Well no, maybe not right away. But surely – possibly even with Marco – there came a point where you could drop the globe-trotting, haven't-a-care-in-the-world, act?'

Kate shoved another whole triangle of sandwich into her mouth and slowly chewed.

'Kate?'

'I may have forgotten to do that part.'

'Oh, Kate.'

'It's not completely my fault. It isn't as if Marco and I saw each other that often anyway. I guess it was easier to fall into the pattern of being two shallow souls meeting up for hot monkey-sex.'

'Well, props obviously for the hot monkey-sex, but, didn't you ever think about a future with him?'

'Honestly? It wasn't until he'd told me he'd found more than that with someone else that I realised I'd been assuming "more" would come along later but without me, you know, having to actually give more.'

'Wowsers. So, lesson learned, then?'

'I guess. So what was your lesson learned?'

'Mine?' Juliet chewed slowly while she pondered how to word her answer. 'Mine's to forget about chasing love and work towards something tangible instead.'

'Love is tangible!'

'Is it? Look at my mum and dad. Look at *your* mum and dad.'

The corners of Kate's mouth turned down and Juliet felt awful. 'I'm sorry. I shouldn't have mentioned your dad.'

'No. It's okay. I actually contacted him after the funeral, you know?'

'No, I didn't know.' Juliet suspected no one else did, either.

'I demanded a visit so that I could ask him why he hadn't come. It took a lot of badgering, but I did eventually get him to agree to meet up. I really prepared for that meeting. Endless home truths were sitting right on the tip of my tongue, but somehow from the moment he didn't recognise me something switched inside of me. I mean, *of course* he didn't recognise me. I was a woman and he remembered a girl crying and clinging and making a show and preventing him from leaving cleanly. We were strangers to each other.'

So much sadness and coming right on top of Kate losing Bea... why hadn't she realised how much Kate had had to contend with.

'He did write Mum a letter, apparently,' Kate continued. 'Explaining how sorry he was and how he'd privately grieved for the young daughter he'd known, how he had told his wife and children and if it wasn't too hard to hear, how he wanted to pass on their condolences as well.'

'And Sheila never said a thing to you about this?'

'Never. I don't even know if she registered it, and if she did, can you imagine receiving condolences from the family you'd been left for? His wife advised him not to come to the funeral. Told him it might be too upsetting for Mum and I to see him there when he hadn't contacted us ever before. And she was right to, I think. He showed me photos of his kids. I asked him if he ever thought there'd come a time when he'd want to get to know Melody, and he was honest enough to say he didn't. There's no connection there and he feels it would be disloyal to his other kids to force one.'

Juliet could only imagine what Oscar would have to say if he ever learned that. 'I can't believe he showed you photos of his life without you. Like you were on some sort of long-lost catch-up instead of a mission to find out why he hadn't gone to his daughter's funeral. What an incredibly crass arse-ball.'

Kate smiled. 'I know. I kept expecting Davina McCall or Nicky Campbell to pop out. But, you know what? There was love in his face when he showed me those photos and I have to hand it to him – he stayed with her. Created something tangible with her. And hey, look at what Oscar and Bea had, too.'

Juliet stared down at her plate, pushing the breadcrumbs from her sandwich into a pattern. 'Mmn,' she said, paranoid a whisper of emotion would show in her voice. 'But look what it left behind when it was ripped away?' It was obvious to Juliet that Oscar was never going to let himself feel that much for anyone ever again.

'Ah, but what about the whole, "It's better to have loved and lost than never to have loved at all," thing?' Kate probed.

'How do you know I'm not adopting the "if you don't look for it, it will come to you" approach?'

Kate snorted again. 'At some point I will get you to 'fess up, you know?'

''Fess up to what?' Juliet said, her mouth going dry.

'To who it was that hurt you. Come on,' she cajoled, 'I shared about Marco.'

'There is genuinely nothing to confess to. I already told you, no one has hurt me.'

'So you're not nursing a broken heart?'

Juliet stretched her mouth into a smile and with a casual shake of her head, stood up to walk over to the kitchen worktop and flip the switch on the kettle. 'Nope. By the way, Old Man Isaac is certain you didn't lose your locket there this morning. Also, he can't remember you wearing it, either, so I'm thinking you probably lost it at The Clock House, or, in the woods. I've left a message with Trudie to check the lost property box at The Clock House after she finishes auditions this afternoon.'

Kate stood up, collected the plates and holding them up in front of her, said, 'Okay, this is me recognising your change of subject and going along with it,' before placing them gently into the butler's sink. 'This afternoon I'll search the woods.'

'I'll come with you and you can talk me through why you now have to put on a summer fete.'

'Oh my God, I can't believe I haven't even told you yet.'

'Start filling me in now – biccies are in the cupboard to the left of you.'

Juliet took the tea into the lounge and curled up on one end of the sofa, waiting for Kate to join her.

'You know what,' Kate said, following a few moments later with the packet of biscuits. 'Oscar had a stack of chocolate biscuits like these sitting on his table and didn't offer me one *and* I had to ask for a cup of coffee!'

Juliet bobbled her mug of tea. Swearing under her breath, she wiped a few drops off her jeans and waited for her heart rate to settle back down to anything resembling normal. When she'd asked to be filled in, she'd thought it would the meeting with Old Man Isaac part, not the meeting with Oscar part. 'I expect he was just surprised to see you,' she tried. 'Plus, you know, he's a guy and guys don't exactly get pulled aside at school and taught hospitality.'

Kate frowned and pulled one of the cushions from behind her to hug. 'But that's just it, his house screams hospitality – but you know – homely as well. And he had all these cushions. Like these, actually,' she said, frowning down at the one in her lap before clicking her fingers. '*That's* what struck me while I was there. They're these exact colours and patterns.'

Juliet blushed to the roots of her hair. 'You know how matchy-matchy I get. When I realised I'd made too many for here I gave him the extra as a house-warming gift.'

Kate speared Juliet with a look like she'd said the most bizarre thing ever. As if she couldn't imagine either her or Oscar not knowing the exact number of cushions a sofa needed. 'You gave him the extra or you made him a set?' Kate asked.

Juliet took a gulp of tea. 'Does it make a difference?' she mumbled, thinking about all the pleasure she'd got from sewing on the appliqué pieces that Melody had chosen and how she'd thought long and hard about sewing in her little 'made with love' labels before chickening out.

'I guess not. So you've obviously seen his place, then?'

'I still help out with Melody a fair bit,' she confessed.

'Oh.' Kate dunked her biscuit into her mug and bit off the soggy half and then chewed thoughtfully.

The longer Kate chewed, the weightier the silence felt, so that she bumbled out, 'I forgot to ask you if he gave you the files?'

'No, he didn't and I'm pretty sure he's not going to either.'

'Is that because you went in too—'

'Hard? No. Honestly,' Kate shot back. 'I promise I didn't. I went in like a marshmallow. But no matter how I am with him, he's still so angry at me and—' she broke off and picked up her mug to clasp it comfortingly against her cheekbone before whispering, 'God, Juliet, you have no idea what it's like – knowing that every time he looks at me, he sees Bea.'

Juliet winced at the pain in Kate's voice. She couldn't

imagine how awkward it must make Kate feel. There were times, even now, when Kate entered a room or called out to her and Juliet would have to remind herself that there was only one Somersby twin now.

How did you cope when your entire existence was separated into when you had a twin and when you no longer did?

You ran, she guessed now.

Ran to where no one knew and you could try and find out who you were as an individual.

'Maybe this time,' she ventured quietly to Kate, 'with you staying around, that will change?'

'But what if it doesn't? I don't know what's worse, the anger I get now, or–' she stopped again and brought her mug to her lap, where she frowned down into it, lost in thought.

'Or?' Juliet pressed.

'–the look in his eyes before I left the first time. You know how big his eyes are–'

Yes. She did. Big and green and incredibly soulful.

'–and when Bea died,' Kate continued, 'they'd see me and fill up with this awful desolation and I couldn't change it – didn't know how to change it. So I just...'

'Left,' she gasped, finishing where Kate had tailed off. 'Oh, Kate, that's really why you left?'

'Partly,' Kate confided. 'I couldn't make it better for him and all the time Mum, Oscar, *everyone*, saw me walking around they were reminded either of Bea or of what had happened to Bea.'

Juliet's heart broke all over again for all of them.

161

'Kate, if I'd known this, I'm not sure I'd have asked you to come back.'

'You didn't ask.'

'I did.'

'Okay, you did. That postcard Jedi mind-trick was genius. It's sweet of you, but you don't have to worry that I'm doing this for morbid reasons. For the first time in a long, long time this really feels like what I'm supposed to be doing, when I'm supposed to be doing it.' She reached out and touched Juliet's hand briefly. 'Do you think Oscar is angry all the time because he's punishing himself for Bea being gone?'

'He's not angry all the time,' Juliet insisted.

'So it's definitely just seeing me, then? I was worrying he might get this angry with Melody.'

'What? No way would he. You're being absurd.'

'Am I? I could tell he was angry she'd written back to me.'

'No. I'm sorry, Kate, but you couldn't be more wrong about Oscar. You didn't hang around long enough after Bea died, and I get why', she added quickly, 'but, he lost the woman who meant absolutely everything to him and within a month the two most important adult connections to her absented themselves as well. It was really hard on him when your mum checked out and you checked yourself onto a plane. He couldn't make his little girl's world better and he had to try and keep the business going.'

'So you stepped in to help him?'

'We *all* stepped in to help him,' Juliet defended. 'He asked all of us for help. Do you know how difficult that must have been for him? I mean, you have met Oscar, right?'

Regret flashed in Kate's eyes and Juliet worried she'd been too harsh.

'You can't get bitter about not being here, Kate. Look what you found. Look what you've done.'

'Yeah. Big wow. I've written some articles. I've reviewed some places.'

'You found yourself, I think. And now you're ready to take on something that means something to you.'

'What do I do about Oscar?'

'He just needs time to see that you aren't going anywhere and that you have no intention of going anywhere even when things get messy.'

'You don't think that's being over-optimistic? Even if I stop reminding him of her, I'll be reminding him of what Bea wanted and didn't get to have.'

'I think this is going to work better if you stop doing him the disservice of thinking he can't get over what happened and start treating him like he's allowed to move on.'

'What? Of course he's allowed to move on. I wouldn't ever want him to feel he was expected to grieve forever. Bea would never have wanted him to, either. Is he – has he found someone, then?'

'No. He's too busy pretending he doesn't deserve to move on.'

'Why wouldn't he deserve to? Unless someone's making him feel like that? He told me he has dinner with Mum every week. Is she making him feel like that?'

'I don't think so. I guess it's, well, it's a small village, isn't it? If everyone keeps thinking of him as The Young Widower of Whispers Wood, how's he ever going to see himself differently?'

'Maybe Old Man Isaac is right about us all losing our mojo, because what is it with us all labelling each other? There's Oscar, The Young Widower of Whispers Wood, and now you, The Crazy Cat Lady of Whispers Wood...' Kate shook her head and then laughed, 'Hey, the two of you should get together–'

'*What?*' Juliet only just managed to hold onto her tea without sending it flying across the room. 'That's crazy!' she spluttered, feeling intense heat suffuse her face. 'He's never going to see me as getting-together-with material. He doesn't even see me.' *Oh, my God, shut up, Jules!* 'Other than a friendly and convenient baby-sitter. I mean – I swear it wouldn't even register if I walked past him naked–' *Shut up. Shut up. Shut up!* Finally her brain caught up with her mouth and got it to stop making words, but with her hands trembling around her mug and her breath coming out choppy and no doubt her face looking like it was actually possible to die from mortification, Juliet had the most awful feeling that she'd let not a cute and fluffy kitten out of the bag, but, rather, a whole pride of exceedingly chatty big cats.

'O-kay,' Kate said, with a look of 'speak very slowly to the crazy cat lady' on her face. 'I was going to suggest the two of you got together to form a support group, where your logo is a picture of a label gun with a giant red 'x' through it, or something. Obviously I wasn't talking about you and Oscar getting *together* together, because that would be, well, insane, right?'

'Right,' Juliet whispered.

Kate slapped her hands over her mouth, her eyes going as wide as saucers. 'Oh my God, Juliet?' She lowered her hands. 'Are you *interested* in Oscar?'

'No. Absolutely not. Because that would be about the most ridiculously stupid thing to do in the world and I'm not stupid. I mean I have qualifications. I have self respect. I have...'

'Oh, Jules.'

'Don't. Please don't,' she couldn't bear the look on her cousin's face. 'I know. Believe me you don't have to tell me how much I know it's impossible. And I swear, I didn't mean to fall for him. I didn't even see it coming. I mean, why would I? I was only helping out. And then, darn it, I got the biggest crush. And I knew,' she said, cradling her tea like a lifeline, 'just knew it was only because we'd been spending a lot of time together and...' The words stopped flowing and her smile wobbled dangerously.

'Jules—'

Juliet tried to centre herself. But her words, when they came out, were laced with disbelief at finding herself in this position. 'Do you know how angry at myself I was when I realised it was becoming more than a crush? I've tried everything, Kate. Really, I have. I even asked Trudie' – she tried to smile – 'you know, under the guise of asking for a friend, if her daughter, the herbalist from Horsham, could make a little anti-love potion.' She tried for a laugh but it missed its mark, judging by the look of pity and compassion on Kate's face.

'You absolutely don't have to worry about this at all,' she said, injecting as much rock-steady dependability into her voice as humanly possible. 'I have it in perspective now. I know what I'm doing. I'm opening a hair salon. I'm putting other things in my life. And I *will*, totally, completely and categorically fall out of love with Oscar Matthews. I promise.'

Chapter 18

Breaking Bread

Oscar

'What'll you have, love?'

'Hi Jen. It's busy in here tonight,' Oscar remarked, needing to raise his voice a little to be heard over the Friday night hubbub coming from the crowd in the hotel lounge area behind him. He took a brief look at the guest bitters on offer and decided on his favourite standby. 'A pint of Whispers Wrangler, please, and can you see if there's a table free in the restaurant?'

'Sure,' she smiled as she held the pint glass under the pump. 'I'll double-check for you, but I'm pretty sure the restaurant's fully booked.'

The way his day was going, he figured it would be. He supposed he could always eat at the bar, but he really wasn't in the mood to do small talk or work-talk and he'd discovered that people found it harder to stop by a dining table and ask him about building regs and 'mates rates' than if he was sitting at the bar eating.

Taking the proffered pint in one hand and his change in

the other, he moved further down the bar to let others place their orders. Shoving his change into his jeans pocket he stared into his pint, letting the background noise soothe. Coming here had been a last minute decision fuelled by the need to recover from Kate's visit, Melody's visit to the dentist, and then a too quiet home after he'd agreed Melody could have a sleepover at her best friend Persephone Pavey's house.

He took a healthy gulp of his beer. Getting told by a dentist, who he was almost certain was younger than him, that Melody needed her first filling had gone down about as well as you'd expect, considering how his day had started.

Melody was only eight!

What the hell had he been doing wrong that someone – admittedly a someone who'd had to study for nearly as long as his daughter had been alive – was going to have to drill into his daughter's mouth?

He'd remembered Melody having to miss her check-up last year because he'd been up to his neck on the Hamilton refurb and guilt had swamped him. Hands down, no way would Bea have ever let their daughter miss something as important as a dental check-up. Honestly, some days it really was remarkably easy to feel like he was failing on every parenting level imaginable.

He'd managed to alleviate the dark mood a little after a sneaky look on Mumsnet had revealed that half the parenting population suffered a major guilt-trip at the news their child needed a filling. But he'd realised if he wanted to keep up the father-daughter Sunday movie time together he was going to have to swap out the treats for fruit or something.

Juliet would probably know what he could make. He made a mental note to ask her, when an even better thought struck him. Persuading her to make them some healthy snacks was bound to turn out tastier than anything he could come up with.

He went for another swig of beer when guilt reared its head again. He probably should stop relying on Juliet so much. She'd been sort of distant with him lately and he thought it was her subtle way of trying to force him to remember she had a life of her own. The problem with Juliet was that she was too nice for her own good. And the problem with him was that he was too damn selfish.

Knowing Kate spent time with Juliet whenever she came back for a visit, he could picture Juliet now, sitting on her sofa, her long, red hair falling softly over her shoulder as she tipped her head to the side in that way she had of making you feel you had her full attention, as Kate told her about how her visit with him had gone.

He still couldn't get over the sheer gall Kate had in coming to his house and asking for Bea's files.

First there was the out of the blue request for them and second there was her reaction when he'd said no.

The first he couldn't get to until he'd stopped feeling so bloody guilty about the second. Not that he should have been surprised by her running. But he would have had to have been a complete unfeeling bastard not to have noticed her poleaxed impression when he'd refused to give her the files and had then called her out for wanting to buy The Clock House. Once he'd calmed down, he'd known he needed to apologise. So he'd rung Sheila, asking to speak to Kate, and more fool him for assuming she'd be staying at her mum's, because it had then become awkwardly clear Sheila hadn't known her daughter was back and therefore didn't know where she was staying.

That was all it had taken for him to be pissed off with Kate all over again.

'Sorry, Oscar,' Jen said, interrupting his thoughts. 'But I'm afraid the last table has already been booked by a Mr Westlake.' She looked over Oscar's shoulder, hoping someone would lay claim to the name.

A voice behind him said, 'Yes, that's me.'

'Great,' Jen said with a quick, apologetic smile for Oscar. 'If you'd like to follow me, Mr Westlake?'

Oscar turned to find a man about his age staring at him.

'Help you, mate?' Oscar said, not really appreciating the intensity of his stare.

'Sorry – I was miles away. You lost out on a table, you say?'

Oscar shrugged. 'I can eat from the bar menu.'

'You're the guy who runs the building business out of Whispers Wood?'

Great! He knew it. Bloody business talk.

'Yeah. That's me.'

'Saw your van in the car park. I'm Daniel Westlake. I just moved to Whispers Wood. I'm buying The Clock House.'

Shock had Oscar's gaze sharpening. 'Is that right?'

As he reached forward to shake the guy's hand he thought about Kate's claim that she wanted to buy The Clock House and set up Bea's business there.

Bea *and* Kate's business. He forced the correction because he knew it had been Kate's idea initially.

Did Kate know someone else was interested in buying the building?

'Look, why don't you share my table,' Daniel offered. 'No sense losing out. I hear the food is supposed to be really good.'

'It is.' And at least this way he could find out what the hell was going on with the sale of The Clock House.

The hotel restaurant was never going to be Michelin-star quality, but compared with other eateries in the surrounding area it was probably one of the better ones. And, Oscar thought, as he and Daniel were shown to their table, at least the ambiance wasn't one of those intimate-surroundings deals that you were supposed to bring dates to.

Not that he'd brought a date here.

Way, way too close to home.

It had been daunting enough to have joined an online dating agency, created a profile and then to have gone on a couple of dates over the past year, without having people he actually knew knowing.

Three.

He'd been on three dates. Four, if you counted the third leading to a second date.

All three women had been really, really nice.

And the relief he'd felt at discovering that had been immense because it meant that the lack of spark with any of them hadn't made him feel as though he was betraying Bea. He'd been able to tell himself he was just meeting new people and that it didn't need to turn into anything.

Yeah.

The whole point in joining up meant that he was ready for 'anything' to turn into 'something'.

And he was.

Mostly.

In the absence of a real spark with any of them, though, it had been easy to put obstacles in his way and tell himself he that he was happy it being him, Melody and the business. So he'd cancelled his membership and told himself that this wasn't failure. It was practical. He was really too busy to feel lonely sometimes anyway.

As they were shown to their seats he couldn't help noticing the empty table for two beside them. 'Excuse me, but this table appears free?'

'I'm sorry, sir. It's reserved, but if they don't turn up, I'll let you know and you can take it.'

'So, what's good here?' Daniel asked, taking his seat and picking up the menu printed on small A5 card.

Oscar sat down in the opposite chair and immediately blew out the small votive candle in the middle of the table. 'You can't go wrong with the steak. The sea bass is really good too.'

Daniel smiled and popped the votive candle on the empty table beside them. 'Brilliant. Don't get me wrong, sausage rolls and pies at Big Kev's are fine, but there comes a point – I've found that to be on the fourth consecutive day, that you start craving protein and vegetables.'

'Right. You don't cook, then?'

'I'm no Jamie, but at the moment I'm staying at the B&B

in Whispers Wood and so it's breakfast and outstanding cream teas.'

'You're at Sheila's place?' Sometimes he loved that small village equalled small world. Forget looking nosy. He'd be able to ask her all about the guy preparing to buy The Clock House at dinner on Thursday. 'She's my mother-in-law. If you let her know, she'll feed you an evening meal, too. She'd hate to think of you having to make your way through the heat-rack at Big Kev's.'

Daniel stared at him for a few moments before shrugging and saying, 'Didn't want to outstay my welcome by asking.'

'So, you'll be moving into The Clock House once the sale goes through?'

'Not at first. Sheila told me about a couple of cottages coming onto the rental market, so I'm going to go for one of those.'

Oscar nodded. 'I did the refurbishments to get them up to rental code. Does this mean you want to do a lot of work to The Cock House?' After balling Kate out about the building he could hardly get precious about it himself, yet the thought that it might have extensive work done made him feel queasy.

'I'll only be needing cosmetic work done, I think. I'm moving into one of the cottages because I met with Old Man Isaac today and, well, let's just say the sale isn't going to go through until I've well and truly proved myself.'

'Ah.' Oscar had to laugh. That was Old Man Isaac, for you. 'So what do you have to do to prove you're,' he made finger quotes, 'Whispers Wood worthy?'

Daniel grinned. 'Immerse myself in village life and raise some funds for a village fete.'

'Village fete?'

'Mmn. Apparently you're getting one, this year.'

'Crafty old beggar,' Oscar said. 'You must really want the place, then? Or really like Whispers Wood?'

'Bit of both, actually.'

'Relocation is quite a big deal, though, or are you keeping another place elsewhere?' They didn't get many tourist or holiday renters in Whispers Wood.

'No. I was in London before but it didn't feel like the place to settle down.'

'So this is a new start for you?'

'You find something wrong with that?'

'Not necessarily.' Although Oscar was never going to understand running away in order to do that. 'What do you want to do with The Clock House?'

'I want to offer affordable and rentable office space. One thing I've learned is how difficult it is to afford business premises or get flexibility with your lease. I want to offer several options. A combination of permanent office space, a desk for the day, or simply a room for a few hours to carry out job interviews or meetings.'

'Actually, that's not a bad idea. Before I moved to the place I'm in now, I was in one of those cottages on the green and it was difficult to get any work done from home. I used to carry all my interviews out in the local pub, but even that's gone now. People probably use this place at the moment.'

'That's why I'm here tonight.'

'Carrying out a little recon?'

'Yep. Their wedding reception room doubles up as a

conference room, but because the building is listed, they'll never be able to add to their existing facilities. So you think the idea is a good one?'

'I do.'

'Great. I've been conducting a little research and so far all the feedback I've had is positive. Apart from someone who likened it to opening up a Starbucks, that is,' he finished with a scowl.

Oscar grinned and looked up towards the double doors that led in through the pub area of the hotel. Two women were being shown to a table and it was impossible not to notice that the surrounding diners' heads were bobbing up like apples to take in the show.

That's what happened when Kate walked into a room... he knew because that's what used to happen when Bea walked into a room.

But then he caught sight of the woman walking behind Kate. He'd recognise all that gorgeous red hair anywhere, so he really couldn't say why the sight of Juliet walking towards him should give him a funny little kick in the guts like it did.

She was wearing a summery dress in a shade of mossy green that was slightly see-through beneath an overlay of tiny sparkly embroidered flowers.

He reached for his pint, suddenly thirsty.

Kate and Juliet were striding confidently towards...

Oscar's gaze swung in slow motion to the empty table beside the one he and Daniel were seated at.

Oh Holy Hell, no way.

Quickly he put down his pint and picked up his menu, holding it right up in front of his face.

When he sensed that movement had ceased around him, he continued to stare intently at the menu, not taking anything in. Maybe he could have if the menu had actually been printed on decent-sized paper. He was all for saving the trees, but, really. At the very least it could have been big enough so that he wasn't aware of the weighty stare of the guy he'd just met sitting opposite him.

Or the weighty stares coming from Kate or Juliet.

Suddenly an index finger was tugging the menu away from his face and he was looking up at the person responsible for being determined to acknowledge this moment.

'Hello Oscar,' Kate said, with a smile on her face. 'Shall we make this even more awkward and pretend none of us know each other?'

By the light in her eyes she'd obviously got over their meeting this morning and any apology he might or might not have taken advantage of giving dried on his lips.

'Kate,' he tipped his head in greeting and reserved his smile for the woman standing next to her. 'Juliet.'

When he glanced at Daniel his gaze was narrowed and shooting back and forth between him and Kate. The poor guy must think he'd stumbled into really bad dinner theatre.

'Juliet,' Kate said, 'this is Daniel. Daniel – Juliet.'

Oscar watched as Daniel rose from the table to shake Juliet's hand and as Juliet put her small, delicate hand in Daniel's, the weird kick Oscar had felt in his guts moved up to his chest wall.

'*This* is Daniel?' He heard her whisper to Kate.

'This is Daniel,' Kate confirmed.

'Wow,' she mouthed silently, which Oscar took to mean she approved and for some ridiculous reason he found himself sitting straighter in his chair, his chest puffing out a little.

'We can both see and hear you, you know,' he bit out.

'Would you like to make this a foursome?' the waitress said. 'It's no trouble to join up the tables.'

'No,' Oscar said.

'Why not,' Daniel said.

'Good thinking,' Kate said.

'Oh, I'm not sure–' Juliet said, at least agreeing with him. But she'd obviously spoken too softly because suddenly everyone was helping to push the tables together. Well, Daniel, Kate and the waitress were, anyway.

Juliet caught his eye and then looked quickly away again.

Fabulous! Kate had probably told her how shitty he'd been to her earlier. Oscar found himself mentally packing to travel on Guilt Trip Number... actually, at this point in the day, he'd lost count.

'Don't worry, this could all be so much more awkward than it is,' Kate announced, smiling at the waitress as she took the menu being handed to her.

'I really don't see how,' Juliet muttered, taking her menu and pretending great interest in the food on offer, just like he'd done a moment ago.

'Well,' Kate said, 'we could all be on a blind-date double-date and at least this way you two,' she added, pointing at him and Daniel, 'don't look like you're on a date with each other, because as it is, Gloria Pavey looks like she's about to have an aneurysm at the thought.'

The needle on Oscar's Awkward Radar edged higher into the red zone. 'She's not here, is she?'

'On your six,' Kate said out of the side of her mouth.

Oscar turned and frowned. He didn't see her.

'Your other six,' Juliet said with a roll of her eyes.

He turned his head and saw Gloria's cat-like eyes fixed on the four of them, completely ignoring the poor man chatting away animatedly opposite her.

'I guess,' Oscar said, turning to face forward in his seat again, 'this explains why Persephone's sleeping at her dad's tonight. Gloria must be out on a date.'

'Does it matter to you if she is?' Juliet queried and he wondered at the bite in her tone.

'Truthfully? I'd love it.'

'Really? Why?' Juliet asked, straightening the edges of her cutlery.

Oscar focused on the coral varnish on her fingernails and thought it might look a bit arrogant mentioning Gloria's new propensity for flirting with him at the school gates, so he went with, 'Because the divorce was really rough on her and she–'

'Of course,' Juliet interrupted with an emphatic nod as she curled her fingers around the tines of the fork. 'Let's all feel sorry for Gloria.'

What the hell?

Juliet had been in Kate's company for five minutes and already she'd turned into bitch-mode? But then he noticed Kate smile sympathetically at Juliet and wondered if, in fact, it had been Gloria being her usual bitchy self that had Juliet acting so out of character.

His nostrils flared at the thought of anyone deliberately setting out to upset Juliet, who was quite possibly one of the sweetest people on the planet.

'It's Persephone I feel most sorry for,' he ended up commenting, before picking his menu up again.

Juliet looked immediately contrite. 'Sorry, you're right. Divorce is never easy on anyone. Is that where Melody is tonight? With Persephone?'

Oscar nodded. 'I dropped her off at Bob's earlier. It must be his weekend and that's why Gloria arranged to come out.'

'Melody will look after her.' Juliet said matter-of-factly.

'And Melody is? Daniel asked Oscar.

'My daughter.'

'I see,' Daniel said with a frown.

'You and Kate obviously know each other – how did you meet?' Oscar asked, looking between the two.

Kate grinned. 'Oh, we had one of those meetings where we completely fell for each other. Ended up horizontal within moments, didn't we, Daniel?'

Daniel choked on his beer and Juliet laughed and Oscar was momentarily caught up in realising it had been a while since he'd heard her soft laugh and how pretty it sounded.

'What Kate means,' Juliet said, recovering, 'is that they bumped into each other at The Clock House.'

'And then I fell on her,' Daniel explained. 'It was completely accidental. Totally innocent. Absolutely nothing sexual about it. At all.'

Oscar looked at Kate, who was staring at Daniel as if she

couldn't decide between being amused at his reaction or disappointed.

This evening was getting more confused dot com by the minute.

'How do you all know each other, then?' Daniel asked.

'Oscar is my brother-in-law,' Kate said.

'Oh.'

Oscar thought that Daniel looked rather relieved to discover this, but then his gaze slid to Juliet's. 'So then, are you his...?'

'Wife?' Juliet looked like she wanted the ground to open up and swallow her. 'Definitely not.'

'She's my cousin,' Kate said, saving the day.

'She died,' Oscar said.

'Are you ready to order, now?' The waitress asked, bouncing up and interrupting the silence.

Chapter 19

A 'Fete' Accompli

Oscar

All four heads moved from the waitress to their menus and Oscar didn't know what the other three were thinking, but he was thinking that he had no clue how to break the pregnant pause and at this rate it was going to last longer than nine months.

He wasn't used to people not knowing or not being warned beforehand, and guessed, in a way, he'd been cocooned. He wondered how Kate dealt with telling strangers. Did she blurt it out like he'd just done?

Then he heard Kate clear her throat and say, 'How about if I order for everyone? It's a talent of mine.'

Oscar took a peek at the waitress, who looked as if she was about one breath from passing out with embarrassment at so obviously interrupting at a *really* bad time.

'So, Daniel,' Oscar heard Kate say, 'do you have any allergies? Are you vegetarian? Vegan?'

Daniel must have shaken his head no, because the next thing Oscar heard was Kate saying, 'fab. In that case we'd like the first four starters on the menu, followed by the last four main courses. We'll divvy them up when they come out.'

'Um... how would you like the steak?' the waitress squeaked.

'Medium-rare,' she answered confidently.

'Thank you. To drink?'

'Two glasses of Shiraz for us girls – anything else we'll order when the food comes.'

The waitress mumbled a 'Thank you' and, snatching up the four menus, left as quickly as she'd come.

Without paper to hide behind Oscar took a deep breath. 'My wife – Kate's sister–'

'Twin,' Kate said so quietly that maybe only Oscar heard.

'Kate's twin,' he corrected, his voice feeling like sandpaper, 'died four years ago. That's how we're all linked.'

'I'm so sorry,' Daniel said staring intently at Kate before turning to Oscar and offering an apologetic smile. 'I didn't know.'

'How could you?' he said ineffectually.

He wanted to say that it was okay.

But it wasn't.

He sighed. It was what it was. What it might always be.

For the first time he could see why people left and went somewhere no one knew them. It had never occurred to him to do that after Bea had died. How could he take Melody away from all her memories and from everything she knew?

'Oscar, you mentioned Melody is having a sleepover at Persephone's tonight?' Kate said, surprising him by coming to his rescue for the second time. 'I'm glad the two of them are still close.'

'Persephone is Melody's best friend,' Juliet added, sending him a quick, reassuring glance and at the same time making a point of including Daniel in the conversation. 'Their BFFship was declared on their first day of nursery, when they realised they both had first and last names that began with the same letter. Oscar's last name is Matthews and Persephone's is Pavey – as in daughter of Gloria sitting over there in the corner.'

'Got it,' Daniel said. 'I think.'

'Oh dear God, she's getting up,' Juliet suddenly muttered.

'Who – Gloria?' Oscar asked.

'Incoming,' Juliet whispered, as she squirmed in her seat. 'Brace, brace, brace.'

'Relax,' Kate said to Juliet. 'I have this.'

Juliet sort of whimpered and Oscar found his hand stretching out to comfort her before he stopped himself. He tried to catch Kate's eye to ask her what was going on, but her gaze was fixed firmly on the approaching woman.

'Well, well. Isn't this cosy?' Gloria said, sidling up. 'Fancy seeing you all here. Together.'

'Evening, Gloria,' Kate said, keeping her expression pleasant and unthreatening. Like a smiling assassin would, Oscar thought. He might have his issues with Kate, but she was very protective of those she loved. Bea had told him once about the time she'd been being picked on in the playground and Kate had wandered up, a smile as sweet as sunshine on her face, before asking if the bully wanted the dressing-down she was about to give him in public or if he'd prefer to receive it in private. When he'd laughed in her face and called Bea more names, Kate's smile had remained in place, before, in a lightning-quick move, she'd yanked down the boy's trousers in front of everyone and declared her 'dressing-down' complete.

'Hello, Kate,' Gloria smiled back, but to Oscar her smile was so much smaller and so much thinner. 'Back on one of your flying visits?'

'Oh, this time I'm parking my broom permanently.'

'Permanently?'

'As in I'm home to stay.'

'Stay?'

'What can I say, I was homesick.'

Oscar frowned, not knowing how he felt about the fact that she might really have been missing Whispers Wood.

'Homesick?' Gloria said.

'Is there a parrot in here?" Juliet murmured.

Gloria pursed her lips into a saccharine smile. 'I didn't think you had a home left to be sick about?'

'That's enough, Gloria,' Oscar said because, in the end, family was family.

Looking about as contrite as Gloria could, she scanned her gaze over Juliet. Oscar caught the dismissive look and was immediately offended on Juliet's behalf. By the time Gloria turned her body in towards him and stroked her hand proprietorially over his shoulder, Oscar was about one step from escorting her back to her table. Finally she moved her full attention to Daniel. 'I don't believe we've met?'

'Daniel,' Daniel offered.

'Daniel...?' Gloria repeated, obviously waiting for him to introduce himself fully.

'Yes,' Daniel simply said, deliberately misunderstanding.

'Are you out on a date, Gloria?' Kate asked. 'The four of us have been wondering.'

'Oh, well,' Gloria giggled, setting Oscar's teeth on edge. 'While I'm flattered you've all been talking about me–'

'Oh, I wouldn't be flattered, exactly,' Kate shot back, her smile widening further.

'Yes, it's never nice to find out you've been talked about,' Juliet said, her chin tipping up defiantly.

Gloria's lips pinched together at Juliet's unexpected retaliation. Then, with a small laugh, she said, 'It's hardly a sin to go out on a date, isn't that right, Oscar?'

Wow. Gloria knew about the dates. He didn't know how she did, but she did and again he felt the weighty stares from around the table. His gaze flicked to Juliet to gauge her reaction. Only because he hadn't told her. Not for any other reason, he told himself.

But Juliet was simply staring down at her hands, and as they were below the table, he couldn't tell anything else.

'Goodbye Gloria,' he said. 'Enjoy your date.'

'Oh look, food's coming,' Kate said, completely ignoring her, although as soon as she was gone, she added, 'I know she's been through a tough time, but for all our sakes let's hope she takes her date home and in the morning makes good use of his Morning Glory-a.'

'Kate!'

'What? Just-sayin'! Anything that improves her mood is bound to improve mine.'

'So what's behind your talent for ordering for others?' Daniel asked Kate as he accepted the plate of scallops on a bed of parsnip purée and pea-shoots she'd passed him.

'It's not really much of a secret,' Kate told Daniel, looking at the black-pudding potato cake with poached egg, spinach and hollandaise, the salt-and-pepper squid and the crayfish and crab pot and passing Oscar the black-pudding potato cake. 'And was kind of borne out of necessity.'

'Ah,' Daniel said. 'You're a secret foodie.'

Kate passed Juliet the squid and Oscar watched as Juliet's mouth turned down before she efficiently swapped her plate with Kate's for the crayfish and crab.

'I've had to review a lot of hotel restaurants,' Kate continued. 'Unfortunately if you start ordering lots of things on the menu you don't get thought of as a foodie – you get rumbled as a critic and suddenly the service goes all sycophantic and the food doesn't come out until it's perfect. I started asking friends along so I could try a few of the dishes without looking like I was at work.'

'Clever. I guess this is my cue to say: would you like a taste?' Daniel asked.

'Sure,' she answered with a slow smile.

Oscar watched Kate's eyes as Daniel fed her a scallop. He didn't dare turn his head to look at Daniel's expression, but if the slightly glazed look in Kate's was anything to go by, it looked as if they both wanted something else as well as The Clock House. The rate this meal was going by the time they all got to the main course, he was going to be suggesting they both, 'Got a room.'

His gaze swept to Juliet's and when he saw the blush bloom on her cheeks, he knew she was thinking the same. They shared a secret smile and then Juliet shocked the hell out of him by offering him a taste of her starter.

Christ! Juliet's eyes had that same innocence in them that he always appreciated, and, yet, lurking in the outer corner of her blue irises was a sparkle of something his brain refused to decipher. Anticipation shot through his system and he'd never wanted a taste of anything so much in his life.

'I'm good, thanks,' he muttered, shoving some food from his own plate into his mouth. Calling himself all sorts of coward for not looking up to see her response, he shoved in another mouthful, not tasting a morsel of it and reached for his pint, which he realised was now empty.

Great.

Please God Daniel wouldn't offer her a taste of his food next and, as if the fates had somehow read his mind, or at least, Juliet had, she took the conversation on with a, 'The food here is one of the things that brings people in. The hotel is great and the rooms are really nice, but it's the food that probably makes their money for them.'

'How do you know what the rooms are like?' The words left Oscar's mouth before he could stop them, or at least, swap out the suspicious tone for idle curiosity.

'Oh. Well, I've been–'

'Hey, a lady never tells,' Kate inserted, cutting her off and giving Juliet a look that said, 'and why do you suddenly feel like you have to tell Oscar everything that happens in your life?'

And making Oscar want to reply, 'What the hell is suddenly happening in her life that she needs to get friendly with hotel rooms?'

The waitress chose that moment to come and clear away their plates and Daniel asked Kate, 'It sounds as if you've travelled extensively?'

Kate threw Oscar a quick look before replying, 'Yes.'

'And now?' Daniel asked.

'And now I'm here, so I'll be travelling much less.'

'Less?' Oscar found himself probing.

'As in, probably not at all.'

'Won't you miss it?' he asked.

Kate skewered him with a look that said, 'and we've all been playing so nicely.'

She lifted her wine glass and swirled the ruby liquid. 'Some things you miss so much you think it's going to break you,' she whispered, before taking a huge gulp of wine and smiling. 'Travelling isn't one of them.'

'Do you have a favourite place?' Daniel asked.

'Let's see. There's a little place in Venice and then there's a gorgeous house on Lake Como that you can rent out...'

As Oscar sat back and listened to Kate and Daniel discuss all the wonderful places they'd travelled to, he thought about his and Bea's honeymoon to Bora Bora in French Polynesia. Two weeks in paradise. They'd used all their savings. Neither had wanted to be sensible; they'd wanted a honeymoon they'd remember forever.

The two of them hadn't travelled anywhere else abroad after that. He tried to decide if that was simply because there wasn't time, with starting the business, and then Melody coming along so quickly, but he couldn't get to an answer.

Melody was getting to the age where she would like to

explore the world a little, though. He shouldn't forget that. Shouldn't get so wrapped up in the business.

The waitress came to put down their main courses and this time Juliet asked if she could divvy out the dishes.

He snuck a look at her as she passed Daniel the lamb, Kate the chicken and him the steak, keeping the asparagus risotto for herself.

She'd been part of Cheryl's business plan since she'd qualified five years ago. He knew she loved her job, but he also knew that, like him, she never stopped. Was she sitting there, listening to Kate and Daniel and thinking she'd missed out?

'Have you ever wanted to get away from it all?' he asked her quietly.

'You mean other than a quickie?'

'Quickie?' Where was that waitress, because he really needed to order another drink?

'You know, two weeks' sun, sand, sea and–' Juliet stopped, picked up a spear of asparagus and popping it into her mouth, sucked.

What the actual?

Had she just…

No.

She wouldn't have.

And if she had, it was surely by accident.

Therefore he had absolutely no business thinking what he was thinking.

With a shaking hand he reached for the pitcher of water and poured himself a large glass. 'You've worked non-stop for years,' he said, when his voice was steadier. 'You've never fantasised about taking off and travelling?'

'God no. I mean it's nice to have a holiday every now and then, but for more than two weeks? I love it here too much. And anyway I'm going to have way too much fun to even think of travelling once I open up the salon with Kate.'

The food in Oscar's mouth turned to sawdust and any remaining appetite vanished.

'What do you mean, with Kate?'

'In The Clock House,' Juliet declared. 'Kate's going to open her spa and I'm going to open a hair salon.'

'That has to be the most–' he stopped himself from saying 'stupid' because he knew absolutely that Juliet wasn't. She was sensible, like him. She was centred, like him. Why on earth would she put her faith in someone who had shown time and time again she couldn't be counted on?

'Why don't you open up in one of the little shops on the parade?' he said, trying to keep the conversation from spiralling out of control.

'Because it doesn't make as much business sense as opening up in The Clock House, with Kate.'

'Actually it makes better business sense.'

'In your opinion,' Juliet stated flatly.

'Come on, Jules. Think about the–'

'Did you just call me Jules?'

'What's that got to do with anything?'

'You never call me Jules.'

'Of course I do.'

'No. You don't. You always call me Juliet.'

'This is not the point. The point is that you shouldn't risk everything you've worked for, like this.'

'Risk?' She was looking at him like he was the biggest disappointment in a friend you could find and, just like that, all the comfort he'd taken from their friendship – all the support he'd taken so that his life didn't centre on the biggest tragedy to befall him, was reduced to Kate and how her comings and goings picked at his wounds until they were raw again.

'I think he means you can't take the risk if I'm part of the equation, Jules,' Kate offered, her voice devoid of expression.

'Is it?' Juliet's head swung back to him, her pretty blue eyes locking onto him like a laser beam. 'Is that what you mean?'

Damn it, she knew it was. How could she go through with this when she must know that Kate would up and leave when the going got rough, leaving her high and dry and her dreams parked indefinitely.

He couldn't let that happen.

'Are you aware that Daniel here has also put an offer in on The Clock House?' he asked.

'Yes. And I know all about the challenge that Old Man Isaac has put to them both. No offence Daniel – you seem like a really lovely guy, but cards on the table – I'm going to help Kate raise funds for the village fete, and I'm pretty good at things like that.'

'No offence taken,' Daniel said, but his eyes were only for Kate when he added, 'May the best person win.'

'You're absolutely set on this?' Oscar asked, appalled.

'Juliet is the one who got me to come back, Oscar,' Kate said.

Meaning she wouldn't have bothered if Juliet hadn't talked her into it? Unbelievable. Why couldn't Juliet see this was a bad idea? He was going to have to show her how easily Kate upped and left when the going got tough...

'Daniel,' he said, turning in his seat to face him. 'You need any help at all with fundraising, you come to me.'

'You can't be serious?' Juliet spluttered.

'Why can't I?' he said, returning her look evenly. 'You're helping Kate. It's hardly a level playing field if someone else from the village doesn't help the other contestant.'

'Look, if this is going to cause trouble...?' Daniel said.

'Oh, it won't,' Juliet said a steely glint in her eye.

'What she said,' Oscar muttered.

'In that case, welcome to team Daniel.'

Chapter 20

Let Them Eat Cake

Kate

Kate was day-dreaming.

What she was actually supposed to be doing was selling cakes.

But during the down-time between customers she couldn't help fantasising about the look she wanted for the spa when it opened.

Nothing too way out – this was Whispers Wood, not a luxury spa hotel in Bali. But she was definitely thinking about the softest, fluffiest bathrobes and towels in the country and the best qualified therapists she could find. Initial budget suggested she could afford three therapists and a receptionist while she studied part-time to qualify as well. Once she'd proved this was all going to work, she could expand to fit the space a bit better.

She'd decided on country-chic as the look... with added opulence so that guests wouldn't feel too out of their comfort zone, but also properly pampered, by the time they left.

Juliet and she had been up until the small hours talking

colours – lots of whites, creams, golds, with hints of delicate rose that would match the eau de nil walls and the rich, warm wooden floors and doors. Furniture – heated beds for the spa, plus she'd found these gorgeous white leather relaxation chairs for pedicures and fabulous matching mirrors for Juliet's hairdressing stations. Together they'd also found this dreamy shop that stocked antique chests of drawers, dressing tables and armoires, which they wanted to have professionally painted in cream so that they could mix and match throughout both the spa and the salon. They'd pored over magazines and websites looking for accessories and, to her delight, Old Man Isaac had allowed her access to the loft, where she'd found the original chandelier that had hung in the main reception room. He'd said it was hers if she won the challenge.

She'd planned out the space and Juliet agreed it would be better for her salon to be on the ground floor, and the spa treatment rooms on the second floor – away from the noise and extra footfall from community events. They would use the third floor for office space, stock space and a small lounge area for staff to take their breaks.

She could see it all so clearly. The understated elegance, the relaxing ambiance, the sense of rightness to what she was doing. The only problem was, she wasn't exactly Little Miss Patience. Once she'd made up her mind about something, she wanted to do it. Right away.

A picture of Daniel formed in her mind.

Oops!

She knew he wasn't supposed to be in there – goodness knows, she had enough on her mind with the spa – but she was finding it harder and harder to kick him out, despite him being the enemy.

A very sexy enemy, whose company she'd found charming, exhilarating and interesting during Dinner-Gate the previous week.

'If you keep sighing like that, you're going to put off the customers,' Juliet told her.

'What customers?'

'We have built it, so they will come, grasshopper,' Juliet said, indicating the tables filled with cupcakes.

Juliet sat behind one of the tables, the very picture of serenity, which was weird because the double-hitter of both Oscar and Gloria at dinner had to have put her through the wringer.

As if by mutual consent, they hadn't discussed Oscar or Daniel, other than to agree they were both going to lose by a country-mile and that when they did, Juliet and she might or might not choose to be magnanimous about it.

While Kate had been day-dreaming about the spa, Juliet had been cutting out triangles of material and pinning them together, because, as she had informed Kate, you could never have too much bunting. Kate was finally realising that Juliet's crafting was the equivalent of spending a whole week in a spa. It inspired her, it comforted her, it relaxed her. In fact, Kate was certain that if Juliet could have got away with knitting while driving home from that meal out the other night, she would have.

'You know what, Juliet? We are going to create a spa experience so great Gloria Pavey will want to visit it every day.'

'God, really?' Juliet looked completely appalled by the idea.

'Yes, really. I know you've been dreaming of the day you

could do her foils and then stand her outside in an electrical storm, but wouldn't it be so much more poetical if she loved the place so much she bought all her friends here and they all parted with their money on a regular basis.'

'I guess.'

'You know I'm right.'

Juliet rolled her eyes. 'She always goes into town to have her hair done, but I have a nasty feeling she's going to be my first booking.'

'At first we'll seduce her with FOMO. But then we'll be so on-point she's going to come back again and again.' Kate got up from the table, stretched and then moved to hover over Juliet's shoulder. 'So how much have we made so far?'

Juliet put her bunting back in the bag at her feet and then grabbed a couple of the donation jars so that she could start counting them out. 'Tell me again why we're counting when we still have four hours left to go?'

'It's good to have an idea of how well we're doing,' Kate murmured, moving to the front of the trestle table to fiddle with the bunting Juliet had hung.

'You are so impatient,' Juliet said, making neat piles of coins.

Kate tugged on the bunting so that the swags were more even. 'Can you blame me? It's dead in here.'

Juliet looked up briefly from her counting. 'I told all my clients. Mum told hers. You put up the posters in good time.'

'Used to be a time where you could count on the weather in this country. It's only weeks to the start of summer proper. Where's the rain? It's beautiful out there. No wonder it's quiet in here.'

'Maybe we should have set up outside.'

'Too risky. Or so I thought. Sorry. You've made all these gorgeous cakes...'

'Not to worry.'

'I can't help it. Now that Oscar's helping Daniel, what if he's got the whole village to stay away?'

'Oscar wouldn't do that.'

'I suppose,' she said, forcing herself to be fair because while it had hurt incredibly to see how much Oscar had hated the thought of Juliet putting her faith in her, she knew she should take heart in knowing he would never set out to deliberately sabotage Juliet's efforts to help.

Clearing her throat, she ventured, 'Interesting how protective Oscar got at the thought of you being dragged into my scheme, don't you think?'

Juliet produced a pad and pen, seemingly from nowhere, and started jotting down figures. 'Not really,' she mumbled. 'That's just Oscar, isn't it?'

Was it, though? Kate smiled to herself. Had Juliet really not noticed Oscar's covert looks at her from over his menu, from across the table, and from behind his pint glass?

The one time he'd caught Kate staring at him while he'd been staring at Juliet, he'd actually blushed and a look of bewilderment had crossed his face. Almost like it had occurred to him that maybe he had feelings for Juliet.

Kate had thought about it a lot over the last few days and she'd concluded that if Juliet could help make him and Melody feel whole again, she could handle it.

'He couldn't take his eyes off you,' she said, studying Juliet closely.

'Of course he couldn't. Had to make sure the little lady was listening while he mansplained business economics to me, didn't he?'

'Wow, angry much?'

'Actually I'm the opposite,' Juliet answered with a determined smile. 'I'm happy. His ridiculous response to me opening up in here with you is making it that much easier to fall out of you-know-what with him. Now,' Juliet pulled another jar of money towards her and tipped it out onto the table to start counting, 'speaking of subject changes, have you been round to see your mum, yet?'

'You know I haven't. I've left umpteen phone messages and an invite hasn't been forthcoming.'

'If you're waiting for your mum to make the first move–'

'Duh – hence the messages.'

'Leaving messages was your first move?'

'No,' Kate said. 'Phoning her was my first move.'

'Any sane person would have just visited. Did you phone her at a time you knew she'd be too busy to phone back?'

'No.'

'Kate–'

'All right. Maybe I did. But I've left messages since. The ball's in her court.'

'Is it? What exactly did you say in these messages?'

'I don't know. Stuff.' Message one had been, possibly, the most randomly worded, underehearsed message ever left on an answering service. Message two, three and four had been much better, starting and ending with: It's me again. Call me if you want to meet up. 'Her not replying is punishment for me not telling her I was coming home. Next comes the part where we finally meet up and she pushes all my buttons before then pushing me away.'

Juliet met her gaze unflinchingly. 'You're not entirely innocent when it comes to pushing buttons yourself.'

'I know. But I was going to try really hard not to this time. I swear. You and your mum keep telling me she's better, but I think that's just with you. She's acting entirely true to form with me.' Out of habit she took out her phone to check she hadn't missed any calls or messages.

Nothing.

She shouldn't have put off dropping round to see her. What was she doing in postponing the inevitable, apart from keeping alive that silly spark of hope that it might be different this time?

'How much have we made, then?' she asked, trying very hard to ignore how much she hated that her mother hadn't called back.

Juliet tipped out the last of the jam jars full of change and started counting. 'Right, total so far is £56.27.'

'That's it?'

'£58.00 if we pretend the foreign coins are English.'

'Someone paid for your delicious cupcakes with fake money?'

'Not fake money, exactly, just not English money.'

'Of all the low-down things to do, putting your leftover holiday money in a donation jar? Old Man Isaac was right; this village isn't the same any more.'

Kate started casting her eye over the few people milling about in the foyer chatting. Maybe she and Juliet should move the tables out there and then people wouldn't have to search them out. Not that wandering into the first room and finding them should be that hard. Especially what with the poster with the giant arrow pointing into the room.

There were only seven more weekends until the fete and if they kept going like this they were never going to beat Daniel and Oscar.

'We should have charged set prices for the cakes instead of putting donation jars out,' Juliet said.

'I thought it would encourage people to be more generous.'

Kate looked at the tempting trays of cupcakes and tried not to feel too despondent as she counted four dozen sitting in their pretty white cupcake holders, decorated with frosting in all shades and with a different hand-crafted sugar flower and cute little bee sitting on top of each one. It was the first of their fundraising ideas and she'd really thought they'd hit the ground running, but they were going to have to get much more serious with the next one.

'So this is where you've been hiding out all day.'

Kate whirled around to see Crispin Harlow walking towards them.

At least, she thought that was him under the tremendously bad rug sitting on top of his head.

'Crispin?' The name came out like a question. She didn't understand. It was like a bunch of squirrels had fallen out of a tree and landed on top of his head. Tearing her gaze away she attempted a normal voice, 'It's so good of you to stop by and support us. All for a worthy cause, I'm sure you'll agree?'

'Oh, I do agree, but don't let me buy any. Diet,' the man said, patting his mostly flat stomach and giving her a wink.

Do not look at his hair. Kate stared un-blinking into Crispin's eyes. 'And where are you off to that you need to get Beach-Body ready?' Maybe he was off to Persia to get a better rug. *Don't you do it, Kate, don't you look at his hair.*

'Technically, nowhere, but with summer around the corner...' Crispin tailed off and looked pleased with himself that he was resisting the cupcakes in front of him.

'Oh summer, shwummer!' she said, waving a hand dismissively, before looping it through his arm so that he couldn't get away. 'Buy the cake and take an extra exercise class.'

'They do look tempting.'

'They're delicious,' she promised, going into full-on sales mode. 'A guaranteed taste of heaven.'

'Did you make them?' A look of uncertainty crossed his face. He was probably thinking about that time she'd mistakenly added salt instead of sugar to the mince pies she'd made for the Christmas play interval.

'Me? Oh no,' she assured him, leaning forward to confide, 'I wanted them edible, so Juliet made them.'

'Ah.' Crispin's face softened. 'The lovely Juliet.'

'Hi, Crispin,' Juliet said and then deliberately looked away, refusing to react to Kate's mad gesturing at Crispin's hair as her face formed unspoken question after question before Crispin turned towards her again, mentioning, 'I'll admit I always take one of Juliet's coffee and walnut cakes to the Easter lunch buffet at the church every year. They're exceedingly good, you know.'

'So Mr Kipling tells her. Here,' Kate plucked one of the lemon cupcakes from a tray and held it out to him. 'Try one on the house. If you like it, take another home for Mrs Harlow.' She was going to flog him some cake if it was the last thing she did. 'I'm sure your lovely wife wouldn't mind you popping a few pounds into the donation jar for the village fete.' As soon as Crispin's hand came out, she dropped the little cake into his palm so that he had no choice but to take it. 'Aunt Cheryl tells me Mrs Harlow took over the hat-judging at the last fete a few years ago?'

'She did indeed,' Crispin said, bringing the cake up to his mouth and pausing to speak again. 'Are you going to have a hat competition, this year?'

'Oh, well,' for a moment Kate was non-plussed. 'Surely that's up to you and Mrs Harlow?'

'Us?' Crispin took a cautious nibble of the cupcake. 'Why is it up to us?'

'Well, won't you be organising the fete?' Maybe the wig had melted a little of his brain. She couldn't think of any other reason why the man who organised everything in the village wouldn't be organising the village's biggest community event of the year.

Crispin finished off the cupcake in two more bites. 'I thought you and that Daniel fellow were organising it?'

'What? No, no, no.' Isaac hadn't said anything about them having to organise it as well. 'We're just the fundraisers. You know, so that we can get you money for the really good, um, fete-stuff.'

'You might want to tell that to Daniel.'

'What?' Oh no way had Daniel offered to organise the fete.

'I must say, he's been like a breath of fresh air, coming into the village and getting us all excited about his plans.'

'What?'

'And the website he's created for the village – genius.'

'*What?*'

'Really, Kate dear,' Crispin said with a reproving look, 'all that travelling around the world, you'd think you'd have picked up a more extensive vocabulary.'

'*Que?*' Kate tried with a smile.

'Don't tell me you didn't know about it?'

'All right, then.' Even though she didn't. How the hell had Daniel managed to produce a website for the village and, more importantly, why the hell hadn't she thought about creating one, first?

Wow, had he lured her in! With his blue, blue eyes that turned hot when he fed her food and his rich deep voice when he'd talked about countries they'd both visited, and the sincere flash of sorrow shooting across his handsome features as he'd learned her twin had died.

Now she discovers that while he'd been staring into her eyes, he'd, in fact, been thinking about... websites?

'Well, that is a surprise,' Crispin commented. 'He popped over last week to go over the details with me. Obviously someone let slip that I was the go-to guy for all things Whispers Wood.'

'I'm sorry, pardon?'

'Maybe you haven't noticed the new lampposts I've had fitted at the entrance to the cut-through and around the green?'

'I have and only you could have pulled that off, Crispin. But, I really need you to tell me what website you're referring to?'

'*The Whisperings* from Whispers Wood, I think he called it. Clever name, don't you think?

Kate wrinkled her nose. 'Hardly original.'

'But effective. And it's going to make my life much easier.'

'It is?'

'Well, you know I've always firmly believed that those of us with leadership capabilities must ensure village life runs smoothly, but I'll admit it's nice to have been offered some help for once. I know I give the impression that it's easy, but it's actually incredibly time-consuming – not that I mind that. But, that website is going to revolutionise my schedule so that I can concentrate on my new hobby.'

'Buying really bad wigs?' the words shot out before she could stop them.

'I beg your pardon?'

'Er, you were saying you had a new hobby?'

'Yes. Golf.'

Kate couldn't believe it. 'I thought golf was a good walk ruined?'

'Well, that's where you're wrong, Kate. I admit I thought it was too until Mrs Harlow suggested we try it together and it turns out it's a wonderfully thrilling game.'

'I don't think it is, Crispin. Unless you're playing strip golf?'

'Of course not.'

'Then, I still say you're giving up organising us all for a good walk ruined.'

'Not giving up, no... but handing over some of the responsibility.'

'To Daniel Westlake?'

'Nobody else ever offered.'

'I volunteer as tribute,' she said immediately.

'What?'

'Don't you mean, "*que?*"' she shot back, but when he didn't look amused she added, 'Let me be your Katniss to his Prim!'

'You know, sometimes I genuinely have no idea what you're talking about. I only came in here to show my support.'

'Sorry. Speaking of Hunger Games... have I given you one of the blueberry cupcakes to try?'

'I just had a lemon one.'

'Well, I'm going to box you up a couple. You don't even have to pay for them, although...' she tucked her hand back through his and looked left and right dramatically, 'you never know who could be eavesdropping. Do you really want it reported on the new *Whisperings* website that you didn't support a community project?'

'Oh, very well.' He took the box in one hand and took a note out of his pocket and shoved it into the jar with his other. 'Sold.'

'The village fete thanks you, Crispin.' Leaning over, she gave him a peck on the cheek and resisted the urge to straighten his wig.

Crispin blushed. 'You know sometimes your language and actions defy logic, but I am glad to see you back and I hear that you're back to stay this time?'

'I am.'

'Well, I'm very glad to hear that and I know Mrs Harlow will be pleased when I tell her, too.'

'Crispin, wait.' She quickly grabbed another cupcake and

rushed over to him. 'Thank you,' she said, hoping her smile didn't wobble as she squeezed his hand in gratitude for his words.

'You're welcome and don't forget you're going to need all kinds of permits to run that beauty spa of yours if you win the fundraising. I hope you're already on top of your research because these things have a habit of taking time to get once you get the ball rolling.'

Gently she turned him around so that he was pointing in the direction of the door and then gave him the gentlest of pushes. 'Goodbye, Crispin, say hi to Mrs Harlow for us,' she called out as he left.

'Wow. You schmoozed him like a pro,' Juliet said, holding her hand up in the three-fingered Mockingjay salute. 'He put a twenty pound note in the jar.'

'What a sweetie.'

'Tell me that again when we open up in here and he's in every five minutes checking we're not breaking some bylaw.'

'Hey?' Kate pointed to her head. 'What's the deal with his–'

'Oh. *The weave*. Not sure anyone has had the guts to mention it.'

'But, I mean, it's not because he's ill or anything, is it?' She was going to have to give him his money back if she'd schmoozed a twenty out of an ill man.

'No. He's healthy as an ox. Mum thinks it's a consequence of Mrs Harlow retiring. You know – his way of keeping things interesting in the bedroom.'

Kate put her hands over her ears. 'Eeww. Stop that.'

'Maybe we'll find the answer in *The Whisperings*.'

'Can you believe that?' Kate pulled out her phone to look up the website that Daniel had supposedly started. 'Of all the devious... Look!' She passed the phone over to Juliet so that her cousin could get a good gawp at the new Whispers Wood website.

'It looks really professional. Wait, did you see, under Upcoming Events it lists a five-a-side football tournament that he's organised for this afternoon, and a fun-run for next week. And there's going to be a Town Hall meeting to discuss themes for the fete.'

'Give me that,' Kate demanded, grabbing her phone back to look at the screen. 'Right. Operation Village Fete is about to get serious.'

'I know you're resourceful, but I don't see what we can do.'

'Oh, I'm going to MacGyver the hell out of this, don't you worry. I'm popping home to grab us some clothes and then we're going to go out there to the punters playing and the punters watching this football tournament of his and we're going to sell all these gorgeous cakes at exorbitant prices.'

'But we're wearing clothes already.'

'Not the kind we need for a serious sales drive.'

'Oh, Kate, I'm not sure about this.'

'That's okay. I'm sure enough for the both of us.'

'But–'

'Do you want Daniel and Oscar to win?'

'Hurry back.'

Chapter 21
Sun Tzu and the Offside Rule

Daniel

'Watch out!'

Daniel heard the words too late. The next thing he knew he was being tackled from behind and face-planting into the grass like a professional footballer.

Mother Hubbard, that hurt.

With a moan, he rolled over and discovered he was lying mostly inside the penalty area. Among the calls for a penalty was one lone, sexy-smoky voice of dissent.

'Dive! Dive! Referee, tell me you saw that.'

Daniel eased himself into a sitting position so that he could get a clearer vision of the side of the pitch.

Unbelievable.

Kate was haranguing the referee like a football coach for the other side.

His team's coach – Oscar – looked like he was being harangued as well. Interesting. After meeting the incredibly sweet-natured Juliet at the hotel restaurant last week, he would have said she didn't have it in her to get overly riled about anything. Looked like he couldn't have been more wrong the way she was jabbing Oscar in the chest.

Taking the offered hand of the player who'd ploughed into him, he grinned his thanks and got shakily to his feet. The running gave him excellent stamina, but getting taken down by the local vet, who looked like he was more used to playing rugby than football, wasn't his idea of fun.

Still, it was for a good cause and up until going down like a sack of spuds, he'd been enjoying himself. No way would he have had the time to organise and participate in something like this if he'd still been running West and Westlake back in London.

He looked over towards Kate again and double-blinked.

Shouldn't there be some sort of law about wearing swim-wear to the village green? If there wasn't, then he was damn sure there was some sort of hygiene and health and safety law about handing out cupcakes while dressed only in a bikini top and shorts.

He blinked again as she took a note in exchange for handing over a cupcake.

Wait a minute, she wasn't handing them out... she was selling them.

At his event!

Ignoring the whistle to resume play, he started to cross the makeshift pitch towards her.

He and Kate Somersby were going to have themselves a little talk about fair play and if he had to personally search her to confiscate her copy of Sun Tzu's *The Art of War*, so be it.

Pow!

Totally didn't see the football coming.

Felt it, though, as it bounced off the side of his head and left him feeling like he'd been on the receiving end of a right hook from a heavyweight.

He felt himself sway alarmingly.

For Footie's Sake! No way was he going to go down for a second time.

Kate was making her way over to him in the next instant. Running across the pitch like some Baywatch-Emmerdale hybrid fantasy and while normally he would have appreciated seeing two of her, the nausea accompanying the double vision was not nice at all.

'Oh my God, are you all right?' she asked, looking horrified for him, or was that at him, he couldn't really tell, what with everything moving.

He planted his feet more firmly, in case it was him moving, dragged in a breath and shook his head a little. Thankfully, when he looked at her again, there was only one of her.

He couldn't begin to imagine what it must be like losing a sibling, let alone your twin, so some of the shadows that made their way into her eyes at times now made sense. He admired the way she forced those shadows back time and time again, as if she didn't want to be claimed by them. It was a survivor's instinct that he found admirable.

Now that he knew she wasn't married to the guy in the photo in her locket, who had turned out to be Oscar, it was even more difficult to stop thinking about her.

When he'd first seen Oscar in the hotel bar, he'd recognised him from the photo and been morbidly fascinated about discovering his relationship with Kate. He couldn't have been more relieved they weren't romantically involved, mostly because it meant he was free to think about Kate, but also because it turned out that he really liked Oscar. Yes, he was a little surly, but there was a solid, hard-working, tell-it-like-it-is integrity to him that you didn't need to question. After being around Hugo, he'd been finding it hard to trust his instincts, so it was refreshing not to be constantly questioning the opinions he formed.

'Seriously, that was quite a hit you took there,' Kate said, and, as if unable to help herself, she reached out and laid her hand softly against the side of his face. 'Are you sure you're all right? How many fingers am I holding up, what happened in the season finale of *The Walking Dead*, who's tipped for *I'm a Celebrity* this year, where's the nearest PokemonGo location, and do you know who I am?'

Trapping her hand against his face, he answered, 'None, have no idea times three and Wonder Woman. And this is getting to be a little old, isn't it?'

'Sorry, still stuck on that Wonder Woman part,' she whispered, staring up into his eyes as though she couldn't look away. 'What's getting old?'

He laughed. 'Us.' He took another step, to close the distance between them. 'You and me and this being unable to remain upright in each other's company for any length of time.'

'Oh.' She licked her lips and he took another incremental step closer. 'We managed okay at dinner last week.'

'Yes. We did. Maybe we should do that.'

'What? Dinner?'

'Sure. I'd love to,' he answered with a grin. 'When do you want to go?'

For a second she looked as if she might ask if now was good and he was absolutely sure his answer would be yes.

But then she called out, 'Medic' and, breaking the spell, stepped backwards to create more space between them again.

That was when he realised they were still in the middle of the pitch. Admittedly the match was being played around them, but in case next time it was her getting hit by a rogue ball, he marched them back to the sidelines.

'I don't need a medic,' he assured her.

'What if you have concussion?'

'What if you were to wear this outfit for our dinner?'

'What if you have detached retinas?'

'Nope, I'm seeing everything in glorious detail, which I'm guessing is the point.' He enjoyed the amber in her eyes flaring with heat and then, regrettably, stepped back out of her space as Ted ambled up to speak with her.

'Hi Kate, thought I'd better let you know the kids have found the unmanned table of cupcakes inside and are preparing to have themselves a feast. I take it they're supposed to be for sale, and not supposed to be given away at er,' he looked down and then as if overly aware of what he'd be seeing if he did, he immediately looked up and then, as if running out of angles to hold his head, looked at Daniel, 'half-time?'

Kate sighed. 'Thanks for letting me know, Ted. I was about to move them to the table I've set up outside. Have you bought any yet?'

'Oh. I will. Um – I can move them outside for you. You look–'

'Busy?' Daniel helpfully inserted.

'Well, if you're sure it's no trouble,' Kate told Ted. 'For that I'm going to give you a discount on the cakes.'

'A discount? Right, well, I guess I could take two.'

'I tell you what... you take three of them and I'll only charge you £15.'

'Fifteen pounds for *three* cupcakes?' Daniel queried, shaking his head again. Blimey, maybe he really was concussed.

'Sounds fair, right?' she said, smiling at both him and Ted.

'Sounds like daylight robbery,' Ted said, without any malice and as if he was used to her smooth operating.

'Oh, but Ted,' Kate pouted. 'It's for a really good cause. You know we're having the summer fete again this year? Those shiny trophies given out for best produce won't pay for themselves, you know? I'm sure you used to win first prize for your marrows.'

'Second,' Ted answered.

'Only second? Now that doesn't sound quite right to me. Surely you should have got first.'

Daniel wanted to applaud.

'I didn't realise you'd be having a Best in Show award for veg this year,' Ted said, and Daniel had to stop himself from miming a fish on a hook being reeled in.

'Of course we will. What's a village fete without a veg contest? How are your marrows, by the way?' Kate asked.

Daniel suspected they were growing bigger by the minute.

'I tell you what, Ted – make it five cupcakes for the £15, but only because it's you.'

Daniel watched as Ted pulled out his wallet. 'I only have a £20.'

'Oh darn,' Kate said, skimming her hands down her shorts, 'I don't have change and I can't take all your money. You keep your twenty, I'm sure Daniel here will have the correct amount.'

Daniel couldn't believe his ears. 'You want me to pay for Ted's cupcakes?'

'Where's your community spirit? Don't embarrass Ted, give me the £15 and let him grab his cakes.'

With a sigh, Daniel unzipped his shorts pocket and took out his wallet. 'Would you believe it? I only have a twenty, too.'

'You are too, too generous,' she said and swiped the twenty out of his hands and stuffed it into her teeny, tiny shorts pocket.

'Thanks, Daniel,' Ted told him with a smile that had him wondering if he'd just been hustled by *two* experts. 'I'll knock it off the garage bill. Kate, I'll take the cakes from the table and put the rest out there over by the refreshments, for you.'

'You are an absolute star, Ted. Thank you.'

As soon as they were alone again, Daniel held his hand to his ear like it was a phone and made a ringing noise, and then spoke, 'Hello, yes – she's right here,' he held his hand in the phone shape out to her and said, 'Lord Sugar is calling.

He's seen the way you sell cake and he wants his Week One, Task One, Apprentice back.'

She laughed. 'Luckily I don't need his investment for my business idea.'

'Yeah?' Curious, he asked, 'How are you going to get the funds, then?'

She tapped the side of her nose as she smiled.

'Hey, it is my business if you're cashing in on my event.'

Kate shrugged. 'It's a free space. Besides, we've been selling cakes all day.'

'You deliberately booked your event the same day as mine?'

'I didn't know you were going to be doing an event today.'

'It was on the website.'

'Ah. Yes. The website. Kudos for that, by the way.'

'Thank you. I think,' he added, in case she was being sarcastic. 'If you want to advertise your events on there, let me know and I'll organise it for you.'

'So helpful.'

'I like to be.'

'Why?'

'What do you mean, why?'

'What's in it for you?'

Offended, he took a step backwards. 'This is supposed to be about helping the community. Remember?'

'And were you going to tell me about the village meeting to find a theme for the fete?'

'Yes, I was going to tell you.'

'Really?'

'Really.' He knew he didn't exactly go into conversations

these days believing everything the other person said, but he was upset that she thought he would deliberately scam her to get ahead.

'When were you going to tell me?'

'When I next saw you.'

'And how did you know when that was going to be?'

'You mean other than the fact that I don't seem to be able to take a step anywhere in this village without bumping into you, or over you, or falling at your feet?'

'I want in on the organising.'

'You – what?'

'If you're now helping Crispin organise the fete, then I want in on that too.'

'How about whichever one of our themes gets picked, gets to organise it.'

'I guess I could work with that.'

'Good. Are we done talking business now?'

'Why, what possible other things could we talk about?'

'Dinner?' He was picking up her repaired locket early next week. He could give it to her over dinner.

'You need an audience for eating crow?'

'So it's back to war?'

'I think it has to be. I've already picked out paint colours.'

'You're sure you wouldn't rather have dinner?'

'I'm sure.'

'Shame. Speaking of being at war,' he said as he picked up on the raised voices from the other end of the pitch. 'Aren't they doing a good enough job without us adding to it?'

Kate swung her head in the direction he was pointing, to where Juliet and Oscar were still arguing. 'That doesn't look good. I should go over there and see if she needs any help.'

'Looks like she's handling herself fine.'

Kate smiled to herself as if proud of Juliet. 'It really does, doesn't it?'

'What happened between you and Oscar that you dislike him so?'

'I don't dislike him. He's my brother-in-law. Why? Has he been sticking the knife in about me to you?'

'Hasn't said a bad word about you. But the way he jumped to Juliet's defence by offering to help me the other night–'

'You saw that too?'

'And there's obviously tension between the two of you.'

Kate sighed. 'He thinks I – it's complicated... well maybe not complicated, exactly, but I suppose understandable.'

'I see.'

'No you don't, but that's okay. To be honest, I'm surprised half the village hasn't already told you.'

'Ah. But I haven't been initiated into the art of village gossip, yet.'

'Darn it. I felt sure Trudie and Aunt Cheryl would have kidnapped you by now, and by the light of the full moon brought you onto the village green and made you sip from the "Nosy Cup".'

'I'll be sure to lock my windows and doors from now on.'

'You're not into discovering all the village secrets? Shame on you. If you're going to be living here...'

'I'll take my chances that if someone wants me to know a

secret, they'll tell me as part of an honest conversation and not as part of idle gossip.'

'Wow. I'm trying not to be impressed.'

'Is it very difficult?'

She laughed and he wanted to lean in and capture the warmth of it with his lips.

In fact, he was leaning towards her when her attention moved to over his shoulder and her laugh turned rich and throaty.

Recovering his forward momentum he turned to see what had her laughing.

'Holy cow,' he muttered.

'Well, Gertrude, anyway.'

'Why is there a cow on the green?'

'Maybe she's making a political statement, you know, like a streaker!'

'Streaker's aren't making political statements, they're just exhibitionists.'

'Not always.'

His head whipped around to meet her gaze. 'Okay, the way you said that really makes me want to ask if you have personal knowledge of this phenomenon.'

She grinned. 'I'm saying nothing at all about my university days.' She stared at the football pitch. 'Maybe Gertrude's your sub, although if she is, she's completely offside.'

'Come to think of it, I think I met her my first day here, but she wasn't roaming around, she was safe in a field.'

'Gertrude gets tired of other cow company and occasionally wanders out of her field and over to where life seems more interesting.'

'Shouldn't somebody do something?'

'Don't worry. Look, she's already making her way off the field of play. She'll be out of the way in a – oh, crap, she's heading for the cake stash.'

And just like that, his Wonder Woman was off and running and yelling to Juliet, 'Hey, Cakes before Rakes,' as she gestured madly to where Gertrude was making a beeline towards their makeshift trestle table full of cupcakes.

Chapter 22

Juliet and Oscar Standing by a Tree, A-R-G-U-I-N-G

Juliet

'It looks hectic in here.'

At the sound of his voice, Juliet looked up from the table, where she was busy laying out how to make patchwork owl patterns.

Above the noise of children filling up the room, she couldn't hear the rain beating down outside, but she'd been secretly pleased the weather had brought in a bigger crowd to take part in the activity-day fundraiser. It was the first Saturday of the school holidays and parents were eager to give their kids something to do.

'What do you want, Oscar? I'm busy.' She tried not to notice the way his jeans and t-shirt always fitted him just right.

'I dropped Melody off and thought I'd stop by to say, Hi.'

'I'm surprised you're letting Melody take part at all after the football tournament,' Juliet told him, placing bundles of material scraps along the table.

Looking up when he didn't leave, she followed his gaze and

saw that Melody had made her way over to Kate's story-time tent. She smiled softly. Kate was going to love realising her niece was in the audience and Melody was in for a treat. Kate had been practising her voices for reading *Fantastic Beasts and Where to Find Them* and she'd spent hours in the woods collecting twigs for the children to customise into wands afterwards.

'Are you sure you want Melody around such bad role models?' Juliet asked tightly.

'Come on, Jules. You took me by surprise. You can't blame me for—'

Juliet stepped away from little ears. 'Oh, I think you'll find that I can. And that I do and as it looks as if Melody's nicely settled there's probably no need for you to stay, so Hi and Goodbye.'

'Actually I also wanted a word with you and to give you something.'

'Sorry. Not interested. Too busy.'

'Surely you can take a break for a few moments?'

'Nope.'

'Trudie,' Oscar called out, 'Can you cover for Juliet? She's been working flat out and needs a break.'

'Of course I can, sweetie,' Trudie said, walking up to the pair of them. 'My improvisation class doesn't start for an hour anyway.'

'Perfect,' Oscar said. 'Thank you.'

'Now, wait a minute.' Juliet tried shaking off the hand that Oscar had gently yet firmly wrapped around her upper arm.

'Juliet, please,' Oscar sighed and stopped walking, but remained holding her arm.

It was the husky 'please', together with the heat that he created from the touch of his hand on her bare arm that had her caving.

Helplessly she looked around the room and took in the interested looks of those around her.

Honestly for a plan to ensure she wasn't bumping into Oscar Matthews every five seconds this helping out Kate with the fundraising so that they could move into The Clock House was backfiring on a colossal scale.

From the moment she'd told him of her plans to open the salon, she'd seen more of him than ever before.

Admittedly, with her dressed in the small yellow bikini top and denim cut-offs at the football tournament, he'd definitely seen more of her than he was used to, too.

And, all right, since she was in the mood to admit things, she had thought about his over-the-top reaction to seeing her dressed like that. She'd thought about it a lot.

She looked over at Trudie, hoping she would read the imploring, 'please don't make me talk to the gorgeous man,' look for what it was, but Trudie was smiling in a way that suggested she was more than happy to settle in for an entertaining show.

With a sigh, she looked back at Oscar and said, quietly, 'Not here, then. Outside.'

As if he was afraid she was going to bolt, he didn't let go of her arm. Instead, he slid his fingers down to encircle her hand and in a move that was either incredibly gallant or suggested they were going to be a while, reached down and grabbed her denim jacket.

It was really bad that whether it was gallantry or that she was going to be spending a while with him, her heart pitter-pattered, and as she let him keep her hand in his as they walked out of the building together, it gave no sign it was going to settle back down.

Outside the rain had eased to a steady drizzle. Releasing her hand, Oscar shook out her denim jacket and helped her into it, and then, half-jogged with her over to the cover of the giant oak tree at the edge of the green.

'So...?' She walked up to the gnarly trunk of the tree and turned to lean back against it. It was quiet out here at the edge of the woods and standing under the tree canopy with him was intimate. 'You wanted to talk?'

'I did.'

He didn't add anything, so she waited; fixing her stare on the pattern of raindrops that had landed across the shoulders of his blue t-shirt.

She waited some more and when she couldn't stand it any longer, said, 'Doesn't talking usually involve using your voice to produce words?'

'Give me a minute, will you?'

Juliet released another sigh. 'If this is going to be another lecture about the perils of going into business with Kate, you can forget it.'

She made to move past him, but his hand shot out and held gently against her midriff, halting any leaving in its tracks. 'This isn't about me lecturing you. This is about me starting with an apology.'

'For...?' She stayed right where she was, caught between

the gentle touch of his hand at her waist and the bark of the tree behind her. She stared down at her fingers clamped around the cuff of her denim sleeve, thinking that if this segued into a lecture then she was going to have to forget about the melting heat at her stomach and get her hand free to sock him one.

'I shouldn't have spoken to you like I did the other day,' he said.

'No, you shouldn't have.'

'You really caught me by surprise.'

She fiddled with the cuff of her jacket sleeve and mumbled, 'If the sight of a woman wearing summer clothes in summer catches you by surprise then you really need to get out more often, or, at least start watching more TV.'

'I don't know what came over me.'

'You acted like a jealous jerk.'

'Exactly. And that is so not me.'

'Right. So not you.'

'You've been surprising me a lot lately. Not that that's an excuse, but maybe it started with you freaking out after seeing Gloria at the restaurant.'

She winced. 'I did not freak out.'

'You actually did a little. I know she's hard work, but usually you're the first one to make us all remember we need to go easier on her at the moment.'

'Yes. Well. That was before.'

'Before?'

'Before she labelled me Whispers Wood's Crazy Cat Lady.' She couldn't look at him. 'You better not be laughing.'

'Of course not,' he said and as she stole a glance she couldn't fail to notice he was biting his lip to keep from smiling. 'Because as insults go I can see how that one is totally unforgiveable.'

'Do you even know what crazy cat lady is code for?'

'Is it code for you having a lot of cats, because Melody mentioned that you'd taken another one in a few weeks ago...'

'Look, it might not seem hurtful to you, but to me—'

'It shouldn't be to you, either. Come on, Juliet. You know her bark is worse than her bite and you're hardly some old spinster.'

'Yet,' she murmured, watching beyond Oscar's shoulder to where the rain was starting to fall heavier again. 'I'm hardly some old spinster... yet.'

'Is this what all of this is about? She pressed a hot button? Are you lonely, Juliet?'

She looked up defensively, right into Oscar's intelligent green eyes.

'Of course not,' she said, aware she needed to be careful. Needed to not let him do what he always did and sneak under her guard and undo her with his gentleness and his need to protect.

'You're not looking to meet someone special?' he asked, his gaze snaring hers.

She licked her lips. 'Like you and your going on dates?'

He jerked away from her slightly and his gaze released hers and moved to the tree bark just above her head. 'You knew about those?'

'Melody let it slip,' she confessed. She'd hardly been able to believe it when his daughter had told her about how her dad had sat her down and asked her how she would feel if he went out on a date. Juliet had wondered what she would have said if he'd sat *her* down and asked her what she thought about him starting to date, and for weeks she'd waited for him to mention it to her. Then she'd waited months. But he'd never said one word and she was never going to try whittling it out of Melody. That wouldn't be fair on the relationship she had with his little girl, no matter how much she'd wanted to find out what had happened.

'Melody told you?' Oscar smiled, a resigned humour, not anger, showing on his face. 'Probably explains why Gloria knew – she must have told Persephone, too.'

'She was worried you didn't believe her when she said she was happy for you to start dating.'

'Of course I believed her. Damn. Sometimes I swear I don't know how I got so lucky with her.'

'I think it has something to do with you being a good dad,' she added gently.

He shook his head, as if he wasn't sure, but she knew he was sincere when he whispered, 'Thank you.'

'So the dates, thing...?' she asked, annoyed with herself because it shouldn't matter to her any more.

'Yeah... and yet... no!'

'You've stopped?'

'Yep.'

'Why?' she asked him.

Oscar shrugged and turned so that his back was against the tree also. He stared out at the rain for a while and then said, 'I guess I'm not ready. I mean, I thought I was.'

'Right.' What could she say to that?

'And you?'

'Me?'

'I can't remember you going on any dates for a while.'

'To be honest, I'm so focused on the fete and setting up the hair salon, it's not even on my radar.' A smile filled her face. 'It's wonderful to think that in a few months I could be running my own business.'

'Yet you haven't once mentioned wanting to do that.'

She turned her head to stare at him. 'Like you didn't mention the dates to me?' Licking her lips she added, 'We don't have to tell each other all our secrets.'

For a moment he seemed fixated on her mouth and Juliet's heart started pounding hard and heavy in her chest. But as if he suddenly grew aware of what he was doing, he lifted his hand to drag it over the stubble on his jaw, frowning, as if his mind was settling back on the problem he had. 'But why would you wanting to go out on your own and open a hair salon be a secret? I can't imagine your mum not approving.'

'Of course she approves,' she said, hoping to make him see it was him, not her who was reacting strangely. 'She's completely supportive.'

'Is it that you're worried you'd be lonely opening up the salon on your own and that's why you're teaming up with Kate?' Oscar probed. 'Because you could do it on your own, you know. You don't need Kate's help. I know you're shy, but you shouldn't let that stop you from—'

'You think I want to join forces with Kate because I'm too

shy to do this on my own?' Juliet dragged in a breath. 'You don't think I could possibly want to be in that building because I've worked out that the premises and location will bring me more business than opening up in the parade?' He didn't look convinced, but she continued anyway. 'You don't think I worked out that it would destroy Kate if she wasn't at least given the chance to fight for The Clock House?'

'Jules–'

'You think I'm just biding my time waiting for "someone special" to come along? That I couldn't possibly be all right with not having time for romance while I'm trying to do something for myself? Something that's going to make me happy? Something that will give me more than some stupid romance that won't last anyway because all the men I meet don't even...' she tailed off, mortified at where she'd been going with her words.

Oscar ducked his head so that it was impossibly close to hers. 'All the men you meet don't what?' he asked quietly.

She shook her head and pressed her fingers against the rough bark. She couldn't believe she'd nearly gone full Sinead O'Connor on him when the one thing she definitely didn't need was a comparison website to know that no one out there compared with him.

Oscar must have mistaken her silence for being lost in thought because he ran a fingertip down her arm to get her attention.

Juliet pressed her fingers even harder to the wood as her heart flipped over and all her other organs sort of melted to form a trampoline net to support its bounce.

'I hate it when we argue,' he told her.

'That's because we never have,' she whispered.

'We must have.'

'Nope.'

'Huh.' He turned his head to stare back out at the rain. 'Weird.'

'Or not,' she said suddenly tired. 'You're only arguing with me because you don't like the fact Kate's come back and it looks like she's sticking around this time.'

'Do you really think that's the only reason?'

Her breath hitched. Could there be... another reason?

No. No. No.

She'd be really stupid to start thinking that it might be because he'd finally seen her in another light and yet, taking a deep breath, the old romantic in her decided to ante up. 'What's the other reason, then?'

She'd surprised him again, she could tell from the way he jerked his hand away so that it was further from where it had been resting next to hers against the bark.

'I don't want to see you get hurt, Jules,' he said finally.

That was it?

Of course that was it.

'I can look after myself, Oscar. And stop calling me Jules. It implies you're—'

'Implies that I'm what – Juliet?'

'Invested.'

He frowned. 'Well, of course I'm invested. We're friends.'

'Right. Friends.'

'We're not friends?'

229

'Of course we are.'

'I swear since Kate's come back it's like we can't communicate with each other at all. I don't like that. And what's with not coming over so much?'

'I didn't think you'd noticed.'

'Of course I have. So has Melody. What did we do?'

'Nothing. I guess I realised you don't need me as much.'

'So, what – that means you don't want to see us?'

'No. It just means there's not a need to.'

'I see.'

'Good.'

'I didn't realise you only stopped by to help out, so I guess I owe you another apology for not treating you like a valued friend.'

But that's all he really thought of her as, anyway. I mean, sure he liked her. Appreciated her. Felt bad that he might not have let her know that. But it wasn't anything more. Or deeper. It was never going to be.

And she couldn't do it any more.

'Well, maybe if you hate hurting me and you hate taking me for granted maybe we shouldn't be around each other so much,' she ventured.

'That's crazy. If anything I think we should be around each other more.'

'What?'

'I've obviously made you feel taken for granted, so I should rectify that. How about you come over for movie-time on Sunday with Melody and me? We'll make you dinner and let you choose the movie.'

She loved spending time with him and Melody. Could see the three of them sitting in front of the TV, comfortable in each other's company. Happy to be spending their free time together. It would all look so natural.

And yet she had to start protecting herself better.

'I'm sorry. I can't,' she said.

'You don't like that idea, then, think of something else we can do.'

'Oscar, what are you going to do if Kate and I win the fundraising challenge and Kate buys The Clock House?'

'Tell me the reason you don't think we should be around each other is because of this ridiculous challenge?'

'You're the one who heard my plans and immediately offered to help Daniel.'

Oscar swore softly under his breath. 'I can't work out if it's sad or ridiculous that you don't believe I can separate Old Man Isaac's challenge from the relationships I've made in the village. Kate asked for Bea's files. I've got them in the back of my car. If you don't want to take them today, let me know when I can drop them round.'

'Conscience appeased now?'

'Damn it, Juliet, what do you think Kate will do when *Daniel* wins and buys The Clock House?'

'You're so quick to think she'll leave? What if she doesn't?'

'But what if she does?'

'It sounds to me like you want to help her along her way by making sure Daniel wins? This is her home, Oscar. Do you still not think she deserves her place here? Why? Because she didn't handle Bea's death in the exact way you needed her to?'

He stepped away from her and she immediately felt the broken connection.

'Kate will do what she wants to do,' he said, his jaw rigid as he shoved his hands into his jeans pockets. 'She always has.'

'You seriously believe that? You seriously believe Kate left because she wanted to? What if she left to make it easier on all of you?'

He looked like she'd just unpinned a grenade and hurled it into the space between them and then he stared at the ground for several moments before finally looking up at her and saying, 'Then she's stupid. Families are supposed to stick together. Running away is never the answer.'

'Running away? God, Oscar, how do you think she could ever run away? All she has to do is look in a mirror to be reminded every day of what she lost – of what you all lost.'

Chapter 23

Is That a Presentation in Your Pocket?

Kate

Perhaps Whispers Wood wasn't quite ready for Powerpoint presentations and she should go with the trusty old flip-chart she could see leaning precariously at the side of the stage. In less than two hours she and Daniel would have presented their ideas for the village fete theme and the voting would be being counted.

Speaking of Daniel...

Where was he? Kate scanned the growing crowd, looking for someone a head taller than everyone, who shot her senses into overload.

'Where should we sit?' Juliet asked Kate.

Kate looked at the rows of chairs set out in front of the stage. Nerves hovered in the pit of her belly. She took out some of the papers from her bag and started fanning herself. It was a balmy summer's evening and although the doors and windows of The Clock House had been thrown open to let air circulate, there were more people here than she'd expected.

'Somewhere near the front?' Juliet asked, 'So you can get to the stage easily?'

Kate promptly grabbed a hold of the fringing on Juliet's jacket to stop her. 'Or,' she suggested, 'somewhere at the back near the exits in case it's a tough crowd.'

'Don't think of it is a tough crowd, think of it as *your* crowd.'

Turning around, Kate spotted seats on the very back row and made a beeline for them.

'Will you at least try and relax?' Juliet said, as she took her seat next to her.

'Yeah, yeah, yeah,' Kate murmured, plonking her jacket and bag on the last two available seats next to theirs so that no one could sit on them. 'Would have been a cinch if you'd let me bring along the hip-flask.'

'You don't need a drink. There's no way anyone could have done more to prepare for this meeting. You are going to rock this, Spa Girl.'

'Call me Wonder Woman and maybe I'll believe you,' she said, scanning the crowd for Daniel again. She didn't dare tell Juliet, but a lot of the time she was 'researching' she was actually thinking about Daniel. Instead of giving herself props for being mature and turning down his dinner invitation, she'd been wondering how to wrangle another one from him so that she could accept. 'Don't you think there's one other person who might have prepared better than me?'

'Who?'

'Who-shmoo, Daniel Westlake, that's who.'

'Oh. Him.' Juliet shook her head. 'Nah. I'm not worried.

You know this place, Kate. You've been to countless village fetes on this very village green. Plus, you've included every blessed idea in every top ten list of how to put on the perfect fete, imaginable.'

'Ladies and gentlemen,' Crispin Harlow's voice rang out across the room as he walked up the steps to the stage and took his natural position behind the podium. 'Thank you all for coming out tonight...'

'Crap,' Kate whispered, hunkering down in her seat, her butterflies getting more serious by the minute.

'What?' Juliet whispered.

Kate shot her a quick grin. 'I forgot the kitchen sink. I was supposed to put it in my Everything-Including-the-Kitchen-Sink Fete Plan.'

Juliet reached over and squeezed Kate's arm. 'Just be yourself. Everyone's going to love your theme.'

'Now before we start on the main reason we're all here tonight,' Crispin said, 'I have a few requests to read out. First, Trudie McTravers would like you all to know she'll be posting who got which part before the next rehearsal on...'

'Ooh, look who's arrived!' Juliet said, nudging her in the ribs.

Kate tore her gaze away from Crispin and looked at the open doorway, where Daniel was standing, looking gorgeous – sorry, *confused* – he was looking confused, to see that the meeting had already started.

He must have been three feet away, but Kate swore she was entering some sort of pheromone heaven. And as if Gloria Pavey could also tell how good he smelled, she turned and waved him over to sit down next to her.

Daniel's smile froze into place and Kate thought seriously about offering him one of the seats next to hers. Unfortunately because teleportation didn't technically work outside of the Starship Enterprise, her thoughts missed Daniel's head and he headed for the seat next to Gloria.

'Sorry, coming through,' he mumbled, as he started making his way over to where Gloria was grinning triumphantly. He'd tucked a large cardboard tube under his arm and was carrying a beaten-up leather satchel bag with papers sticking out of it. 'Shit,' he mumbled and turned as the tube he was carrying hit Ted squarely on the top of his head. 'Sorry Ted.' He turned and immediately the other end of the tube hit the person sitting across the aisle. 'Shit, shit, shit. Sorry.'

Kate giggled and turned to Juliet. 'Forget the hip-flask, did you bring the popcorn?'

'I'm not sure this is supposed to be entertaining. Poor Daniel.'

'Ah, Daniel, I see you've finally joined us.' Crispin's voice rang out from centre stage in all its pedantic glory. 'You're late for a meeting you organised, if I remember correctly, so thank you for finally turning up, but I hope you're not aiming for the chair next to Gloria's – that's where I'll be sitting.'

'Right. Apologies everyone,' he said, turning around. Kate wondered if he was as nervous as she was and that's why he didn't notice people automatically ducking again to avoid being hit with what were presumably his plans for the fete, as he searched out a spare seat. 'I must have the wrong time.'

And then he was standing in front of Kate and it was like

the butterflies inside of her caught the giggles and had decided instead to dance with joyous abandon, the traitors.

Pointedly he looked at the spare seats beside her. She moved her jacket, but before he could hit her with his tube, she grinned and asked, 'Is that a plan in your pocket, or are you just pleased to see me?'

'Hilarious,' he replied, sitting down beside her. 'I don't get why I'm late. I checked my watch and set off in good time.'

She leaned towards him in order to impart the sad truth in her most helpful voice. 'Crispin has Isaac move the hands of the clock forward ten minutes on meeting nights, so that no one is late.'

'Huh.' Daniel shook his head at the information. 'You think someone might have let me know.'

Kate made a hash-tag sign by laying the two fingers of one hand over two fingers of her other and said, 'Whispers Wood Wisdom. I guess it's something you know if you've, you know, lived here all your life.'

'Great.'

Mary, the school chaplain from the private boarding school in Whispers Ford, turned around in her seat to face them both. 'Can you be quiet, please?'

'Sorry Mary,' Daniel said, charm personified as he bestowed her with a sheepish grin.

She sort of sighed out a giggle and turned back around, leaving Kate frowning hard at her.

'How do you know who Mary is?' she asked him as Crispin started talking about putting extra dog-litter bins around the green.

'Oh. It's about getting to know the people who live here. Sort of, like, you know, something you do if you haven't lived here... all your life.'

He raised his eyebrow in challenge to her and with a quick poking out of her tongue, Kate said, 'Shh,' and deliberately stared resolutely ahead.

He let out a quiet laugh and settled his papers across his lap. After a few moments Kate gave up staring at Crispin's hair and tried to read some of the print in Daniel's presentation.

'I see you went Old School instead of embracing modern technology,' she whispered out of the side of her mouth as she indicated the papers on his lap.

'You're going Powerpoint?' he gave her a look that suggested he was impressed and a little nervous.

'All will be revealed.'

'Which one of us is going first?'

'You are.'

'Because Daniel comes before Kate?'

She placed a hand on his arm and said, 'You know there are things that can help with that, these days.' Out of the corner of her eye she saw Juliet bring her hand up to her mouth to hide her smile.

Daniel rolled his eyes. 'I meant in the alphabet. Is that how it was decided?'

'Sure. If that's what you want to think.'

'Honestly,' Mary turned around again in her seat. 'The pair of you are like children at assembly! Can you not save your chatter for persuading us which theme to go with?'

'Sorry Mary,' Kate said.

'Sorry Mary,' Daniel said.

After a few moments, Daniel leaned in and when she automatically leaned away with a suspicious look in her eyes, he grinned and beckoned her closer so that he could whisper to her.

Wow.

Okay.

Did he really think a sexy grin and a forefinger beckoning her closer was going to bend her to his will?

Apparently he knew her body better than she did because in the next moment she found herself leaning towards him so that the Village Fete Whisperer could work his magic into her ear.

'So, what should I be thinking?' he asked.

Kate shivered as the warmth of his breath became heat snaking from his mouth into her ear canal, and slithering straight to all the needy parts inside of her. She swallowed and tried to remember the question. Oh yeah. With a smile she said, 'I bribed Crispin to let you go first.'

'What with?' He moved his head back to stare at her lips and she couldn't have answered if her life depended on it. But then he was moving to whisper against her ear again, 'What with?'

This time it was her mimicking him by beckoning him closer so that she could whisper into his ear, 'Juliet's going to teach him to cook something nice for Mrs Harlow.'

He groaned low and gruff and Kate would have given anything to know if his response was from what she'd said or how she'd said it because, okay, her lips may have deliberately brushed against the outer shell of his ear as she'd spoken.

'Did I happen to mention Oscar's doing Crispin's extension?' he said, his voice a little above a whisper now as he spoke without leaning in.

'No. You didn't.'

'Yes. Crispin let me see the plans when I went over to discuss the website with him. I casually mentioned my idea for a theme while we were talking. I'm surprised you didn't hear about it before the meeting, the rate I've heard him championing it with the residents.'

The butterflies in her belly stopped their flirty dirty dancing and immediately started muttering nervously about her presentation instead.

'—so without further ado,' Crispin announced, 'Daniel, if you'd like to make your way to the front and tell us all about what you've come up with for our fete this year.'

Daniel snapped to attention and started gathering up his things. As he made his way to the front she couldn't help admiring the rear view as much as she'd admired the front.

The crowd was silent as they watched the newcomer set out his papers and pop the lid on his tube. Kate actually leaned forward in her seat so that she could see better.

'Wait a minute,' Juliet murmured. 'Is that a—'

'Oh my word, he's had a banner made.' She turned her head to exchange a we-can't-let-ourselves-be-too-impressed-with-this look with Juliet as Daniel pinned it to the flip-chart and covered it up again.

He cleared his throat and Kate was almost certain she

wasn't the only one to release a sigh of appreciation when he pulled out a pair of glasses and put them on to read from his notes.

He looked so completely sexy-geek in them that she actually squirmed on her seat.

'What the actual?' Juliet gasped.

'Quite,' she agreed.

'That is some next-level sex appeal, he's got going on.'

Kate let out a whimper. 'How am I going to top that?'

Juliet held up her hand in a calming manner and started rooting around in her bag. The next thing Kate knew she was shoving a pair of oversize cat-eye nineteen-sixties-style white sunglasses with yellow daises on the side into her hands.

Perfectly Zooey Deschanel *New Girl* on Juliet, but on her...

'What else have you got in your bag?' she asked, handing them back.

'Oh. I know.' Juliet grinned. 'You could bribe them with... oops...'

Kate saw people turn and look down as Juliet lost her grip on the bag of sweets she'd produced and Skittles scuttled noisily across the floor.

'What is going on back there,' Crispin moaned as he rose to his feet to look over.

'Sorry,' Kate said. 'We had a Taste The Rainbow moment get out of control on us. Everything's fine now. Swear,' she promised, smiling her bestest smile before shooting Juliet a look that she hoped could clearly be read as, 'If this is you helping, thanks, but no thanks.'

'Right, I think I'm all set up and ready to go now,' Daniel's voice rang out, and everyone immediately faced forward again to hear him speak. 'It really means a lot that you all came to listen to Kate and myself. I know I haven't been in the village for long, but the welcome I've received has been wonderful. And, actually, it's the word "wonderful" that got me thinking...'

Kate, along with everyone else in the room, watched him walk over to the flip-chart he'd put in the centre of the stage. She was almost certain there was a collective in-take of breath as he flipped open the cover page to reveal his banner which read: Whispers Wood's Wonderful Wonderland, in gorgeous olde worlde writing.

'Yes, fetes are about raising money and who knows – perhaps at this year's we'll raise enough to win us Best in Bloom again or buy more Christmas decorations for everyone to enjoy. But I don't want to focus on what we'll get from the fete... so much as the fete itself. I've never lived in a village before now,' he went on to say, 'but I believe a fete should be about bringing the community together to celebrate and have fun. One wonderful day where everything is about Whispers Wood. As a newcomer I've been looking into some of your wonderful history. For instance, did you all know how Whispers Wood got its name? Or about the ghostly sightings around Knightley Hall in the 1920's? Or that fairy rings only turn up under one of the trees on the green?'

Immediately several people started talking excitingly, shouting out a few of the answers.

Juliet turned to Kate. 'Did you know all this stuff?'

'No,' Kate answered with a sinking heart because now she

wanted to know all this stuff and find out lots of other stuff and basically celebrate All The Stuff with everyone. 'What a swot.'

'Sexy swot.' Juliet nodded.

Kate hissed, 'He's just a man, standing in front of an audience, asking us all to love him.' She listened to the excited chatter going on around them. No way was her theme going to win now.

'I have to admit I'm pleased by your response,' Daniel chuckled. 'But I'm sure there'll be a few questions and I'll do my best to answer them...'

'How much is this going to cost?' Crispin immediately asked.

'Well, the more money raised at our fundraising events the more money can go into renting equipment and tents. Our imagination is limitless. It wouldn't cost much to dress up in your favourite bygone Whispers Wood style, and we could have lots of memorabilia stalls, story-telling stalls, face-painting, classic games, wood whittlers, flame eaters, jugglers, paper lanterns, the usual. And we could set up a decorating committee...'

'Sounds like you're expecting us to put on a Tim Burton production.'

Kate hadn't realised she'd said the words aloud until she felt all heads turn in her direction.

'I guess that's a fair point,' Daniel said. 'I may have got a little carried away. We can scale back. My point is that a village is supposed to have an individual identity, and we do. Why not celebrate the weird and the wonderful amongst us?'

As the residents of Whispers Wood applauded Daniel's presentation, Kate felt weird, she did not feel wonderful.

'Kate, would you like to come up here and tell us about your theme for the village fete?' Crispin asked as Daniel collected up his papers and removed his banner from the flip-chart.

No, she would not like to.

And, as if Juliet was thinking what she was thinking, she reached out and put her hand over Kate's shaking ones. 'Hey, this is *your* crowd, remember?'

But it hadn't been her crowd for a long time.

This was supposed to be an opportunity to win them over.

With a sigh she picked up her plans and as she stood, caught Oscar's eye.

She couldn't read his expression, but her knees were properly knocking together as she made her way to the stage.

Chapter 24

All the World's a Stage and
Now I Get Stage-Fright?

Kate

Kate stared out over the crowd, wondering if they'd turned up in their droves to support her or watch her fail. The thought that it might be the latter had her so churned up she didn't even think she could do her presentation. Unrolling her speech, she popped it on the lectern, praying for her words to somehow make sense again, as she addressed everyone.

'Good evening,' she said, 'you all know me, so I won't bother with an introduction–'

'Although it's been that long,' Gloria trilled out, 'perhaps you should remind us.'

A good comeback – indeed any kind of comeback – failed her as deep, familiar and overwhelming panic embedded itself into nerve-endings, knowing exactly how best to flood her nervous system with one very succinct message: run – run like the wind.

And then Kate heard Oscar clearly say from his position

at the very back of the room, 'Wait a minute, I didn't get the memo about heckling being allowed. Anyone else get it?'

Kate watched as people shook their heads and Gloria turned puce. 'No?' Oscar said. 'Okay, then, Kate, feel free to proceed in the heckle-free zone.'

Kate's gaze shot to Juliet, who leaned forward slightly in her seat so that she could offer Oscar a shy but approving smile. Oscar dipped his head in acknowledgement as Juliet added a silent 'thank you' and when his gaze lifted to Kate's for once she saw neither anguish nor anger in his huge green eyes. She hardly dared believe that Oscar was coming around to the idea that she wasn't the worst person on the planet, but then he had given her all of Bea's files, hadn't he?

She didn't know if he'd chosen to do that or if Juliet had convinced him because Juliet had remained characteristically shtum when she'd handed them over and then left her alone for a few hours so that she could pore over them uninterrupted.

Bea's neat, cursive handwriting had flowed across every piece of paper. Emotion had poured on top of emotion as Kate read the work her sister had completed on working formulas for adding raw, organic honey to shampoo and conditioners, lip balms, moisturisers and other products, which if produced for the spa would help create a lasting and luxurious brand. There had been books and books filled with Bea's notes and Kate had been shocked to realise how secretively, efficiently and, admittedly, somewhat obsessively, Bea had been working on her plans while studying for her diploma in spa therapy. It looked almost as if she'd been keen to get all her thoughts down on paper while she could – as if she'd felt time was running out.

Kate hadn't wanted to think her sister had been living with any sense of premonition, so she'd quickly looked through all of Bea's business plans for The Clock House instead. These had been much more basic, but then it had been Kate whose job had been to get the business qualification, so it was hardly surprising if cost projections were ignored or the fact that without something extra like Juliet's salon helping to fill such a large space, or leaving some room for community events, their little spa business would have been lost in a building the size of The Clock House.

Logically Kate knew the village would feel happier about her being back to stay if she opened the spa alongside Juliet. Whispers Wood loved Juliet. They loved her sweet nature. They loved how hard she worked. They trusted her judgement.

So did Kate. And Juliet believed in Kate, so she owed it to her to give the best possible presentation and take one step closer to securing The Clock House.

Clearing her throat, she pasted on what she hoped was a confident smile and started talking.

'I too think our fete should be for the whole community and that's why I'd like our theme to be...' she hopped back to the chart and pulled the covering piece of paper away to reveal her floral, honey and bee theme.

No one said anything remotely negative.

There were even some murmurs of interest and pleasure.

But there wasn't the breathy excitement that had whispered over the room when Daniel had done his unveiling.

She stared down at her speech, the words blurring a little. The fake-it-til-you-make-it confidence she'd used to get her through new situations over the last few years deserting her now that she was amongst people who knew her and could turn her idea down on the grounds that they didn't see her as a safe bet.

No matter how much she had tried to turn her attention to formulating a plan for if that happened; her mind had determinedly shied away from the exercise over and over again. She had absolutely no back-up plan for a scenario in which she didn't win and open up in the clock house.

Panic layered over panic. Her head jerked up to scan the room for an exit and her gaze collided with Oscar again. She wondered if he had stationed himself at the door purposefully.

Now she thought she could decipher his expression perfectly. It was unwavering and knowing, telling her that, as always, it was her choice to run, to escape, to evade. It wasn't his style to impede.

But he would judge her for it.

And find her wanting.

She reminded herself she'd come back because she was ready. Ready to stop the world from changing that one little bit too much. On a deep breath she began talking about how the theme she'd chosen meant residents could embrace and celebrate the fact that it was summer in Whispers Wood. She talked of having a vintage feel to the fete with competitions for jams and honeys. She talked about floral competitions that would rival the Best in Bloom award. And she talked about bees and their plight and how important it was to educate everyone. And bunting, she talked a lot about bunting.

By the end of her presentation there were, thank goodness, a lot more sounds of interest, and as she looked out over the sea of faces she saw a lot more warmth.

'So, if any of you have any questions you'd like to ask me?'

'I do,' Daniel stated, standing up so that he could be heard. 'I was wondering how you came up with the idea?'

Silently she thanked him for the tame question to start her Q and A session. 'It was a combination of thinking about what would suit all ages, and researching into what makes a good fete work and...' her words tailed off. She shouldn't have said the third 'and' because with all eyes on her she couldn't for the life of her remember the actual flash of inspiration.

'And bees?' Daniel queried helpfully.

'Right,' she nodded. 'And bees.'

'You've spoken a lot about bees and honey tonight and I can't help feeling as if you're subliminally trying to influence residents about your plans for The Clock House.'

'What?'

Over Juliet's, 'Hey, that is below the belt,' comment, Kate's gaze shot straight to Oscar's. He was looking grim, but he didn't say anything. Was that because he was on Daniel's side because when he'd given her Bea's files she'd thought he was coming around to the idea of her being home...

'Daniel makes a fair comment,' Gloria chimed in. 'Everyone knows about the competition between you and Daniel for The Clock House. Daniel's theme doesn't have anything to do with the business he wants to set up, whereas you want to set up a spa using honey in your treatments. Honey from the bees behind The Clock House, right?'

Kate blanched.

Was Daniel right?

She'd been trying so hard to fit back in, but was everyone now thinking she was pushing her own agenda? Or worse, were they all still in What-Katie-Did-Next Land, waiting for her to leave?

Her hand shook as she twisted the top off of her bottle of water, so that she could take a calming sip, but as she brought the bottle to her mouth Gloria asked if she was going to provide an answer this century and fumbling the bottle, she felt cold liquid seep into the fabric of her top.

Her white cotton, now transparent, top.

As she grabbed the front of her top to pull it away from her trembling body, the only thing missing from the awful sense of déjà vu was the warrior-like response she'd made last time she'd dropped water down her front.

'I really, um, just wanted to create a theme you would all like,' she said, hoping the quiver she could hear in her voice was only in her imagination. 'I never for one moment thought I was taking what I want to do with The Clock House and coming up with a way to shove it down your throats. I'm so sorry. If you'll excuse me,' she gathered up her papers and with a quick, 'Don't forget to vote,' she jogged down from the stage, the open doorway fixed firmly in her sights.

Chapter 25
Queensberry Rules

Daniel

'Kate, wait.'

Damn it, the woman could give Usain Bolt a run for his money.

Extending his arm forward he wrapped his hand around her upper arm as she reached the gates of The Clock House and stopped her in her tracks.

The papers she was carrying dropped to the ground and fanned out as she whirled around to face him and in the light shining out from the building behind them he could see she was pale.

'Nice sucker-punch you have there, Daniel. My mistake for thinking we'd adopted Queensberry rules for the challenge. You reeled me in, laughed with me, joked with me, *whispered* in my ear and then–'

'I'm sorry. Really. It hadn't been my intention to–'

'Make me look like Derren Brown in front of the whole village? Now they all think I've been pulling the wool over their eyes and that my idea is some sort of carefully constructed illusion to get them onside with the spa.' She sounded exhausted and baffled. 'Do you have any idea how hard I've been working to fit back in here? Of course you don't. How could you? You're too busy trying to ingratiate yourself into the community so that people will approve of what you want to do here.'

Daniel felt his jaw clench tight. 'You know we could bring back fighting fair any time now.'

'Don't pretend you haven't been doing exactly what you accused me of doing in that meeting. Dropping by to see Crispin. Tripping the light with Gloria Pavey.'

'Hey, the only tripping I've been doing here is over you.'

'Chewing the cud with Ted,' she carried on as if he hadn't spoken, 'Negotiating supplies with Big Kev. And is there any ear you haven't bent when it comes to market research for your business idea? I bet you even ran it past Gertrude.'

'Well, don't pretend you haven't been flirting your way around the village, wearing next to nothing and smiling and giggling at me and Ted and Crispin.'

'Unbelievable. Trust a man to bring an argument down to sex. It's not like I haven't seen you running all over the place in your tight-fitting t-shirts and running shorts.'

'Hello? I'm dressed like that because I'm running. I'm a runner. As in... I run. Did you or did you not wear what you wore to my football tournament with the deliberate intention of getting more cake sales?'

'All right. Yes. And that was wrong, which was why I didn't do it again during your fun-run last week.'

For a moment Daniel couldn't speak. Had she just admitted

she was wrong? He'd known people who had gone to actual prison still not admitting what they had done.

Two. He'd known two people.

But he really, really didn't need to be focusing in on that at the moment, other than to internally acknowledge that Kate had recognised what she'd done because she had more spark and more grit and more guts to think about how her actions affected others than those two people put together and as he remembered the loss she'd suffered he also realised that maybe Whispers Wood had skewed her sense of perspective and proportion.

'Look, we both want to win,' he began carefully.

'No we don't,' she shook her head sadly. 'You want to win. I *need* to win. It's not the same at all.'

'Want and need – they're just semantics.'

'No. They aren't. Why are you here, Daniel? You obviously don't have any ties. And why don't you, by the way? How can you reach the age you are and not have anybody to belong to? And being that you so obviously don't, why can't you go somewhere else and start there? Why does it have to be here specifically?'

Because I met you...

The thought stunned him. Is that what was really driving all of his decisions? Was he trying to, what, impress her? Win her over? Win her heart?

'Because,' Kate continued, 'I can't do what I want to do anywhere else, Daniel. This is my home.'

And I want this to be my home too...

This thought didn't stun him as much as thinking he was

253

doing this all for someone other than himself. He loved it here. Felt like he could add something worthwhile to the community here.

For the first time he wondered what Kate would do if he won. Oscar had hinted she'd pick up the bags she probably hadn't even unpacked and jump on the first plane. He knew he wouldn't enjoy opening up his business knowing he wouldn't be bumping into her. And if *she* won? Would he stick around? He needed to make money. He wouldn't be able to do that here. He'd have to leave. Would she miss him? Or would she be too busy being happy setting up her spa?

He didn't like thinking this village might not be big enough for the both of them and shoved his hands into his pockets. As he did so his fingertips brushed over the slim jewellery box he'd put there. Her locket. When she'd asked him if he was pleased to see her earlier he thought she'd guessed what was in his pocket, but then he'd realised she was simply making a joke about the banner he'd been carrying.

Taking the box out of his pocket now, he passed it to her.

She took it suspiciously. 'What's this?'

'Call it a peace offering.'

'I don't understand.'

'I know. You will. Open it.'

He didn't know what he'd expected, really. Maybe a rueful smile and then a 'thank you'.

Certainly not the awful silence as she opened the lid and stared down into the contents.

'This is my locket.' She lifted wary-as-hell eyes to him. 'You've had my locket all this time?'

'You lost it in there,' he said, jerking a thumb behind him, 'the first time we met.'

'But why didn't you just give it back to me? Why would you keep it with you all the time knowing I must have been looking for it?'

'Calm down, I wasn't being creepy. I didn't give it back because I was busy getting it fixed for you.'

If he thought she'd been pale when he first caught up to her, it was nothing compared with the white-sheet look she was giving off now.

'Fixed?' she whispered. 'Fixed?' The box dropped unheeded to the floor as she took out the necklace. She opened up the locket and stumbled forward. 'No, you didn't,' she cried out. 'Oh my God, you got it fixed? How could you? Why would you? I can't even—'

Daniel watched as with shaking hands she ran her finger-tips over the now perfectly smooth watch face and as she felt the surface her entire being seemed to fold in on itself. Dimly he was aware of footsteps crunching over the gravel towards the two of them, but he couldn't tear his eyes from her face.

'I *hate* that you did this,' she spat out, shaking from head to foot.

'Kate, he didn't know,' Oscar said, reaching the two of them. 'He couldn't possibly have known.'

'Known what?' Daniel asked, feeling like something was very, very wrong here but not having a clue. He stared back down at the locket dangling from Kate's hands. 'I thought I broke it when I fell on you.'

'It was already broken,' she whispered, her breathing

shallow. 'It belonged to Bea – my sister, Bea. She was wearing it when she crashed her car into a tree. She was wearing it when she died. And now you've taken it and made it–'

Daniel thought he might be sick. She was telling him that he'd taken something of hers and wiped out its past by making it new again, wasn't she?

'Kate, I–'

'No.' She shook her head and her words gained in volume and loathing as she unleashed them. 'Don't you say anything to me. If it wasn't for you I wouldn't have lost it in the first place. You with your coming to Whispers Wood and breaking down and having a wander around and impulsively deciding this was the place for you. I mean who does that?' She looked behind him to where he now realised a small group had gathered outside the main doors. 'Oh, right,' she said, slapping her forehead, 'I mean, apart from me, right? Because that's what I do, isn't it,' she shouted out. 'You all think I swan all over the globe, picking up and putting down without a care in the world.'

'Kate, you have to stop now,' Juliet said quietly, walking up to stand beside her. 'Please,' she laid a hand on Kate's shoulder, but Kate shook it off. 'Stop or you're going to make it worse and then afterwards you'll hate yourself for it.'

'Juliet's right,' Daniel agreed, wanting to wrap her up in his arms and make it all better for her. He stepped much closer to her, not wanting to crowd her, yet wanting to block their audience's view as much as possible. 'I'm so sorry about the locket. Why don't the four of us go somewhere private and talk through–'

'Oh now you want privacy?' Kate shouted, clutching the locket to her chest. 'Now that you've had your public meeting where you get to tell everyone how brilliant you are for the village. Well, you know what? I don't need your sympathy. I have this in the bag. You really think the village is going to support someone who has City written all over him and whose idea of permanent residency is my mother's B&B?'

Chapter 26

Parallel Universes

Kate

Kate stared at the selection of wines Big Kev stocked and tried to get her brain to engage with the task at hand, namely – getting drunk. Very drunk. So drunk she'd become numb to the white-hot emotion bubbling beneath her skin. So drunk she'd empty her head of Oscar telling Juliet to 'leave her be for a while' as she'd run across the green into the only place that was open. So drunk she'd put off processing what Daniel had done with Bea's locket and how the feel of the metal beneath her fingertips felt different now, as if it had lost Bea's imprint. And definitely so drunk she could put off being reminded of how she had reacted in front of him and half the village.

Furiously she blinked through her blurred vision and started twisting the bottles on the shelf so that their labels were all lined up pillar-straight.

Zombie-like she turned the bottles, unable to believe she'd run away like that. Admittedly she'd only run halfway across the village green, but still.

She shouldn't have come back to Whispers Wood.

If she hadn't she would never have crashed into Daniel and never dropped the locket and Daniel would never have found it and got it repaired – *fixed*.

Nothing felt fixed since coming back.

With a sigh she pulled a bottle of Shiraz off the shelf. Probably as soon as tomorrow she'd start seeing artwork appear for Whispers Wood's Wonderful Wonders everywhere. Except not. Because she planned on being desperately hungover by that point. So hungover she wouldn't even want to leave the house.

The sound of low voices followed by tinkling laughter brought her out of her cycle of self-pity and, curious, she made her way to the end of the narrow aisle and peered around the corner.

'Mother?' Horrified, Kate clapped a hand over her mouth.

What kind of crazy parallel universe was this? There was no way that back on Planet Earth, Sheila Somersby and Big Kev would be... The bottle of Shiraz slipped from her fingers and smashed against the shop's tiled floor.

'Kate?' Her mother stepped forward awkwardly. 'What on earth are you doing here? Shouldn't you be at the meeting?'

Kate opened her mouth, but no sound was forthcoming. Her mother had been smiling.

Smiling.

But now the pretty flush on her mother's face was mutating back to its usual pallor and Kate wanted to have slipped away unnoticed so that her mum could have had those extra moments of smiling and flirting and enjoying life before the sight of her one remaining daughter sobered her so.

'You look ill, are you ill?' Her mother queried, awkwardly. 'Is that why you left the meeting?'

'Wait – you knew about the village meeting?'

'Of course. Oscar had to cancel Thursday night dinner to attend. Kevin and I were just discussing it and I – decided not to come.'

'Right.' So ironic that a family dinner she *wasn't* part of was cancelled so that they could attend a meeting she *was* a part of but hadn't called. Because the thought made her feel even more crap, she got brave enough to start button-pushing. 'Why?'

'Why didn't I come?' Sheila stood a little straighter, a little steelier. 'I didn't want the first time we saw each other in months to be across a stage, in a room full of other people watching us.'

'Wow. Okay,' Kate couldn't believe it was something her mum would have even noticed. She wondered if she'd notice the bitterness coming through now when she said, 'Well, as usual, thank you for your support. And while we're at it, thank you so much for not returning any of my phone calls, either.'

Now colour came into her mother's face again. 'Maybe what I had to say couldn't be said on the phone.'

'We're standing in front of each other now, Mum. What did you have to say to me?'

Sheila pursed her lips and, after a moment's silence, shook her head and stated, 'I'm not prepared.'

'You need to prepare to speak to your daughter?'

'I...' Sheila tailed off and Kate's hand clutched around Bea's

260

locket. She needed to remember she was back to stay and what that meant.

Into the uncomfortable silence she dragged in a breath and prepared to try and try again. 'I could pop around tomorrow for a visit?'

Sheila frowned. 'You know I have bridge on Fridays.'

The scent of spilled wine mingled with the creeping sense of hopelessness. 'So when would be a good time for you?'

'How about now?' Big Kev intervened, finally stepping forward and opening his arms up for a hug.

Kate practically ran into them because Big Kev was as tall as a large oak tree, with a heart the size of a small country.

'It's good to see you, Kate,' the gentle giant with the gruff voice said. 'Sorry we didn't make it to the meeting tonight. We were,' he stopped abruptly and with a quick look at her mother, turned back to Kate and said, 'well, Sheila's already explained. Here, step aside and talk to your mother while I clean up.'

'Oh, I don't want to intrude and I really have to get back to Juliet's. She'll be worried about me.'

'Why?' her mother said.

'Why?' she repeated, like she was a parrot.

'Why will she be worried about you?' That her mother looked her up and down, her gaze lingering on her face, had Kate worrying that some of those tears she'd forced back down inside herself had somehow leaked free without her being aware.

'It's not a big deal,' she said, knowing her mother couldn't cope with big deals any more. 'The meeting didn't go quite as I had planned, that's all.'

'What happened?'

Which part, she wanted to ask. The part where I got my presentation handed to me in a sling by the handsome dude who rode into town all Jack Reacher-like a couple of weeks ago. Or the part where I lost my locket and heart to him, only for him to hand the locket back fixed and my heart broken.

Kate searched for an answer that didn't sound insane – because obviously she hadn't lost her heart to Daniel Westlake. She didn't even know Daniel Westlake. He was just some usurper threatening her business venture. She had to start keeping him in that box or life was going to get even more screwed up. 'I think everyone liked Daniel's plans more than mine,' she explained lamely.

'That's a shame,' Big Kev commiserated. 'I'll just put this lot out the back and fetch you another bottle.'

Alone again with her mother, she returned her scrutiny, shocked to see her out of black. And in Sheila's eyes she caught a glimmer of something that didn't stack up against the usual catalogue of sorrow and soul-destroying blankness her mother usually looked at her with. Scrambling around for something to say, she went with small talk. 'So, are the two of you off somewhere nice after Big Kev locks up?'

'Don't be silly,' Sheila answered, looking uncomfortable. 'I'll be going home. Alone. Kevin has hours left on his shift tonight.'

Kate saw the look Big Kev gave her mother as he put a fresh bottle of Shiraz on the counter for Kate and was gobsmacked when her mother flushed scarlet and looked apologetic. That her mother was showing emotion – good, bad or ugly – was such a new concept for Kate to digest, she thought she could grow to like this parallel universe.

'So you're staying with Juliet, then?' her mother asked, after another awkward silence.

Kate nodded and popped a note onto the counter to cover the cost of both the broken bottle and the new bottle of wine.

'Probably for the best,' Sheila said, looking anywhere but at her. 'I'm afraid I'm booked solid.'

'That's okay. I'm fine at Wren Cottage.'

Sheila nodded. 'You'll pop by tomorrow?'

'I'll stop by after bridge.' Death grip on the new bottle of wine, she turned at the shop door. 'Mum?'

'Yes?'

'You look pretty in that colour.' Scooting out the door, she didn't stop to gauge her mother's reaction. Too afraid she'd see disapproval or the haunting hue of grief.

Chapter 27

Conversation Starters For One

Kate

At some point between visits, her mother had exchanged the old front door of the chocolate-box cottage that had once been home for a new one in a soft sage green colour with black ironmongery doorknocker and letterbox. Two huge glazed maroon pots either side of the door held specimen box clipped into pyramid shaped precision. To soften the look, her mother had planted pretty purple and yellow violas at the base of each pyramid and to the left of the front door was a neat oval sign with the name of the B&B.

Part of Kate was incredibly proud of her mother.

Part of Kate hated what grief could accomplish.

Taking a deep breath, she prepared to walk up the front path and go in.

She was dressed in a summer dress that she had actually bought this time, a wrap-around soft jersey casual dress... in her favourite confidence-boosting scarlet. She hoped it said 'something I threw on', not 'something I agonised over in case I saw anyone on the way over'. Bea's locket was her only accessory and she was trying hard to get used to the clock ticking away as it sat over her heart.

Instead of getting royally drunk last night, she'd crawled into bed emotionally spent and, to her surprise, had slept like a log. Waking up early, she'd decided to go into town, do a little shopping and check out the local competition by getting a massage and now she was feeling much more relaxed.

Well, she was feeling relaxed enough to offer the appropriately sized gargantuan apology to Daniel as well as trying to navigate spending a little time in her mother's company, at any rate.

Opening the front door of the B&B she walked in, deliberately making her way past the front room, sure she would never grow accustomed to the low murmur of strangers' voices.

Ribbons of the past draped themselves across her defences and tugged. Memories of her and Bea watching DVD's, setting up their nail varnish stations, gossiping about girls, fantasising about boys, munching on junk food and arguing about which university courses to take.

She found her mother in the kitchen. Standing as still as a statue in front of the window that looked out over the back garden. Kate knew she wasn't seeing the crazy-paving patio with the fairy-like balls of moss and the miniature daisies growing between the cracks. Or the climbing roses around the pergola that divided the lawn from patio. Chances were her mother wasn't seeing anything. Visiting, as she was, the past, where memories of her late daughter comforted.

Kate fought against the curtain of invisibility settling silently over her shoulders. As always it choked. Cutting off her ability to remind her mother she had another daughter, who might, conceivably, still need her. Not that she would ever let herself ask, even if she could.

A sigh must have escaped her because her mother turned around sharply. 'Kate. Have you been standing there long?' Her voice was rusty and her hands clutched against her apron.

'Not long,' she reassured, feeling her heart race. After her argument with Daniel last night and then bumping into her mother and Big Kev doing... whatever they had been doing, Kate was finding it difficult to lock down her emotions. 'How was bridge?'

'Oh, my mind was really on all the baking I had to do today.'

Kate tried not to let it bother her that it was easier for her mother to provide all the surface requirements her guests might need than worry about or look forward to her daughter's visit.

Another awkward silence ensued while Sheila fussed with the edges of a freshly baked cake set on a cooling rack.

'So, um, is Daniel around?' Kate eventually asked.

'Daniel?'

'Pieces of eight,' Kate said like a pirate.

'What?'

'I thought – if we're going to be doing the parroting thing again, I should mix it up a little.'

Her mother looked lost and Kate wished, not for the first time, that her automatic defence mechanism wasn't flippancy.

'Daniel moved out last week,' Sheila commented.

Kate's mouth dropped open. 'But-but, where has he gone?'

'He moved into Mistletoe Cottage on the green.'

'He...?' She couldn't believe it. Last night she'd accused him of not being serious about living here permanently and all the time he'd moved into an actual property in the village? What was bigger than gargantuan because now she was going to have to increase the size of her apology appropriately.

'I think it's nice he's putting roots down in the village. He really is a very lovely man.'

Really a very lovely man? This might possibly be the first time her mother had ever made a personal comment about a guest, but Kate had to admit her mother hadn't lost her intuition. Because not once had he retaliated last night – when she'd gone too far and been unable to rein herself in.

'Would you like to tell me how the meeting last night really went?' Her mother asked.

Unused to her mum's interest, Kate faltered. 'Um, like I said, it didn't really go as planned, but it was fine.'

'Fine?' Her mother looked at her. *Really* looked at her and Kate shifted uncomfortably. 'That's not what Cheryl told me today at bridge.'

'What did she tell you?'

Her mother ran her hands down her apron again and Kate looked down at the floor. It was bad, then.

'What, exactly do you know about The Clock House challenge, Mum?'

'Oh, you know how people talk in a small place like this. I assume I know it all. Certainly Kevin and I have been discussing it.'

'What else have you and Big Kev been doing?'

Her mother flushed like a schoolgirl and Kate pulled out one of the kitchen chairs and plonked herself down on it. If the world was going to keep shifting on its axis like this, it was probably safer to be sitting down.

Still agog, she watched her mother wipe her hands down her apron again and move to the larder, re-emerging with a jar of jam and a bucket of renewed emotional distance. Taking the large sponge cake off the cooling rack, she efficiently sliced it in two and began slathering one of the halves with the preserve.

Into the silence, Kate ventured, 'What did Big Kev think of my buying The Clock House?' As a resident and business owner in Whispers Wood, Kate was genuinely interested in his opinion, and if, in a round-about way, she also happened to garner her mother's opinion on the subject, how very handy.

The rhythmic jam-spreading stopped. Then, tentatively, her mother said, 'He's not opposed to the idea.'

'But...?'

'No one wants it to become an empty shell.'

Right. Because there were enough empty shells left behind. A lump formed in her throat, making it hard to push out the question she now desperately wanted the answer to. 'And you? What do you think of the idea?'

Her mother cast her gaze down at the jam jar she'd picked up. Slowly she set about replacing the lid and then picked up the bowl of cream she'd set aside earlier. Kate's hands crept up to grab a hold of her locket.

Three large dollops of cream had to land in the centre of the cake before Kate heard a quiet, 'I think Bea would have been proud of you.'

The size of the lump in Kate's throat doubled as, with every bit of her being, she wanted to ask her mother if Bea had somehow sent her a sign or somehow 'told' her that.

She couldn't – wouldn't ask her mother, though, in case it sent her further away from her again when it felt like maybe, just maybe, they were having their first real conversation in forever.

When she was sure she had a better grip on her voice she said, 'If I do all this, you know it means I'd be staying in Whispers Wood permanently.'

'You won't miss all the travelling?'

'I won't miss it.'

'I was never sure if you did it because it was easier than being here, or if you did it because you really enjoyed it?'

Kate felt the heat of the metal locket against her skin. 'I did it because it was easier than being here, Mum.'

Her mother gave a short, accepting nod of her head. 'And do you think you might find it easier being here now?'

Kate met her mother's eyes. Aware of just what it was costing her not to look away because it was costing all of her courage too. 'I'm hoping it will be, yes.'

Her mother blinked and gave another short nod.

The top went on the cake and was followed by a dusting of icing sugar. 'Well, then,' she said. 'I suppose settling back in Whispers Wood will help the both of us become better at this.'

Another drifting of icing sugar wafted down over the cake her mother had made for her guests before Kate watched her move to flick the kettle on and then take out two small plates.

As she set them out in front of the cake, Kate realised it was for the two of them! Maybe Aunt Cheryl's advice to come and see her mother for herself might have been right after all. Maybe her mother really was finally shaking off the shackles of grief. Maybe the two of them really were about to sit down and try tea and cake...

'You know, Kate,' her mother said, slicing into the light and springy cake and delivering two large pieces to the plates. 'If you're really happy to settle back here, you should think seriously about moving out of Juliet's tiny place and moving into Myrtle Cottage.'

Chapter 28

Past Tense, Present Tense, Totes Tense

Kate

Kate didn't take time to peruse the contents of the drinks trolley set up discreetly in the corner of the room. One hand made a grab for the decanter, the other upturned one of the matching crystal tumblers beside it.

Removing the stopper from the container, she took a quick, cautious sniff.

Yuck.

Sweet sherry. Still. Beggars couldn't be choosers. Needs must, and all that...

'Kate? What are you doing?'

Kate whirled around at the voice and stared in dismay as Oscar's gaze settled on the sherry. Brazening out the fact she'd been at the B&B approximately three minutes and was supposed to be in the cloakroom instead of the formal guest lounge, she pointed to the alcohol and said, 'I'm grabbing my cup, putting some liquor in it.'

'Christ, Kate. Only you could try and *Uptown Funk* your way out of Thursday Night Dinner.'

'Thursday Night *Family* Dinner,' she corrected him. He obviously had no idea how freaked out she was to get the invitation. And why would he be? *He'd* been having these dinners with her mum for ages.

'What? You can't run away, so you're going to drink your way through the evening?' Oscar asked. 'You've been here less than five minutes. You're not even trying. Is it really so hard to be included?'

'Oh, not at all,' she replied, putting the sherry carefully back on the trolley. 'Between Mum being a gigantic bag of nerves and the permanent scowl on your face whenever you see me, I'm sure to have the loveliest time.'

'Come on. Wouldn't you be nervous if you were in her shoes?' he asked, conveniently ignoring the remark aimed at him.

'Wouldn't you be nervous if you were in mine?' she added pointedly. 'Exactly,' she answered before giving him the chance to agree. 'Ergo, alcohol.'

'Trust me, drink is not your friend in this situation.'

'It's not?' She looked at him disbelievingly. 'What is, then?'

He sighed and shoved his hands in his pockets. 'Just be you.'

Kate's jaw dropped open. 'Wow. Okay. Just be me. Genius. If only "me" wasn't guaranteed to say the wrong thing.' *And if only "me" didn't remind you all of who is missing from the table.*

'I'm sure we'll make allowances when that happens – *should* that happen,' he quickly corrected.

She watched him as she turned the crystal tumbler back over. 'Why are you being so nice to me?'

He stared down at the floor for a moment and when he looked back up at her there was a sheepish expression in his eyes. 'Juliet reminded me how drunk I got the first time I brought Melody along to one of these family dinners.'

'You got drunk?'

Oscar winced. 'I bypassed your lightweight sherry option there and went straight for the bottle fourth from the back. Potato vodka, I think. Twenty million per cent proof. Ought to be outlawed. Or buried deep in a chest freezer that comes with a chain and padlock.'

Kate stared fascinated as he paled before her, then shuddered and swallowed a couple of times in quick succession, before adding, 'Sheila had made trifle for dessert.'

A giggle burst through her wall of nerves. 'Oh, no way.' No way had he got sick on potato vodka at her mother's house. But the way his hand crept over his stomach definitely suggested he had. 'You didn't?'

'I did. Right into the trifle. Which promptly made Melody sick too. Also into the trifle. Bad night all round.'

'And you came back the following week? I mean, Mum actually allowed you back in? Cooked for you again?'

'I think she thought my utter humiliation in front of my daughter was punishment enough. I still can't eat trifle.'

'Or drink vodka?'

'Warped or what,' he confessed, with a rueful smile playing at the outer edges of his mouth.

'Well, you might like this instead,' Kate said, walking over to the bag she'd placed on the coffee table. Nervously she withdrew the bottle of Tequila and passed it to him.

273

Oscar took the bottle of Cuervo she was holding out to him and stared down at it suspiciously. 'You bought me a present?'

Kate forced herself not to wring her hands or pull at her clothes. 'Yes – I remembered... Bea used to buy you this sometimes.'

He smiled and then threw back his head and laughed.

Kate stared. 'What?'

'I hated this brand.'

'Shit.' She made a grab for it.

'No.' He held the bottle up high. 'It was sweet of you. Thank you.'

Mortified to have chosen something he didn't even like she jumped in the air, trying to get a hold of the bottle. 'I'll get you something you do like. Give it back.'

'What on earth are you two doing in here,' Sheila said, coming fully into the room. Consternation pinched her facial muscles tight, making the nerves that had just started to dissipate re-gather tsunami-style in the pit of Kate's stomach.

'Nothing, Mum,' she answered automatically. 'I was just giving Oscar a gift. Here,' she went to her bag and pulled out a bouquet of roses in pale pinks and creams. 'These are for you.'

Her mother stared at them as if they were going to bite.

When she didn't take them, Kate couldn't help the words, 'Don't tell me you hate roses now?' from spilling from her lips. Damn it. Her gaze flicked with embarrassment to Oscar's and then back to her mother's as Sheila reached out awkwardly to accept the bouquet.

'Don't be silly,' Sheila murmured, staring down at them as

if she really didn't know what to do next. 'Who could dislike roses? They were Bea's favourite, I think.'

'They were Bea's favourite because they were your favourite, Mum.'

Sheila paled.

Kate looked at Oscar as if to say, 'See? This is where me being me gets us all.'

With the awkwardness sitting between them and practically holding its belly from laughing so hard at how pathetic they all were with each other, Kate forced air into her lungs and clearing her throat, told Oscar, 'I bought Melody a little gift too. I hope that's okay?'

'Why?' Oscar asked.

Kate swallowed. 'When you're the guest you should bring gifts.'

'For the host. Not everyone.'

'Yes. Well.' She stared hard at both Oscar and her mother. 'I wasn't sure whose idea this had actually been.'

Her mother's shoulders sagged with disappointment before they set rigid again. 'I'd better go and put these in water and then see to the food.'

As soon as Sheila left the room, Oscar said, 'It was your Mum's idea, obviously.' As if there was no earthly reason why he would ever have suggested it. 'She's trying–'

'I know,' Kate said fiercely before taking a deep breath. 'I know she's trying,' she repeated, forcing the words to come out softer the second time around. 'So am I, believe it or not. So fine. No alcohol.' She moved towards the hallway. 'And I'll try to be "me" but not too much "me".'

'Hey, how come you're in here?' Melody asked, poking her head through the door. 'I'm starving. Come on, Auntie Kate. I want you to sit next to me.'

Kate allowed herself to be dragged into the kitchen, where she stared at the simply laid table, with the old William Morris flowery placemats set out. 'We're not eating in the dining-room?' Without thinking, she sat down at her old place at the table and ran her finger over the faint indentations in the surface of the mat. Biro marks from when her mother had used to insist they did their homework on top of a protective surface – not the actual table, in case she ever needed to add it to the five in the dining room if she had extra guests.

'We sit in here because Gran says it's less formal.' Melody sat down next to her. 'And I sit here because this is where Mum used to sit.'

Kate shot a quick look to Oscar, but he simply shrugged as if to say he'd had way more awkward battles to fight. Her gaze went to her mum, who was busy filling a pitcher with water and appeared unfazed by Melody's simple remark, so Kate finally turned her attention back to Melody.

Love unfurled deep in her chest, spreading warmth to muscles and nerves cramped tense in a twisted brittle mess. The little girl's chatter was familiar. Easy. Sweet.

And blessedly uncomplicated.

Like a gift.

Trying not to feel too much for fear of emotion getting the best of her, Kate reached over and put the little white velvet box with a pink satin bow tied around it onto Melody's place-setting.

Melody looked at it and then with huge green eyes that were so like her father's stared up at Kate. 'What's this?'

'A gift. From me to you.'

Melody turned to look at her father, as if waiting for permission.

'Go ahead and open it,' he said and Kate hoped she was the only one who could tell his smile held a hint of trepidation.

Kate leaned forward in her seat, her hand sneaking up to clutch at her locket. What if Oscar would think she was trying to bribe his daughter or offer consolation for being an absent aunt?

Melody made short work of the bow and snapped open the jewellery box.

'Oh wow,' she gasped, reaching in excitedly to remove the necklace and hold it up to the light. 'I love it, I love it, I love it.'

'I'm so glad,' Kate whispered, determinedly swallowing back tears.

'Better say thank you, then,' Oscar firmly suggested to his daughter.

Melody leaned over and flung her arms around Kate's neck and squeezed. 'Thank you Auntie Kate. I'm going to wear it every day.'

'Or maybe at the weekends,' Oscar said. 'It looks far too expensive to wear to school.'

'Listen to your dad,' Kate said when Melody immediately pouted. 'Do you know what these represent?' she said, taking the simple silver chain and pointing to the three gemstone charms strung onto it. 'The dark red is a garnet – that's your dad's birthstone. The blue is a sapphire – that's your birthstone. And the pearl is–'

'Bea's birthstone,' Sheila whispered. At some point while Melody had been unwrapping the present, Sheila had picked up a serving plate filled with salad and now she stood, as if taking part in a mannequin challenge, at the head of the table.

'A pearl is for June?' Melody asked, looking at Kate for confirmation.

'Uh-huh,' Kate answered, praying her mother was going to unfreeze sometime that evening. Tearing her gaze from her mother she looked back at Melody.

'So it's like we're all together?' Melody asked, getting up from the table and holding the chain out to her father so that he could help her put it on.

'Uh-huh,' Kate said again. Unable to look at Oscar, unable to look at her mother, she pushed up from the table. 'Mum, you sit down. Let me dish up,' she mumbled and disappeared behind the island unit to pick up the platter of roast chicken that went with the salad.

'That means it's your birthstone too,' Melody said into the silence. 'So I have you on my necklace too, right?'

Kate's hands trembled as she laid the white oval china dish down in the centre of the table and turned to reach out for the one her mother was still holding.

'Of course it's my birthstone too,' Kate said, answering Melody but eyeing her mother warily. 'But the three on your necklace are just to represent you, your dad and your mum, okay?'

'Okay,' Melody answered, as if Kate's logic was faultless.

Sheila's brown eyes finally collided with Kate's and Kate hated herself because she could see the retreat in her eyes. In the set of her shoulders. In the angle she held her head.

'When I'm not wearing it, I can put it in the jewellery box you gave me, Gran.'

Sheila shook her head slightly and seemed to gather herself. 'Of course you can, darling.'

'Look, Aunt Kate – I have a photo of it on my phone. It's completely ill.'

'That means it's good,' Sheila said, with a pleased face, as she sat down.

Kate returned to the table, dutifully looked at the photo and tried to get onboard with her mother getting down with some slang. Somehow the knowledge wasn't nearly so difficult to cope with than the way her mother had successfully rallied at totally shutting down at the mention of Bea.

Later, as once again by tacit agreement the three adults let the child lead the conversation, Kate thought that she should have stayed – shouldn't have run. Not the first time, or any of those other times.

If she'd stayed she would now be in the same place the rest of her family was. That special place where the grass was greener and the sun shone brighter. Where answers to the mildest of questions weren't tempered, stilted and second-guessed.

The place where her mum could gently talk about Bea.

The place where Oscar let her.

If she had stayed she could have muddled through with them.

And maybe it would have got worse before it got better.

But wouldn't she rather be in Nirvana alongside them – able to remember Bea from a place of happiness and healing – instead of feeling like she was being ripped open. Her memories being dragged from her before she was ready as she scrambled to catch up with them all.

'What's for pudding, Gran?'

Kate was pulled from her reverie as Melody stacked her plate on top of Kate's and took them to the sink.

'Who says there's pudding?' Sheila asked, stacking her plate on top of Oscar's and getting up from the table as well.

Kate heard the teasing note in her mum's voice.

All she'd wanted for the longest time was for her mum to get better.

If she'd stayed... pushed it... made her put up with her presence, would she have broken through? Or was sweet Melody, the next generation, the only one who could have possibly snuck under her mother's stoicism and started the healing?

'There's *always* pudding,' Melody confided to her as she sat back down at the table.

Kate dragged in a breath. 'Well,' she said, picking up her spoon, determined to be in the moment and enjoy it. 'I, for one, certainly hope it's trifle!' She grinned with delight as Oscar, Melody and, yes, even Sheila, groaned.

Chapter 29

The Girl Next Door

Daniel

Daniel chucked his front door keys onto the hallway stairs and toed off his running shoes.

For the record, twenty-nine degrees celsius was too hot to be chasing a cow around the village. Next time Gertrude fancied a chomp on Cheryl Brown's prize-winning dahlias, he would calmly continue his run and then put into the kitty with the rest of the residents so that she could by some new ones.

Thank God Oscar had driven by when he had because chasing Gertrude back to the farm had rapidly turned into Gertrude thinking it the most fun ever to turn back on herself and set about chasing *him*. As he'd jumped into the van he swore he'd seen the bloody thing laughing at him. Oscar had definitely been laughing at him. No doubt by tomorrow it would be all over the village that Gertrude had tried recreating the Running of the Bulls from Pamplona with him. Knowing his luck, there'd be photographic evidence of the incident put on the *Whisperings* website.

At the sound of the doorbell, he sighed. Already halfway up the stairs and dreaming of standing under the shower spray, he debated simply ignoring it. Not that standing under the spray could be considered the technically correct term. This was a tiny cottage and the shower over the bath, although perfectly power-showered up by Oscar as part of kitting out the cottage properly for the rental market, was still fixed to the wall at a height that meant he had to duck a couple of feet to get his head wet.

He hadn't thought about the height of cottage ceilings when he'd signed the lease. He'd been too pleased about not once having second thoughts to get a place of his own here.

The doorbell rang again and he ambled down to answer it because it was too hot to rush.

He opened the door.

Speaking of hot...

Kate was dressed in another pair of ought-to-be-outlawed denim cut-offs, this time in white. By the time he managed to move his gaze up he saw that she'd teamed the shorts with a skimpy scarlet red vest top.

Was she trying to kill him?

Probably.

He definitely deserved payback for getting her locket fixed. His gaze sharpened when he saw the chain lying against her honey-toned skin. It had to be a good sign that she was wearing it again, right?

'Howdy neighbour,' she announced, beaming.

Neighbour?

She brought one of her hands from behind her back and

passed him a cup. 'I thought I'd return the cup of sugar I borrowed.'

Daniel frowned and contemplated the symptoms of heat-stroke. 'I didn't lend you any sugar.'

'And I stumbled across this humble pie sitting on the doorstep,' she said, bringing her other hand round from behind her back. 'So I figured I might as well bring that in too.'

Daniel stared down at the pie in her hand and then stared back up at her, the beginnings of a smile playing at the corners of his mouth. 'What kind of pie did you say that was, again?'

'Humble. As in...' and that was when her patience ran out and she sighed, 'Oh, for goodness sake, I'm here to apologise, now are you going to let me in or am I to melt in the heat? If it's option number two it's going to be you who will end up clearing up the mess.'

He wiped some sweat from his brow. 'You are, without doubt, the most–'

'Kindly, thoughtful neighbour a person could have,' she finished for him. 'I know.'

'So, I guess, come in, then?'

'Thank you.' She stepped over the threshold and Daniel inhaled the cloud of flowers and honey that floated over him like a gentle summer breeze. The scent was somehow sultry instead of sweet on her and it had him craving a long, cold drink.

He grabbed the pie and sugar from her and wandered through to his kitchen, assuming she'd follow him.

'So...' She stared at the pie as he placed it on the countertop. 'I'm going to need to work my way up to the apology proper.'

He looked at her and she smiled and waved her hand about. 'In other words,' she added, 'feel free to make neighbourly chit-chat with me first.'

'Right.' He opened his fridge and took out a carton of fruit juice, holding it up and raising his eyebrow in query.

'Mmmn. Thanks.'

He took down two glasses and filled them with juice. 'So... neighbourly? As in you're living?' he jerked his head to the side.

'Yep. Moved into Myrtle Cottage this morning. Do you know, when Bea and I were growing up we had a friend who used to live in this cottage. Turns out Myrtle Cottage is exactly the same layout. Oscar's company has done a really good job of modernising the kitchen and bathroom, although have you noticed the shower-head in your bathroom could do with being a bit higher? Mine hits me right in the—'

'Whoa,' Daniel croaked out around a mouthful of juice. He squeezed his eyes shut to aid the 'down boy' command he gave his imagination. Maybe her plan was simply to wait until she'd killed him before she offered her apology and that way he wouldn't actually hear it. 'I'm sorry, but I don't consider talking about showering, neighbourly, or chit-chat.'

'Oh. Okay. Um,' she glanced at him as though she could tell he'd been heading straight for the shower before opening the door to her. Her eyes darkened and he knew she was fighting making another comment about his running gear or showers or being all wet and he wondered what he'd say back to her if she did because this flirting that spilled into the atmosphere around them whenever they were together was beginning to feel as normal as breathing. But then the heat in her eyes was chased away, as if she'd remembered why she'd come round to visit. 'Shall we take these through to the lounge?' she asked, picking up her glass.

'Fine.' As he followed her out of the kitchen he forbade himself to look lower than at the very top of her head.

'You've been in, what, two weeks now,' she commented as she looked around. 'When does the rest of your stuff arrive?'

'I already went back and got everything.' He'd been dreading it. The grotty studio apartment testimony to where he'd ended up after the court case, but it had actually been cathartic organising for the few bits of furniture to be delivered before giving notice on the lease. And driving back in Monroe with a couple of bin liners of clothes, he'd felt like he was coming home.

'This is it?' Kate queried, scanning the room, nothing missing her attention. 'This is you?'

Daniel considered the frothy bit of juice at the top of his glass. 'I guess I travel light.' He glanced up and caught Kate's nod.

'Me too.'

That made sense. She'd spent years travelling from one job to the other. He guessed you quickly learned what was important and what was just excess baggage.

He looked around the lounge. Only the shortest end of his brown leather L-shaped sofa had fit and the only place it fit was under the window. He was using one of the other sections without its back as a makeshift coffee table and above the fireplace he'd fitted his small-by-most-standards forty-inch flat-screen TV.

'At least your TV suggests you're not compensating for anything,' Kate said with a smile as her gaze swept over it.

Daniel smiled and then fought and lost the need to explain his lack of furniture because it was important to him that she understood he didn't consider this move temporary. 'I rented a semi-furnished place in London, so I didn't have that much to bring with me.' He considered the juice left in his glass because there was explaining and then there was divulging that he'd sold most of his stuff when he'd sold the modern penthouse with views over the Thames in order to repay clients every single penny Hugo had stolen from them.

'I could give you a list of shops in the area where you could pick up a few good pieces.'

'Hey, I have the sofa and the TV, what more could I possibly need?'

She looked at a pile of paperbacks stacked precariously beside a battered cardboard box holding his phone, tablet and laptop chargers.

'To be fair, there's only really one more thing I think you need.'

'Yeah, what's that, then?'

She smiled. 'Storage.'

'Ah.' He tried not to be disappointed she wasn't saying the one thing he needed was her. 'I suppose I could do with a wardrobe to put my clothes in.'

'What are you using at the minute?'

'The bed.'

'What are you sleeping on?'

'The bed.'

Kate rolled her eyes and grinned. 'If you're using the bedroom at the back of the house, like I am, it's going to be hard to fit a wardrobe because of the sloping ceiling. If I was on better terms with Oscar I'd hassle him to make me a fitted wardrobe. As it is, I'm not, so I guess this is where I KonMari the hell out of the situation.'

'Con who?' Daniel asked, everything inside of him going still as his brain computed how likely it was that every single person on the planet was out to con the next person.

'You know – the Japanese art of folding clothes à la Marie Kondo?'

Oh. Okay. His internal organs started whirring back to life, his brain going into overdrive at the realisation that Whispers Wood had all but deleted his propensity for going into a new situation waiting for the con. He wasn't sure whether that was bad or good.

Looking at his hands, he held them out to Kate and said, 'I'm not sure these are built for origami. If I can't get a wardrobe to fit, I'm going to use a bin liner.'

'Yes, because nothing sounds more permanent than living out of a bin liner.'

She had a point. 'So have you unpacked yet?'

'Give me a chance. I only moved in this morning. But I will. Actually, I'm really looking forward to it. I've already made a list of what I need to buy.'

Her smile became soft and he found himself wanting to get her to smile like that at him. 'So you're going shopping at the first available opportunity?'

'Yep.'

'Great. We might as well go together.'

'I guess we could. Of course the person we should really take is Juliet, because her taste is outstanding.'

'Kate?'

'What?'

'No offence, but I don't want to go furniture shopping with the whole of the village.'

What he wanted was to spend the time getting to know her because no matter how much he tried shutting down the awareness between them, and no matter how often she said something that brought him smack-bang up against his issues, he was drawn to her like a moth to a flame. He knew it was bad. Knew he was competing against her for something he had every intention of winning, but now she was living next door to him and he knew which bedroom she would be sleeping in and, yeah, his good intentions to protect himself – protect her – kept flying right out the window. 'I trust your judgement, okay?'

Kate looked at him as if some days she didn't even trust herself to get out of bed, but she nodded and then she undid him completely with her quietly intense and sincere, 'I really am incredibly sorry about the way I reacted the other night.'

'That's okay.'

'No, actually. It isn't. I behaved appallingly.'

'You had every right to react the way you did.'

She glanced down at the locket, brought her hand up to stroke her fingers over the metal. 'I should have had this repaired a long time ago. I'm not sure why I didn't. It was–'

she shrugged her shoulders, as if helpless to come up with an answer. 'I don't know what it was.'

'It was that you weren't ready,' he replied simply. 'I took that choice away from you and for that, I'm deeply sorry.'

'No lasting damage,' she said shyly.

'I'm glad.'

'I should congratulate you on winning the vote.'

'Thank you, but you know you didn't lose by that big a margin.'

She nodded. 'Aunt Cheryl gave me the details. Your theme really is a great idea – you deserved to win.'

'I thought yours was good, too. I know you said you wanted in on the organising. Is that something you still want?'

She grinned. 'Bitten off more than you can chew?'

'Oh, trust me I can handle myself when it comes to work-load.'

'Yeah? I can handle a list or two if you want to throw some work my way.'

'Okay. Did you want a piece of pie?'

'Would love a slice, but I can't. I have to start getting ready for tonight. Are you coming along?'

'Absolutely. Great idea, by the way.' Credit where credit was due, his football tournament and fun-run had brought in a lot of money, but he had a feeling her latest fundraiser was going to knock his two out of the park.

'Thanks. I wrote a piece on a hotel that used to put on outdoor movie and barbecue nights in the summer. I rang the manager and explained what I wanted and not only did he lend me all the equipment, he's going to show me how to set it all up. That's why I need to be available.' She hesitated and then added, 'Otherwise I could definitely do pie. With you.'

'We'll do it another time.'

She looked at him as if she too didn't know what to make of the fact that all the time they were being nice to each other and making arrangements to spend time together the competition between them felt like it was slowly being eroded away.

'Okay. Another time, then,' she replied and walked back into his kitchen to set her glass down next to the pie. She turned around before he was prepared and slammed into him.

'Oops,' she whispered, her hands landing on his chest. 'I should be more careful.'

'I don't mind.' At his words he felt her hands move restlessly against his chest and creep higher towards his shoulders.

At the top of his shoulders they squeezed and a groan rumbled through his chest. He managed to stop it before he voiced it, but he suspected she was aware that their accidental embrace might not be considered so accidental and carefully she stepped away from him.

With a delicate clearing of her throat, she glanced up at him and said, 'Well, thank you for accepting my apology. Very neighbourly of you. I'll, um, see you tonight. Don't forget to bring what you want to eat for the picnic part.'

'Will do. See you later, then.'

'Yep.'

'Great.'

In the confined space of the kitchen she managed not to touch him as she stepped around him.

''Bye then,' he told her, as she reached the front door.

''Bye.'

He watched as she opened the door and walked out and when, at the very last moment, she turned to wave to him, she bumped into the little wrought-iron gate and called herself an idiot, and he couldn't help it, the grin slipped out and spread across his face in delight.

He shut the door and bounded up the stairs for a cold shower.

Chapter 30

Life Isn't Like in the Movies

Oscar

Oscar watched Melody swing the picnic basket back and forth as she hopped ahead of him on the walk from the barn to the village green.

'It was great seeing Auntie Kate at dinner last night, wasn't it, Dad?'

Oscar offered a non-committal, 'Mmmn,' and thought about how he really owed Kate a conversation.

Family dinner hadn't been the right time, but maybe he'd be able to find her later.

'And Gran didn't have a heart attack or anything when she accidentally swore.'

'Why are you so certain it was accidental,' he asked, without thinking.

Melody thought for a moment. 'Because she's different when she's around Gran. You know, quieter and, like, more reserved and stuff.'

My daughter, the observationist, he thought, suddenly seeing all the other times Kate and Sheila had been in the same room after Bea had died and realising that Melody was right.

So maybe the conversation needed to be more of an apology. She'd tried so hard to cover her apprehension at dinner, but it had only made him super-aware of just how long it must have been since she'd been around family.

'Tonight's going to be great, isn't it? Are you excited about watching the film?' Melody asked, hopping to her next subject as efficiently as she hopped down the lane.

'Sure,' he answered easily.

'Really?' she spun around and walked backwards so she could read his expression. 'You're really excited to be watching *Finding Nemo*?'

'Wait. *Finding Nemo*?' He turned left then right as if he couldn't work out where he was or why he was where he was. 'Who's Nemo?' he said, in his best Dory impression. 'I thought we were watching *The Godfather*?'

Melody giggled. 'As if you'd let me watch *The Godfather*.'

'One day, sweet pea, one day.'

'Dad? Do you think Kate's going to stay this time?'

'Maybe.' Although life wasn't like it was in the movies, and even though he knew Melody already knew that subconsciously, he shouldn't ever think that just because she'd lost her mother at such a young age, she was prepared for everything life could throw at you. 'Melody, you know, you can't always hold onto people if that's not what they want. Sometimes you have to give them the space to choose to stay. So we mustn't crowd Kate, okay?'

'But how will she know we want her to stay if we don't tell her?'

'Sometimes it's more important not to pressure a person.'

'Okay. But I really hope she chooses to stay. Hey, it looks as if everyone got here before us.' Melody tugged on his hand as she stepped onto the green. 'Come on, or we'll never find a good spot.'

The open-air cinema experience tonight was the latest of Kate's fundraising events and Oscar had to admit it was a brilliant idea. It looked like the entire village had turned out to spend the evening together. In fact, squinting against the fading light, Oscar could see that more than a few people from Whispers Ford were in attendance tonight as well.

He assumed Kate was somewhere around making sure everything was working to plan, but he hoped he'd get the chance to talk to her.

In all honesty, it had torn him up inside to see her reaction when Daniel had given her back the locket. At first he couldn't understand why she'd never had it repaired, but then it had begun to dawn on him.

He could still remember the helplessness he'd felt when the only thing she'd asked to have of Bea's was her locket. She could have asked for pretty much anything else and he'd have made sure she got it, but it had never occurred to him she'd ask for something from the clear plastic envelope he'd had to sign for at the hospital. He'd given the locket to Bea for her twenty-first birthday and she'd never taken it off. From Kate's reaction when Daniel had given it back to her repaired, she obviously hadn't taken it from around her own neck since he'd handed it over four years ago.

'Oh, there's Persephone,' Melody squealed, spotting her near where the huge projector screen had been set up. 'Can I go and sit with her, Dad. Please?'

Oscar wondered if Melody was aware that she was clutching the new necklace that Kate had given her in exactly the same way he'd seen Kate clutch Bea's locket at dinner last night.

He looked over to where Melody had pointed and saw Gloria taking out plastic punnets of food from the local supermarket. She was lining them up next to paper plates and plastic knives and forks, but he didn't have a hankering for processed food, plastic and Gloria. He had a hankering for homemade, real, and... Juliet.

Oscar tripped over someone's trailing leg and mumbled an apology.

Surprise, closely followed by guilt for letting the thought slide in, zinged through him.

Obviously he didn't *want*, want Juliet.

And yet... damn it to hell because he'd hardly been able to think about anything else since that teeny-tiny yellow bikini-wearing incident.

'So can I, Dad?'

'Can you what?'

'Sit with, Persephone?'

'You don't want to sit with Juliet?' he asked, and could have kicked himself. Could he not get her out of his mind for even five seconds?

'We just saw her yesterday, Dad.'

True.

They'd stopped off in Big Kev's after dinner at Sheila's so that they could pick up some treats for the picnic and had bumped into her paying for a bottle of wine and a box of chocolates.

Polite.

That's what they'd been with each other. So polite that Melody had asked what was up with the two of them. Juliet had gently assured her that nothing was amiss and that she was just tired and looking forward to her evening at home researching new hairstyles. Then, she'd smiled weakly at Oscar and hurried out of the shop.

'You know you only saw Perse a few hours ago at school,' he told his daughter.

'Yes, but we have things to discuss.'

'Evening Oscar,' Crispin said from next to them. 'Hello, Melody.'

'Hi Mr Harlow,' Melody answered, 'Wow, I like your table.'

Oscar looked at the crystal glasses in Crispin's hands and then his gaze strayed to the linen tablecloth over the dining table. 'Evening, Crispin. Going all out, I see. Where's Mrs Harlow?'

'Oh, she's nipped back home. Can you believe we forgot the taramasalata?'

'Right. Because what's a little *Finding Nemo* without the fish roe.'

Crispin nodded, clearly not seeing the irony and beside him Melody was now speaking into her phone telling Persephone that she was 'working on it'. Unsure he wanted to know what 'working on it' meant, he nevertheless couldn't ignore the parental radar pinging to alert.

'We'd better go and find a spot to sit down,' he told

Crispin. 'Have a great evening and say 'Hi' to Mrs Harlow from us.'

Crispin waved an acknowledgement as Oscar and Melody picked their way across the green. When it became impossible to find a decent pocket of space for the two of them he told Melody, 'Okay you can go and sit with Perse and Mrs Pavey. Take the basket with you.'

'But I meant for you to come and sit too.'

For an awful moment Oscar got the feeling his daughter and Persephone were colluding on getting their respective parents together and there was just no way he had time for that amount of 'awkward' in his life.

'Sorry sweet-pea. I promised Kate I'd check if she needed extra help.'

'But what if she doesn't? You can't sit on your own. Oh – why don't *you* go and sit with Juliet?'

Out of the mouths of eight-year-olds... At least she wasn't going on about him spending the evening with Gloria.

'You promise me you'll stick with Perse and Mrs Pavey, okay?'

'Promise.'

'You have credit on your phone?'

'Yes, Dad.'

'No wandering off on your own. You want to go to the toilet, you do the girly couples thing and go with Perse, okay?'

'Yes, Dad.'

'And no talking to strangers.'

'Dad, it's Whispers Wood. There are no strangers.'

'If you're going to get sarky then I'm going to re-think...'

'Okay, I promise. No talking to strangers. No wandering off on my own. If I need you I'll phone or text you. And if I can't get hold of you I'll try Kate or Juliet.'

'Good girl.' Whispers Wood was a good place to grow up in but it was also a small place to grow up in. If he didn't at least remind her of the big wide world, he'd be remiss. It was hard enough feeling like at any moment she'd be wanting to catch the bus to go shopping in town with her friends or to meet dates and he was going to have to let her. He shuddered and prayed for a little more time before he had to start worrying about that. 'Evening, Gloria, is it all right if Melody joins you for the picnic and movie?'

'Of course.'

Gloria might have the ability to be a complete bitch, but there was no doubting how much she loved her little girl and she was always generous and welcoming to Melody. 'Here,' she said, shuffling along the blanket she'd spread out, 'there's plenty of room for you too.'

Whether it was fate but Kate chose that exact moment to walk past.

'I'm sorry, Gloria, I promised I'd help Kate set up. Melody, I'll meet you back here before the end of the film, okay?'

'Okay Dad, say thank you to Kate for the necklace again for me.'

In his daughter's eyes, Kate could never do any wrong and maybe he should examine why she felt so at ease to believe that. After Juliet's words the other day, he must admit he'd been starting to examine why he'd always found it so easy to believe she would. And after seeing her at dinner last night, maybe her always choosing to leave hadn't been a case of 'like father like daughter' after all.

'Kate, wait up, are you free to talk?'

'Talk?'

He supposed he deserved her incredulous look. 'I know you're probably up to your neck in things to do. I figured I could help and we could talk at the same time.'

'But don't you work for the other side?'

'I come in peace, I promise.'

'Um. Okay.'

'Great. So what do you need doing?'

'To be honest, I was about to take a break. We can't put the film on until it gets much darker or the definition will get screwy. Everyone looks like they're happy starting their picnics.'

'This is a really great idea, Kate. You've done a fantastic job.'

'Thank you. Daniel's a tough act to follow, but at least my previous work experience came in useful for this one.'

Oscar nodded thoughtfully. 'Melody has hardly stopped talking about all the places her aunt has visited.'

'Oh, I'm sorry. I should have thought – I guess I really rambled on last night, didn't I?'

'You did fine.'

'And to think I was just being me,' she teased nervously.

He bit back the retort that she'd be more practised at family dinners if she'd chosen to stick around and instead thought about what Juliet had said about Kate only needing to look in the mirror to be reminded of what had happened. Why on earth had that never occurred to him? Too lost in his own grief, he supposed. Definitely too quick to see her as an easy target for all his anger about Bea dying.

'I thought the dinner went really well, actually,' he ventured and felt her turn her head at him in surprise before she looked straight ahead again.

'Me too. Even if I am hoping it'll get easier. If I'm invited again, of course.'

She said it with amusement, but he knew if it was him he wouldn't be laughing at having to wait for permission to have dinner with them. Shoving his hands into his pockets, he looked around him. Without either of them being aware of it, they'd walked around the back of The Clock House towards the beehives. He hesitated and then sat on the bench he had built a couple of years ago.

'Thank you for the necklace you gave Melody,' he said. 'It was really thoughtful.'

Kate sat down and said quietly, 'I had always intended at some point to give Melody Bea's locket. It should go to her, rightfully. Bea was her mother and... But then I thought that you might think I was trying to manipulate my relationship with her.'

He sighed. 'You don't ever have to give Melody the locket, Kate. I consider it yours. How are you feeling now? About Daniel getting it fixed, I mean?'

'I'm okay. Getting used to it. It's different now, but then I guess everything is.'

'Yes.' Except for this place, he thought, as he gazed out over the meadow grass, where even though he couldn't see them in the fading light, he knew the wild flowers were, their petals closed up tight for the night. 'It's okay that you wear it, Kate. Okay that you need that link to Bea. I have Melody, so...'

'I know. She's the best link to Bea, isn't she?'

He nodded and then shoved his hands through his hair, as if that would help him feel his way through their conversation. 'I feel really terrible that I never thought about how hard it would be for you being around here after she died. There's no excuse.'

'Actually, there is. Grief is such a, I don't know, a displacement, I suppose. Like we all got picked up and thrown onto separate life-rafts and we all bobbed along in the ocean, on the same journey, but separate.'

Oscar picked a long blade of grass and rolled it between his fingers. 'Juliet said something to me, and well, in case she was bang on the money, which she kind of has an annoying habit of being, I need you to know that never once did I, or do I, look at you and *only* see Bea.'

She turned her head to look at him. 'Really?' she whispered.

'Really, and while I get why some people would – especially your mum – you have to know it was different for me. Bea was–'

'Your boo.'

'Huh?'

'You know, your bae.'

'What the hell is a bae?'

'Bea was your boo, your bae, your Bea.'

'God, you're going to be teaching my daughter all kinds of weird urban shit aren't you?'

'Affirmative,' she grinned.

He hesitated and his voice was sombre as he asked, 'Do you look at you and see only Bea?'

She turned away from him to stare out into the distance and he wondered if he'd taken them too far too soon.

'The first time I left I dyed my hair fire-engine red,' she suddenly confessed. 'I didn't look in the mirror for months and when I caught reflections of myself it was always a shock. I'd wonder who this person was staring back. For a while being shocked was better.'

'And then?'

She pushed out a breath. 'And then I'd come back home and it would be the same, or I guess I would *feel* the same and no one acted like it was ever going to be any different.'

'You always looked the same when you came back.'

'I know. I would dye it back. I should have got it all cut off but–' she threw her hands up in the air and shuddered.

'Ha,' he said immediately remembering. 'When Cheryl gave Bea that bob.'

'Exactly. Who knew we perpetually tipped our heads to the side, like that?'

Oscar grinned. Bea's bob had got shorter and shorter the more Cheryl had tried to even it out. 'She didn't speak to me for two days because I laughed when I saw her.'

'Only two days? She didn't speak to me for two weeks because I refused to get mine cut the same.'

'Two weeks? Wow, she didn't mention that.'

'And how could she have when she wasn't speaking to you. Although let me tell you that two days is nothing.'

'Well, I suspect I had different ways of getting around her.'

There was a short, shocked silence and then they both burst out laughing.

It was probably the first time they'd laughed together and shared a memory of Bea. And when he thought he heard Bea's gentle laugh in his ear he moved his hand up to ease the ache in his heart.

'So I hear you've moved into Myrtle Cottage?'

'Yes. I told you I was back to stay.'

He was silent a moment and then asked, 'Can you promise me something?'

'I'll try.'

He guessed that was a good enough start. 'Can you please come to me and tell me if you're thinking about leaving again?'

She looked upset that he thought she might still go and maybe he'd been wrong again to ask for that because maybe she wasn't like her dad after all. However he had to protect Melody and he knew if she wanted to go he wouldn't stop her, but he might at least try to find a way for her to stay.

As if Kate decided it was better to choose your battles, she simply answered, 'Okay.'

'Thank you. And something else... I actually think Daniel would understand if I pulled away from being his official helper.'

'No way. It's enough we're going to try understanding each other a bit more. That is what we're trying to do here, isn't it?'

'It is.'

'No deserting Daniel, then,' she said. 'Hey, since you've been

303

here and I haven't... Are my mother and Big Kev having a...'
She brought her hands up to hide her face. 'Oh my God, I
can't even say it.'

Oscar chuckled. 'A dalliance?'

She brought her hands down. 'Yes. Okay. Dalliance. I think
I can cope with that description.'

'It began after she started getting better, but I don't think
she's ready to admit it.'

'So if it wasn't Big Kev, what made her improve like she
has?'

'I think it was just time.'

Kate nodded. 'Time.' Her hand brushed over the locket.
'Oscar, do you ever think about having a dalliance with
someone?'

'What?' The question threw him completely off-guard. And
the fact that the first person who popped into his head was
Juliet had him breaking out in a sweat. Here they were having
their first civilised conversation, both warm from their memories of Bea, and suddenly he was picturing Juliet.

'Quid pro quo time. I promised I'd speak to you first if I
thought about leaving. Your turn to promise me something.'

He really didn't feel comfortable with that, but he supposed
it was fair. 'I'll try,' he repeated her words back to her.

'It's been four years, Oscar. You shouldn't feel any guilt
about the prospect of moving on.'

He inhaled. 'I don't feel guilty.'

'Really? Because that's not what Juliet thinks.'

Chapter 31

By The Light of the Silvery Moon

Oscar

To the sounds of *Finding Nemo* blaring out across the village green, Oscar searched the crowd for Juliet. Not because of what Kate had said. More because... okay, it was a more solid excuse to base his search on than merely the need to seek her out.

Citronella lanterns had been placed at intervals and everyone in the village who owned solar-powered garden lights had been asked to bring them to line the edge of the green. As he searched for Juliet, he thought about how romantic the place looked and then stopped in his tracks because what the hell was he doing thinking something looked romantic? This was a family event. He swapped the word for 'magical' and that's when he saw her.

She was sitting on her own, candlelight teasing out the gold highlights in her red hair. She'd thrown a wrap in silvery grey casually around her shoulders.

By the time he reached her he was grinning from ear to ear because he'd worked out why her bowed head was illuminated.

'Juliet Brown are you literally reading by candlelight?'

She started and even in the soft light he could tell he'd made her blush.

'Ssh,' she said. 'No talking at the cinema.'

'What are you reading?' he asked, squatting down beside her.

'If I tell you, will you go away and leave me in peace?'

'Probably not,' he grinned.

'I'm reading next year's fashion trends. I couldn't not come and support Kate's event tonight, but this is the only chance I've had to get ahead of myself in weeks.'

'And what's going to be hot next year?' he asked, settling himself down next to her.

Her blue eyes shot daggers. 'I have a feeling mullets are coming back.'

'Yeah?' he ran a hand through his short hair. 'I look forward to putting myself in your hands. Or should I say scissors?'

'You've had the same style for years and I don't remember inviting you to sit down,' she grumbled as he sat down beside her, stretching his legs out in front of him.

'I took the decision for both of us.' He immediately felt the air thicken between them.

'Do you think that I like that sort of talk or something?'

'Yes.'

Her eyes got huge and her shocked 'What?' came out decidedly breathy.

'Yes, I think you like it,' he declared, his heart beating faster.

'Well, you're completely mistaken.' She looked down and he noticed her fingers clenching in her lap.

'Juliet, I was teasing. I'm sorry.' He hated thinking he'd made her uncomfortable. This is why he needed to work on his reactions to her. He was going to curb the flirting and the need to touch her if it killed him.

Juliet sighed and closed down her tablet. 'Shouldn't you be watching the film with Melody?'

'Please don't make me go over there, she's sitting with Persephone and Gloria.'

'Ah.'

Oscar caught the small smile she gave before she lowered her face to hide behind the slide of her hair. Completely forgetting his rule not to touch her, he reached out and tucked her hair back behind her ear. 'What's that smile for?'

'Nothing. I just heard that Gloria had been hanging around the school gates and searching a certain someone out recently.'

He lowered his hand and frowned. 'Who did you hear that from?'

'Mum, of course. She got it from Trudie's daughter, I think.'

'The herbalist from Horsham? But she doesn't even live around here. How did she hear?'

'So it's true, then?'

'No.' He winced. 'Maybe.'

'And you're not interested?'

'Please. It's Gloria.'

'Too close to home?'

If she wanted to hear about too close to home he should tell her about how when Sheila had talked about asking someone to family dinner his first instinct had been to ask her, before he'd realised Sheila was talking about asking Kate.

'No, it's not about being too close to home. It's about being Gloria,' he repeated and after looking at him for what felt like an eternity, she dropped her gaze and he breathed again. 'Hey, did you know Crispin is somewhere around here eating taramasalata?' he asked, bringing one knee up to rest his elbow on.

'Of course. Because what's watching *Finding Nemo* without a little fish roe?'

Oscar grinned. 'That's exactly what I told him.'

Juliet grinned back. 'Let me guess. He didn't get it?'

'Nope. I guess I shouldn't,' he nudged her, 'bait him.'

'That's terrible.'

'You got it and I got it, though. What do you think that means?'

'We both have a really stupid sense of humour?'

'Either that or you've been hanging out with me too long.'

'If you have a problem with that it can be rectified.'

'No. I don't. In case you haven't noticed, I've been trying to get you to hang out with me more.'

'Oscar, I already accepted your apology the other day. You don't have anything to make up for.'

He nodded and watched the film a little before getting around to asking, 'Are you lonely now Kate's moved out?'

She looked at him strangely. 'I was living on my own before Kate came home and I was perfectly fine.'

Was she, though? She did so much for everyone else... Spent most of her days listening to other people's problems as part of her job, which actually, he realised, she used as a good way of deflecting when she didn't want attention turned on her.

'I guess I'm wondering who hears your dreams, who listens to you at the end of a long day?'

'What on earth has got into you?'

'Nothing. I've been working through some stuff with Kate and it got me thinking.'

'But that's great,' she exclaimed, leaning towards him and clasping hold of his hand to squeeze. 'Oh, I'm so happy.'

'Are you?' His fingers tangled with hers as he stared into her pretty blue eyes and although it was dark under the midnight-blue sky, he thought he could see clouds forming. 'Before Kate came back, who listened to you, *really* listened to you?'

She blinked. 'You did. We talk. It's not only one-way, okay? Stop feeling guilty.'

What wasn't only one-way?

His gaze slid over her.

What would happen if he broke every rule in the book and leaned forward to press his lips against Juliet Brown's? He leaned a little closer to her, dropping his gaze to focus on her mouth. Her lips.

They'd be soft and giving.

'Dad?'

And maybe wild and a little wanton against his.

'Oscar.'

He watched her lips form his name and couldn't look away. Yeah, definitely a little wild.

'*Dad.*'

His daughter's voice finally broke into his consciousness and he sprang away from Juliet and shot to his feet. 'Melody?'

'We're not interrupting anything are we?' Gloria said, looking interestedly at the pair of them.

'Absolutely not,' Juliet muttered, hurriedly gathering up her things and standing up. 'We were just coming to look for you, weren't we, Oscar.'

'Yes. That's exactly what we were about to do.'

Chapter 32
Nocturnal Habits

Kate

Kate opened the back door and stepped out into the sweet summer's night. She was exhausted. But happy-exhausted, she acknowledged, stretching muscles aching from hours hunched over the table she'd set up in the spare room.

Her lab, she'd affectionately labelled the space when she'd finished setting the room out like a production line, complete with pots and jars with labels she'd designed herself.

Oscar had given her honey from the beehives and after testing Bea's recipes for the past two weeks, she'd spent today making up bottles of shampoo and conditioners and filling pots with body-scrubs and moisturisers. She was going to ask Daniel if she could book a stall at the fete and sell them.

Her gaze strayed to the waist-height stone wall separating both gardens. Disappointment washed over her when she realised he wasn't already out here, waiting for her.

She'd become ever so slightly addicted to their nocturnal meetings.

They'd started the night of the cinema fundraiser. She'd

been too excited to sleep when she'd got back, so she'd stolen outside to have herself a relaxing look at the stars before turning in.

Daniel had been in his garden doing the same and the next thing she knew he'd been nipping back into his kitchen and coming back out with two plates of pie. They'd chatted while eating. Talking quietly about inconsequential things as the magic of the night had wrapped itself around them. By the time she'd gone back inside it had been to the loveliest sleep she'd had in a long time.

The next day she'd told herself she'd slept well because the fundraiser had gone so well and because she and Oscar and she and her mum were taking the time to work out some of the tangles between them.

But deep down she knew it was because she'd spent some time under a blanket of stars, talking to a man who made her forget they were competing against each other.

Every night since, they'd ended up in the same space, at the same time, chatting over the garden wall before turning in for the night.

Opening her locket, she saw that it was only slightly before ten o' clock, so it was still early. She could smell moisture in the air. It hadn't rained for weeks and although she knew the gardens could do with a soaking, she made a bargain with nature that she'd work extra hard and eat healthier if the rain held off so that she and Daniel could have their time together.

With the dry grass tickling her bare feet, she hopped over to the pretty white wrought-iron café table and chairs her mother had brought over as a house-warming present. Pulling out the chair that faced the house, she moved it so that it was ever so slightly closer to the wall and sat down. A second later and she was up again, positioning the other chair so that she could prop her feet up.

In the light spilling out from her kitchen she contemplated the 'Rumba Red' nail varnish on her toes. She supposed she could pop back inside and grab her pad and pen and start adding all the things that kept popping into her head about the spa. It was crazy that she kept adding to the list instead of ticking things off. Even crazier that she wasn't panicking like mad about that. But being home and easing back into the pace of country living felt so right that worrying seemed silly.

Home.

She was trying so hard not to think too far ahead and scare herself with scenarios where she didn't win The Clock House because she was truly starting to feel as if she'd finally unpacked some of the rocks she'd been carrying around.

The lights in Mistletoe Cottage suddenly flicked on and Kate's heart did a triple back-flip before sliding back into position, where it started its pulsing beat for him.

Moments later the back door opened and out he stepped.

'Hey,' he said, 'finally saw a YouTube video on that KonMari stuff. Life is definitely too short, so are you up for that shopping trip tomorrow?'

'And good evening to you too, Daniel.'

He smiled. 'I like that we simply start our conversations. It's very–'

'Gilmore Girls?'

Daniel sighed. 'Who? I'm going to have to go back to YouTube aren't I?'

'Hang on, I'll nip back inside for my Pop-Culture stick. One good whack from that and you'll be good to go again.'

'Can you grab something to drink while you're getting it?'

'Absolutely. Oh, that reminds me,' she said getting up. 'I actually do have something for you to drink.'

She scurried inside to the kitchen and opened up her fridge. Diving in to the cold air, telling herself she was only hot because of the temperature outside and not because of how Daniel looked at her, she retrieved the bottle of IPA beer and took it out for him.

'You mentioned this was your favourite the other night and after the whole eye-crossing, staggering-about, off-your-face incident after only a couple of sips of one of my honey martinis, I thought you'd better stick to this.'

She passed him over the beer and watched as he took it and inspected it. 'You found me a bottle of Red Flag?' His grin was huge as he hurriedly twisted the lid off, lifted the bottle to his lips and took a healthy swig.

He groaned with delight as if it had just kissed his throat and as Kate watched his Adam's apple bob up and down she felt her own mouth go dry.

'You didn't get one for yourself?' he asked.

She shook her head and he offered the beer for her to taste. Without stopping to think, she reached forward, wrapped her hand around his and slowly brought the bottle to her lips. Gently he tipped some beer into her mouth so that the hoppy liquid could slip down her throat.

'What do you think?' he whispered, staring at her mouth, his eyes turning obsidian.

She swallowed and smiled, releasing his hand. 'I think the only thing I like about it is that it has a name that sounds like a nail varnish. Actually I'm wondering if it could strip nail varnish.'

'Philistine.'

'Ha. Says the man who seems to actively steer clear of culture.'

'Pop culture is different.'

'Do you even watch the news?'

'Yes, I watch the news. But I steer clear of all that tabloid and gossip crap.'

'Why is that?'

'Because I'm a man?'

Sensing a story, she added, 'Even Crispin knows who the Kardashians are.'

'I suspect even salmon-fishers in the Yemen know who the Kardashians are.' He cocked a hip against the wall and stared down into his beer for a few moments. 'I was really busy for years. I didn't do free time. I just did work.'

'No relationships?'

'Okay. I did relationships.' He looked up, his smile loaded as he confessed, 'Well, not relationships, exactly.'

'Wow. So you do realise a relationship is more than swiping right.'

'You must know what it's like dating in London.'

'I'm thinking it's the same as anywhere else.'

'So what about you? Any long-term relationships?'

'A few.' She bit her lip and thought about Marco. 'One, and while we're being so open and honest, I guess it was more of an on-off relationship.'

He searched her face. 'It must be hard to keep something going when you're travelling so much.'

'You know what?' She ran her finger over some of the daisies spilling from the cracks in the stone wall. 'It was easier. We both travelled. Which meant the time we did get to spend together was...'

He nodded. 'About one thing and one thing only.'

'Yep.' She stopped stroking the daisies and, forcing herself not to fidget, placed her hands on top of the stone wall.

'Keeps things clear and simple.' His hand crept towards hers. 'But then you wanted to move it into being about more than one thing and it turned out he didn't want to?'

'No, the other way around. Except it turned out he wanted to turn it into something more with someone else.'

'Was he an idiot?'

He looked proper shocked and her heart kept right on doing that pulsing, beating thing for him. 'It's lovely of you to think so, but he helpfully explained that I wasn't enough.'

'Dick,' Daniel said, low and disgusted. 'I can't imagine you not being enough, Kate.'

She lifted her hand and wagged a finger at him. 'You didn't know me then.' Although maybe no one had. Ever since she'd had the meltdown in front of half the village, people had started taking the time to ask how she was. Was it really that all she'd had to do was show a little vulnerability for people to want to move past the small talk and get real? Was getting real what Marco had thought she'd never be able to do? 'Either way, I wasn't even given the chance to become more.'

'So you're nursing a broken heart.'

'Not at all.' She felt the top of her nose wrinkle as she confessed, 'Although I was nursing a wounded ego for a bit. And you? You never wanted to turn some of that casual dating into something more?'

'I think I assumed I'd get around to it. I went to work every day, brought work home with me every night. And when I wasn't working I was running.'

'From what?'

He shook his head at her. 'Do I have to explain the running gear again? I run.'

'Yes, but from what? Apart from cows, that is.'

'God, who told you about that?'

'Please. This is a village. My point is no one wakes up one day and thinks: I think I'll get into running. They run to get fit. They run to compete. They run to be on their own and think. They run to get away from something. Are you running from something, Daniel?'

'Not really.' He paused. 'Maybe.'

'You didn't enjoy your work? What did you do anyway?'

'I was partner in a small firm of accountants.'

'You're an accountant? Wow. So didn't picture that.'

'Why not?'

Yeah, why not? She realised if it wasn't for these nocturnal habits of theirs she'd still know next to nothing about him.

'I guess I assumed you were expanding on what you already had – a co-working franchise.'

'Who knows, one day I might really have a franchise.'

'You're a regular accountant? Not in an Affleck way?'

'Not even remotely.'

'I wouldn't have thought there's much room to be creative in that field.'

'Oh, you'd be surprised.'

'Huh?'

'Sorry, I said, you seem really surprised. Don't see me as a facts-and-figures man?'

She stared at him thoughtfully. 'Maybe. What made you leave?'

'Didn't have a choice. It no longer exists.'

'Oh. Well, I guess that's some catalyst for ending up here.'

'I've been thanking the catalyst gods ever since.'

'So we're both moving into fields we have no experience in.'

'Must be something to do with this place.'

'Or we're both wildly impulsive risk-takers.'

'Mmmn.' He moved so that he was leaning over the wall more. 'You want to take a risk right now?'

'With you?' She couldn't have torn her gaze from his if her life depended on it.

He reached out and slid his hand into the hair at her nape. 'Absolutely with me,' he whispered, his thumb stroking across her cheekbone. He inched closer, pulling her in with the look in his eyes until his head was blocking out the large opal disc in the sky and the world was reduced to him and her. Daniel and Kate. Two semi-friends. Two definite rivals. Standing in the darkness of the countryside, oblivious to everything bar the need to take a risk and sink into each other.

'You smell of honey,' he told her, his voice gruff and full of awareness that made her heart pound and her insides dance.

'It's my shampoo.'

'It's you. It's like nectar.'

'Daniel? What are we doing?' she whispered, needing verification somehow that this wasn't premeditated. That this wasn't about The Clock House. She wanted Daniel's kiss so much her lips were tingling and she thought about Marco telling her she didn't give enough and she thought with Daniel it would be so easy to give more. Maybe even the most.

'We could call it being neighbourly.'

'Or too risky.' Because what if the risk had fallout she hadn't even thought about?

She didn't realise she'd pulled away until she felt Daniel's sigh against her skin and then felt him press a gentle kiss to her forehead before stepping back.

'I'm sorry,' he murmured. 'I really enjoy our chats and I don't want to complicate or jeopardise this.'

She licked her lips as if she'd be able to savour his breath on them and at least have that. 'We both have other things to concentrate on at the minute. We'd be stupid to lose sight of that so close to the finishing line.'

'Maybe when the race is over…'

'Maybe.' Although then there'd be a winner and a loser and wouldn't it be even more complicated?

Sadness washed over her because she still had every intention of winning The Clock House and after the open-air cinema event she was fairly sure she was ahead of him. But if she was truly ahead of him in the fundraising stakes, if she was the winner of The Clock House, then what would he do? Would he leave right away?

He was where she had been before this summer, she realised. Footloose and fancy free. Able to pick up and go at a moment's notice. There wouldn't be anything to hold him here if she won.

'Shopping tomorrow, though?' he asked quietly.

'Sure. I'd better go in and get my beauty sleep.'

'From where I'm standing, you don't need it. But okay.'

''Night Daniel.'

'Kate?'

'Uh-huh?' She turned back. She'd never regretted being sensible so much in her life.

Daniel hesitated and then smiled. 'Nothing. Thanks for the beer.'

Chapter 33
Money, Money, Money – It's So Funny...

Daniel

'I thought the world's most expensive place to shop was 5th Avenue. Turns out it's an out-of-town shopping outlet in a barn.' Daniel stared at the price tag attached to the pile of wood that appeared to have pictures of animals stuck all over it.

'It's not that bad. Besides, this is an investment piece,' replied Kate.

'You consider this... what is this, anyway?'

'It's a coat-stand of course.'

'Of course,' he said, looking agog at her.

'Okay, maybe it's not an investment but it is rather pretty, so I might have to buy it. Now *this*,' she said, forgetting all about the coat-stand and moving to a chest of drawers. 'Is definitely a statement piece. Isn't it gorgeous?'

Daniel looked at the piece of furniture in question. It was painted grey and all the handles were made out of glass that looked as if they'd shatter if you so much as touched them. Why was everything painted? What was wrong with plain old wood? Leaning forward he saw the price and winced. 'I think I'm having a heart attack.'

'Poor baby.'

'I might need CPR.'

'Well, don't look at me. We already agreed on no lip-locking.'

'Stupidest decision we ever made.'

'Or wisest,' she said bending over a table lamp to get a look at the bulb inside.

'Nope,' he said, secretly working out how to get her to change her mind about the no kissing. 'Stupidest decision ever.'

She looked up at him, her gaze softening, like she too was regretting them not having at least one taste of each other. Had she lain awake last night thinking about him? Feeling happy, hot, challenged, intrigued and attracted as hell?

Because he had about her.

He watched her swallow and realised with delight that she had and wild horses couldn't have stopped him from moving closer, until he saw the moment common sense invaded her thinking, saw the regret leave and a steeliness enter. 'Decision made. I'm definitely buying this.'

Maybe that on-off relationship she'd talked about had her thinking she wasn't going to find someone who wanted more from her. And, as common sense flashed through him he realised he was hardly in a position to offer her more himself while they were competing for the same thing, so he quashed the flirting and looked at the table lamp she was looking at. 'Seriously? You're going to pay £359.00 for a pewter pineapple with a lampshade thrown over the top of it?'

'You know, I'm suddenly totally getting the accountant thing.'

'What you're getting is the sensible, logical, plough-every-penny-into-the-business, thing.'

She picked up a silver candlestick and with a gentle 'tsk' looked at him and said, 'Are you worried about my money management, Daniel? Because you really don't need to be, you know.'

'Why, you win the lottery or something?'

She flushed scarlet and fumbled the candlestick. It dropped from her hand and landed on his foot. Yelping in shock, he hopped around and then stopped abruptly – completely fixated on Kate's expression.

'Holy first-world problems,' he whispered, 'you really won the lottery, didn't you?'

Uncomfortable didn't begin to describe how she looked as she bent down, picked up the candlestick and clung to it. 'Please. As if you would have forgotten this,' she squeaked out, moving her hand across her body, 'photographed with one of those giant cardboard cheques?'

He stared and when her smile faltered, he said, 'But then I don't take notice of tabloids and gossip, remember?'

She didn't say anything to deny or acknowledge what had been a flippant comment and he couldn't fail to notice her hands were trembling as she set the candlestick back on the shelf and started fussing with making sure it was lined up neatly with the others.

Shock reverberated through him. It would certainly explain why she was able to buy The Clock House and start up a business and never appear worried about financing either.

He wasn't sure why he was so unsettled by the possibility Kate could have a large amount of money to her name. Was it because he... didn't? Not any amount that wasn't completely accounted for at any rate.

Music jingled into the air between them.

'Saved by the bell,' Kate croaked out after visibly jumping at the sound of her phone ringing.

Daniel watched her smile grow warm and heard her say, 'Hello, Isaac.'

He looked around the barn they were in. She'd appeared incredibly at ease with buying up a small estate's worth of expensive hand-crafted furniture, but what did he know? He'd never seen her get showy with money and had mistaken her ease with buying things for excitement and, if he was being totally and hugely arrogantly honest, he'd put the sparkle in her eyes down to being around him.

And why rent a cottage if you could buy a mansion? Unless you really were intending on ploughing everything you'd won into your business?

A thought slammed into him...

If she had lottery winnings sitting around, then why the hell didn't she simply put it towards the fete fundraising, to ensure she won? Was it because she'd needed to win over the village first and she'd known splashing the cash wasn't the way to go about that?

To think he'd been feeling guilty about not mentioning why West and Westlake no longer existed, but now he was doubly grateful he hadn't confessed.

'Daniel?' Kate called his name, uncertainty radiating out

from her. 'Isaac wants to know if we can pop over and go over the fundraising and fete organising?'

Daniel didn't trust himself to speak, so he simply nodded. All this time he hadn't been paying attention to the nagging worry of what he'd do if he didn't win The Clock House challenge. Somewhere along the way he knew it had become too simple to say he'd simply relocate his idea to somewhere else if he lost. Whispers Wood was his home now. He thought about the order he'd placed for the sleek, functional, wardrobe Kate had picked out for him earlier. He'd bought furniture, for God's sake.

'What time shall I say?'

'Tell him we'll go over as soon as we finish up here. That is, unless you want to buy up the whole of the other two shops on your list first?'

Hurt flashed across her face and he turned away, pretending some stupid lampshade had caught his eye.

He had to get it together because if he was falling for Kate Somersby as hard as he'd already fallen for Whispers Wood, he was going to be left with egg on his face if she was only playing with him and intending to use her money to win The Clock House challenge.

Now he was glad he hadn't completely let down his walls with her. There was even still time to lay a few more rows of bricks while he thought about what he was going to do if she did wade in right at the end and throw down an amount of cash that lost him what he'd been working towards.

He was aware of her putting away her phone and then

quietly and with less enthusiasm organising delivery of the items she'd bought.

'Daniel?'

He turned around to face her, his gaze colliding with hers before scudding away from the confusion and embarrassment on her face.

'Are you ready?' she asked.

No, he wanted to shout.

No, he wasn't.

He wasn't ready to stop thinking about kissing her, but neither was he ready to lose The Clock House.

The anger that had fizzled out over the weeks returned. Damn her if it turned out they'd never been playing on a level field. She couldn't let slip she had secret funds she could tap into to get her over the finishing line and not expect him to come out fighting.

Chapter 34
You've Got To Be In It To Win It

Kate

Kate chased the block of ice around the kitchen countertop, going full *Psycho* on it with a kitchen knife. She wasn't really listening to Juliet. She was too busy wondering if Daniel wasn't talking to her because he'd found out she had money? Or if it was because she hadn't told him she had money? Or if it was because technically she'd neither confirmed nor denied she'd won the lottery?

With a sigh she managed to catch the block of ice before it slid off the counter.

'What do you think about that, then?' Juliet asked.

'Sorry, what?' Kate said as she opened a drawer and took out a clean tea-towel and laid it out underneath the block of ice. She picked up the knife and began hacking off tiny shards to go in the cocktail shaker.

Juliet started decanting the tray of empty martini glasses she'd brought in from the garden. 'I said, so then we had sex in the field beside Knightley Hall with Gertrude looking on approvingly.'

The words finally filtered through, so that Kate paused in her stabbing action and looked at Juliet, open-mouthed.

'Ha. I knew you weren't listening.'

'You haven't been off having sex?' Kate double-checked, tired of feeling one step behind every single conversation this evening.

Juliet took the knife out of Kate's hand and gently shooed her away, pointing her in the direction of measuring out alcohol instead. 'As if I have time,' Juliet laughed, 'In a field or anywhere else. Do you know how much bunting we have to finish tonight? And we absolutely have to come up with a good idea before I leave.'

Kate completely concurred with the coming-up-with-a-good-idea part of the evening. After the most awkward non-conversation conversation with Daniel, the two of them had got back into Monroe and driven in silence to meet Old Man Isaac, who'd sat them both down and explained that they nearly had enough money raised for the best fete ever, but that 'nearly enough' wasn't quite good enough.

Those had been his exact words.

Kate knew he hadn't meant to imply she wasn't good enough or that her efforts weren't good enough, but as she'd sat next to Daniel, worried about his reaction to her in the shop and worried she suddenly wasn't good enough somehow, she'd found herself agreeing to one more fundraiser.

Which was why, at this very moment, outside in her garden, sat her mum, Aunt Cheryl, and Trudie. Team Kate's Operation Fete was having a critical planning meeting.

Squaring her shoulders, she determined to concentrate on the evening ahead and not on what Daniel thought of her.

Pouring shots into the cocktail shaker she said to Juliet, 'But to clarify... if you were Netflix and chilling in a field – it would be with Oscar, right?'

Juliet had obviously been watching Kate's efforts with the ice closely because she too started stabbing away at the block like a woman possessed.

'Because you should know that if it was,' Kate added gently, 'I would approve.'

The stabbing motion stopped as an emotional Juliet looked back at her. 'You would?'

'I would.'

'Oh, that's–' Juliet sniffed and pulled herself together. 'Not that we are. Not that we would. Not that he even thinks of me. Except, well, *maybe* he does. The night of *Finding Nemo* I really thought... I mean, he was looking at me. You know. Really looking at me in a 'where have you been all these years' way? But this is all ridiculous anyway, because I've made up my mind about what I can have. And it isn't that.'

'What if you could have both?' Kate asked, adding a couple of extra shots of vodka because she'd lost count.

Juliet remained silent.

'You don't think you could handle both?' Kate prodded, screwing the cap on the bottle and then unscrewing it and adding a couple more shots to be on the safe side.

'I tell you what I couldn't handle and that's becoming Transitional Girl,' Juliet admitted.

Kate wanted to tell her that wouldn't happen, but what did she know. She'd kind of been that for Marco. Or maybe they'd been that for each other, she suddenly thought, liking that idea much better. 'For the record, Oscar has been looking at you differently from the moment I came back. My advice is to try not to catastrophise transitioning into a different relationship with him.'

Juliet scooped up ice, plonked it into the shaker and wiped her hands down her denim pinafore dress. 'I don't know, Kate. All this time I've been so busy putting the salon between me and him. I honestly think I might be imagining all of this simply because I'm so tired from doing hair all day, thinking about the salon, and then working on the fete.'

Kate drizzled honey into the shaker, her heart heavy. 'I'm sorry I caught you up in all of this fundraising.'

'Hey. Don't even, okay. If anything, you should be angry with me for dragging you back and landing you in this.'

'Or we could both be angry at Daniel instead. He was the one who threw a spanner in the works. If it wasn't for him—' she stopped and concentrated on squeezing lemon into the cocktail mix. She still couldn't believe he'd stumbled across the truth like he had. He'd been joking about her winning the lottery and if she'd had her wits about her, if she hadn't been so distracted by him or so wrapped up in him, she'd have been able to laugh off his words and that would have been that. But instead of shaking it off or even bluffing her way through, she'd blustered and flustered and made it so that it was impossible for him not to realise she had, in actuality, won the lottery.

Confession: This might be tough to believe but there had been large periods of time where Kate had almost been able to forget she had 1.4 million pounds sitting in the bank. In truth, she hadn't ever thought she'd *ever* be able to spend the money she'd won just before her sister had died. Four years was a long time to leave it there untouched.

Claimed, yet not.

'If it wasn't for Daniel... what?' Juliet asked.

She could tell Juliet that Daniel had found out about her win and now he was acting weird. She could ask for advice on how to broach the subject with him and how to make it so that afterwards they never had to talk about it again. But telling Juliet would only worry her and from the sounds of it she had more than enough on her mind. 'Nothing. Like you I'm nervous about coming up with another fundraising idea and making it work before the fete in three weeks.'

'Between us all, we'll come up with something,' Juliet said, striving for positivity.

'Or get pissed trying,' Kate replied, as she picked up the tray of martinis and stepped out into her back garden.

'More?' Sheila said, eyeing the glass being passed to her. 'I really don't think—'

'Exactly,' Cheryl told her sister. 'Don't think, just drink.'

'And how will getting drunk help us come up with another fundraising idea?'

'It'll loosen our inhibitions and free up our creativity,' Trudie declared, whipping a glass from the tray and settling it next to one of the three sewing machines Juliet and Cheryl had brought round.

'As if you need any inhibitions loosening, Trudie McTravers,' Sheila said but Kate noticed there was a teasing note in her voice.

'Here, Mum, have one of these mini quiches to sop up some of the alcohol,' Kate told her, passing her the party tray she'd picked up.

'Oh,' Sheila eyed the plate. 'There's no more cucumber sticks for the dip. I'll make some more to go with it.'

As Sheila stepped across the extension cables strewn across the patio for the sewing machines and disappeared back inside, Kate worried. Should she pop in and check on her? Would it be appreciated or was she the very last person her mum wanted to see if she was trying to pull herself together.

Sod it, she thought, and followed her inside. 'Mum? Is everything okay?'

'Of course.'

Of course. Racking her brains for something to say, she ended up going with, 'Thanks for inviting me to family dinner again.'

'The last time I checked, Kate, you were family.' Sheila's hand clenched against the fridge door. 'Sorry. I'm sorry. That came out the wrong way.'

Kate's heart clattered to the floor. 'That's okay,' she ventured and then had to push. 'Did you catch yourself thinking about Bea just now?'

'No.' Sheila shook her head. 'No, that's not why I came inside. It's – I'm still learning how to take part, I suppose. I get a bit flustered. Let's face it; I was never the life and soul of a party, was I?'

'No that was Dad, I guess.' Kate grimaced. Great time to mention the D word.

A shriek of laughter came through the window.

'Actually it's always your Aunt Cheryl and Trudie who're the life of a party.'

'True,' Kate said with a smile. 'Well, I'll let you have a minute.'

'Kate?'

'Yes?' she turned back at the kitchen door.

A worried look crossed her mother's face. 'I know I hardly have the right to ask but who are you doing all this for? The Clock House, I mean?'

'For everyone.'

Sheila pursed her lips. 'It should mostly be for you, you see.'

Oh, Wow. 'I do see that, Mum.'

'Good. Well, I'll just get the cucumber and then I'll follow you out?'

'Okay. And Mum,' Kate waited until Sheila poked her head out from the fridge and was looking at her. 'You do have the right to ask. You're my mum.'

'OMG,' Juliet whispered, exchanging a shocked look with Kate only moments later as Sheila emerged from the cottage and started sliding down the shrink-wrap cellophane on the cucumber, 'your mum is working that cucumber like a—'

'Don't say it,' Kate muttered in horror. 'Do not say it.'

'Evening ladies,' came the deep voice from over the garden wall.

'Evening Daniel,' four voices trilled back, leaving Kate feeling left out because it seemed her voice had stopped working the moment he'd stepped out of his cottage and into her line of sight.

'Having a bit of a party?' Daniel asked, focusing in on the tray of martini glasses, jam jars and cocktail shakers.

'Actually we're finishing off the decorations for the fete,' Juliet explained.

'Great. That's something I can tick off my list, then,' he said with a wink and then grinned at Trudie. 'Nice work pulling that tire across the green this morning. Impressive circuit-training skills. Cheryl,' his grin turned charmingly apologetic, 'sorry about your dahlias, I hope Gertrude didn't get them all.'

Kate wanted the ground to open up and swallow her as Daniel's gaze slid to her mother's hands holding the cucumber. 'Looks like you've got your hands full there, Sheila.'

Sheila looked down and burst into laughter.

Unused to the sound, Cheryl, Trudie and Juliet stared at her, shocked. Kate was shocked too. Even more shocked as she felt the tears forming. Her mum was really, truly coming back to life and Daniel seemed to know how to gently tease her and to get her to laugh at herself.

'Well, I'll let you get back to it.' Daniel's eyes drifted to Kate and she burned under his gaze, wishing she could go back to how things had been between them before their shopping trip. 'Kate,' he acknowledged, tipping his head in her direction.

'Daniel,' she said, finally finding her voice and tipping her glass to him.

She watched him disappear back inside.

Maybe now that he knew she had money he considered he didn't need to know anything more about her?

Frustration inched up her spine, making her feel ridiculous, because if it turned out that assumption was the case then she had no business missing their chats over the garden wall.

No business missing the way his gaze would hold hers as they talked deep into the night.

No business missing... him.

'If I was twenty years younger...' Cheryl sighed when the patio doors closed behind him.

'Right ladies,' Kate said, cutting off anyone else agreeing, 'shall we brainstorm while we sew? Who wants to do triangles, who wants to do tassels, and who wants to do pom-poms?'

It was her mother who was first to come up with an idea as she sewed triangles onto bias binding. 'How about a netball competition?' she said.

'Daniel already did a football tournament,' Kate said, handing Juliet strips of flowery, polka-dotted and checked fabrics for her to tie into colour-co-ordinated tassels that she then attached to garlands that matched the bunting.

'What about a sponsored walk?' Cheryl asked, winding wool around pom-pom makers.

Kate sighed. 'Daniel already did a–'

'Fun-run,' Cheryl said. 'Right. Um...'

'Ooh, I know... How about a bachelor auction?' Juliet threw out.

'A bachelor auction?' Trudie looked like someone had mentioned her two most favourite words. 'Sweetie, that is a fabulous idea.'

'Do we have enough men, though?' Juliet wondered aloud.

'Of course we do,' Cheryl declared. 'All the married men can still take part and the wives can bid for them to do something around the house.'

'I wouldn't waste my bid on Nigel doing something around the house,' Trudie said.

'Depends on what your understanding of Doing Something Around The House is,' Sheila said, giggled and then frowned as the sewing machine stopped. 'I think I broke this.'

'Okay, that's enough alcohol for you,' Kate said, moving the glass away from her mother. 'And Juliet, it's a brilliant idea, but I'm sorry, we can't have a bachelor auction as our fundraiser.'

'Why not?' Cheryl asked.

Kate looked guiltily around the garden. 'Because it's too sexist.'

'Too sexist?'

'It objectifies men and Juliet and I already turned up to Daniel's football tournament in bikinis selling cakes, thus making ourselves objectionable.'

'Doesn't she mean objectifiable?' Cheryl murmured to Trudie.

'No bachelor auction?' Trudie pouted.

'No bachelor auction,' Kate insisted.

'I suppose we could have a sponsored readathon?' Cheryl said, snaffling a couple of the cucumber sticks and using them as cocktail stirrers.

'A readathon?' Juliet looked thoughtful. 'Melody Matthews would love that idea.'

'That's true – my granddaughter always has her head in a book,' Sheila said proudly.

'I love that about her,' Juliet agreed.

'Yes, it's sweet,' Sheila told her and Kate silently shoved the martini glass back into her mother's hand, hoping to distract her from the contemplative glint that had come into her eyes as she'd connected Juliet to Oscar.

Sheila took a large sip and then looked up at her daughter. 'Have you booked your stall yet? Maybe we could have an evening selling all the products you've made?'

Kate shook her head. 'If I flood the village with stock before the fete, they're just going to think I'm subliminally trying to get them on-side again.'

'Don't be silly, they wouldn't think that,' Aunt Cheryl claimed loyally.

'To be fair,' Juliet grimaced. 'Gloria Pavey might.'

Trudie groaned and shook her head. 'I swear what that woman needs is a good–'

'O-key dokey, then,' Kate said cutting Trudie off. 'Shall we revisit the readathon idea?'

'I'm worried it's a bit insular. Isn't the idea to bring everyone together?' Cheryl said.

'Damn.' Kate considered the pool of alcohol sitting in her belly and imagined a large swan swimming in it, paddling like mad and getting nowhere. 'We're five intelligent women. We must be able to come up with a really good idea.'

'Ooh, I have it,' Trudie said, leaping up from the table, sending ribbons and fabric floating down to the ground.

'Yay.' Kate grinned. 'What is it?'

Trudie held up her empty glass. 'I think we should all have another round!'

Kate looked around at her team. 'At this point, why not?' She stood on slightly wobbly legs. At the kitchen door she turned and swore that this batch was going to be the tastiest yet. Four women in various states of drunkenness all roared as one. She laughed and waved her hands at the sewing machines 'When I come back I want to see steam coming out of those machines.'

But when she did come back out it was to find all four of them not at their posts but standing in front of the garden wall dividing Mistletoe Cottage from Myrtle Cottage.

At the sound of her putting the tray down on the table Cheryl turned around and with a huge smile announced that they'd put their heads together and come up with the perfect plan.

'You have?' she asked suspiciously.

'We think you should find out what Daniel's idea is.'

Kate stared at them all. 'Your idea is to find out what Daniel's idea is and, what? Beat him to it, or something?'

Trudie nodded vigorously. 'All you'd have to do is put it on *The Whisperings* website first and it'll become your idea.'

'And how am I supposed to find out what his idea is…' suddenly her alcohol-addled brain fused and sparked, 'oh, okay. I can't believe we didn't think of this earlier. Juliet, phone Oscar, he's bound to know.'

Juliet shook her head. 'I am not phoning Oscar at close to midnight. I'll wake up Melody.'

'So how do you propose I find out what his idea is, then?'

'Easy. Look,' her mother said, pointing at Daniel's kitchen patio doors. 'All you have to do is break in when he's gone to sleep and get a good look at his plans. I'll get the password for the website from Crispin.'

'You lot are insane. Or drunk,' she announced, bringing her own glass to her lips because when it came to insanely drunk or drinking insanely they all seemed to be ahead of her. 'You're proposing I commit a crime?'

'You want to win, don't you?' Juliet said.

Kate took another sip of her martini. 'Boy, has living in the country changed since I was last here. I can't walk into his house,' she said, coming to line up with them at the wall. 'While he's asleep,' she added, looking through his patio doors and turning towards her team with a huge grin on her face, 'And steal the plans that look like they're sitting on the kitchen table.'

'Shee,' said Juliet lisping slightly, 'that definitely looks like them, right?'

'Is it breaking and entering if you have a key?' her mum whispered.

Kate turned to stare at her mother.

Sheila shrugged elegantly. 'While I get the password from Crispin, I could ask him for the spare key.'

'No you could not. Oh my God, you are all really serious about this?' Her gaze fell on the sewing machines and how you could barely see what you were doing with the soft yellow light spilling out from her patio doors. Once all the lights were turned off... 'And how exactly do you Einsteins propose

I see to get into his house in the dead of night? Once I've scaled the wall, that is?'

'Oh sweetie,' Trudie whispered, turning away from the wall to walk over to her bag. 'I have the perfect accessory to help you with that.'

Chapter 35

The Curious Incident of the Plan
in the Night-time

Kate

Ouch!

Kate pulled herself to her feet, rubbing her coccyx as she did so. It turned out that scrambling over the dividing wall between hers and Daniel's cottages was harder than it looked when you were drunk as a skunk.

A giggle escaped her.

Could skunks get drunk?

Kate smacked her lips together, intrigued at how numb they felt and gave up on the drunk skunk conundrum to devote her attention to the real burning question: how the hell had Trudie got her hands on a pair of night-vision goggles anyway?

She'd mentioned something about birds and twitching, but Kate had been none the wiser and as she steadied herself against the wall she could only come up with four viable theories.

One: Trudie was ex-SAS.

Two: Trudie knew someone who was ex-SAS.

Three: Trudie knew Daniel Craig and *he* knew someone

who was ex-SAS. They'd probably got chatting away at a wrap party or a red carpet event when Daniel had grinned and asked Trudie if she wanted to see his favourite prop from the latest Bond film and voila! One pair of night-vision goggles had ended up in her clutch bag.

Of course the theory that was most plausible was the fourth: that Trudie had purchased them off eBay. But Kate made a mental note to mention Daniel Craig within Trudie's earshot and then watch closely for her response.

Bringing both hands up to fasten the goggles more securely to her head she nearly gave herself a heart attack when she saw movement through the lens and it took more than the usual amount of time to catch on that it was her own hands moving about in front of her face.

Putting a hand to her racing heart, Kate was learning fast that this SAS stuff was a lot more tricky than she would have thought. Although possibly actual SAS studs didn't carry out their duties while inebriated.

Boring!

Didn't they know everything felt much more doable after a few glasses of nectar? Oh! Daniel had told her she smelled like nectar. Now that they weren't talking it was going to be harder to help him see that she tasted of nectar too. She pouted. Or maybe she dribbled. She couldn't really tell since all sensation had left her mouth after the last drink.

Quietly she tip-toed Pink Panther style across the grass, taking extra care to be quiet as a mouse when she reached the patio. If only she had a comms unit to go with the goggles. She could radio in when target was acquired.

When Trudie had first taken the goggles out of her bag, everyone had gasped in wonder, as if they were looking at a pair of one-off Jimmy Choo wellies rather than a piece of intelligence equipment. That was when Kate had decided to call an end to the thinking-planning-strategic part of the evening. If committing a little B&E was really the best they could all come up with, then they were well and truly stuffed. She'd suggested everyone get some sleep and come back to it fresh the next day. They'd spent a giggly half an hour clearing away the bunting and finishing off their drinks and then bid her goodnight, waving their torches and shushing each other as they'd left.

The garden had seemed eerily quiet after they'd all gone and to combat the sudden loneliness she'd poured herself a nightcap.

Two nightcaps later and her gaze had fallen on the goggles.

For a laugh she'd popped them on. Not really getting the point until the lights had gone out in Mistletoe Cottage and suddenly it had seemed like the best idea ever to climb into Daniel's garden and see if she could see the plans through his patio doors because ethical, shmethical, Daniel had consistently come up with good fundraising ideas and she was all tapped out.

'Shh,' she told herself as she pressed her face up against said doors and heard the goggles clunk loudly against the glass.

She squinted at the large piece of paper on his table, piqued when she couldn't make out any of the words. Her hand reached for the door handle because maybe he hadn't locked the door and she was so, so close now, it would be silly to follow the *abort, abort, abort,* instruction chiming through her head.

'Waaahh!'

Kate clamped a hand over her mouth to stifle the wail as blinding white light knocked her on her arse. Whipping off the night-vision goggles she squeezed her eyes shut.

What the actual?

Opening her eyes, she realised that the kitchen lights had flicked on and there standing in all his butt-naked glory was Daniel Westlake.

She blinked.

How very dare he walk around his own house in the nude.

Like a camera capturing an image, she sealed the sight of Daniel Westlake with nothing on, onto the hard-drive of her memory.

As she sat staring open-mouthed in at him, the night-vision goggles somewhere on the grass behind her, she wondered why he didn't burst out into the garden and call her every name for voyeur under the moon. Or why he wasn't calling the police. Or the mental health services.

And then she got it.

Once the lights were on he couldn't see her out in the garden.

She watched him saunter – yes, saunter across his kitchen, over to his fridge, open the door and get out a carton of juice and she watched even more as he tipped his head back, the corded muscles in his neck working overtime as he drank thirstily. She was helpless to look away as his hand came up to scratch absentmindedly at abs that put the board into washboard and the sex into ripped.

He was completely. Utterly. Bare-arsedly beautiful.

And she was hungry like the wolf.

Suddenly he lowered the carton and went absolutely still, staring straight at her.

Holy sex on a stick. Any moment now she'd be detected.

And then he was looking at the countertop for his glasses and putting them on while she was scrambling back out of the well of light and hugging the garden wall – like if she wished hard enough she could find her cuttlefish Indominus Rex gene and camouflage herself against the wall.

Do NOT walk around that kitchen island unit.

She screamed the words silently on loop because if he did she'd be able to see... everything he had to offer and as he already had a lot, she wasn't sure she'd be able to handle it.

But, then, as the seconds clicked by, she realised her mantra had changed to:

Okay, if you absolutely have to, walk around that counter unit...

She was sick.

And bad.

So sick and so bad for now willing him to walk around the counter unit and stand in front of the doors and then possibly open the doors and beckon her inside.

She should at least close her eyes.

She had that control, didn't she? But as she stared at him she knew that, caught between wanting to see more and knowing she shouldn't even have seen what she already had, it was obvious why she'd drunk such a stupid amount tonight.

She'd been drowning her sorrows because for all of her backing off and being sensible last night, she wanted him.

Really wanted him.

Whether he was talking to her or not.

The problem was that wanting The Clock House as well meant that she couldn't have what was now staring her in the face.

Because in spite of what she had told Juliet earlier about her having the salon *and* Oscar in her life, Kate knew that wanting The Clock House and wanting Daniel was different. Like one of those physics-science things, where outside of inside her head, the two couldn't occupy the same space without causing a catastrophic event.

Honestly, you waited years for one dream to come along and then two diametrically opposed dreams hit at the same time.

She felt her bottom lip quiver, which might mean she was sobering up.

Never had she been so disappointed yet pleased when he simply turned around and switched off the lights.

She waited a few minutes.

And when she was certain her legs would be able to support her, she grabbed the goggles and climbed back over the wall and dragged herself into the cottage.

On the way up to bed she poured herself the largest glass of water.

To help with the hangover she was sure to have in the morning.

Not because she had a raging thirst she needed to abate.

Chapter 36

Thanks For Nothing, Mr Tumnus

Kate

Along with the maddening earworm of a Duran Duran song going around her head – and why she was singing 'I'm on the Hunt and After You' over and over, she didn't know – Kate was also feeling distinctly sorry for herself.

The glass of water hadn't helped with the hangover.

Nor had the breakfast she'd tried to get herself to eat.

Nor, even, the painkillers.

She'd nearly accepted that the pounding in her head and the roiling in her stomach was apt punishment for last night, but as she ventured outside and the sunlight tried to melt her eyeballs she vowed that never again would she so much as take a sip of alcohol.

A nice steady walk in the fresh air was going to get her all the way over to Wren Cottage, where she would spill the beans to Juliet, because if she didn't talk about what she'd done it would be way too easy to pretend it had never happened and acknowledging that she'd been reduced to *spying* on someone was surely going to prevent her from ever attempting anything like that ever again.

Slowly she made her way across the green, the only thing to pull her focus the incessant and highly invasive sound of birds cheeping. Talk about way too much stimulus for her delicate state of mind. Kate groaned as she wished sorely for a pair of earphones.

And a pair of sunglasses.

And an intravenous line of strong coffee.

She sensed him before she actually saw him.

Turning her head gingerly to the left, she took in Daniel's supreme form as he ran the length of the green. As he turned the corner, his gait smooth and experienced, he drew closer and all she could think was that she knew what was under those shorts and tee... Had been close enough to touch what was under those... BANG!

Wow.

Okay.

That wasn't at all mortifying!

Who the hell had put that lamppost there?

She staggered back a step and brought her hands up to double-check that her head was still on her shoulders. It turned out it was, which meant the next step, while holding back the nausea brought on by her abrupt halt, was to try wrapping her head around the fact that she'd just walked into a lamppost in full view of The Running Man.

Speak of the devil because in a heartbeat he'd made it across the green to stand in front of her.

'Jeez, are you okay? That looked brutal.'

All she could do was mumble out an, 'Ow,' as she stared between her fingers down at his feet.

'Here, let me see,' he instructed, and the next thing she knew she could feel his warm, gentle, large hands tug at the ones she was holding in front of her face. 'Doesn't look like there's damage,' he said, tipping her face up to the sun. 'Although you do look really red.'

'Of course I'm red in the face. I head-butted a lamppost.'

'I think the redness might be down to embarrassment,' he said.

'Or abject misery,' she moaned. 'I am going to kill Crispin. Taking it upon himself to erect lampposts on the village green without holding a meeting first. Hasn't he got anything better to do of a morning?'

'Actually, I'm pretty sure this lamppost was already here,' Daniel said.

'Pretty sure?'

'Make that definitely sure.'

'Oh me. Oh my. Leaning against a lamppost, in case a certain lady walks by? Aren't you just a regular Mr Tumnus.'

'Yes, Lucy Pevensie. I live for lampposts. In fact I attached a poster to this very one only this morning.'

Kate couldn't even look at the eye-searingly fluorescent orange poster for fear of being sick. 'So if you've been here all morning leaning against this lamppost it must have gone up in the middle of the night. This is beyond the pale. I'm telling you, Crispin has to be stopped.'

Daniel didn't even bat one of his long Spanish eyelashes when he said, 'I imagine there's all sorts of shenanigans go on in the middle of the night in this place.'

Kate's head shot up at that.

Ow again.

Daniel was looking down at her with a knowing sort of glint in his eye.

Her insides all mushed tightly together. No way was he referring to *her* shenanigans in the night?

'Got a bit of a sore head this morning?' he asked, as her hands crept up to rub at her temples.

She pointed to the lamppost. 'Is it any wonder?'

'There isn't another reason?'

Other than nearly knocking herself unconscious? She opened one eye to look up at him. 'What other possible reason could there be?'

Daniel leaned in close. 'I can smell the alcohol on your breath,' he whispered helpfully.

'Don't you mean nectar?' The words slipped out and, as his gaze settled on her mouth, her hangover melted into the background because the way he was looking at her made her forget about feeling yucky. Forget about fundraising. Forget about money. Forget even about The Clock House.

Well, maybe not those last three, but at least the first one for long enough that she could attempt to clear the air properly between them.

She licked her lips. 'Daniel, I know things have been a little off since,' she closed her eyes briefly and steeled herself to follow through, 'since you said what you said.'

Daniel folded his arms. 'Said what I said about what?'

'You know,' she whispered, 'about me winning the lottery.'

'Right, the lottery. Couldn't be anything else as well, could it?'

Jiminy Cricket was he expecting her to mention their

stare-off last night as well? She dragged in a breath. So be it. But first she had to explain her response to him guessing how she had the funds to buy The Clock House. Make him understand somehow. 'It's only that no one here knows about the money and I would really appreciate it if—' she broke off as her gaze struck the poster again. She blinked and read the bold black print. 'Wait a minute...'

A high-pitched hissing sound made her wince and then wince again when she realised she was the one emitting it.

'You're holding a bachelor auction?' she squawked.

Daniel's grin took on epic proportions. 'Great idea, huh?'

'A *bachelor auction*?'

'Yep.'

'In The Clock House?'

'Yep.'

'This is your big fundraiser idea?'

'Yep.'

'Your fundraiser idea is to steal Juliet's fundraiser idea and pass it off as your own?'

'Well, I wouldn't want to put it quite like that. Would you? Want to put it like that?'

'Yes, I bloody well would.'

'Huh. Interesting,' he said conversationally. 'How you can interpret the word 'steal', I mean. Because it's hardly as if I climbed into your garden in the dead of night to steal the idea right out from under you, is it?'

Kate's mouth open and closed. Several times.

'I mean, who would do that?' Daniel asked.

'Look, Daniel – I—'

'Morning Daniel, morning Kate, isn't it the loveliest day?' Crispin chirped as he came to a stop beside them.

'Morning Crispin,' Daniel greeted, his voice full of the joys of spring. 'I agree. It's gorgeous. Not sure Kate agrees, though. Very upset with you for building this lamppost on the edge of the green.'

'This lamppost?' Crispin frowned up at it. 'But it's been here forever.'

'That's what I told her. Didn't I, Kate?'

'Mmn,' Kate managed to get out.

'Between you and me, Crispin,' Daniel leaned forward, 'I'm not sure she's really with it this morning. She looks like she got hardly any sleep at all.'

Crispin looked her up and down. 'You do look a little peaky.'

'Ask her why?' Daniel said.

Kate no longer cared about her dehydrated eyeballs as she stared daggers at Daniel. 'It's all right,' she smiled. 'I think I just have a really bad case of stink-eye.'

Daniel smirked and turned to Crispin. 'Thanks for putting up the details of the auction on the website for me. I've been flat-out putting these up all morning.' He pointed to a roll of posters tucked under his arm and Kate couldn't believe she hadn't noticed them before. Too busy fixed on his body and not being able to un-see what she'd seen last night.

'Very enterprising, I must say, Daniel,' Crispin said. 'It's got Mrs Harlow all excited.'

That news got her attention and she whipped her gaze to Crispin's. 'You don't think it's sexist?'

'Sexist?' Crispin looked bemused.

'Yes.' She nodded and felt her head pound. 'You know sexist, as in, parading men about on a stage and getting women to bid for them.'

Crispin appeared thoughtful as he scratched his jaw-line, but then bitterly disappointed Kate by saying, 'It is on a volunteer basis only, so I hardly think the men taking part or the wives bidding on them are going to complain.'

'Okay, maybe sexist is the wrong word,' she argued back, determined to get her point across, 'Let's try suggestive instead? I assume the event is open to all ages. What example are we setting for children?'

'The event is in the evening and Daniel has already organised separate entertainment for children. I really think the men can take it, Kate. It's a bit of fun and the most important thing is to raise enough money to put on the best fete possible. It's not long to go now and we need every penny we can get.'

Kate hung her head, fuming. But then she spotted another pair of feet walking by and uncaring of her hangover, suddenly stepped in front of the chaplain's path. 'Mary. Thank God.' Literally, she thought, triumphantly. 'Mary, please feel free to tell Daniel here exactly why this idea is so wrong.' She pointed to the poster and gestured for Mary to read it pronto.

Mary stopped and stood in front of the lamppost, reading the poster word for word. Kate had faith while she waited for her to finish. The Lord working in mysterious ways and all that. Even if some of His vessels appeared to be very slow readers.

Finally Mary turned to Daniel and smiled. 'What fun. Are you going to be auctioning yourself, Daniel?'

'Absolutely, Mary.'

'Great,' she said.

Kate didn't understand. 'Great? Why is that great, Mary?'

'To be honest, I could do with a bit of muscle help installing the new games equipment that's been delivered to the school during the holidays.'

Kate blinked. 'But don't you think an auction sends completely the wrong message?' she asked, tapping her foot impatiently.

Mary looked confused. 'I think it's only fair to pay someone to help me move the equipment and it's wonderful if what I pay goes straight back into a community project.'

'Oh. My. God.'

'I beg your pardon,' Mary asked.

'Nothing,' she mumbled.

'Well, I must be getting off. Daniel, would you like me to take some of those posters and give them out for you?'

'Would you, Mary? That's so thoughtful of you.'

As he handed over about a million of the offending articles to the school chaplain, Kate had a feeling it was only her who could see the devil in the detail of his grin.

'I should be off, too,' Crispin declared.

'Wait,' Kate added sarcastically, 'You don't want to take any posters off his hands, as well?'

'Oh, good idea,' and taking a handful, off he went.

'Here, give me the rest,' Kate sighed, making a grab for them.

'No way,' Daniel said, raising them above his head so that they were out of reach. 'I'm not handing these over so that you can shove them down a drain or something.'

'I would never,' she gasped mortally offended. She'd been thinking of the recycling bin by the bus stop.

'Right,' Daniel snorted.

'Well, don't blame me if this idea of yours completely bombs.'

'Finally admitting it's my idea, now?'

'Only because you stole it, Mr Idea Stealer. You can hardly say the idea came to you in the middle of the night.'

'Actually, I can absolutely say that.'

Her jaw snapped shut.

'Wise,' he murmured.

Unable to let him have the last word, Kate raised her head defiantly and promptly plumbed new depths. 'I raised a gazillion from the open-air cinema night. I can't see you topping that with a few men standing awkwardly on stage while their better halves pay money for them to put up a shelf they could just as easily put up themselves.'

'But there's no way you have enough time to come up with a better fundraiser, so I don't see how you can possibly stay ahead of the game now.'

Game?

Was that all it was to him?

'This isn't about who has the most funds to buy The Clock House,' he continued. 'This is about who has the most stamina to raise money. Do you know how much stamina I have, when it comes to something I want, Kate?'

She had a feeling she was about to find out. Still. She couldn't let him have the last word.

'I'm very confident about the amount of money I've raised. People are still talking about that night.'

'I'm going to raise more. What's more, it's all going to be meticulously accounted for.'

'What's that supposed to mean?'

'It means I've asked Isaac to count our winnings based on ticket sales and receipts and separately account for,' he raised his hands to finger-quote, 'any amount of money handed over' at the end of each fundraiser.'

'What the hell are you talking about,' she asked, finger-quoting him back 'any amount of money handed over'. You make it sound like I've been handing over brown envelopes of mafia money or something.'

'Not mafia money – but I don't expect to see any lottery winnings as part of your pot, either.'

This was why he had distanced himself from her?

He thought she'd cheat her way to The Clock House? Granted, donating funds to the fundraiser probably wasn't really cheating, but in her eyes it was. Not to mention the fact that the only way she'd been able to become okay with spending the money in the first place was to spend it solely on Beauty @ The Clock House.

It hurt more than she would have thought that Daniel didn't think she was above playing a game, stringing him along and throwing down a winning hand at the end.

'I know we haven't known each other long,' she said, 'but I would never, ever, do something like that.'

'Well, I'd as soon neither of us had to worry about it. This way it stays a level playing field.'

She obviously wasn't going to be able to convince him. 'Fine then. Try not to be too upset when I beat you fair and square.'

'Like I said – it's all about stamina, and if you don't mind me saying, you don't look like you've been sleeping.'

'Neither do you.'

'I suppose it did take a while to get back to sleep last night. I kept feeling like I was being... watched.'

'Watched?'

'Like the wildlife of Whispers Wood was staring at me.'

'Maybe it was your ego that has you thinking that.'

Daniel's laugh was rich as he leaned down and whispered in her ear, 'Oh, I'm pretty sure it wasn't my ego they were staring at.'

Chapter 37

Going Once, Going Twice... Sold

Kate

'So we're both agreed?' Kate checked as she walked into The Clock House with Juliet and saw the stage set for the bachelor auction.

The room was packed and Kate couldn't help thinking of the last time she'd been in this room and what had happened.

'Agreed,' Juliet said. 'No bidding. Either of us.'

'Right,' Kate said. 'We'd rather eat worms than bid at this auction.'

'Absolutely.'

'We're here to show our support for community projects. That is all,' she said, shoving the bag of sweets further down into her bag so that they weren't on show.

'And to smirk about how we would have done it better.'

'So much better.'

'Oh, look.' Juliet pointed to the front row. 'Let's grab those two seats for the best view in town.'

As they settled in their seats, Juliet leaned towards her and whispered, 'So I brought a little refreshment for this evening.'

'Great. What have you got? I brought sweets.' Kate's eyes grew bug-shaped round as Juliet lifted up her jacket to reveal a hip-flask. 'You brought alcohol? Oh, Jules, I've really led you astray.'

'I know.'

'I don't know what to say – wait, I do,' she grabbed the hip-flask, took off the top and raised it to Juliet. 'Chin-chin.'

They grinned at each other and suddenly she was passing it back to Juliet to hide because Crispin was standing in front of them and saying, 'Ladies, you need to get your paddles.'

'What?' Kate said, the grin still on her face, 'You want us to get paddled? You want to paddle us? I knew this event was going to get out of hand. Crispin, I'm going to have to tell Mrs Harlow about this.'

'You know very well I wasn't referring to some sordid sexual act.'

Kate gasped. 'Did you just say sordid? And sexual? At a family event?'

'You need paddles for bidding.'

'Oh. Right,' Kate shook her head at him. 'No thank you. We don't intend to bid.'

'Don't intend to bid?' Crispin frowned. 'Then why are you here?'

'For the entertainment factor,' Juliet said.

'What she said,' Kate agreed and then grudgingly added, 'And to show our support at a community event.'

'But you simply have to bid,' Crispin implored, his frown rising as high as his weave.

'Um... no we don't.'

'But it's our turn to look after Ant and Dec, so Mrs Harlow is going to phone in her bid and you have to bid for me or she'll have no one to bid against.'

'Ant and Dec?' Kate looked at Juliet.

'The school goldfish,' Juliet supplied. 'They get passed around whoever's free during the school holidays. I had to decline.'

'Well, of course.' Kate nodded. 'Because that would really have put the cats amongst the fish.'

Juliet gave her a mock sour look. 'I was going to say because I was coming here but okay if you want to endlessly bring up the cats then go ahead.'

'*Everyone* is here tonight,' Crispin said, looking simultaneously pleased and scared. 'It's only because Mrs Harlow couldn't bear to think of them home alone that she offered. It was very good of her.'

Kate snorted at a village who was worried about two fish being left home alone. 'Should have called them Kevin and everything would have been fine.'

Juliet laughed, but Crispin looked as if he was going to have a heart attack.

'Okay, okay, okay,' Kate muttered. 'Consider us paddled into submission. We'll bid on you.'

'Oh, thank you ladies. I'm number 006.'

'Double-oh-six?' Kate laughed. 'Priceless. Who's 007?'

'I think that's Daniel.'

Unbelievable.

Kate coughed out the word, 'Fix.'

Crispin looked at her like this was completely the wrong

360

time to give him a cold. 'Can I trust you two to get your forms and paddles while I go and get changed?'

'Changed?' Juliet asked.

'Into my bachelor outfit.'

'He's making you all wear outfits?' Kate asked.

'Barbaric,' Juliet hissed out, unable to hide her smile.

'Hey, Crispin, if you come back out dressed as Christian Grey I'll up my bid.'

'Really, girls,' Crispin tutted disapprovingly as he moved away.

'But Crispin,' Kate said, standing up and raising her voice, 'all you'd need is a paddle and you'd be all set.'

Crispin didn't even bother turning around.

Kate grinned down at Juliet. 'So I guess I'll be moseying on up to the table and grabbing us two paddles and forms?'

'As long as we're agreed that it's only because Crispin is forcing us into it. Otherwise we totally wouldn't be bidding.'

'Right. That man is such a tyrant.'

'I'll save your seat.'

'Back in a mo.'

Kate waved 'Hello' to a few people as she made her way to the table and once there tapped the lady in the flowery summer dress on the shoulder. 'Hi, Mum.'

Sheila whirled around. 'Kate! I wasn't expecting to see you here.' She looked nervously around her. 'I'm only here to support the event. That is – I–'

'It's all right, Mum,' Kate cut her off. 'I think I know who you'll be bidding for when the auction starts.'

Her mother turned beetroot-red. 'It's only that Kevin is very worried no one is going to bid for him, so I said I would.'

'It's okay, Mum. I think it's nice.'

'Nice?'

'Um, you know,' Kate's mind raced, 'Everyone appreciates it when friends support each other.'

Sheila relaxed a fraction. 'Friends,' she said with a nod. 'Yes. Good. Well. Who are you picking up paddles for?'

'Crispin.'

'Not Daniel?'

Kate looked at her as if she was insane.

'I'm going to bid on Daniel,' Cheryl said, as she sidled up to them.

Kate picked up a form and started reading the terms and conditions in earnest. Anything to pretend Cheryl bidding on Daniel did absolutely nothing to her insides.

'What are you doing?' Sheila asked her.

'Familiarising myself with the rules,' she mumbled, head down, hoping the flush on her cheeks would kindly "do one".'

'It says you can bid on more than one person, you know,' her mother added helpfully.

'Really?' Kate's head shot up and then dropped back down to the piece of paper.

'Really,' Sheila confided and then tentatively put a hand out to push Kate's hair back over her shoulder. It was an old habit that startled Kate into feeling warm and happy. 'Kate, I know this isn't your fundraiser, if you would prefer it if none of us stayed tonight...'

'Don't be silly,' she asserted, pushing down the emotion. 'It's absolutely fine that you're all here. This is about raising money for the fete so we can then raise oodles more money for the village. Gold at Best in Bloom next year isn't going to win itself without a serious injection of cash and fighting spirit, is it?'

Sheila smiled. 'Well, if you're sure?'

'I'm totally sure.'

Her mother and Cheryl looked at each other excitedly and Kate was reminded of her and Juliet.

'All right, then,' her mother said, 'Obviously it's going to be difficult to beat your cinema night, but, it's rather fun to have a calendar full of these events, isn't it?'

Kate looked around the busy room and felt the buzz in the air. Everyone looked so happy to be here and she realised, for the first time, that she didn't feel like an outsider tonight.

Suddenly she knew it was going to be important not to let this sense of renewed spirit amongst the residents of Whispers Wood stop as soon as either Daniel or she moved into The Clock House.

'We'll have to come up with some more ideas that get the whole village together after this is all over,' she told her mother and Cheryl.

'Great idea,' Cheryl said, skewering her with a pointed look. 'I know you're helping out the Harlows, but I think you should bid on Daniel too. If you won, you could use the time together to... brainstorm,' she added with a waggle of her eyebrows. 'Sheila, shall we go and take our seats?'

Back at her own seat, she handed Juliet her paddle. 'You have to write your name across it and fill out this form if you successfully bid for someone.'

'So much hard work,' Juliet said, grabbing the marker pen Kate was also shoving into her hand.

'Did you know Trudie is the auctioneer?' When Juliet took out her phone she added, 'Who are you phoning?'

'No one, I'm tweeting: Beyond outrageous, to @AFlairForTheDramatic.'

'Stop. Knowing our luck, Trudie will reply and then the evening will start trending.'

'Good point. Drink?'

'Definitely. Sweet?'

'Absolutely.'

Suddenly the room lights went out and a spotlight appeared centre stage.

Ha. School-boy error, thought Kate. If it was going to be as dark as this Trudie was never going to be able to see the name on the winning paddle. Kate squirmed in her seat to make sure she was as comfy as possible.

And then she squirmed some more as Daniel walked out onto stage to stand under the spotlight.

'Wow,' Juliet whispered. 'I guess at least he's wearing clothes, right?'

Those weren't 'clothes'. That was a tuxedo that looked like it had been tailor-made.

As Daniel put on his glasses, Kate's hand wandered into her bag of sweets. She needed something to whet her whistle. Or at least make sure she didn't whistle. Or cat-call. Or pant.

'Good evening everyone,' Daniel crooned into the mic.

There was no feedback from the mic. No muffled sound.

Just Daniel's deep, throaty, charming voice pouring over her senses like runny honey.

'I'd like to thank you all for being here. This is for the fete and of course I want us to raise an enormous amount of money tonight, but I also insist on you all having fun. Bearing that in mind, I'd like you all to remember that the bachelors stepping onto this stage are all nervous, so be gentle with us... but also, dig deep and spend hard. It's for a good cause. And now, over to our auctioneer extraordinaire, our hostess with the mostest... Trudie McTravers.'

The auction was into its well-organised stride by the time Crispin ambled onto the stage.

'Bachelor No 006,' Trudie announced, peering through her half-moon glasses at her notes. 'Ladies, what will you give for this very well-groomed, very experienced – at least in all matters Whispers Wood – silver-foxed orator? Oh, and I'm supposed to add here that there's a 'secret' bidder on the phone. Mary? Have you got the bidder on the phone?'

'I have, we can begin, Trudie.'

'Right, so um...'

'Twenty pounds,' Kate shouted out, holding up her paddle.

'Twenty pounds bid, do I have more? Mary?'

'Twenty-one pounds,' Mary said.

Kate looked at Juliet, who looked back aghast, obviously agreeing that they couldn't let Crispin go for a cheap-skate twenty-one pounds when even Ted had gone for sixty-five.

'Fifty pounds,' Juliet shouted, smiling up at Crispin.

'Fifty pounds I'm bid. Do I have more Mary?'

'Seventy-five pounds,' Kate piped up before Mary could say anything. 'Hey, this is fun,' she said out of the side of her mouth to Juliet.

'Seventy-five? I think you're supposed to let Mary bid next, sweetie.' Trudie looked amazed as her gaze slid to Mary standing at the side of the room with her phone.

'I can't help myself, Trudie,' Kate said, winking up at Crispin.

'Um... Mary?'

Mary was talking quietly into her phone and then, after a moment, looked embarrassed as she countered with, 'Seventy-six pounds, Trudie.'

'One hundred and twenty pounds,' Juliet shouted out, grinning from ear to ear.

'Whoa, are you sure?' Kate whispered, shocked.

'This is the best fun ever.' Juliet waved her paddle about wildly. 'Besides,' she added quietly, 'Mrs Harlow is bound to offer one more pound.'

'I hope for your sake she does.'

'Mary?' Trudie asked, her voice faint but hopeful.

Mary turned her back on the room to talk in a hushed voice into the phone.

'Psst, Crispin?' Kate called up to the stage.

Crispin inched closer. 'What?'

'Do something.'

He lifted his hands helplessly.

'You text Mrs Harlow right now and make her bid one pound more, or Juliet here is going to give this,' she circled her hand up to her head to indicate hair and then pointed to his wig, 'a buzz cut'.

Crispin took out his phone and started texting.

Finally Mary turned around and triumphantly shouted, 'I have one hundred and twenty- one pounds from Mrs Harlow, um, I mean, the bidder on the phone.'

Trudie smiled gratefully and then stared down at Juliet and Kate, 'Am I bid any more?'

Kate put her hand over Juliet's in case she got paddle-happy again and after a few moments, Trudie happily shouted, 'Going once, going twice,' and with a tap of her gavel, said, 'Sold, to the bidder on the phone.'

Crispin left the stage to a round of applause, his head held high.

'And now for bachelor number 007...' Trudie looked down at her notes.

The crowd fell silent and Kate found herself holding her breath.

'Bachelor 007,' Trudie introduced, her voice dropping a seductive octave, 'holds a licence to... drill.'

'Huh?'

And then Juliet let out a whimper because onto the stage walked not Daniel but Oscar. Kate relaxed a little as she realised Crispin must have got the numbers all wrong.

'Yes, that's right, ladies,' Trudie continued, 'our resident builder comes fully insured to knock your foundations out from under you... and then rebuild them brick by brick.'

'Wow, do you think Trudie wrote these, or do you think the bachelors did,' Kate turned to Juliet to offer her a sweet but Juliet didn't notice on account of her eyes looking like they were out on stalks. 'You can bid if you want,' she said gently.

'No way. I promised.'

'He looks pretty good in that suit, though,' Kate whispered.

'Stop it. I am steadfast. I am hard-core. I am—'

'Fifty pounds,' Gloria shouted out.

'Bitch,' Juliet muttered.

'She's just upset because Bobby bid successfully on Bob, reminding everyone who was left on her own. Hey, you want me to bid for you?'

Juliet looked as though she really wanted her to, but shook her head determinedly and for extra measure, sat on her hands.

'Oh, come on, ladies,' Trudie said, 'you all know how talented this fine specimen is. Why, I bet he can fix all your needs.'

On the stage, Oscar winced and turned red.

'Seventy-five pounds,' Kate said, grabbing Juliet's paddle and holding it up. Juliet snatched it right back off her and Kate was worried she was going to whack her about the head with it until Gloria said, 'One hundred pounds.'

Immediately Juliet's paddle went up as she stood up, turned to stare at Gloria and shouted out, 'One hundred and fifty.'

'One hundred and seventy-five,' Gloria bid back.

'Two hundred,' Juliet countered.

'Two twenty-five,' Gloria sneered.

'Three hundred.' Juliet raised her paddle once more.

'Three hundred and—'

'Five hundred.' Juliet voice boomed across the room.

Kate's gaze slid to the stage, where Oscar was standing open-mouthed. Finally he shoved a hand through his hair and stared at Trudie, and Kate could see he was willing her to end this madness.

'Five hundred I'm bid,' Trudie said. 'Going once...'

Juliet cocked a hip and stared Gloria down.

'Going twice... Sold to Juliet Brown.'

Kate heard Cheryl's whistle above the sound of applause and watched proudly as Juliet nodded, turned and gracefully sat back down in her seat. She met Oscar's eyes, nodded again as he tipped his head in a thank you and walked off the stage.

'Whew. I think I need a cigarette,' Kate murmured.

'I can't breathe,' Juliet whispered shakily. 'Also, I think I might need to borrow some money.'

'Relax, friend. I've got you covered. But I'm going to keep hold of this for you for a while, okay?' And reaching out she grabbed Juliet's paddle from her.

''Kay. Thanks.'

'And now for our last bachelor of the evening...' Trudie said as Daniel stepped out onto the stage.

Kate barely heard Daniel's sales pitch. She was too busy fiddling with the edge of her own paddle, the form sitting on her lap, and her bag of sweets.

'Fifty pounds,' Mary said.

'One hundred pounds,' Cheryl said.

'Kate, come on, you can't let the night end on an anti-climax,' Juliet insisted. 'I think you need to bid for him.'

Kate turned to her cousin, shaking her head sadly at her. 'The Paddle of Power has gone to your head.'

'Two hundred pounds,' Gloria bid.

'Kate stick your paddle in the air and bid.'

'Three hundred pounds,' Cheryl countered and as Kate turned to watch she couldn't help noticing the concern on her mother's face.

'Three hundred and twenty pounds,' Gloria shouted out.

Oh for Heaven's sake.

With a hugely dramatic sigh she started rummaging in her bag, pulled out her purse and started counting coppers.

'One thousand pounds,' she said, her intention clear as a bell despite her voice being muffled by her bag.

There was a gasp in the room.

'One thousand pounds?' Trudie asked her. 'Sweetie, are you sure?'

Kate shook her head and held out her hand, 'No. Wait. One thousand pounds and sixty-three pence.'

'Am I bid any more?'

'No,' Daniel said succinctly as he stared at Kate. 'You aren't.'

Trudie grinned from ear to ear. 'All right then, everyone, going once... going twice... Sold to Kate Somersby. That concludes the auction tonight. Thank you to our fine group of bachelors and congratulations to Kate Somersby and Juliet Brown for providing our largest bids of the evening.'

As the audience filed out of the room, chatting excitedly with each other, Kate looked at Juliet.

'So,' Juliet said. 'That happened.'

'Uh-huh.'

'This evening did not go to plan.'

'Not at all.'

'We sucked at not bidding. I'm very tired now. I think I'll go home. Feed the cats. Soak my head.'

'And tomorrow we'll figure out what the hell we're going to do with them.'

Chapter 38

How to Lose a Guy in Zero Dates

Juliet

When Catty McCatface's paw swiped at the magazine for the third time in as many minutes, Juliet sighed and tossed the latest issue of *In Style* onto the coffee table.

'All right,' she said, staring pointedly at feline number five. 'One more look in the mirror, but then I swear I'm not moving from this spot until he rings the doorbell.'

As she got up to walk across the room and grab her compact from her bag she felt the nerves jingle-jangle and sighed for what felt like the millionth time that morning. She had the strongest urge to bound up the stairs and check out her outfit in her full-length mirror. An urge she wasn't going to succumb to. It was bad enough that this was the sixth outfit she'd changed into this morning because it also happened to be the first outfit she'd agreed on with Kate the night before. She should have trusted their instincts because all the changing had only served to get her even more hot and bothered.

The azure-blue sky held no clouds, only a soft haze, indicating it was going to be another scorcher, so the white denim shorts, turquoise silk camisole and crocheted poncho that was really more of a fine lace net of daisies worn casually over her top and shorts, was going to have to do.

'I bet Trudie or Bobby or Mrs Harlow didn't feel like this when they had their dates,' she muttered, checking her minimal makeup hadn't melted off already, before turning back to the cat and exclaiming, 'Ha. I know this isn't a date. That was a trick statement.'

'Hi,' Oscar's voice had Juliet whirling around, her compact snapping shut with a shocked click. 'The door was open, so I wandered in, hope that was okay?'

'The door was open?'

Catty McCatface padded over to wrap her body around Oscar's legs, giving Juliet a look that said, 'You're welcome.'

'Yeah,' he said, bending down to pick up the cat. 'At least you're getting a little through-draft in here as a result. It's already damned hot outside.'

As Juliet looked at Oscar standing in her cosy lounge, holding one of her cats in one hand and his beaten-up metal toolbox in the other, all she could think was that things were looking 'damned hot' inside as well.

'So who were you talking to?' he asked, putting Catty McCatface back down.

'Myself. Obviously.'

'Not the cats?' His grin hinted he was teasing, but Juliet didn't think it would help her case any if she admitted she'd gone back to talking to them now that Kate had moved out.

'You brought your tools?' she said instead, nodding at what he was still holding.

'You were expecting me to turn up in the tux?'

Darn that tux and all the gorgeousness therein contained, that had her acting so completely out of her comfort zone, thought Juliet. 'Of course not. This isn't a date.'

'Have you ever had a date turn up at your door to take you out dressed in a tux?'

'Nope,' she said, waiting a heartbeat before teasing, 'I don't own a tux.'

Oscar grinned. 'You said you had a list of things for me to do around the house?'

'Yes. Yes I did.'

'So...?'

'Right, number one is to hang a curtain rail in the bedroom.'

'You don't have curtains in your bedroom?'

'Spoils the view,' she said, catching the surprise bounce into his eyes. 'Of course I do. I think the cats decided to play with them and now the rail is coming down,' she finished lamely, trying to breathe past the nerves. Today was supposed to be about keeping her 'date' with Oscar as far away from feeling like a date as possible. That was why she and Kate had agreed that Juliet would keep Oscar busy doing things around Wren Cottage and Kate would keep Daniel busy decorating The Clock House in preparation for the fete.

Kate could organise oodles of legitimate work for Daniel to do.

Juliet on the other hand?

Why on earth hadn't she suggested the four of them spend the day working on The Clock House together? She and Oscar would have helped get the work done in half the time and the place was big enough that she would have been able to breathe without – she eased out a breath – breathing him in.

'Thank you for outbidding Gloria.' Oscar said as he followed her out of the lounge.

'You've already thanked me. I remember something about being saved from a fate worse than death?' she threw over her shoulder as she ascended the stairs.

She could feel him behind her and why on earth she thought it appropriate to add a little extra sway into her hips was beyond her, yet when she heard him drag in a breath, the smile that broke out over her face was pure feline.

'Isn't there that thing where if you save someone's life they're responsible for you?' Oscar asked.

'I think it's the other way around.' She paused on the threshold of her room because although she knew he meant it as banter, she didn't want him to feel responsible for her. She wanted him to feel...

He scooted around her and then stopped inside her room.

She tried to see her private space as he was seeing it. Three walls in soft dove grey and the feature wall behind her bed in a warm dusky rose that glowed when the acres of cream fairy-lights that she'd twisted around the iron bedposts were switched on at night.

Juliet swallowed, wondering what he was thinking. Other than that her space was really girly. She snuck a look at him from under her lashes. Her pulse quickening when she realised the feminine softness of her room only made him look all that more masculine. Her gaze swung to the white embroidered bed linen he was staring at and her heart beat out a triple-time rhythm when she saw the satin bra she'd forgotten to put away.

'I've never been in your bedroom before,' he said, his voice gorgeously rough as it teased at her equilibrium.

'Well, why would you have?' Goodness, her tongue felt thick in her mouth.

'You've seen mine,' he added, tearing his gaze away from the bed to stare instead at her lopsided hanging curtains.

'That was different,' she commented, thinking of all the design work that had gone into rebuilding the barn.

He was so tall that he could reach up to wiggle the curtain pole in his hands. 'Blimey. I see what you mean about it being loose.'

'Exactly.' It had taken her and Kate hours to unscrew all the fixings so that the rod hung just so! 'You know Melody could have come with you today,' she told Oscar as she watched him put his tool box on her bed and reach up to tug on the rail with both hands.

'She got a better offer,' he said, pulling the rod away easily and laying it on the floor before reaching into his tool box for a pair of pliers.

'Ouch,' she said, searching automatically for a strip of the right size rawl plugs as he used the pliers to pull out the old ones.

'Sorry, you know she loves spending time with you, but she's actually gone to the lido in town with Persephone.'

She looked up from the rawl plugs she was deciding on to find him studying her.

Was he imagining her in a bikini? Her hand dropped to

the edge of the fringing on her lacey poncho and when his gaze followed the movement she felt the tingle of goosebumps against the top of her thigh and tried to decide if it was the heat in his gaze or the tickle from the poncho's tassel she was brushing back and forth.

'I hope she remembered to take sunscreen,' she managed to get out.

He smiled. 'Please. It was the next thing she put in her bag after her Kindle and backup book. Then she checked to make sure I had some with me too.'

'Good girl.'

'Yes. Hand me those rawl plugs, will you? Thanks. Good choice, these are a much better fit for the hole.'

To stop herself watching the play of muscles under his t-shirt as he set about pushing them home with a tap from his hammer and then lifting the rod and fixings back into position, she searched his tool box for the right sized screwdriver, smiling when she came across not one but two bottles of sunscreen.

'Kate showed me a picture of the necklace she got Melody,' she said, handing him the screwdriver, together with two new screws when he held his hand out. 'Does she like it?'

'Are you kidding? She hasn't taken it off. It was a nice idea and this way Kate gets to keep Bea's–' his hand paused as he screwed in the fitting, 'I mean, *her* locket.'

'You should have seen her when she thought she'd misplaced it,' Juliet mused, automatically grabbing more screws for the other end of the curtain rod. 'I thought my heart was going to break.'

He stopped what he was doing to stare at her, his huge green eyes searching hers, as if he was looking into her soul and seeing a lot more than she wanted him to.

'I'm sorry,' she gushed out. 'I shouldn't have said that.'

'Don't be silly. You have a big heart, Jules. No one wants to see it breaking.'

She let it slide that he'd called her Jules. Had to when he was looking at her with a quiet thoughtfulness.

'To be fair,' he said, turning back to concentrate on screwing the remaining end of the curtain pole to the wall. 'I felt the same when she found out that Daniel had got that locket fixed for her. I hadn't realised how hard I'd been on her, or how hard she worked to hide her grief until she was shocked into letting some of it go, like that. It's funny because I always thought of Kate as emotional – dramatic, I guess. But I've just been realising lately... Have you noticed that since Bea... whenever she's with Sheila, she just sort of mimics her behaviour back to her?'

'Yeah. She sort of fell into that when Sheila stopped responding to any talk about Bea. Patterns, I guess.'

His head bowed as he stood in front of her window. 'Yeah. Patterns. Actually I did know how hard I was on her. Makes me feel like scum to think I treated her so badly, simply for not, like you said to me, reacting to Bea's passing in the way I thought she should.'

'Hey.' She reached out to lay a comforting hand on his back. 'It's okay–'

'It's not, Jules.' He sighed and then slowly turned to face her. 'And when you made me see the truth, instead of thanking you I stormed off on you. I'm s–'

That was one of the things she loved about Oscar. The fact that he listened and analysed. Oh, he might over-react initially, but she knew he always did the person the service of weighing up their words. Without thinking, she reached up to lay her fingertips against his lips. 'Ssh. There's absolutely no need to apologise or feel guilty for being human. I know Kate's pleased the two of you are talking again...' her words drifted to a close when Oscar reached up and took her hand from his lips.

'Juliet?'

'Yes?'

'Are we going to spend our whole day together talking about Melody and Kate?'

'Um,' Juliet wondered if he knew he still had her hand in his and that his thumb was sweeping gently back and forth across her knuckles, creating all sorts of havoc with her breathing.

'Because I could talk about my daughter all day, but it occurs to me you seem to find it difficult to let people say thank you to you.'

'What?'

'So I'm wondering how else I could say it.'

Juliet tried to swallow. Did he even know he was staring down at her lips as if he was contemplating whether a kiss was a good enough way of saying thank you?

Chapter 39

Out of the Barbecue, Into the Fire

Juliet

'B-barbecue,' she stammered out and could tell from the look on his face that that was the last thing he was expecting her to say.

'Barbecue?'

'That's how you can thank me,' she said. 'It's the next thing on the list. I have this barbecue set I've been meaning to put together for ages.' She headed out of the bedroom, knowing she was rambling but unable to stop. 'I'd love to be able to come home from work and sit out in the evening with a glass of wine and something cooking on the barbecue. So, if you're all finished up here?'

Oscar blinked. Shook his head as if to recover from the verbal whiplash and took a last look around her room before closing up his tool box and stating, 'Lead the way.'

Talk about playing with fire, Juliet thought moments later as she watched Oscar take in the grill, which consisted of a drum and two sets of legs. A few seconds later and he was looking back at her as if he knew she could have put this together for herself in a heartbeat.

What was she going to say when he asked her why she was giving him things to do that hardly matched the amount of money she had paid for him for.

She had to keep it together. Nowhere on any plan she had did it say that flirting with Oscar Matthews was okay.

But then, what if he put the barbecue together in ten minutes and then left because she had nothing else for him to do and she started missing him and regretting not pushing the boundaries?

'Can I make a suggestion?' he said, folding up the instructions and stuffing them into his back jeans pocket. 'It's going to take me about fifteen minutes to put this together for you and then it's probably not going to last much longer than that and I can't help thinking about the bricks I have in the back of the van. I could build you a brick barbecue that would last forever and look better.'

'But where would it go?'

'On the patio, so you can see it from the kitchen? If I build in a few extra shelves, you could put pots on it in the winter.'

'And how long would that take you to build?'

'Anxious to get rid of me?'

She fiddled with the hem on her poncho again. 'I'm concerned about the heat, that's all.'

'I have sunscreen. It won't take me that long. Maybe a few hours. What else have you got for me to do?'

Juliet thought about the rest of her non-existent list. 'I suppose I could sacrifice the rest of the list for you doing this.'

'Great.' In one smooth move he reached for this t-shirt and whipped it off.

Shock had her croaking out, 'Whoa, at what point did I order The Naked Barbecue Builder?'

'Relax. I'm just putting on sunscreen. You got a pad and pencil? I'll want to make a few sketches and take some measurements.'

When she returned she wished she'd brought out the superglue as well so that she could glue her gaze to the design appearing on the page before her and not Oscar.

'What do you think?'

'Delicious.'

'So you're happy with the design?'

She hadn't been looking at the design. She'd been enjoying the concentration on his face. The way his forearm flexed as he changed the angle of the pencil...

She looked down at the simple barbecue drawing. 'Can I borrow the pencil,' she asked and quickly extended a couple of lines on his sketch. 'Could you make it so that I can tile this area? That way I have a preparation area as well.'

'No problem. Speaking of preparation,' he bent down and picked up a bottle of sunscreen, tossed it to her and turned around to present her with his back.

Juliet licked her lips and stared down at the bottle now in her hand. Slowly she took the cap off the bottle and sprayed some onto his back, fascinated by the rippling of his muscles as the cool lotion hit his skin.

Was she supposed to slap it on and rub it in or dare she

let her hands do what they ached to do and slowly glide over every inch of his skin?

Catching her tongue between her teeth, she laid her hands softly against his back.

The instant she made contact he tensed. Her fingers splayed to soothe and after a second, his head dropped to his chest and he stood there patiently while she rubbed in the lotion.

'You have freckles,' she whispered, tracing the dusting across his shoulders and down his back and revelling in the feel of his hot skin over the solid strength underneath.

Oscar stepped away abruptly. 'I can handle it from here.'

'Oh.' Juliet was grateful he didn't turn around to see her blushing beetroot red. Had she overstepped the mark? Shown him with her touch that she was enjoying the experience a little too much? 'If you're sure?'

'Never been more sure of anything in my life,' he muttered quietly. He moved his hand back to grab the bottle from her and set about covering his front with sunscreen and cleared his throat. 'You probably have stuff to do inside... I don't want you to feel you have to spend all day watching over me.'

Juliet stepped back, sadness washing over her. That was the problem between them, wasn't it? They did an exemplary job of watching over each other. But that was where it stopped. 'I'll put some lunch together for when you're finished.'

She'd put the washing on, cleaned the bathroom, made two dozen scones, whipped up a salad for lunch and, most importantly, got herself completely back under control by the time he stepped back into the kitchen.

Darn it, it might be that she'd only achieved the first three, she thought desperately, as her gaze followed a bead of sweat trickling over his sculpted torso. Collecting herself she tore her gaze away and forced herself to stare somewhere over his shoulder.

'You need to leave the mortar to set and you need to buy some grill shelves for it, but otherwise it's all finished,' he announced.

'Great. Thank you. Home-made lemonade?'

When he nodded she passed him a glass and tried not to devour him with her eyes as she watched him drink thirstily.

'Are these your plans for the salon?' he asked, wandering over to the kitchen table to check out the designs.

'Yes, it's taken me ages to work out what I really need and how to get it all to match with Kate's colours. It's going to be fabulous.'

'Can I have a look?'

'Of course. I'd actually love your advice. I'm worried about having to move some of the electrical sockets and well, one of the walls.'

'Sounds mostly cosmetic. I'd have to check to see which walls are load-bearing – especially if you want to move this wall to create more room.'

'Darn. I knew I should have had you help out at The Clock House today. You could have looked at the walls and given us your expert opinion.'

'I'm pretty sure Daniel is appreciating the time alone with Kate.'

'Really?'

Oscar looked up from her plans. 'You have seen how they are with each other, right?'

'Oh.'

'Exactly. Besides it would have been awkward giving both you and Daniel my expert opinion over wall-moving.'

'Oscar? If Kate doesn't win the challenge, I'm going to open up in one of the empty units on the green, like you said.'

'You should. These ideas prove you're too good to let your talents go to waste. Does Kate know this?'

'In theory she does. But I truly think she's going to win The Clock House challenge and it won't be an issue.'

'Despite the fact that she paid one thousand pounds for Daniel and you paid five hundred pounds for me?'

'I didn't *pay* for you, pay for you.'

'Didn't you?'

The air turned hot and heavy again.

'Not the way you're thinking.'

'What way am I thinking?'

She wanted to moan. He was making it impossible for her to keep her head straight. If she flirted back, if she left herself open, would he respond in kind or would he back away like he'd done in the garden?

What was it Kate had said about her finding it difficult to push herself forward? Maybe she should take the tiniest risk now?

She put her hand on the middle of the plans and leaned in towards him. 'Oscar, are you trying to tell me you have some extra services I could avail myself of?'

His grin turned downright dirty and she found herself a

millimetre away from his lips when suddenly the room was shrieking at her and Oscar was flinging himself backwards, grabbing her plans off the table and wafting them under her smoke detector.

'Lawks. The scones,' she said, suddenly smelling burning.

'Damn it, Juliet, how can you be baking in this heat?'

'What part of the fact that it's the Whispers Wood fete *the day after tomorrow*, did you miss?'

Yanking open the oven door, she grabbed the nearest tea towel and took out three trays of scones. 'Please be all right,' she prayed, wafting the tea towel at them. 'Phew. Only a tiny bit of scorching around the edge of the top tray.'

When Oscar remained silent, she forced herself to turn around and face him.

His gaze scooted up to the smoke detector and she tried to interpret his expression. Was he thinking divine providence they'd been interrupted. She wasn't sure her heart could take much more of this. For a start she realised she still had another four dozen scones to bake before the fete.

'Look, why don't you nip upstairs and grab a shower and then sit down in the lounge and have a rest, while I sort these scones out and then plate up some lunch for us.'

He looked as if he was weighing up whether to comment on what had been happening before the game of scones episode. 'Actually,' he finally said, 'a shower sounds really good.'

'There are clean towels in the cupboard next to the bathroom at the top of the stairs.'

He looked relieved and at the doorway turned to put the

plans back on the table. 'You know, you should be really proud of yourself. You figured out what you wanted and you went after it.'

But she hadn't.

Yes, she was getting her salon either way. But as for wanting Oscar...

She'd taken another batch of scones out of the oven and plated up the salad before she realised she hadn't heard any sound coming from the bathroom in a while.

Wiping her hands on a cloth she took off her apron and popped her head into the lounge and stopped at the sight before her.

'He sleeps,' she whispered, smiling.

He looked so big on her small sofa, sitting with his head tipped back. He'd put his t-shirt back on and as she crept closer her smile grew. He smelled of the honey and coconut body-wash Kate had bottled up for her.

Did he dream, she wondered, as she perched on the edge of the sofa? She reached out to push her hand into his hair. He probably had no idea his eyes would always close on a sensuous rush whenever she touched his hair before cutting it. Or how much watching that would make her heart beat faster.

He sighed at her touch and lifted his body slightly, as if blindly searching for more of her.

She couldn't resist his unconscious plea and not allowing herself time to think, slipped from the sofa arm to straddle his lap and push both her hands fully into his hair.

Oscar groaned, his hands going straight to her waist as

he shifted under her. He was all heat and muscle and she was all molten and lithe. Stretching over him, she lowered her head to nuzzle at his exposed neck. Her lips trailing soft, barely there kisses that caused goosebumps on his skin, and made her smile against him. He swallowed, groaned again and this time he held her like he was never going to let her go as his hands pushed down on her hips as he rose up.

'Jules.' His head moved, his mouth searching for hers now. 'Give me one taste. Just one. That's all I'll ever ask for. I promise.'

She pulled back at his words and the movement must have been enough to wake him up properly because, as his hands tightened against her, she saw the shock of what he'd been about to do – what they'd been about to do – perforate the seductive spell.

A second later and he was squeezing his eyes shut.

When he reopened them sensible, sane Oscar was present again.

'Jules.'

For the second time that day she pressed her fingertips against his lips. She didn't want to hear it. One taste? *One?* That would be all he'd permit? As if she was some curiosity that could be fixed and dealt with?

She tried to breathe. Closed her eyes so that she wouldn't have to witness the regret and the guilt building within him. He went still as a rock beneath her, his hands sliding away to drop passively to the sofa and after a few moments she steeled herself to push away from him and when her stupid poncho got caught on his stupid belt buckle she thought she might die from the awkwardness.

'Shit,' she whispered, her hands trying to untangle herself.

'Let me help.'

Help? Help would have been stopping her before she'd put herself out there to be rejected. Help would have been the smoke detector going off again and waking her up to herself. And most of all it would have been him not looking at her like he didn't want to hurt her after he already had.

His hands covered hers, but she brushed them off.

'There. You're free of me,' she stated.

He inhaled deep into his chest at her words and she took that as her sign to climb as elegantly off him as she could. Refusing to look at him she said, 'I think you should go now.'

'Jules. This isn't your fault. I was sleeping and you were so... I forgot to think – just responded and–'

'Please leave.'

He hesitated and looked as if he was going to press another apology on her, so she turned and closing herself off from him, sat down on the sofa and grabbed the magazine off the coffee table.

He left before the first tear slipped down her face and as she heard the van pull away she promised herself she wasn't going to cry into the cats that gathered to comfort her.

Chapter 40

Gonna Swing From the Chandelier

Kate

'How do you know it's going to rain?' Daniel asked Kate as he hefted in the last box and added it to the growing pile in The Clock House foyer.

'Hello? Have you not seen Gertrude and friends sitting down in the field?' Kate dragged the box he'd just put down over to the adjacent pile so that all the decorating equipment was together.

'What's that got to do with the price of fish?'

'Science isn't it?' she said, picking up her clipboard to calculate numbers of trestle tables. 'Cows sitting down when it rains. Ted's arthritis playing up. Red skies and all that jazz.'

'Red skies? Okay, now you've completely lost me.' Daniel grabbed the pen out of her hand and added the five tables he'd tripped over in the other room to her tally.

'Red sky in morning, shepherd's warning,' Kate said. 'I'm telling you don't be surprised if at dawn you start seeing shepherds arriving in their droves, wandering about wagging their fingers and pointing to the sky.'

'You're paranoid.'

Kate chewed on her bottom lip as she stared down at the list. 'I just want it all to go perfectly.' She heaved out a sigh. 'I can't believe it's nearly here.'

'It's come around quick.'

Too damn quick, she thought she heard him add under his breath.

Was he, like her, feeling all jittery about being on the cusp of achieving what they'd set out to do? Was he wondering what was going to happen when the fete was over? When one of them got to move forward with their lives in this fabulous building and the other... didn't?

'Between Crispin and Isaac there's three pages of A4 notes,' she muttered. 'I know we'll divvy out the rest of the setting-up tasks at the village meeting tomorrow night, but I really wanted to get most of this place decorated in case of rain on the big day.'

'Are you absolutely sure we have enough decorations?'

'Trust me. Juliet made enough bunting to decorate all of England.'

Daniel smiled. 'We should have roped in her and Oscar to help us today.'

Kate snorted. 'I don't know if you've noticed–'

'The smouldering looks they give each other?' Daniel said, looking up from what he was doing to stare at her.

'When they think the other isn't watching?' Kate stared back at him, barely managing to keep her own smouldering banked.

'Yeah,' he said, his gaze cutting deep, his voice going deeper. 'I've noticed.'

Kate wanted to fan herself with the clipboard. 'That's why I think it's better if they spend today together without anyone intruding, if you know what I mean?'

'And I suppose spending such a large amount of money entitles you not to have to share me.'

'Oh that.' She flicked a bit of pretend lint from her ripped cut-offs. 'How much did I spend again?'

'One thousand pounds.'

She heard the bemusement in his voice and felt the corners of her mouth lift in a grin. 'And sixty-three pence. Don't forget the sixty-three pence.'

'Right. Because, look after the pennies...'

'Exactly. Do you miss all that?'

'Looking after the pennies? You make me sound Dickensian. It's more of a surprise how little I miss it, to be honest.'

'You won't go back to it after the fete?'

'Kate, you know I'm going to win The Clock House challenge.'

The knowledge hung in the air between them, but for her to admit it fully out loud would mean having to deal with the emotional meltdown it would surely bring. 'Maybe. Maybe not.'

'You paid one thousand pounds and sixty-three pence for me. I've won.'

'You're so sure I didn't pay with my lottery winnings and therefore skew the figures?'

'Yes,' he said, his gaze on her, now steady and confident. 'I'm sure.'

It set all the worry she'd had about seeing him today to

bed. That he had come to the realisation, without her having to ram it down his throat again or go out of her way to prove it to him that she wouldn't spend her lottery winnings on the fundraising, meant a lot to her. She didn't know what it was that had changed his mind about her but she was grateful for it. 'Thank you.'

'Out of curiosity, why did you pay so much for me?'

'It was worth it to see the look on Gloria's face.'

'I think it was more than that.'

'You're right. I got carried away.' So completely carried away by him.

'I'll say. That's a lot of money, Kate.'

'So, get to work or I'll be seeing Isaac about a refund.'

He gave her a mock salute. 'I'm going to go outside and mark out where the stalls are going, because I did actually see the weather forecast and it's not going to rain.'

'Forecast, shmorecast. And, wait, marking out where the stalls are going to go isn't until page three of the notes. You're going to have to settle for stringing up lights and bunting instead. Come with me.'

She didn't grab his hand to steer him up the sweeping staircase, but she wanted to.

This wasn't a date, she reminded herself.

So there was no need to touch.

Definitely no need to kiss.

The only kiss she needed to keep in mind was the Keep It Simple Stupid kind.

At the top of the staircase she saw Daniel pause, obviously thinking she was going to choose either the left wing of rooms or the right wing of rooms to take him into. Instead she smiled mysteriously and beckoned him across the landing to take the set of stairs from the third floor up to the attic.

At the attic door she shoved her hand into her pocket to retrieve a brass key.

'What are we doing up here?' Daniel asked from behind her.

'You'll see.' But as she unlocked the door and opened it she was unprepared for the wall of heat that greeted her. Surprised, she took a step back, right into Daniel's arms.

'Whoa, steady. Okay?' he mumbled in her ear.

She was very okay. In the sense that what wasn't to be okay about tingling and throbbing awareness of a person? 'I'm sorry, I didn't think about how hot it would be up here.'

Great. She'd already broken the no-touching rule. Although, to be fair it was him touching her.

'I can handle the heat if you can,' he said.

Kate wasn't actually sure she could, but she certainly wasn't going to back down from the challenge. Besides. They needed all the strings of lights that were kept up here. 'Into the attics we go, then.'

At the top of the narrow stairs she switched on the single light, breathed in the hot, musty air and walked into the middle of the large pitched-roof attic space.

'I never thought to check these rooms when I looked around before,' Daniel said as he came into the space. 'It's amazing.' He didn't seem to care about the poor light quality or the heat as he moved around, creating mini tornados of dust motes wherever he went. 'You could turn this space into another set of rooms easily.'

Straight away he was poking his head through the archway at one end of the attic and then walking to the other to investigate.

'God, this building speaks to me,' he said. 'What does it say to you?'

Before it had said: *Home and Bea and new start.*

Now it said: *I'm so sorry but you've lost.*

Kate swallowed hard. Was her story to be her always losing what she loved? She couldn't accept that and instead clung desperately to the hope still fluttering in her heart. She must remain positive but that was going to be harder to do up here, shrouded in intimate light that left her feeling exposed.

'At the moment it's saying one word: *stifling*,' she muttered. 'Let's get what we came for, namely boxes of fairy lights, and go.'

'I can't explore a little first? Look in the room that houses the clock mechanism? Come on, I bet you've been hotter?'

Kate thought back to pre-Clock House challenge when she'd been wandering around street markets convinced she was going to expire from heat. 'A while ago I was in Tobago and it was about forty degrees in the shade,' she mentioned. Had it really only been a few months ago, she thought, stunned.

'Now, that's hot. What's the coldest place you've visited?'

'The ice hotel in Sweden.'

'I've heard about that place. Don't they rebuild it every year? Did you see the Northern Lights? I'd love to do that.'

'Me too. I didn't get to see them but I did go on a horseback moose safari.'

'Sounds strangely scary. How did you end up getting to visit all of these places to review them anyway?'

'After Bea died it was,' she chewed on her bottom lip as she thought how to phrase it, 'difficult for me to be here. At university I'd written a few reviews and articles for the newspaper. I don't know what made me get back in touch with the editor.' It suddenly occurred to her that it could have been a sign from Bea. But that would be silly. Wouldn't it? 'Anyway, I did, and he knew someone who knew someone who was looking for a guest reviewer on their travel blog. I wrote a few pieces for them and they liked my work and then I got asked by a travel company if I'd be willing to be one of their mystery guests and it grew from there.'

'That's amazing. So where's the most romantic place you've ever been?'

'Romantic?'

Kate watched Daniel lift the corner of the dust sheet hiding the glorious chandelier she wanted to put up in the main reception room downstairs. She thought about how Isaac had told her she could have it if she won.

'Yeah, romantic,' he said, dragging the cover completely off the chandelier.

Tiny pin-holes of light filtering through the roof met the artificial yellow light and danced off the chandelier's glass nuggets and beading, sending sparkles shimmering across the attic. Daniel grinned over at her. 'How crazy magic is that?'

He laughed gently and then picked up a piece of jewelled

glass that had become detached and held it in his hand, twisting it to catch more light.

Where was the most romantic place she'd been?

She chewed on her tongue because she really wanted to say right here, right now. In the magical light of a fusty attic room, cosseted in stifling heat, with Daniel Westlake holding a jewelled piece of glass in his hand as if it was a ring.

But she daren't because that totally went against her new Keep It Simple Stupid ethos.

She cleared her throat and stared at the glass. 'There're these caves in St Croix that are amazing in their own right, but then you can swim through and come out the other side into your own little perfect oasis. What about you? Where's the most romantic place you've ever been?'

He carefully reattached the teardrop of glass and re-draped the dust sheet over the chandelier before stepping back with a sigh. 'I guess it depends who you're with.'

'I guess.' She kept her eyes wide open so she couldn't wrap herself in daydreams of swimming in the cove with him in St Croix, or staring up at the northern lights from a luxury igloo, or sitting in a café in Paris, or being in this room with him with its heat and dancing light.

'Are these what you were looking for?' He said poking into some wonky cardboard boxes.

'Yes.'

'Why don't you grab those two and I'll carry the rest. We'll be out of here and back in the fresh air in a jiffy.'

Back on solid ground. Well, the ground floor of The Clock House anyway.

Downstairs in the foyer Daniel put the rest of the boxes with the others. 'So I guess the first thing is to unravel all the lights and plug them in and check they're all working?'

'Mmmn. I was thinking it would look really good if we draped the lights, bunting and garlands from each corner of the room up to the central ceiling rose.'

'Sort of like the inside of a circus top?'

'Exactly like that. Do you think that's doable?'

'Hi guys, sorry to interrupt.'

Kate whirled around. 'Oscar?' Her hand came up to clutch at her locket. 'What are you doing here? What's happened?' He looked pale as he stood hovering in the doorway, his hands shoved in his pockets, his shoulders hunched forward and tension shooting off every line in his body.

'Kate, I was wondering if you could maybe pop back to Wren Cottage and check on Juliet?'

'Check on her?'

'Please.'

He looked like he'd had a really big shock and automatically she walked over to comfort him. 'It's all right. I'll go and check on her now.'

'Thank you. I can help out here if you want.'

Kate cast a worried frown at him. Maybe getting stuck into some physical work and chatting with Daniel might help. She swung back to Daniel, who took one look at Oscar and gave a nod and a smile. 'Great,' he said. 'Kate? You'll come back later to make sure we got it right?'

'Sure.'

Oscar stopped her at the door. 'I really fucked up.'

'I'm sure it's not as bad as you think.'

'I hurt her and that's the last thing I wanted. I have a feeling I've taken something complicated and made it even more–'

'Complicated?'

'Yeah. She won't speak to me – she might not even want to speak to you. But I'd feel better if she had a friend around.'

'I'll see what I can do.'

Chapter 41

Red Sky at Night

Daniel

'I'm in here,' Daniel answered, his heart bouncing against his chest wall as he heard Kate call to him. She was back just in time, he thought, glancing out of the window at the fading light before turning to find her standing in the doorway. 'What do you think? Does it look how you wanted?' Unsure what to do with his nervous hands, he shoved them into his jeans back pockets.

'It looks even better.' Her eyes sparkled with delight as she looked up at the multiple strands of tiny white light bulbs interspersed with red pom-pom garlands and blue cotton bunting. He'd anchored them from the corners of the room so that each swag draped up into the middle of the huge chandelier he and Oscar had hung up.

'We checked with Old Man Isaac and then Oscar ensured the light was all in working order before we installed it,' he explained as she stared at the glass chandelier.

'I knew it would look fabulous in this room.'

'There'll be plenty of time to put the tables up later, but

for now,' he moved away from where he'd been standing to reveal what else he'd been working on, 'I'm glad you came back, otherwise I was going to have to eat all this on my own.'

Her gaze strayed from the light to what Daniel had set out under it. 'You made a picnic?' She took a couple of steps forward to take in the feast of cheese, bread, pastries and fruit that he'd laid out on a blue and beige picnic rug Big Kev had lent him.

'I thought you might need a little pampering.' By the time Oscar had gone to pick up his daughter, Daniel had been left with enough time on his hands to remember Kate's face when he'd asked about what she'd do with the space in The Clock House attic and for a split second she'd looked lost and vulnerable. After putting the finishing decorative touches to the rest of the rooms, he'd wanted to do something special for her.

'Are you hungry?'

'Starving.'

'Come and eat. How was Juliet?' he asked as he waited for her to sit down on the blanket he'd laid out.

'She'll be okay. She took a risk and it didn't pay off, which left her feeling pretty wretched, but by the time I left she was feeling more philosophical.' Kate reached out to pluck a parmesan and olive pinwheel from the selection plate of mini pastries, tarts and quiches. She bit off a piece and moaned. 'These are so good. How was Oscar?'

Daniel started loading up one of the blue plates he'd found in the kitchenette. 'Kicking himself for not following through on that risk you're talking about, I think.'

'Well, I certainly hope you told him to think long and hard about what he's done.'

'Actually, I told him to think long and hard about what he *didn't do*.'

'Ha. Even better.' She shucked off her flip-flops, stacked them neatly at the edge of the picnic rug and then crossed those incredible long legs of hers. Her soft white top flirted with the top of her shorts, giving him tantalising glimpses of tanned, taut flesh. Next she reached up to take the band out of her hair and then fluff out the tresses so that the waves could rest freely across her shoulders. After that came a stretch and a, 'What a day', and as she set about relaxing and getting comfortable he figured she had absolutely no idea how sexy she was.

'Yeah,' he sighed, finding it next to impossible to swallow his mouthful of bread and cheese when his mouth was watering for something else entirely. 'I thought, given how hot it's been I should go for a drink that was cold and bubbly... want a glass of champagne? I stored it in the kitchenette fridge so it should be perfect now.'

'Sounds like heaven. You know you really didn't have to go to all this trouble,' she called out as he went to retrieve the bottle.

'What, nip across the green and grab something to eat and drink?'

Okay.

He might have asked Big Kev what Kate's favourites were. And when Big Kev told him to wait a moment before he'd disappeared upstairs, Daniel had told himself that this picnic idea was merely a sensible reaction to being hungry. But when Big Kev had come back downstairs with a punnet of strawberries, a picnic rug and a huge smile on his face, it had been Daniel who'd impulsively swapped the bottles of beer for the bottle of bubbly. In the kitchenette he searched high and low for glasses and when he made his way back to Kate it was to find her nibbling on a strawberry.

The glasses, which were actually little blue cups and the only thing he could find, clunked clumsily against each other as his grip tightened in reaction.

'I feel pampered,' she said, taking another bite of the strawberry. 'Throw in a shoulder massage and I'll think about hiring you for the spa.'

He walked towards her, settling himself opposite and passing her both of the cups so that he could open the bottle. 'Working in your spa might be a good option for me if I don't win.'

'Becoming your office manager might be a good option for me if *I* don't win.'

The silence was palpable as they both looked at each other and then there was the pop of the cork and Daniel was pouring champagne into the cups.

'I have an idea,' Kate said. 'Instead of toasting to this place, I mean.' She blew out a breath and raised her head to look him warily in the eye. 'Tonight let's not talk about The Clock House or winning. Or losing, either.'

'Okay.' His answer was automatic as he clinked his cup against hers. Focusing on a decision being made about this place would only start the countdown to ending whatever this journey was that they were on together.

* * *

As Kate finished recounting zip wiring through the Chiang Mai rain forest in Thailand a fascinated Daniel turned his head to look at her. Was it any wonder she'd found the courage to nip over the garden wall in the middle of the night, hoping to get a squiz at his plans for fundraising. He bit back a smile. Women genuinely didn't seem to realise how loud they got when they were together – especially when alcohol was involved. If anything, he had been the adventurous one to wander downstairs and seek her out... He halted his thoughts in their tracks because mentioning that escapade might lead to talking about the fundraising and this place and while they were lying next to each other on the picnic rug, only a tipple of champagne and some strawberries left of their feast, apart from the lick of awareness caressing his thoughts every now and then, Daniel couldn't remember feeling more relaxed.

Or enchanted.

'I can't believe you've done all those things,' he told her.

'Sometimes neither can I.'

'I don't think I've ever met someone as adventurous as you.'

He couldn't help wondering how Whispers Wood could ever feed that aspect of her personality and, as if she could tell what he was thinking, she turned her head back up towards the ceiling, frowned and focused intently on the chandelier above them before she quietly said, 'Some people might say the things I did were more dangerous than adventurous. Some might even say foolish.'

'What do you say?'

There was another long silence and when she spoke again, despite the fact it was only the two of them in the large room and they were lying close enough to touch, he had to strain to hear her. 'I say I didn't know who I was without Bea. I say that when I first started saying 'yes' to doing things I never once stopped to consider whether they were safe to do–' she broke off, frowned up at the light again. 'I say that that might have been because I wanted to join Bea – like maybe I had a death-wish.'

The words left her lips on a whisper of shame and guilt and a shocked Daniel turned fully onto his side so that he could reach out and gently tip her face towards his. How could she ever have thought that? She was too full of curiosity for life. 'You didn't have a death-wish. You *don't* have a death-wish. Trust me. I know someone who has and you are *nothing* like him.' He feathered his fingertips across her jaw-line, refusing to let her look away. 'Perhaps you were doing those things for your twin, because you knew she wouldn't ever be able to. Sort of like an homage. Have you thought about that?'

Some of the darkness left her eyes and she reached up to hold his hand against her face before easing out a breath and dropping her hand back to the blanket. 'I like the sound of that.'

His fingers moved to play with the tips of her hair. Soft. Strong. Beautiful. Like her.

'Were you and Bea identical?' he asked.

She nodded and whispered, 'There's this tangible connection present with twins that's hard to explain. And there's a confidence you lose when that connection is severed.'

'Do you know who you are now? Without her, I mean?'

She shrugged. 'So many of my dreams were Bea's dreams, it never occurred to me I had additional dreams until...' She went back to staring up at the ceiling. 'Until I bought a lottery ticket and won and suddenly some of them were given oxygen to breathe. When we realised I had a winning ticket it was Bea who screamed louder and jumped higher for joy. Straight away she was talking about how we could buy premises for the spa. How we'd be open in months. How all our dreams had suddenly come true and I–' she stopped, gave her head a little shake of denial.

'And you?' Daniel prompted.

'I sort of hesitated and didn't answer.'

This time when she tilted her head to meet his gaze it was with a look of disbelief that she'd done that, but he thought he understood. 'Kate, I've done accounts for people who suddenly come into a lot of money. It takes time to process the responsibility.'

'It wasn't that, really. Owning our own business... Opening the day spa had been my idea in the first place. That's what we were working towards.' Her fingers started toying with the edge of the blanket. 'But I think I expected we would fit some life experience in first, you know? Suddenly Bea was imagining us cutting the ceremonial ribbon on somewhere like this place, whereas I was dreaming about where to travel to first.'

Reaching over her head she grabbed two of the remaining strawberries, passed one to him and bit into the other. 'It wasn't the first time we'd argued.' She cast him a brief smile and twirled the strawberry stalk nervously in her fingers before adding, 'but usually afterwards we'd laugh about how it was good we weren't exactly the same or life would be boring. This time when we calmed down and apologised to each other it was different, though. We didn't laugh about our differences and I felt Bea looking at me as if everything had changed. As if she was worried our dreams would never be in sync.' She shoved the rest of the strawberry into her mouth, chewed, swallowed and breathed out. 'Then some stupid drunk-driver ran her into a tree and she was gone and Mum had a breakdown and Oscar had to look after Melody and his new business and I was left sort of rudderless and anchorless.'

'God, Kate. I'm so sorry.' No wonder she hadn't been able to spend the money. And no wonder she'd had to go away and find out who she was before she could come back. 'Shall I tell you who I think you are? I think you're brave and strong and resourceful and alive with life.'

Something small dropped to the ground behind them, making both of them roll away from each other in shock.

'What the hell was that?' Daniel scanned the floor. It had sounded like glass tinkling against wood.

Kate gasped and reaching out, picked up the teardrop of glass that had fallen off the chandelier earlier.

Daniel looked worriedly up at the chandelier. 'Do you think for safety we should take it down?' When she didn't answer he looked over to find her smiling softly at the glass.

'No,' she said, as if hugging a secret to herself. 'I think it'll be all right.'

'You're not scared the whole thing could come crashing down?'

She shook her head. 'The chandelier's safe. We'll pop this back on before we leave.'

'Okay, but,' he leaped to his feet, picked up the end of the picnic rug and pulled so that both it and, more importantly, Kate, weren't directly under the light.

'Feel better now?'

He nodded and lay back down on the blanket, grabbing the last two strawberries and passing her one. He'd just bitten into his when she turned onto her side to face him and asked, 'Who was the person you thought had a death-wish?'

His chest tightened uncomfortably but he thought he managed to sound somewhat sane when he said, 'My father.' He stared down at the remainder of the red fruit in his hand and went for broke. 'He's in prison.'

'Oh. Can I ask what for?'

'Originally tax evasion. This stint? Fraud.'

'That's why you became an accountant.'

His smile was rueful because, yes, he'd responded to his father's behaviour in an obvious fashion and wasn't that the real reason the job had only ever felt like a job and not his passion? And wasn't that why it had been so easy to follow Hugo? Hugo, who reminded him of his father – made him feel closer to his father?

Daniel shoved the rest of the strawberry in and as he bit down tried to concentrate on the sweetness of the fruit, not the bitterness thoughts of his father always brought. 'You ever heard of the racing car driver, Danny Westlake?'

Kate gasped in recognition. 'That's your father?'

'Yeah. The press had a field day when he was arrested. He'd been retired from racing for years, but everything he ever did was to excess – except for being a family man. Being tied down with a wife and kid was never part of who he wanted to be.'

Daniel eased himself up onto his elbow and reached for the champagne bottle. Silently he held it out to Kate, but she shook her head and gestured for him to go ahead and finish it. He upended the bottle into his cup and took a swig. 'The racing season I turned thirteen he had a bad crash, but when he got back into the car the next race it was with zero fear. It really shook me up, though, and I begged to travel with him the next season. I didn't even question why he agreed. It turned out the team thought I'd calm him down, help him accept mortality and race more cleanly. Not take so many risks. Unfortunately my being there had the opposite effect. The more constrained and contained he felt, the more he courted danger, and if he couldn't go full-out on the circuit, he'd do it on the open roads. We're all very lucky he didn't hurt anyone. Long story, short, he was caught for speeding, lost his licence, got dropped from the team and sent home with his tail between his legs. He wasn't qualified for anything except chasing thrills and living beyond his means. Oh, he did discover he had one other talent. By the time I was nineteen he'd scammed almost everyone in our home town. When he was finally arrested on tax evasion it seemed like such a conservative crime compared with how he lived his life. By the time fraud charges were brought, Mum accepted the news stoically.'

'And you?'

'After watching what years of worry had done to her I never wanted her to think history would repeat itself. So I worked

my arse off and started an accountancy firm with my best
friend.'

'But then it closed down?'

'I shut it down.' He swallowed down the rest of the champagne, wishing it was something stronger. 'That is to say, I
had some help from the authorities in shutting it down.' He
grimaced. 'Kate, my business partner – my so-called friend
– is also in prison.' He saw her awkward disbelief and, like
ripping off a plaster, got out the rest of the words as quickly
as possible. 'He stole from our clients.'

'Oh, Daniel, you must have felt so betrayed.'

'I swear to you I didn't know.' Hang on? 'You aren't worried
I was in on it with him?'

'No way. Although now I think I understand your reaction
when you found out I had undisclosed funds sitting in a bank.'

'I should have worked out what he was doing sooner, but
I'd started acting more like an employee than a partner in a
business. I've spent the last year in court, extricating myself
from the fallout, losing my business reputation and selling
most of everything I owned to pay back the clients he stole
from.'

'You paid them back?'

'Of course.'

'That's going beyond, Daniel. It's honourable and admirable.'

'I had to make it right. And it's obscene how much money
property in London goes for.'

'But The Clock House? Your new business? Do you have
enough left?'

'I have enough left.'

'Because I happen to know someone with some spare funds...'

'I have enough,' he repeated gently, wondering if she even knew what she'd offered him – not in terms of financial help – although that showed the size of her heart – but more in her utter belief in him. 'I thought we weren't going to talk about The Clock House tonight?'

'Oops.'

'Mmmn.' He grinned and, reaching out, he hooked his finger into one of the rips in her impossibly sexy cut-offs and tugged, dragging her closer to him. 'It's funny, but this isn't quite how I'd intended for this evening to end.'

'No? How had you intended for it to end?'

'I thought we'd chat over the food and finish the rest of the champagne.'

'I'd say baring our souls constitutes chatting. And we did finish the food and the champagne. So check box to those.' She reached out and drew a tick shape on his chest. 'What else?'

He thought about the risks he swore he wouldn't take until he was secure in the business he was running. He thought about Oscar's face when he'd realised he'd let an opportunity pass right on by. He thought about Kate and how enchanting, enthralling, exciting he found her.

'I keep telling myself to let this go – that it would be silly to get into something before or even after the thing we've agreed not to talk about, but I'd be lying if I hadn't thought about stealing a kiss at the end of the night.'

'Yeah?'

His heart expanded and his blood pounded. 'Well, you are wearing these,' his fingers slipped through one of the frayed rips to stroke the silky smoothness of her thigh. 'And an accountant can only take so much.'

'Let's see how much,' she whispered, wriggling closer still.

'I couldn't help noticing the sunset as I was standing on the ladder fixing the last garland to the chandelier. What does red sky at night mean?'

'Shepherd's delight.'

'Yeah,' he said, lowering his lips to hers. 'Shepherd's delight.'

Chapter 42

Sign of the Times

Kate

The things Daniel had whispered to her...

The way he'd touched her... kissed her... held her...

Well, before they'd both remembered there were in what was essentially a public building that someone could walk into.

Still.

It had been so good and Kate knew she wanted more.

Much more of all the kissing and touching and holding. And much more of the quiet talking into the night.

She shivered with delight, hugging her happiness as she walked back to Myrtle Cottage.

'So here we are,' he said as they reached their respective cottages.

'I can't believe we've done the walk of shame right through the village and nobody said anything.'

He frowned down at her as he tucked her hair back behind her ears. 'Are you feeling shameful? Or ashamed?'

'Absolutely not,' she shot back. Hauling herself up onto

tiptoes she laid her lips against his, packing as much sweet, soothing reassurance into the kiss as she could.

'Spend the day with me?' His voice was sexy and cajoling when he came up for air and she'd have given a lot to sneak away with him. Go somewhere they could embrace the blue skies and each other's company.

'I can't,' she moaned. 'Aside from packing all the stock for the stall, Mum's coming for lunch and I could do with a shower and enough time to get this big fat grin off my face.'

'I guess I'll be taking a shower too. A cold one. Promise me something?'

'Okay.' This morning she'd expected to feel sad that what they'd shared would naturally come to an end after the fete, but being with him had given her all these ideas and there was this glow inside of her thinking that maybe instead of finishing something, they'd started something.

'Promise me tonight at the village meeting you'll wear something that covers up these incredible legs of yours, otherwise I'm not going to be able to concentrate on anything Crispin says.'

'You know the meeting tends to be a lot more fun when you're not concentrating. You won't believe some of the things we've voted on without realising.'

'But I'm not sure I can cope with Mary seeing me look at you like I can't wait to...' He waggled his eyebrows suggestively, making her burst into laughter.

'Okay. Jeans it is.'

'Jeans that go all the way down to the ground, yes?'

She rolled her eyes. 'Boring.'

'Just think of how non-boring it will be afterwards.'

'I'm going to hold you to that. Oh, don't forget Isaac will set the clock forward, so make sure you aren't late.'

'Okay. Say hi to your mum for me.'

She watched him push open the gate to his cottage.

Heard him whistle and the happy sound slipped joyfully into her heart.

Her mother was either nervous or restless. Kate couldn't work out which. All she could do was register the fidgeting, because it was what she did too, and try to work out how to fix it. Determined to hold onto the positive vibes from last night, she looked at her mum across the garden table and tried not to worry she'd been too relaxed about her progress.

'Mum, what's wrong?'

'Wrong?' Sheila's hand trembled as she brought the sparkling mineral water to her mouth. 'Nothing's wrong,' she added, putting the glass down, but immediately picking at the edge of the chicken satay sticks lying on her plate of half-finished food.

'Something is wrong,' Kate said, leaning forward and forcing herself to confront the issue, even if that meant she was about to receive the wall of silence of old.

Sheila looked out over the pale pink anemones that Kate had forgotten to water. Getting up, she walked over to the garden tap and filled the watering can. On her way back she caught Kate's pointed stare and with a wave of her hand explained, 'Everything is changing again.'

Kate watched her mother water the flowers and when she

went to refill the watering can to move on to the next batch didn't stop her. Instead she tried a gentle, 'Everything changes all the time.'

'You're right. I know you're right. I don't know why I get so nervous about that.' She knelt down in her pristine white linen trousers and tugged at a weed in the shallow flower bed.

Kate rose to her feet, grabbed the trug that was on the patio and brought it over to her mother. Kneeling down beside her she grabbed what she hoped were some weeds too. 'You've been heartsick for a long time. It's bound to make you feel jittery coming out the other side of that.'

'Heartsick?' Sheila paused in her weeding and looked at her daughter in surprise. 'Kate, I swear I don't know how you could so generously describe me having a breakdown after Bea died as simply being heartsick.'

Kate's heart thudded. It was the first time her mother had ever admitted to what had happened. She shook the dry earth from the dandelion root and mumbled, 'It was understandable, Mum.'

'Was it?' Her mother searched her face. 'You understood, did you? All those times I ignored you. Refused to communicate with you? Retreated inwards?' She looked down at her hands. 'It's what I did when your father left, so I guess it's what you knew.' She lifted her eyes to Kate's. 'I need you to know how sorry I am. For not being the mother you needed. For not letting you talk about Bea.'

Kate licked her lips. 'It's okay. I understood.'

Sheila shook her head in wonder. 'Who taught you to be so forgiving? Because it certainly wasn't me.'

'Maybe it was Bea,' Kate said carefully. 'You know how she was after Dad left.'

Sheila grimaced. 'Yes.' She pulled out another weed. 'I'm afraid I couldn't forgive him so easily.' She stared down at the trug between them. 'I've just been so angry that she had to leave as well.'

'Mum,' Kate's rebuke was soft as she reached over and took the weed out of her hand. 'It wasn't like she could help it.'

Sheila lifted the back of her hand to her cheek as if to elegantly pat away perspiration. Or an escapee tear. 'I suppose I've almost accepted that,' she said. A smile crossed her face. 'I was so pleased for her when she found Oscar. They were such a good match. They were going to make it. Not like me with your father.'

'Is that what you've been feeling? Dad abandoned you and then so did Bea?'

'Haven't you felt that?'

Kate gave a helpless nod. 'Yes. I think so. Of course, then I left you too. And maybe I shouldn't have. It was just easier to tell myself that I didn't want to make things harder for you – remind you all the time of Bea and that she was gone. I think now I should have done what Oscar did with Melody. I should have forced your company. But every time I came back, well, as usual, my timing was all off and it was easier not to try.'

'You were grieving too. And I didn't give you any other choice and for that I'll always feel terrible. I'm so sorry, Kate.'

Kate lifted her hand to touch the locket dangling from her neck. She thought about the postcards Juliet sent. The ones she kept tucked inside her folder of spa leaflets. She thought about the pebble rising high in the air and landing vein-side up and she thought about the teardrop of glass from the chandelier appearing in the attic and then again when she and Daniel were lying underneath it.

And she thought about why signs and the passage of time mattered so much to the living.

Now that her mum had started coming back to life, Kate really hoped she might see some of those signs and be comforted by them and start to sense time passing, but be able to enjoy living in the present.

'I worry that you're too much like me,' her mum said.

'What, you think I'll end up on my own?' Maybe she understood why her mum thought that. From the moment her dad had left and it had become just the Somersby Women, Sheila had led the way in showing the world they could cope with anything. There had been no public out-crying and to be strong for her children, Sheila hadn't done any private crying. No wonder when Bea had died, she hadn't been able to cope with the emotional turmoil.

'You know what – I am like you. Resourceful, proud, inde-pendent,' Kate acknowledged. 'But we're not on our own because that's our lot, Mum. We're on our own because we can be. Bea couldn't do this. She couldn't wait. She had to have everything straight away, you know she did. And she was lucky. So lucky to find Oscar, because if she hadn't I'm not sure she could have been happy. So I'm pleased that she found love and didn't have to be on her own.'

'Melody–'

'Melody is half of Oscar. And she'll become who she becomes and that'll be fine too.'

Her mother looked out into the distance and then bravely back at her daughter. 'Oscar is looking at Juliet.'

'She's looking back. Do you think you're going to be able to cope with that?'

Her mother looked as if she was struggling, but then after a moment she said, 'He deserves to be happy.'

'Yes, he does. We all do.'

'Kate?' Her mum hesitated and then squared her shoulders. 'Have you thought about what you'll do if you don't… '

'Get The Clock House?' Kate helpfully finished for her.

'Yes.'

'Actually I have.' If she didn't get to open up Beauty @ The Clock House it would be because Daniel owned it – which would mean he'd be staying in Whispers Wood. And she really liked the sound of that. 'Juliet and I have put so much work into the businesses. I'm sure if we needed to we could find other premises.'

'Other premises?'

She heard the jump of panic in her mum's voice and smiled. 'Of course they'd have to be close by because I couldn't consider moving again. Not now I'm home.'

'Oh. Well. That sounds,' her mother sniffed, 'very good indeed.'

'It does?'

'I've a lot to make up for.'

'We have the time to work it out. Oh,' she said with a snap of her fingers, 'I know what we could start with.'

'What's that?'

'We could start with you telling me what's really going on between you and Big Kev!'

Sheila Somersby raised her eyebrows, but the smile that spread across her face was soft and secretive and lovely.

Chapter 43

All For One and One For All

Kate

By the time Kate and Daniel wandered into The Clock House for the village meeting that night there were only single seats left. With a quiet smile for each other they silently parted ways. Daniel sat three rows ahead of her to her right while she...

Crap! If she'd been paying attention she wouldn't have ended up next to Gloria.

She hugged her bag on her lap and pasted an awkward smile onto her face.

The smile was not reciprocated.

In fact it wasn't even acknowledged.

Gloria was too busy reading.

Naturally, Kate wanted to see what work of literature Gloria Pavey would enjoy. Imagine her surprise to discover it wasn't *Zen and the Art of Motorcycle Maintenance*. Unless they'd changed the cover for a woman in a Victorian crinoline smiling coyly from behind her fan.

So Gloria loved a bit of romance.

The evidence had her softening a little towards her.

She leant sideways a little, hoping to read over her shoulder and shuffled backwards guiltily when Gloria huffed out a breath and snapped the book shut.

All right. Jeez. She had zero problem concentrating on Daniel anyway.

She smiled when the first thing she saw him do after he sat down was gaze up at the chandelier. She knew what he was thinking. They'd forgotten to put back the glass droplet that had fallen last night. She opened her bag to double-check she'd put the sparkly talisman inside. She had and taking out her phone she texted him: *I'll reattach the crystal once everyone's gone home.*

Her phone buzzed and she opened the text: *Forgot to ask you… why aren't you wearing jeans that go down to the ground?*

Feeling light and playful, she texted back: *Turned out I don't own any. #SorryNotSorry Don't worry when I open the spa I'll be wearing a… uniform!*

She waited for a text but it didn't come. Instead Daniel disappeared from view for a moment and she got distracted by Crispin making his way to the front of the stage.

When her phone buzzed a few moments later the text read: *Sorry, I dropped my phone. You've got to warn a guy when you start talking uniforms.*

She texted back: *Text.*

And got back: *Huh?*

She smiled and her fingers tapped away: *You mean when I text something like that. Or did you mean when sexting? Ooh, you want to sext? P.S. I told you the meetings were more fun if you didn't concentrate on what Crispin was actually saying.*

At the first vibration of her phone she looked down at his reply: *They definitely are. However, in case I accidentally discover I've volunteered for the stocks and sponge stall, I'm saying no to sexting and putting my phone away now.*

She stuck out her bottom lip and texted: *You're no fun* And got back: *Wait 'til later.*

And then: *And put your phone away.*

She looked up to find him staring at her with a knowing grin and with a roll of her eyes she held her phone high in one hand and her bag in the other and made a great show of putting it inside.

It was the super-loud huff from beside her that clued her in to the fact that Gloria had probably been reading over *her* shoulder the whole time, but the grin that Daniel gave her made her heart kick with excitement and then he was turning back to concentrate and she had nothing else to do except pay attention to what Crispin was saying.

'Everyone manning a stall tomorrow please be aware you have thirty minutes and thirty minutes only to unpack and set up before those cars and vans need to be parked away from the green.' Crispin looked specifically at Oscar and Kate realised it was his van parked right in The Clock House gates as they were walking in. By the time they left this evening Crispin would probably have anointed it with one of the special 'inconsiderate parking' stickers he'd had printed up.

While Crispin went through the list of what stalls there

were going to be and where the catering was going to set up and when the various competitions were going to be judged, Kate looked around the room and spotted Juliet sitting with Aunt Cheryl and her mum. She caught her eye and although Juliet's smile wasn't huge, Kate was thankful that she'd at least felt up to coming tonight rather than sitting at home alone with the cats.

Looking around, she scanned the crowd for Oscar. It wasn't until she'd twisted right around in her seat that she saw him, in his usual place, propped up against the open doorway, his arms folded, his gaze unwavering on Juliet.

'I have something to say, please.'

Kate jumped and swung back around in her seat at the announcement shouted into her ear. And then she realised Gloria was addressing the meeting, not just her.

'Is it about the fete, Gloria,' Crispin asked, his tone tired and yes, Kate thought, her gaze narrowing on Gloria, a little wary.

'You asked if there was any other business and what I have to say concerns all of us,' Gloria said defiantly.

'Very well. Perhaps you'd like to stand up so that everyone can hear you?'

'Of course.' Gloria rose to her feet, and then went one better by standing heavily on Kate's foot as she moved past her and out into the aisle.

Why not go the whole hog and get on the stage, Kate thought, rubbing her foot.

'Firstly I want to say that I've done a lot of soul-searching,' Gloria said.

'What's that?' Kate quipped, beyond annoyed with her already. 'Your soul has gone missing?'

Gloria threw Kate a look that said, Oh, you did not want to have done that, and Kate's heart started to hammer inside her chest.

She turned her head left and caught Juliet's worried frown and then she turned around in her seat and watched Oscar take a step forward, almost to protect everyone from what Gloria might be about to say and as Kate looked at Daniel, Gloria started speaking in earnest.

'Like I said, I thought long and hard about whether I should share the information I have… It's not a secret that I looked upon Daniel Westlake's ideas for The Clock House favourably. Let's face it, no one really expects Kate to actually stick around and commit to living in the village.'

Kate's mouth dropped open as she felt the eyes of everyone settle on her.

'Aside from Kate's incurable wanderlust, Daniel's idea to provide a hub for business owners is innovative, commercial and, in a place like Whispers Wood, a step in the right direction to putting us on the map.'

Had Gloria suddenly become a cartographer, then? What, exactly was she going on about?

'Gloria,' Crispin interrupted, 'This meeting is about the fete tomorrow, not about who wins The Clock House challenge.'

'What he said,' Kate said aloud.

'Ah,' Gloria smiled in a way that suggested she was enjoying the spotlight. 'But when certain information that could directly affect opinion comes to light... well, isn't it my duty to pass on that information?'

'Residents aren't voting on anything to do with The Clock House,' Kate replied. 'And what you have to say would make no difference to how people think about Daniel.'

'No?' With a sudden twist of her head, Gloria's gaze shot straight to a tense-looking Daniel. 'Daniel, is it true that your business collapsed as a result of charges brought against your business partner?'

A gasp went up throughout the audience and all heads turned as one to look at Daniel.

His jaw was clenched tight and his eyes were like ice as he stared her down.

'No comment?' Gloria's smile turned self-satisfied and saccharine sweet. 'Is it true that he was found guilty of stealing from your clients and is currently in prison?'

Again Daniel remained silent and Kate couldn't believe it. Was he too much of a gentleman to respond? She looked closer and saw the look of resignation on his face.

'And is it true your father is also in prison?'

'That's enough,' Kate spat out. 'The one has absolutely nothing to do with the other and neither has anything to do with Daniel.'

'How do we know, though?' Gloria asked, swinging her gaze back to Kate, the light of victory shining in her small, mean eyes. 'How do we know this new business idea of his isn't a scam? How do we know it wasn't his intention all along to settle here, where no one knew him, and start deceiving us?'

'You can't possibly think that,' Kate asked quietly. She looked about the room, panic bleeding into her speech. 'Daniel has never done anything to make any of you believe that. He wouldn't. That is not who he is.'

In the silence of the room, Daniel rose to his feet and made his way into the aisle. Blocked by Gloria he ground to a halt and Kate rose shakily to her feet.

Gloria stood her ground, careful to look everyone in the eye. 'I can't risk supporting a person or his business idea under these circumstances and I don't think any of you should either.' She had to tilt her head to meet Daniel's gaze but she did it. 'Still no comment?'

'Step aside, Gloria.' Daniel's voice was calm but full of warning.

'You can't just–'

'Step aside or I will lift you bodily out of my way.'

Even under her dodgy spray tan, Kate could see Gloria pale and after a couple of seconds she moved out of his way.

'Daniel, wait.' Kate stepped out into the aisle. 'Please.'

'Did you tell her?' he bit out.

'What?' How could he possibly think that? 'No. Of course not.'

'Did you tell someone else?'

'Absolutely not.'

She could tell from the look in his eyes that he wasn't sure whether to believe her. Oh, he wanted to, but that was different, wasn't it? Wanting to trust someone wasn't the same as actually trusting them.

'Let me pass, Kate.'

'Daniel,' she said his name softly. Reached out to put a hand on his chest. But he side-stepped her and carried right on walking out of the room and she was only dimly aware of Oscar going after him because she was whirling back to Gloria with anger shooting through her veins.

'What the hell is wrong with you that you would repeat such bitter gossip publically?' Kate threw at her.

'It's not gossip. I have proof.'

'There's no way you have proof Daniel's done anything criminal. You can't just stand up in the middle of a public meeting and spew private information about a person who has done *nothing* to you. And none of us,' she said, turning around to address everyone, 'should be letting her. It's not right.'

Chapter 44

The Writing on The Clock House Wall

Daniel

Humiliation, anger, bitterness and mistrust all banded together, forming a ball of bile that stuck in Daniel's gullet, making him feel sick. The doors slammed shut behind him and, leaning against the wall for a moment, he struggled for control.

Half his life he'd had to get used to people wondering if the apple fell far from the tree and all damn year he'd worked to separate his name from Hugo bloody West's.

The only person he'd told in Whispers Wood was Kate and after he had, after she'd listened – he'd thought without prejudice – he'd actually felt like the past was in the past and that his future was looking much brighter. She'd made him feel as if all the bad times had brought him to this point and made him a better man. Hell, after last night he'd spent the day without thinking about business once. Instead he'd thought about her. Only her.

Had he got it wrong again?

Put his faith in the wrong person?

Again?

'Mate?' Oscar came into the foyer. 'You need to get back in there and listen to Kate.'

Daniel shook his head and said quietly, 'What I need to do is get out of Whispers Wood.'

'I think that would be a mistake.'

'I'm not sure I care what you think.'

'Well, thanks. I live in Whispers Wood too and I'm going to be really pissed off with you if you think I believe a word of what Gloria has been spouting off.'

'Even if I tell you every word of what she said is true?'

He saw the shock, despite it being quickly masked.

'You did not come here to scam us,' Oscar insisted. 'I won't believe it.'

Some of the tension left Daniel's shoulders. 'No. I didn't. But the bit about my business partner being in prison is true. The bit about my father being in prison, also true.'

'I assume from Kate's reaction she knows all this?'

'I told her last night.'

'Well, she's still here, isn't she? She didn't run at the news. So get the hell back in there and support her defence of you.'

As he said it raised voices coming from the meeting could be heard by both of them.

'Come on,' Oscar insisted, 'Before Crispin goes full Speaker of The House and starts shouting "order".'

From the doorway, straightaway he could hear the frustration in Kate's voice. She'd made it up onto the stage and was standing tall and righteous in those ridiculously short shorts that had been driving him insane from the moment he'd first driven into Whispers Wood.

'I'm sure plenty of details about Daniel's father have been twisted into gruesome gossip by the tabloid press,' she said. 'But I suggest if you're that fascinated about the man, you get your facts from public record.'

'Is public record going to show he started a business with a crook and that his father is a criminal as well?' Ted asked, standing up.

Christ, if Gloria had got laid-back Ted all riled up, Daniel could only assume the rest of the residents weren't far behind. Ted was probably thanking his stars he'd been paid for Monroe's repairs with real money!

Kate's hands went to her hips. 'Again – what does that have to do with who you know Daniel to be as a person? He's paid his bills with you on time, hasn't he? He even paid for those cupcakes you bought off me. I'm sure Isaac can tell you Daniel delivered all his fundraising money without quibble. If he was really out to con us, don't you think he'd have run off with the money by now?

Isaac stood up. 'Kate's right. Not only did you all vote for Daniel's idea for the fete theme because you believed in him. Every single penny of money he collected was accounted for properly.'

'We don't all automatically turn out like the family black sheep,' Kate paused and eye-balled several of the meeting's attendees, 'No matter how many of you have been convinced at one time or another since Bea died that I was only going to end up like my father and leave and never come back.'

Daniel felt Oscar tense beside him and wondered how many times Kate had had to battle this particular assumption. It was human nature, he knew, but still, he'd begun to think of this place as different. Maybe it would be best if he set up the business in a bigger, more anonymous, place. He'd thought he could contribute here, but that would be impossible if underlying his every interaction was a layer of distrust.

'These are the only facts you need to know,' Kate asserted. 'The rest is *no one's* business, unless Daniel decides it is. Firstly, it was Daniel who went to the authorities as soon as he worked out what was happening. Secondly, he took it upon himself to *personally repay every person his friend stole from*.' She paused to let that fact settle in and Daniel felt his heart melt. 'Thirdly, he didn't choose Whispers Wood as his next victim. His car broke down. That is all. Fourthly, he fell in love with a village down on its luck. He's a man of integrity who has as much right to live here as anyone. And fourthly, if I get The Clock House, it will be because I've won it fair and square and not because you lot didn't support the best person for it.'

Into the silence Daniel said, 'Fifthly.'

'What?' Kate was breathing hard after her impassioned speech. Her chest heaving in and out. Her cheeks rosy. Her eyes sparkling with determination.

His goddess-warrior looked completely beautiful, and he felt utterly undeserving.

'You already said fourthly,' he told her. 'You meant fifthly.'

'Right. Um. Fifthly.'

The entire village of Whispers Woods sat staring at Kate and Daniel like she was Baby Houseman and he was Johnny

Castle and at any moment she was going to leap off the stage and into his arms, and then they were all going to dance off into the sunset.

But what if they'd already shared the only sunset they were going to have together?

She'd just stood up for him in front of the whole village. She'd proved that she put people ahead of business. She deserved this building they were all congregating in, much, much more than he did.

He held up six fingers to indicate 'sixthly' and not taking his gaze from hers, mouthed the words, 'Thank you' and then brought his hands to his heart briefly before turning on his heel to leave.

'No. Wait, Daniel, don't go.'

He heard her, but he couldn't stay.

He had to make this right. You didn't have to be an accountant to know which fundraiser had raised the most money, but he was one and he knew the bachelor auction had pulled in twice as much as Kate's events. Knew also that it only had because both Kate's and Juliet's donations had been so large.

'Daniel?' This time it was Oscar. 'Give her a minute to get through the crowd.'

Daniel glanced back briefly to see that Kate's mum and Juliet and Juliet's mum had surrounded her as she made her way from the stage.

'I can't.' If she walked out of this building with him, what if she then decided to sacrifice everything she'd worked for here and leave with him? He couldn't have that on his conscience. 'Tell her I need some space to think.'

Chapter 45

On That Fete-ful Day

Kate

It was one of those rare and perfect English summer days. Sort of.

Rare in the way that a village in England was holding their summer fete and it wasn't raining.

Perfect in the way that the village green was bursting with pretty tents in all shapes and sizes, showing off scrumptious homemade produce and exquisite crafts, all tucked under a canopy of pom-pom garlands and bunting. Flower boxes, worthy of first place in Best in Bloom had been put up at each of the windows of The Clock House and lanterns and streamers hung from all the trees.

And 'sort of' in the way that as Kate looked up from her Bea's Bee Beautiful stall for what felt like the millionth time, Monroe was still absent from its parking spot outside Mistletoe Cottage.

Trying not to dwell on the fact, she wrapped a bottle of shampoo and conditioner in pale pink tissue paper, popped them into a pretty white organza bag and smiled at Mary. 'I hope you enjoy them. There's a feedback card in the bag.'

As soon as Mary left, Kate stepped out of her tent to stare across the green.

Where was Daniel?

She'd thought she'd understood his need for space after the meeting last night. But surely a need to let the anger settle couldn't have turned into him deciding to leave? At the thought he might have left without saying goodbye a large knot formed in her stomach.

'Wow, Kate, everything looks amazing.'

Finding it hard to fight the melancholy, Kate watched Melody bound into the tent with Persephone.

'You're in a dress,' Persephone said in awe.

Yes.

How stupid to swap her perfectly serviceable shorts for her scarlet summer dress.

How stupid to think its cheerful colour and confidence-boosting cut would help her keep smiling when she accepted defeat during Isaac's speech later.

How stupid to look her best for the absentee newcomer.

'Thank you,' she said, following them back inside. 'You both look fabulous. Fancy-dress competition later?'

'Uh-huh, we're fairies from the fairy ring,' said Melody. 'Juliet's going to do our hair in a bit.'

'Prepare for a full-on glitter-and-flower fest, then,' she said, her heart melting as Melody ran a finger over one of the labels on her moisturiser pots. Her expression was all joyful reverence, making Kate doubly pleased she'd talked to her and Oscar about naming her product line after Bea. Melody was already certain the line would go *totes stratospheric* and be found in spas the world over! 'So, how are you enjoying the fete so far?'

'It's the best one we've ever had,' Persephone said, shyly.

'I think so too,' Kate agreed, sharing a smile with her because it wasn't her fault her mum was a complete nightmare. Speaking of whom, though... 'Did your mum come today?' The last thing she needed was Gloria sticking her beak in.

'She's gone into town to get her hair done, so she won't be back for hours.'

Only Gloria could instigate Fete-Gate last night and calmly get her hair done this morning, but Kate was absolutely fine with not having to worry about seeing her.

'Dad's around, though,' Melody said. 'He'll be here in a minute, but first he had to speak to Trudie.' She and Persephone exploded in giggles Kate thought dolphins might be able to hear, and fascinated, she wanted to know more.

'Sounds like you have some gossip to share with me, girls.'

'He wants to talk to you about something vitally important,' Melody said.

'Yes,' Persephone nodded vigorously, 'vitally important.'

Oscar chose that moment to pop his head into the tent. 'Girls, you haven't got long before the fancy-dress parade starts. You don't want to keep Juliet waiting, do you?'

Persephone giggled again and Oscar looked suspiciously from her to his daughter, who grabbed hold of her friend and they exited the tent with shouts of, 'Bye, Dad' and 'Bye, Mr Matthews.'

With a quick, nervous smile for Kate, Oscar focused his attention on the products Kate had displayed in a mixture of shabby-chic wire, glass and wooden milk crates. 'These look great, Kate. Bea would have loved them, wouldn't she?'

'Yes. I think so.'

'So...' He ran a finger across some of the labels the same way his daughter had done.

'The girls tell me you have something vitally important to talk to me about?'

In return she thought she might have something vitally important to talk to him about. Namely: Daniel. She wanted to ask so, so badly if Oscar knew where Daniel was. But then, she didn't want to give Oscar the impression she was now divided about being back in Whispers Wood. They'd made progress, she and Oscar. The last thing she needed was to set their relationship back because he suddenly thought she was getting antsy about staying.

'So, you know I told you I wasn't feeling guilty about moving on?' Oscar asked quietly.

'Biggest lie ever, but I got it.'

'Bea... Bea will always be part of my life – our lives.'

He looked pensive and vulnerable and suddenly she realised. This wasn't about Daniel. This was hopefully about Juliet. 'Oscar?'

'What I'm trying to say is...'

'Oscar, you don't need my permission or my blessing 'though it's awfully sweet of you to ask for them.'

'It's important to me that you don't think I didn't value what I had.'

'I know you did, Oscar. You loved her unconditionally. When you fall you fall deep and it's perfectly permissible to love deeply more than once,' she paused and gently added, 'She would want you to be happy, you know.'

He nodded, his smile watery. 'I know.'

'So you don't need it, but you absolutely have my blessing.'

Oscar swallowed. 'Even if it's with someone you know?'

'Especially if it's with someone I know.'

He grinned and it was one of the best nothing-held-back, nothing-tempered grins she'd seen from him in a long time.

'In that case, I don't suppose you could do me a massive favour and get Juliet over to the fortune-teller's stall before midday?'

Two hours had passed by the time Juliet finally made it into Kate's tent and by then Kate was a bag of nerves.

'Hi, sorry it took so long, I only just checked my phone for messages. What's up?'

'Have you seen Daniel?'

Darn it. That wasn't what she'd been supposed to say at all.

'No, I haven't,' Juliet said, pulling clips from the neckline of her white cropped top and shoving them into her flowery skirt pocket. 'But he must be super-busy so it's not exactly weird.'

'It is weird,' Kate insisted.

'You mean because of last night?'

Kate turned pots of moisturiser to make sure all the labels were facing outwards. 'I mean because the night before we...'

'You... *Oh*. Oh, that's fantastic.'

'Is it?'

'It isn't?'

'I don't think it is. One day after and suddenly the whole village knew his business. And now he's not answering his phone and Monroe's not here.'

'Not here?'

'Not there.' She grabbed Juliet's arm, steered her out of the tent and pointed to the cottages in front of them. 'See?'

'Kate, I know it looks bad, but Daniel wouldn't leave without telling you.'

That's what she would have thought, but…'What does he owe me, really?'

'The way you stuck up for him last night, a lot.'

Her voice was pitifully small when she asked, 'What if he decided no one wants him here except for me, and what if he decided that's not enough to keep him here?'

'That won't be it, Kate. Truly. He's probably just as busy as the rest of us. You look like you've been flat-out here and I've only just finished helping Mum with the fancy-dress entrants and in about twenty minutes I need to set all my food out for the baking competition.'

Kate glanced at her locket watch and then from under the table whipped out a 'Gone Fishing' sign to pin to the front of her tent. 'If you have a break let's have a wander around. Otherwise we'll never even get the chance to experience what everyone else is experiencing.' She could get Juliet to the fortune-teller and search for Daniel at the same time.

Chapter 46

Fete-fully Yours

Juliet

Juliet thought she was getting a bit better at breathing through the mortification that was leaning in to kiss Oscar and him... leaving.

What didn't kill you, made you stronger and all that.

Thanks largely to Kate listening and rebuilding her self-esteem with chatter about all their plans and how excited she was to go into business with her; she'd ended up feeling okay.

Still a total idiot for making a fool of herself like she had.

But not enough of a sorry case that more stray cats had started congregating at her doorstep.

'Perhaps Daniel's with Oscar,' she said, fishing to see if Kate knew where Oscar was.

'He's not,' Kate answered, steering a course through the crowd. 'I saw Oscar with Melody, earlier.'

They hadn't been together when she'd done Melody's hair. Great! Oscar had just the right amount of stubbornness to make avoiding her last forever. She ought to be grateful. Instead she was peeved she wasn't in control of when she saw him.

It had been hard enough seeing him last night at the meeting. All brooding protector. Thank goodness she'd had Kate to fuss over or she might have found her resolve slipping. Might have bounded up to him with some sort of declaration just to see if that made a difference.

Thanking herself for not making the situation a thousand times worse, she slid her arm through Kate's, and asked, 'Are you prepared for later when Isaac makes the announcement?'

'You mean when Daniel's declared the winner? I guess. You can't fake the numbers, Jules. And look what he's achieved, here today. His theme to celebrate the weird and wonderful about Whispers Wood was perfect. I've never seen such a turnout and that's despite Gloria's revelations last night.'

At the popular stocks-and-sponge stall Kate sighed and Juliet knew she was imagining putting Gloria in them.

'I think you should make a special face-pack for Gloria out of one of Gertrude's cow-pats.'

'Loving that idea,' Kate said. 'I'm definitely going to introduce her to the latest Russian beauty trend. A massage that involves being hit with branches. Hard.'

'What?'

'Yeah, I read about it or made it up or something,' Kate said with a grin. 'Ooh, perfect,' she added, coming to a stop in front of a tent. 'Let's get our fortunes read.'

'We already know our fortunes – to open up the best spa and hair salon this side of Sussex, even if it's not in The Clock House.'

'Come on, it'll be a giggle and, goodness knows, we both need one of those.'

Trudie's tent – sorry, *Madame McTravers'*, tent looked fabulous covered in swathes of navy velvet and leopard print fabrics pinned together with silver fringing.

Inside, there was a peacock chair, wicker table and loveseat, all of which were covered in more navy or leopard print. On the table sat the portentous crystal ball.

'Trudie, how on earth are you managing in here? It's sweltering,' Juliet said immediately, pulling at the neckline of her top.

'Hhhooo eez this Troody you speek ov?' Trudie said in an accent not immediately recognisable by anyone on the planet.

'Oops. Sorry. Forgot.' Juliet considered herself appropriately chastised. 'Darn, I haven't got any silver to cross your palm with.'

'No matter,' Madame McTravers said in her thick accent, fanning herself a little as she sat down, her kaftan billowing out around her. 'You are so special, I tell your fortune for free.' Madame McTravers waved at Juliet and Kate to sit down. 'I give palm-reading and look in crystal ball. All will be revealed.'

'Can't wait,' Juliet said under her breath and after receiving an elbow in her ribs for her sarcasm, added a gutsy, 'Fab.'

'Give me hand,' Madame McTravers commanded, her turban wobbling precariously atop her head. 'Ah yes. Kind hands. Skilful as well. Soft, even though you work with them every day.'

'That's Kate's lotion. It's wonderful.'

'You are very creative. Very talented. I see success in your future. Wonderful success. Now I see into the crystal for your love life.'

'Oh, there's no need for that.'

Trudy ignored her. 'The mist is very telling. It is showing me all. A-ha,' she exclaimed.

Juliet jumped at Trudie's 'A-ha,' but threw Kate a grin. Kate was right, this was exactly the kind of giggle they needed.

'A-haaaaa,' Trudie exclaimed again, starting to move and sway like Kate Bush as her hands hovered over the crystal ball. 'Yes. The crystal is very specific. The most specific it has ever been in fact.'

'Really?' Juliet felt a silly flutter in her chest.

'You have only to open your heart and by the end of the day you will be kissed by a man who's fallen head over heels in love with you.'

Juliet's breath hitched. 'Today?'

'Yes. Most definitely. Today.'

'I see. Um. How brilliant for me.' And then, before she started entertaining thoughts of being kissed by Oscar she quickly turned to Kate. 'Your turn.'

Madame McTravers passed Kate a panicked look.

'I think we should stick with yours, Juliet,' Kate insisted.

'Yes. Stick with yours,' Madame McTravers instructed. 'And remember, by the end of the day you will be kissed by a man head over heels in love with you.'

'Lucky me,' Juliet said faintly, ready to leave the tent and all its hot air.

Outside she took a deep breath. There was nothing like the aroma of hog-roast to bring you back down to earth. 'So. That happened.'

'It did indeed.'

'I guess I should find space on my mantelpiece for a little gold cup. I've a feeling the head judge of the baking competition is going to fall head over heels in love with my scones and kiss me.'

Hours later The Clock House clock told Juliet she had time to stop at the floristry tent and see if her mum had won first place, then quickly dump all her equipment back at the cottage and make it back for Kate when Isaac made his announcement.

Shoving combs, pins, hairspray, bands, clips and anything else that remotely looked like a hair accessory into the capacious holdall she used for her work, she was about to zip it shut when she realised she could also cram in the little gold cup she'd received for coming first in the baking competition.

The judge had indeed fallen head over heels in love... for her scones and homemade sweet summer strawberry jam.

She'd even received a peck on the cheek.

Madame McTravers had really excelled at her fortune-telling skills this year.

As Juliet stretched her arms up to the sky to ease out a couple of kinks, she battled to stem the aching disappointment.

It wasn't Trudie's fault she'd tumbled into the seduction of her fortune being told to her and the hope she'd thought quashed had fluttered to life again.

Nope. This was all *her* fault. And she absolutely had to stop this silly watching and waiting and hoping for Oscar.

As she wheeled her Cath Kidston Forest Bunch holdall

across the village green olde-worlde signs invited her to roll-up, roll-up and play a traditional fair game with a Whispers Wood twist. The whole community had really come together wonderfully and there was a buzz about the place that wasn't solely from Bea's bees. Ever since Daniel and Kate had got everyone involved in The Clock House challenge, Whispers Wood had come back to life.

And soon she'd be occupied with planning and running the salon and... she came to an abrupt halt, staring open-mouthed at the new stall being set up at the edge of the green.

'Hello, Juliet.'

Whirling around, her eyes nearly popped out of her head. 'Oscar – what are you doing? Why are you dressed like that?'

'I'm putting the finishing touches to my stall.'

'Your–' her mouth opened and closed like a guppy. She whirled back around again to take in the beautiful carved wooden arch. 'Your stall is a kissing booth?'

'A very special kissing booth,' he said, reaching around her to ensure the sign sat right in the middle of the arch. 'And I'm wearing the tux because I thought you might like it.'

'You look really hot.'

'Thank you.'

His grin made her heart beat about a million times a minute. 'No. I mean–' She'd meant it was way too hot to be dressed in a suit and, looking at the tilt of his mouth, she suspected he knew that.

His voice grew husky as his gaze swept over her. 'You look very pretty today, Juliet.'

'I–' She couldn't speak. Could barely think. Other than to

ask herself why was Oscar dressed in a tux, standing by a kissing-booth and flirting with her?

Reaching out he took hold of her hands, his gaze a soft caress. 'You looked pretty when you won first place in the baking competition,' he murmured. 'You looked pretty when you were doing Melody's hair and you looked pretty when you were coming out of Madame McTravers's tent.'

Flustered, she couldn't meet his gaze. Instead she stared at the little bee buzzing around the cupid cherub carved into the arch of the kissing booth. The bee flew off and Trudie's fortune flashed into her head and her fast-beating heart started dipping and diving.

'I don't understand,' she whispered.

'Neither did I,' Oscar replied. 'Not for a long time. And then I did and while I was trying to un-know I hurt you and I'm so sorry, Juliet.'

'You keep calling me Juliet.'

'I didn't think you liked it when I called you Jules.'

'I needed to protect myself,' she answered truthfully. From those little slips that put them on a more intimate footing. Those little slips that flamed the hope, even when she knew she should be stamping it out.

'Did you like the fortune you were told today, Jules?'

By the end of the day you'll be kissed by a man head over heels in love with you.

Hope bloomed out of control and crazy-big in her heart and she couldn't help herself, she looked up into his face and nodded, yes.

'I made this kissing booth especially for you. To show you.

To tell you. God, Jules, you have no idea how much I wanted to kiss you that day in your lounge.'

Confidence took a nosedive as the hurt that was still too close had her staring down at her feet. 'I got that from the way you pushed me away and fled.'

'I was–'

'Stupid?' she suggested, sneaking a look at him from under her lashes.

'Confused.' He reached out and tucked a wisp of hair behind her ear. 'I don't think it was one-sided – the heat that had been building between us. Was it?'

The thrill of hearing him admit it meant she could too. 'No, it wasn't all one-sided.'

'From the moment I stepped into your house and heard you talking to yourself, all the lectures I'd given myself about how I absolutely wasn't going to steel furtive glances, or touch you unnecessarily or flirt with you in any capacity, flew out the open door. One look at you and I was right back on that stage during the bachelor auction, trying not to beat my chest with pride that the smartest, strongest, sweetest girl in the room had stood up in front of the village and basically made me feel like she was staking a claim.'

'Then why…?'

'Before I fell asleep I was staring at the photo you have of your mum and you at the opening of the hotel in Whispers Ford. It reminded me of the similar photo that I have. Only my one has my parents in it… with Sheila.'

'Oh.'

'Mmmn. *Epic-scale awkie* as my daughter says. I fell asleep

446

worrying about how Sheila would react if you and I started something. And how Melody would react... And how this would all work and stay working because I'd somehow started thinking of you as my future and then you were touching me and kissing me and I–'

'You were flooded with guilt.'

'Yes. And you deserved more than me taking without knowing what I could give.'

'I thought I'd misread the signs. I thought I'd embarrassed you. Made you feel uncomfortable.'

'I knew I'd given you mixed signals and I felt awful.'

'So this kissing-booth you've made?'

'Is about showing you one signal. I started falling for you a long time ago, Jules. You're sweet, kind, loyal and passionate. Slowly, softly, wonderfully sweetly you slid into Melody's and my hearts. It feels like we've slid into yours too. I'm not wrong about that, am I?'

'You have. Oh, you both have. For the longest time you've been in my heart. I don't think I ever really believed I could be in yours. But do you think Sheila will understand?'

'Well, after a long chat with a very excited Melody, I had a long chat with Sheila. And then Kate. And even though I would have pursued what's between us because walking away from you the other day taught me I couldn't do it again, it's nice to know we have their support.' He dropped his head so that his forehead rested against hers and took a deep breath. 'So what do you think?'

Juliet smiled. 'I think you owe me a kiss. I think I owe you a kiss. Basically, I think there should be kissing now.'

'Did I mention how much I love the assertive side of you that goes after what she wants?'

'Oscar?'

'Yes.'

She rose up on tiptoe, placed a kiss to his throat and whispered into his ear, 'I love you.'

He inhaled deeply, his fingers tightening against hers as he lowered his head, and just before he captured her lips with his, whispered back, 'I love you, too.'

Standing toe to toe and holding hands, Juliet sighed against Oscar's mouth as his lips brushed once, twice, over her lips, learning their shape with slow, drugging kisses that sparked into heat and had him deepening his exploration, so that her heart soared and her bones melted.

By the time he lifted his head to gaze into her eyes they were both trembling.

'Wow,' he whispered, with a chuckle.

'Ditto,' she said, grinning from ear to ear.

'You know, I never told a woman I loved her before even taking her out on a date. Melody is sleeping over at Persephone's tonight. After the fete, I could turn up to your door...'

She ran a hand down the lapel of his suit. 'But you have nothing to wear.'

He threw back his head and laughed. 'I could turn up to your door in my tux. We could have dinner and–'

She rose up on tiptoe, already hungry for his mouth again and capturing his laughter on her lips, she smiled against his mouth and sighed, 'Yes. Dinner and!'

Chapter 47

Clocking Off

Kate

As she packed away the few remaining bottles of Bea's Bee Beautiful stock, Kate knew what she was going to do. She was going to nip back home, climb over the wall between Myrtle and Mistletoe cottages and spy through Daniel's patio doors to see if he'd packed up and shipped out.

Pleased she'd come up with a plan, she gave herself an extra point because she couldn't even accuse herself of acting impulsively. She'd thought this through for the last ten minutes.

Picking up the box, she got to the entrance of the tent and hesitated.

Did she really want to find out? All the time she wasn't certain she could keep the little kernel of hope in her chest aglow.

She liked that little kernel. It kept the crashing disappointment at bay.

No pebble to help her decide this time.

No symbols she could turn into signs to help guide her to making the right decision.

449

She sighed. Finding out was the grown-up thing to do. With a quick glance to make sure she hadn't left anything behind she exited the tent and bumped straight into Crispin.

'Kate, there you are. Isaac's ready to make his big announcement. Come on, we're doing it on the main stage beside The Clock House.'

Kate felt her grip on the box loosen.

'No. Crispin, you'll have to stall him.'

'I will not,' Crispin argued. 'The dancing starts on that stage in an hour. We have a schedule to maintain.'

'You don't understand. Monroe's gone, taking Daniel with him.'

'Who on earth is Monroe?'

'Daniel's car.'

'Daniel calls his car Monroe?'

'As in Marilyn.'

'But that makes no sense.'

'Doesn't it? If you'd been subjected to the whole village hearing second-hand about your past wouldn't you have kept right on moving along?'

'No, I mean – that car of his isn't a blonde.'

Only a man would get stuck on a detail like that. 'Well, that's Daniel all over, isn't it? Illogical. Impulsive.'

That made Crispin look at her with an expression she understood only too well. She was the illogical, impulsive person here, not Daniel.

Daniel was admirable and to be admired.

And she did admire him.

So much.

She knew from experience that it took energy and balls to start afresh – especially if you were still reeling from aftershocks and believed you only had yourself to count on. And looking those clients in the eye and repaying every one of them showed immense strength of character.

'But where would Daniel go,' Crispin asked.

Good question.

A dejected Kate walked back into the tent to set down the box. He was probably travelling along in Monroe, not even knowing where he'd end up next.

She couldn't believe how much it sucked that he hadn't asked her along on the adventure with him. Even if she would have had to decline because here was where, it turned out, she fit best.

But then all they'd shared was a summer fling – not even a summer fling. Why *would* he have asked her? They were two strangers who had wanted the same thing. That was all.

And the fact she was missing him already needed to become fiction, fast.

'...how did he get out of the field, anyway?'

'Huh?' Kate looked up at Crispin, who was scratching his head, sorry, weave!

'I saw Daniel's car – Monroe, in the field less than an hour ago.'

'What field?'

'Really Kate, what's the point of turning up to village meetings if you're not going to listen? The field we use for spill-over parking on fete day so that people can move around without traffic.'

'Oh.' Kate remembered Crispin's lecture the night Oscar's van had been parked right in The Clock House gates. 'That field.'

Wait. Did that mean Daniel hadn't left? Had he been here all day and she'd just made an Everest-sized mountain out of a mole-hill? Excitement bubbled under her breast.

'Shall we get to the stage, then?' Crispin asked as if he and patience were about to unfriend each other.

'Crispin, your wish is my command.'

Crispin's eyebrows arched with disbelief.

'Let's get this show on the road,' she said, shooing him out of the tent.

'Are you going to be like this all the way to The Clock House?'

'Where you lead,' she started singing her favourite Carly Simon song. 'I will follow.'

Crispin immediately walked faster.

Kate smiled and sang louder, 'Any – anywhere.'

'Good grief,' he muttered.

'That you tell me to.'

'Stop it. People are staring.'

Wow. They really were. Kate sobered as she came to a stop in front of the stage, realising most of Whispers Woods had congregated for Isaac's announcement.

Automatically, she scanned the crowd like a traffic camera linked to Computer in *Person of Interest,* but not one of the heads in the crowd showed up on her brain with a little red box around it and a number identifying as Daniel Westlake.

Where the hell was he?

'Kate,' Isaac smiled at her. 'If you'd like to accompany me up to the stage.'

'Where's Daniel?' she asked, but she didn't think he heard her as he mounted the steps to the stage and a large round of applause broke out.

Crispin gave her a little push and, feeling slightly nauseous, she followed Isaac.

She stared at the sea of faces in front of her. From the centre front row her mum watched carefully. Big Kev towered beside her, talking quietly in her ear, reassuring her and making her smile. Aunt Cheryl was a few rows back with Trudie, the two of them looking guilty and Kate made a mental note not to drink the punch later.

Mary was to their left, offering Ted and his wife some scones she'd bought.

And there, standing off to the side, were Juliet and Oscar.

They were looking up at her with huge grins on their faces, their arms wrapped around each other.

She smiled back.

At least she hoped she did.

She was happy for them, so why were stupid tears forming behind her eyes? To stop them leaking out for everyone to see, she stared at The Clock House.

Are you mine?

Are you mine because Daniel isn't?

More tears formed.

Panic spread its wings and the urge to run licked at the blood pumping through her veins.

'Isaac,' she whispered, trying to get his attention, but he was focused on his speech.

What was happening here?

Was she about to be given The Clock House as a consolation prize?

'Good afternoon, everyone,' Isaac said into the mic. 'And what a good afternoon it is, yes?'

A roar went up from the crowd and Kate wondered if everyone could see her knees shaking.

'It's been a good morning,' Isaac said. 'And I have every reason to believe it'll be a fabulous evening. Things have got better in Whispers Wood, haven't they?'

The audience gave another cheer.

'I know we lost the Best in Bloom award this spring,' Isaac continued. 'Coming so soon after the hotel opening in Whispers Ford, I understand why that was hard to take. But we shouldn't need to win something to feel special. And we shouldn't feel lost when our neighbouring village moves forward. Luckily, thanks to two special people who have breathed fresh air into an old idea, the fete is a huge success, we have enough funds to ensure days where the whole community can come together aren't a one-off, and we're about to move forward with new business coming to our village as well.'

Everyone cheered and Kate worried she wouldn't be able to contain the conflicting emotions churning inside her. She cast her mum a worried look and Sheila just stared calmly back at her, a lovely smile on her face.

Some of the emotion levelled out and her breathing came a little easier.

She'd done all her running.

She could trust in herself.

It didn't matter if everyone saw her become a blubbering mess.

'This beautiful building,' Isaac pointed to The Clock House, 'has been in my family for over a hundred years and it's no secret that I have no family to pass it onto. Except it turns out I do because family doesn't have to be blood. And I know the person who's going to take it over loves The Clock House and Whispers Wood as much as I do. She's the sort of person who puts others' needs before her own... In fact she walked away in order to do just that.'

Oh. No. She stared down at the ground.

She couldn't accept The Clock House this way. It was too, too bittersweet.

'She thought she'd be letting those she loved heal more quickly,' Old Man Isaac continued, 'and in our grief some of us found it hard to tell her how much she was missed. I'm sure we'll all be very proud to watch her open Beauty @ The Clock House. Kate? I don't know if you've prepared any words...?' he stepped away from the mic and indicated for her to take his place.

Everyone was expecting her to give a thank you speech, but all she could think of to say was, 'There's been a mistake. Isaac, there's no way I raised more money than Daniel.'

She saw movement out of the corner of her eye and apart from the gentle breeze lifting her hair and ruffling the hem of her dress, it seemed to Kate as if everything stopped as Daniel made his way to the stage, a huge bouquet in his hands.

'Congratulations, Kate.'

His voice was deep and she remembered the way it had whispered promises to her as they'd lain under the chandelier in the building beside them.

She stared at him. Stared at the bouquet.

'Why haven't you been answering your phone?' she asked, forgetting she was still by the mic and wincing as her words echoed out over the green.

Daniel lowered the bouquet of flowers and with a frown started patting his pockets. 'I remember having it when I spoke with Gertrude last night.'

'Really? You couldn't speak to me but you could speak to a cow?'

'I couldn't speak to you, last night, Kate. Not when I was thinking–'

'About leaving? Right. I get it. So what?' her hand lifted to indicate her beloved Clock House. 'This is some sort of going away gift?'

'No. Kate this isn't a mistake. You're not second-choice. You're the *only* choice to own The Clock House.'

'Because you've taken yourself out of the equation.'

It had been easy to get used to the idea of him owning it if it meant he was here to stay. But now she'd won it and lost Daniel, because what was there here for him now?

Fat tears rolled down her cheeks and through the blur she saw him look pained as he took a step towards her.

'That isn't the reason, Kate. It's yours because when you told the whole village that I loved this place – that I was one of you, and didn't deserve to be judged for others' actions, you proved to all of us that you put people before business.'

'But you raised the most money. This whole fete was your idea.'

'Actually it was Isaac's. My idea was just the theme. You're right – I was going to leave. I thought if I stayed in Whispers Wood and opened up in The Clock House, not only would you lose out on opening the business of your dreams, you'd also be subjected to all the gossip surrounding my past. And then I thought that if you opened up in The Clock House and I stayed, that gossip could still hurt your business.'

'But that's just gossip, Daniel. I knew the truth. You weren't even going to give me the chance to prove to you how much more we could be than fodder for gossip?'

'For about five seconds I was going to leave. Five stupid seconds and a serious moo from Gertrude and I knew I was being an idiot. You didn't circle back here because you ran out of options – you came home. I – all of us,' he said, indicating Isaac and the crowd, 'want you to be happy about getting The Clock House. Because we know it was a dream long held and because we know you want it now for yourself and Juliet just as much as you wanted it for Bea. Please don't cry, Kate.' Slowly he reached out to cup hold of her face and she felt the tender brush of his thumbs as they stroked away her tears. 'I want you to be able to accept The Clock House with an open heart.'

'So you can leave with a clear conscience?'

'No. So I can put one more challenge to you.'

'Challenge?'

'I want you to rent me the top floor of the building you're going to own. I want to open Hive @ The Clock House. If you don't think it makes good business sense to open my co-working business idea with the spa and hair salon we can discuss it or I'll find something else to do in the area because I don't want to leave. I want to stay. And build something. With you.'

A cheer went up from the crowd, but Kate wasn't even aware of it. She was only aware of Daniel. Standing in front of her and telling her... She licked her lips. She thought he might be telling her he wasn't leaving.

Daniel put his hand over the mic a moment and told her quietly, 'I went to see my ex- business partner at Ford Open Prison today.'

That's where he'd been?

'He wrote to me before I came here, but I wasn't ready to hear what he had to say. I think I knew it was going to be some sort of apology and I was still too angry with him to hear it. I *needed* to be angry with him and use that as a force for change.' His hand slipped from the mic to hold her again. 'Yes, I was embarrassed when Gloria opened up her bag of secrets last night, but more than that I hated what it might mean for you. I don't know if you've figured it out from how I've been falling over my feet around you, but I've been trying to impress you ever since I first saw you. I know we have tons to work out but I'm falling for you, Kate-of-the-shortest-shorts-Somersby. I think you're falling for me too. If I'm completely and utterly wrong about that then take a step backwards and I'll leave right now.'

She wondered if he knew there was a bee buzzing at his mic, but she didn't need the sign. Fascinated by his words, she took a step, not backwards out of his arms, but closer towards him.

'When I finally figured out that leaving probably wasn't the best way to impress you, I went to see Isaac and explain why you're the best person to own The Clock House. I came to Whispers Wood looking for a fresh start and found a home. You came back home and found your heart. I was kind of thinking that if we joined heart and home together it could stand throwing in working together too. Are you up for the challenge?'

'I think so – no I *know so*,' she said, winding her arms around him. 'I fell for you the day I met you. And I say challenge accepted.'

'Seal the deal with a kiss,' Aunt Cheryl shouted out and a laughing Trudie chanted 'Kiss, kiss, kiss,' until everyone joined in.

Kate grinned as Daniel swept her into his arms, twirled her around and then dipped her dramatically and then the cheers and whistles faded into the background as he lowered his mouth to hers.

Dear Reader,

I hope you've enjoyed reading The Little Clock House on the Green. Bringing the village of Whispers Wood to life... letting the characters take their first breath... discovering what secrets they kept and what camaraderie they shared has been such a fun adventure.

Confession: For the longest time I wanted to write a book with a clock house in it – and for the longest time I had no earthly idea why. It took my husband pointing out that it was probably because I walked past one every day for the penny to finally drop. I know – he's super-clever that way!

The clock house that I pass on my *solvitur ambulando* (gorgeously snazzy Latin phrase for my plotting peram-bulations) is really more of a clock tower and forms the main turret in a beautiful block of apartments that was once an asylum built over a hundred years ago. Through the passage of time the building must have seen myriad changes and had its use adapted to meet those changes, yet all the while the clock has remained. Tick-tocking along. Something in me finds this notion so romantic and somehow so hopeful as well.

Put this together with my love of quirky small town/ village settings full of heart and a spark ignited. Suddenly all I could think was: who doesn't want to live in Stars Hollow, or on Three Sister's Island, or in any of the Midsomer Murders villages (minus the murders part)?

And so the village of Whispers Wood with its little

clock house on the green was born and grappling with all the things that had changed in the village (and all the things that hadn't) was Kate Somersby. With hope in her heart her new life wasn't going to be about going big or going home, so much as *going big and coming home*. Home to Whispers Wood, her beloved clock house and a dream business.

Over the course of writing The Little Clock House on the Green, Whispers Wood, its characters and its clock house built such a strong home in my heart that I'm not ready to let it go – and hopefully neither are you because...

This winter, you are all cordially invited to the grand opening of The Clock House.

Step through the doors, grab yourself a honey martini and celebrate Christmas with Kate and Daniel, Juliet and Oscar, and two new characters... Emma Danes and Jake Knightley.

As Emma and Jake help with preparations for the grand opening, you can expect snowflakes and sleigh-bells, spas, salons and office shenanigans, Christmas, chandeliers and a family curse!

If you love your books to come with a helping of humour, a touch of quirk, lashings of romance, oh, and Jane Austen... then step inside the pages of *Christmas at The Little Clock House* – out this winter!

Love and little clock house kisses,

Eve xx

Return to the Little Clock House this Christmas for mince pies, mistletoe and plenty more romance...

Christmas
AT THE Little
CLOCK
House

EVE DEVON

Acknowledgements

Huge, heartfelt thanks to the super-duper team at HarperCollins HarperImpulse: Kimberley Young for your vision and inspiration. Charlotte Ledger, editor extraordinaire, for sharing the excitement and saying YES to *The Little Clock House on the Green* and for your lovely support this year, Helen Williams for showing me how to make my words even better and Holly Macdonald for my gorgeous cover.

Thank you to Emily Benet for the giggles and the camaraderie while we both BICHOK'ed our way through our respective daily writing lives.

Thank you to my dear friend Suzi Olohan. Our cinema/lunch/can't-possibly-fit-shopping-in-as-well-and-yet-ooh-look-at-that-gorgeous-dress days saved my sanity on more than one occasion.

Thank you to all my friends and family for your rallying and championing this year – it means so much.

And the most gigantic big-feelings and heart-full thank you to my very own hero, Andy – for having a heart as deep as the ocean, a spirit as strong as the willow tree, and the ability to belly-laugh with me as we dance through the rain.